The HOUSE *of* HIDDEN LETTERS

Izzy Broom

PENGUIN BOOKS

PENGUIN BOOKS

UK | USA | Canada | Ireland | Australia
India | New Zealand | South Africa

Penguin Books is part of the Penguin Random House group of companies whose addresses can be found at global.penguinrandomhouse.com

Penguin Random House UK,
One Embassy Gardens, 8 Viaduct Gardens, London SW11 7BW

penguin.co.uk
global.penguinrandomhouse.com

Published in Penguin Books 2026
002

Copyright © Izzy Broom, 2026

The moral right of the author has been asserted

Penguin Random House values and supports copyright. Copyright fuels creativity, encourages diverse voices, promotes freedom of expression and supports a vibrant culture. Thank you for purchasing an authorised edition of this book and for respecting intellectual property laws by not reproducing, scanning or distributing any part of it by any means without permission. You are supporting authors and enabling Penguin Random House to continue to publish books for everyone. No part of this book may be used or reproduced in any manner for the purpose of training artificial intelligence technologies or systems. In accordance with Article 4(3) of the DSM Directive 2019/790, Penguin Random House expressly reserves this work from the text and data mining exception.

Set in 10.92/15.05 pt Palatino LT Std
Typeset by Six Red Marbles UK, Thetford, Norfolk
Printed and bound in Great Britain by Clays Ltd, Elcograf S.p.A.

The authorised representative in the EEA is Penguin Random House Ireland, Morrison Chambers, 32 Nassau Street, Dublin D02 YH68

A CIP catalogue record for this book is available from the British Library

ISBN: 978–1–804–95786–8

Penguin Random House is committed to a sustainable future for our business, our readers and our planet. This book is made from Forest Stewardship Council® certified paper.

Izzy (Isabelle) Broom is the author of twelve escapist books and has been published in fourteen overseas territories. In 2015, she won The Great British Write Off with her short story, *The Wedding Speech*, which was later adapted into a prize-winning short film. Her fifth novel, *One Thousand Stars and You*, was awarded Contemporary Romance Novel of the Year at the 2019 RNAs. Formerly a Book Reviews Editor at *Heat* magazine and *Woman & Home*, Izzy still works for magazines on a freelance basis and is an editor and mentor at Curtis Brown Creative. She currently lives in Suffolk, surrounded by books, family, unruly dogs and a rooster from the farm next door, who has inexplicably fallen in love with her.

Praise for *The House of Hidden Letters*

'Whisk away to Greece . . . the perfect escapist read.'
Veronica Henry

'Atmospheric, romantic and mysterious . . .
perfect for fans of Victoria Hislop.' **Cesca Major**

'Completely captivating and utterly enchanting . . . truly timeless.'
Daisy Buchanan

'Absorbing, beautiful and devastating. I loved every page.'
Chris Whitaker

'Engaging characters, evocative setting, emotional journey. I was captivated from the first page to the last!' **Cathy Bramley**

'A gorgeous, sun-soaked treat.' **Sarah Morgan**

'Gorgeous . . . the perfect holiday read . . . Loved it.' **Liz Fenwick**

'Rich and intoxicating . . . Brimming with authentic Greek heart and soul' **Louise Candlish**

'A gorgeous and evocative tale of love, loss and unexpected friendships . . . Pure and blissful escapism.' **Lucy Clarke**

'Captivating and beautiful . . . A sparkling gem of a story.' **Debbie Howells**

'Gripping and emotional . . . rich as the best souvlaki . . . Enjoy!' **Milly Johnson**

'Compelling and captivating, this is the perfect holiday read.' **Kate Gray**

'Terrific . . . joyous page-turner . . . a really delightful read.' **Jane Johnson**

'Rich, lush and evocative . . . When you can't escape to a Greek island in reality, reading Izzy Broom is the next best thing.' **Kate Thompson**

'Wonderful . . . I loved this beautiful book.' **K L Slater**

'[A] rich, evocative tale of courage and hope. Atmospheric, moving, captivating.' **Amanda Jennings**

For my nephews, Zephyr and Atlas

1

It was only a key.

Slim. Grooved. Silver.

But pressed into Skye's palm, it felt like something more. A beginning.

A paper tag dangled from it, a number inked in thick black strokes that matched the one on the plaque by the door. *Her* door, she reminded herself. *Her* house.

She slid her thumb along the stem, rotating the key until it caught the light, a white-hot flash that made her pupils contract. The fierce heat that had greeted her at the port was dogged in its pursuit, and Skye shifted beneath the weight of it, senses alert as she breathed in the scent of dust, heard the distant buzz of a tinny engine, looked down to see lilac petals strewn in artful heaps along the stone pathway; a beauty so raw as to be insolent.

Change your life for €1, the headline had read, and Skye had clicked on the link – of course she had clicked on the link. Following similarly successful schemes launched in France and Italy, the municipality of a remote Greek island was offering six individuals the chance to buy a house for one euro. There were stipulations, naturally. The new owners must commit to spending a minimum of two years on Folegandros and must renovate their properties – all six of which had been abandoned since the end of the Second World War – in a manner that was in keeping with the traditional village setting. Demand was expected to be high, and in order to give every person an equal chance of winning, there would be a lottery. The button to place a one-euro bid had been at the bottom of the article, the deadline for entries just hours away. It had felt like fate.

Skye had the key in the lock when she heard the crunch of approaching feet and turned in time to see a man coming towards her. When she recoiled, he stopped, raising both hands in the universal gesture of surrender.

'English?' he asked, in a voice that was heavily accented.

Skye agreed with a murmur that she was.

'You are one of the lottery winners,' he said.

There was no upward inflection to the statement, and Skye did not immediately reply. Instead, she allowed herself a few beats with which to study him, take in the heavy brows above shrewd dark eyes, pale short-sleeved shirt tucked into belted jeans, workmen's boots knotted tight. He was taller than her, but not so tall that it was notable, and seemed harmless enough. Though didn't they always?

Skye folded her arms.

'You heard about that then?' she said, to which he nodded briskly.

'Of course. We are all' – he paused, chewed over his next word; searching, perhaps, for the correct one to use – 'eager to see who is coming.'

'Am I the first?' she asked, though the question was rhetorical. The woman who'd presented her with the key had told her as much. Skye had registered a slight reticence on her part, as if by turning up one day prior to the agreed moving date of 3 June, she'd upset the proverbial apple cart. It was unclear whether the locals had been consulted about the scheme, though she had to assume some form of permission had been granted. If the village of Ano Meria's existing inhabitants were hostile towards their new neighbours, it would very quickly become impossible for them to live side by side, let alone harmoniously.

The man rubbed a hand across his stubbled jaw, smoothing out the beginnings of a smile.

'In Greece, we have a saying for those that like to be early,' he said. 'It goes something like "the children of the wise cook before they go hungry".'

Skye considered this. 'Where I'm from, we say it's the early bird that catches the worm,' she replied, and was rewarded with a gravelly laugh.

'Where do you live in England?' he asked.

Skye motioned to the house, then more widely into the space around them.

'This is where I live now,' she said. 'What came before no longer matters.'

'*Entáxei*,' he said. 'So, you want to become a Greek?'

'I don't think that's possible.' Skye unfolded and refolded her arms.

'If you say you are a Greek, then I promise not to argue with you.'

'Thank you.'

'But you must understand that we do not have many Greeks here with hair like yours.'

Skye patted her blond locks self-consciously.

'And you will have to work on your accent.'

She narrowed her eyes, and he smiled, extending a hand.

'I am Andreas. Andreas Vithoulkas.'

'Skye.'

Their fingers slid together briefly, and he repeated her name several times.

'It's Skye with an "e",' she explained. 'I was named after an island, which feels ironic.'

Andreas cocked his head to one side. 'Are you going to have a look at your house?' he asked, gesturing at the still-locked door.

'In a minute I will.'

When he failed to take the hint, Skye drew in a long breath and exhaled it sharply.

'Ah, sorry.' Andreas pressed a hand to his forehead. 'I have not explained myself. I am a contractor,' he said. 'A builder. I am the one who will be helping you finish the house.'

'Oh, you will, will you?' Skye replied. 'And do I get a say in this, or . . . ?'

He shifted from one foot to the other.

'Of course, you are free to hire another person, someone from Santorini, or the mainland, but that will take a lot of time. I am the only person doing this job who lives here, on the island.'

His presumption stung, however well meant it might have been, and the sigh that escaped Skye's lips was laced with mild frustration. How best to communicate politely that what she wanted was to look around her new home for the first time alone, without some stranger in tow? He was friendly, yet he was still a man – and as far as she was concerned, that meant he was also an unknown entity. An awkward silence bloomed, during which she did little more than stare at the ground.

Andreas cleared his throat. 'I am intruding,' he said. 'Sorry. I will come back tomorrow, if that is OK with you?'

Skye drew herself up, faintly ashamed of having so clearly communicated her displeasure. 'Of course,' she said, though before she had time to say more, Andreas had nodded and turned away, quickly disappearing from view between the boundary of her modest property and the larger one beyond. She waited, rooted to the spot, unsure whether he would return. Why had she left it to him to figure out what was playing on her mind? When it came to corralling a classroom full of children, she never used to have any such qualms. But then that had been before; she had changed over the past few months in ways she didn't want to admit, was not yet ready to accept.

'Get a grip, MacKinnon,' she muttered, fumbling to get the key into the lock. The door was stiff, and she had to shoulder it to get it open, flakes of blue paint falling over the threshold. It was dim inside, faint light streaming in from around the shuttered windows. She located a switch on the wall, blinking as a lone yellow bulb flickered into life from a cord in the middle of a cracked wood-panelled ceiling. The open-plan living space was empty save for several piles of timber and a scattering of bricks, while the thick shaft of a defunct fireplace banked up from one corner. Stairs leading up to the second storey hugged the wall closest to the door, though there was no banister. Someone had left a stack of newspapers on the bottom step. Skye made her way towards an open archway at the far side of the room, through which she discovered a kitchen, or the approximation of one. The plug sockets appeared new enough, as did the crude strip lighting, but the uneven slate tiles were scarred by another time.

There was a second door in the kitchen that led outside, a brass key that opened it on the sill. Skye went into what she supposed was her garden – a rectangular waste ground hemmed in by a tumbledown stone wall. The wall would need to be repaired, the weeds pulled up and the numerous heaps of what looked concerningly like animal droppings cleared away. She could not fault the view, however, and stood for a few moments to admire the sweep of mountain set against its cobalt backdrop, the confetti-like smatter of pale rooftops, and the faraway ribbon of sea beyond. A church was perched high on a distant cliff, pure white and softly edged, reminiscent of a fallen cloud.

The enormity of her decision astounded her afresh,

though Skye knew that regardless of how much work was required, being on Folegandros was preferable to the alternative. She could never return to the place she had left behind.

A light breeze shifted the leaves of an overhanging tree, and the sun broke through with dazzling clarity. Turning back towards the house, Skye bent to retrieve one of the fallen rocks from the ground and held it in her hands, feeling its warmth, the uncompromising strength of it. As the sound of bells began to ring out across the hillside, she took the stone and slid it back into the wall.

All that was broken, she would rebuild. One small piece after another.

2

⁂

Lottery wins did not happen to people like her.

That had been Skye's first thought when the email arrived, her second that she must have fallen foul of an elaborate hoax. She called the number provided with disbelief, and only when the man on the other end calmly confirmed that yes, she was one of the six that had been selected, and no, he was not a fraudster who'd somehow hacked the entry list, did Skye accept that it was real.

After that, she'd had a month to make the necessary arrangements, though with no job to resign from, and only a meagre collection of possessions to pack, the only real task on her to-do list had been sourcing the means by which to fund her new life, and that sizeable hurdle had come close to unravelling her completely.

Relief in having made it to the island had diluted any excitement she might otherwise have felt, but as the first hour slid by, Skye began to feel the tingles of something close to pleasure. The house was hers, every roughened stone and cracked tile of it. The wildflowers spilling out between the gaps in the walls were hers, as were the old latches on the internal doors, the stained marble basin in the bathroom and dappled glass in the window frames. She hummed to herself as she moved from room to room, a pad in hand on which she jotted down a list of jobs that would need to be done, furniture that would need to be purchased, holes that would need to be filled.

Sometime later, when she was in the process of inflating the single airbed that she'd mercifully thought to bring, a knock sounded at the door. Skye crossed to the window and peered down, immediately recognising the broad shoulders of Andreas. He had returned sooner than promised and was carrying two large carrier bags.

Scribbling *security chain?* at the end of her steadily growing list, she went downstairs to see what he wanted.

'*Geia sou*, hello.' Andreas held up one of the bags. 'I have brought you a kettle, some coffee, milk and a little sugar.'

'Oh, wow.' Skye thawed slightly. 'You didn't need to do that.'

Andreas reached into the second bag and produced a toaster.

'I had a spare one at home,' he said, when she started to protest. '*Ela re*, take it.'

'I don't know what to say.' Skye opened the door a fraction wider. As well as the kitchen appliances, Andreas had brought two chipped mugs, a selection of cutlery and basic utensils, a rather burnt-looking frying pan and some sort of plug-in stick blender.

'For making frappé,' he said, as she examined it.

'You will not fool people that you are a real Greek unless you learn how to make proper coffee.'

'I can pay you for all this,' she offered, but he shook his head.

'We are living on the same island now. We are friends, and in Greece, we look after our friends.'

Skye's mind went fleetingly to her previous neighbours, their collective gazes dropping to the pavement as she passed them, twitching curtains that remained resolutely shut.

'Thank you,' she said haltingly to Andreas. 'This is really kind of you.'

He lifted a dismissive hand. 'Do you have anything to eat? Klodi closes his shop at three o'clock.' Extracting a mobile phone from the back pocket of his jeans, he squinted at it and grimaced. 'The taverna will open in a few hours and—'

'It's OK,' she assured him. 'I have bottled water, and now coffee, thanks to you. I'll survive until morning.'

'Your fridge and oven will arrive tomorrow?' He had posed it as a question, though clearly, he did not need her to confirm it. If anything, he appeared to know more about the moving-in schedule than Skye herself.

'Sooner the better,' she said. 'It does feel a bit sparse in there.'

A frown passed over his features, and Skye glanced down, her attention momentarily snagged by the eagle-head buckle of his belt. She recalled the row of motorcycles she'd seen down at the port, a battalion of polished chrome and sun-cracked leather.

'Do you like the house?' Andreas asked.

'Well . . .' Skye considered. 'It still needs work, as you know, but yes, I like it. I wouldn't have bought it if I didn't.'

'For one euro,' he intoned.

A scruffy ginger cat had stalked up the path from the village while they'd been talking and now sat itself down in the shade of her boundary wall. Andreas clicked his tongue, and the animal stretched towards him, yawning as he stooped to pet it.

'*Geia sou*, Tigri,' he murmured.

Skye bent to pick up the bags. 'I should put all this away,' she said. 'It really was kind of you to bring it here.'

Andreas straightened. 'Slowly, slowly, the unripe grape becomes honey,' he said, almost as if to himself, then smiled at her. 'If you change your mind about eating at the taverna, you are welcome to join me, although of course I understand if you would prefer to be alone on your first evening.'

'I think I would,' she agreed, 'but thank you.'

Skye remained where she was, watching as he strode back the way he'd come, exuding a nonchalance she could not help but envy. The cat, Tigri, fixed its pale eyes on her, yowling as she closed the door on it. There was no point inviting it inside, not when she had nothing to offer save for affection, and even that would have taken considerable effort to muster. It had been a long day, a journey that had begun not hours but months ago, and all she wanted now was to sleep.

The donated items, she took through into the

kitchen, dumping each bag on the floor before going back upstairs. The airbed was in the larger of the two bedrooms, though rather than returning to the task of pumping, she took the ladder up to the attic room, a space she'd run a cursory eye over earlier and deemed too hot, dark and cramped to use for anything other than storage. There was only one window, a slim dormer that offered an unblemished view of the sea. Skye pushed hard against the wooden frame until it swung open, breathing in the scent of salt and warm air.

Dust motes swarmed and long abandoned spiderwebs hung drab in corners. Ducking to avoid the beams, she stepped cautiously over floorboards that creaked in protest, pausing when she encountered an indentation in one of the supporting struts. It was a letter 'K' neatly carved. Whoever had engraved it must have stood exactly where she was standing, their brow furrowed in concentration, thinking not of any future inhabitants who would stare upon the mark they made, but only of what it meant to them, in that moment. Skye knew that the house had been empty for more than eighty years – had 'K' been its last occupant, or were they someone from long before that? It felt suddenly important to know.

'Who were you?' she whispered, trailing her finger across the wood.

No answer came. There was no sound at all save for the faint thrum of crickets drifting up from the garden and then, so abruptly that she gasped, another loud knock at the front door. Swearing under her breath, rubbing her head where she'd banged it against one of the low beams, Skye went once again to answer it.

There was nobody there, only a lidded cool box, inside which she discovered half a loaf of bread, a generous pat of butter wrapped in wax paper, a wedge of moist goat's cheese, one small bottle of red wine and a folded note that read: *Real Greeks like to eat. A.*

For the first time in what had been an undeniably peculiar day, a real smile found its way onto Skye's face.

3

July 1940

The curls of sawdust fell silently, tickling the tops of Katerina's bare feet. She gritted her teeth, concentrated hard on the final flourish of the kappa, keen not to make more sound than was necessary. If Baba were to hear and catch her, the scolding would be severe.

'Go, carve your name into a tree,' he would cry, 'leave my house out if it.'

Katerina understood why he thought the house belonged to him and him alone, but she would not accept it. This was also her house – her home. The only one she had ever known. Surely it was hers enough that she should be able to leave her mark upon it. Who cared if it was forbidden? Besides, it was too late now, the deed was done, a 'K' inscribed for Katerina that would now remain for ever.

Scooping up the evidence, she hurried across to the window and tossed the wood shavings out into the dawn, watching as they twisted and whirled, spiralling downwards like the birds in the fields as they snatched up insects that hovered late in the day, their bodies fat with pollen, lazy with heat. Summer had been heavy and relentless; at night she turned over across cotton dampened with her own agitation, seeking a cool spot on the mattress yet finding not one.

She would hear the rumble of Baba's voice below, as he sat with other men from the village, heads bent together as they grumbled about war, about provisions, about that man from another land, the one with the moustache. Katerina had seen a photograph in her father's newspaper and wondered at the man's apparent power. He seemed so small, a nondescript face amongst so many others, of less interest to her than the dirt she scraped out from beneath her fingernails. Yet Baba's concern was real enough to unsettle her, and, unlike her mama, who cooed and cajoled, he never pretended that she should not be worried – that they all shouldn't be.

The sky outside was pink dipped into yellow, her beloved Aegean alive with the first dapples of light. She fastened her shoes as the bells rang out in the church, heralding the hour of five. Most of the villagers would sleep for another hour, but her goats would not. Katerina needed to milk the nanny, or there would be nothing on the table for Mama when she awoke. It was also her job to check the animals for any injuries, maladies, or small rocks caught in hooves. The herd was modest, only six in total, five full-grown and a late-season *katsikáki* that had been born with a leg missing. She had named her Chrysí, on account of the goat's golden fur. On the weeks when her father travelled across to old Thira – he could not think of it as

Santorini, though that was the name most people now used – Katerina would sneak the baby animal into her room overnight, soothed by the gentle bleating of its contented slumber. Her sister, Leni, had clutched her sides when she found out, though her merriment had turned to pity when Katerina confessed the truth, that she craved the goat's comfort because Leni was no longer there. Her sister had left the family home a year ago, when she married the baker's son, Michalis, and although Leni lived close by, and Katerina still saw her most days, she felt her elder sibling's absence as keenly as she might a missing arm or leg.

'You will understand,' Leni assured her, whenever Katerina began muttering murderous thoughts about 'that thief, Michalis'. 'When you fall in love, *koúkla*, you will understand.'

Love. Such a stupid thing. She was eighteen, strong, healthy, and free to roam between her chores. A man would not let her behave in such a way – he would want to own her, as Michalis did Leni. Trap her at home in the kitchen, give her his dirty shirts to scrub while he sat with his wine or whisky. Nothing about that life appealed to Katerina. She did not want to end up pinned in a book like a captured butterfly.

But she should not think of such things, not when the day was so gilded by beauty, the land hers to explore as she saw fit. The herd had strayed further than usual up the mountainside, and the burn in Katerina's lungs matched that of the muscles in her thighs as she trudged her way up towards them.

'*Geiá sou*,' she sang, scratching at the spot between

the nanny's ears, a smile hitching up as the goat pressed its warm head against her. Fingers still working, she counted the rest, frowning when she came up short. Chrysí was not among them, and Katerina began calling her name, softly at first, then with greater insistence, fear making a mess of her insides. She turned helplessly to the nanny goat, who stared dolefully back, her big kind eyes the colour of ripe figs.

'Where is she?' she pleaded. '*Pou eínai aftí?*'

It was then that she heard the bleat.

Katerina followed the sound, her body tense, chin jutted forwards. There was a roughly hewn pathway going further up the mountain, and she broke into a run, pebbles skittering away underfoot as she got her first glimpse of the young goat above. Chrysí was perched on the very edge of a high outcrop and bounced on her three hooves when she saw her mistress come into view.

'*Óchi!*' Katerina screamed, gripped by terror. The goat was not a strong mountaineer, her balance off on account of her missing limb. If she fell, Katerina would never forgive herself. Taking a deep breath, determined to remain at least outwardly calm, she called up, telling the animal to wait, that her mama was coming, that everything would be fine.

Climbing was easier barefoot. Katerina kicked off her boots, rolled up the sleeves of her shirt, and tucked the heavy folds of her skirt up into her undergarments. This area of the mountain was notoriously treacherous. In the spring, a boy had fallen while trying to pick wildflowers for his mama. Katerina had heard the woman's howls of anguish when his small broken body was carried back to the village, and her agony had hit hard as an arrow.

Glancing up for one final time, she saw that the little goat had wisely lowered itself into a kneeling position. Good. That was good. She scoured the rocky terrain, looking for natural holds, places where the turf was deeply embedded. Stepping off the flat ground caused her arms to shake with effort, but with a grunt, she pulled herself further up, fingers curling between cracks, nails breaking on the hard edges of rocks, skin splitting as she trod hard on jagged stones. Chrysí's bleats rang out, high and shrill. Katerina cursed as she lost her footing, her toes scraping desperately for purchase, and then she was stable again, moving faster, gaining pace, her confidence growing with every step.

'*Ela*,' she crooned, as she reached the goat, breathless with relief, though it was short-lived. She still had to get back down, and now she had the added weight of Chrysí, slung across her shoulders. The goat snuffled at her neck, warm body quivering. Katerina descended slowly, not once looking anywhere but towards the next foothold. Such was her relief when she made it back to the path that she lowered the goat to the ground and fell to her knees beside it, her whole body shaking as she fought to quell the tears.

'Bravo,' drawled a voice.

Katerina was on her feet in a flash, wheeling around, shock making her yell out. The man who had spoken did not so much as flinch, nor did he seem unduly alarmed by the state of her, with her skirts tucked and dark hair plastered across her cheeks. Yanking out the former, she glared at him, daring him to comment, to repeat his mocking appraisal. She had pushed over boys taller than him before, and she would do so again without thinking twice about it.

'Very impressive,' he said, cocking his head to one side. 'That goat owes you its life.'

Katerina narrowed her eyes. 'You saw me?'

He nodded. 'Of course.'

'And, what? You did nothing – did not try to help me?'

His nose was large, the shape of it pleasing; a beard beneath it dark as night. Katerina opened her mouth, but any further reprimands were gone, her words lost, taken like dust by the wind. She looked past him then, back down towards the village, part of her expecting the view to be different, altered in some way as she had been, by his presence.

'What is your name?' he asked.

Katerina felt a trembling in her arms and folded them tightly across her chest.

'Tell me yours first.'

'Stefanos,' he said smoothly. 'Stefanos Lazaridis.'

She nodded curtly but said nothing.

'Are you going to tell me your name,' he asked, 'or will I guess it?'

Chrysí let out a shrill bleat, and Stefanos laughed.

'I think she is trying to give me a clue,' he said. 'Maybe your name is Katsikaki . . .'

'I am not a little goat!' Katerina exploded.

'Do not forget that I have seen you climb,' he said,

dodging backwards as she stomped towards him. 'When I came up the hill, I thought for a moment that someone had dressed their animal in human clothing.'

'*Malaka*,' she hissed, to which he laughed, loudly and with great amusement. If only her face would stop burning, if only he would stop staring at her with such glee.

'My name is Katerina,' she muttered.

'Katerina,' he repeated.

Hearing the word come from his lips caused an odd sensation in the deepest part of her.

'You think I am a goat,' she said, but Stefanos shook his head, moving closer, so close that she could feel the warmth of him.

'What I think,' he said slowly, as his eyes trailed over her, 'is that you, Katerina, are exceptional.'

4

Skye woke with a start, heart leaping into her throat and arms thrashing.

The airbed had slowly deflated during the night, and she winced as she eased herself up into a sitting position. Beneath her, the floor was hard, the boards uneven and slightly damp to the touch. Blinking, she rose, staggering on still-slumbering feet to the nearest window, which was blocked by a wooden shutter so decrepit that it let in more light than it blocked. The sun was yet to rise fully, and clouds lay like smudges against the mountain.

So often, in recent months, she'd found herself starkly aware of her breath. The drawing in and letting go of air should have been the most natural thing in the world, and yet it felt finite, as if by acknowledging it, she was daring it to cease. Skye stood for a few minutes, watching the dark wash of distant sea, waiting until the sensation of panic abated. The room she'd slept in was all straight edges and flat walls, though the plaster was flaking away in patches and there was no shade covering the single bulb.

There had been nowhere to hang any of her clothes the previous day, and having rooted through her suitcase, Skye extracted a pair of shorts and a simple black vest top. Her crinkled blond hair she tied back off her face without bothering to brush it first, and having eyed her cosmetic bag with disdain, she left it in the bottom of her case untouched. Nobody to dress up for here; nobody expecting her to look a certain way. Sun lotion, however, was a non-negotiable, and this she lathered on thoroughly, remembering to smear a dab on the tops of her ears and along her hairline.

Downstairs in her barren kitchen, she boiled water for coffee, deciding not to risk the milk, but sawing a few slices of bread from the loaf and coating them in soft, tangy goat's cheese. These she balanced in one hand while she unlocked the back door with the other, stepping out into her modest garden with its overhanging tree and fragmented stone wall. Steam swirled from her cup, and bringing it up to her lips, she blew gently, taking a tentative sip, followed by a bite of bread, then another, her hunger returning with a rush of ravenous enthusiasm. Skye paid no heed to the crumbs that tumbled down her chin, nor to the cheese that oozed between her teeth; she chewed loudly, swallowed noisily, smiled broadly at the simple pleasure of eating unobserved, consuming what she'd prepared so fast that her throat swelled, leaving her with no choice but to belch. The resulting sound was so loud, and came from so far down in her gullet, that Skye burst out laughing.

What would her mother say if she could see her now?

Back in the kitchen, she put her empty mug in the sink and frowned at the half-melted pat of butter she'd left on the side. Her fridge could not arrive soon enough, ditto the oven, though she had no crockery save for the two cups donated by Andreas, and nothing in the way of furniture. For a moment, Skye thought longingly of the old wing chair she'd inherited from her father. He had re-upholstered it in orange velvet, doing all the work himself, right down to the final stitch. The grooves of his body had still been visible in its cushion surround when it arrived at her small flat in London, and for weeks, she could not bear to sit in it, could not have borne the guilt of having altered any remaining part of him.

In the end, she'd had to leave it behind; she'd had to leave everything behind.

The space she was in felt suddenly stifling, the walls closing in as her hope began to fade. Before the sensation could consume her, Skye fled, pausing only to fetch her purse and mobile phone. She had not seen a single bar of signal since arriving in the village and was glad of it. What better excuse for ignoring the world than being – quite literally – cut off from it? Once outside, the sun raised her spirits somewhat, as did the sight of Tigri, who was back in his spot next to the wall. This time, she bent to scratch him behind the ears, and having responded by squirming against her, the cat let out a contented purr.

'It's a tough life, isn't it?' Skye said wryly, before turning to look back at her house. Of the six situated up on the hillside, hers was one of only two with a hip roof. The other four were flat-roofed, and only a handful had more than a single storey. The largest, which was the closest to her own, had what looked to be a long, barn-like building at the rear, and its façade was freshly whitewashed in the traditional Cycladic style, bright as a brand-new veneer. Skye studied the faded frontage of her more modest abode and noticed for the first time that there was a dark stain running up and around one corner, as if someone had sparked a giant match and held the flame to the stone.

She continued to stare, disquieted by the silence, wondering why she had not thought to question more deeply the abandonment of this place, and the reasons why nobody local had taken ownership of the houses before now. Folegandros might not be as popular as its Aegean neighbours Santorini, Mykonos and Naxos, but there were a handful of hotels on the island, and rentable apartments dotted around. Why had no property developers homed in on this tiny hamlet? The explanation provided by the municipality in charge of the lottery had been vague – perhaps deliberately so – but Skye could not shake the sense that there was more to the story. She thought again of the 'K' inscribed so carefully in her attic. Someone had loved that house, been proud enough of it to leave their mark. She wanted to know what had happened to them.

The sun continued to crawl steadily upwards, a single throb of gold in a gradient sky. Loose earth and pebbles trundled down the path ahead of her, while the far horizon shimmered in a haze. It took less than ten minutes to reach the island's single stretch of tarmacked road, and Skye followed it down towards the centre of the village, admiring the criss-cross veins of stony walls, gnarled olive branches and occasional splashes of vibrant colour from a painted shutter or potted plant. The sea was her constant companion, visible in snatches of blue, and the wind coaxed loose strands of hair across her cheeks.

It wasn't until she reached the first taverna that Skye saw another person, and while the elderly woman sweeping the terrace returned her smile, she made no attempt to speak. There were further signs of life outside a small bakery, and she stopped for a moment to inhale the scent of fresh bread. A vast bougainvillea was draped in splendour over the wall, a shower of papery pink petals below it.

Skye shook her head. It was as if she had walked into the pages of a travel brochure, only this was not a two-week vacation, it was her life, the scene in front of her not a picture postcard, but her home. She knew it was nothing more complex than luck that had brought her to the island, but it felt more profound than that, more as if someone, or something, had intervened to make sure that it happened.

The road led her onwards, past acres of sparse grassland and dust-coated parked cars, until eventually, perched on the very edge of a bend with the sea spread wide far below it, she found the mini market.

'*Kalimera*,' called a voice as she pushed open the door. Skye glanced up to see a slight, dark-haired man clutching a punnet of figs. For a moment, she was thrown, unsure what to say. The man put the tray on the top of a chest fridge and came towards her.

'You are on holidays?' he asked, and Skye shook her head.

'I've just moved into one of the houses at the top of the hill.'

'Ah.' He beamed at her. 'The lottery houses.'

'You heard about that?'

'Everybody in Ano Meria heard about that,' he confirmed, beckoning to her. 'Come, come. What do you need? I don't have many English foods, but here there is teabags. And you will need some milk, perhaps bread also.'

He took a red plastic basket from a stack beside the till and passed it to her.

'Are you Klodi?' she asked, and his smile grew even wider. 'I met Andreas,' she went on, and he nodded.

'Andreas is a great man – the best. He has not stopped working on the houses. For many months now, he is there every day, making things ready.'

'He didn't tell me that,' she said. 'I assumed that, well, I don't know what I assumed. Did the houses need that much work?'

Klodi looked at her as if she'd said something funny.

'Of course,' he exclaimed. 'Nobody except the goats had lived in them since the end of the war. Everything had to be done, there had to be power, and water' – he ticked each off by tapping his hand – 'and there is still a lot of things to finish.'

Skye pictured her cracked floorboards and broken shutters, the mound of rubble in her garden and the holes in her walls, and agreed that there were. Klodi ushered her towards a display of fresh fruits and vegetables, pointing out the best grapes, the plumpest peppers and the shiniest tomatoes.

'We grow a lot of these things ourselves,' he told her, with obvious pride, 'and we have a lime tree in our garden, the fruits from which are the sweetest in all of Greece. Ah,' he went on, as a diminutive woman in a pale-yellow dress and apron emerged through an open doorway at the rear of the shop, 'and here is my wife, Cora.'

Skye smiled a greeting as the woman came towards them, murmuring a *'Kalimera'* that she followed with a timid 'Hello'.

'Geia sou,' Klodi said to Skye. *'Geia sou* is how we say hello in Greek.'

Skye did her best to repeat the words, feeling at once embarrassed to be so inept and encouraged by the Greek couple's earnest expressions.

'You are living here?' Cora said, making the leap more rapidly than her husband had. 'In one of the old houses? Very good. *Poly kala*. They have been empty for too long, ever since I was a girl.'

'Did you both grow up on the island?' Skye asked, helping herself to several aubergines. Klodi shook his head.

'I was born in Thessaloniki, but I came here, to Folegandros, one summer with my family. We went for swimming one day, at the beach in Livadaki. I have seen Cora there and' – he smiled warmly – 'I was a lost man from that moment. I knew that she was the one for me.'

'Just like that?' Skye said, looking at each of them in turn.

Cora glanced at her husband. 'It was the same for me,' she said, pressing a hand to her chest. 'I felt it, inside. And you?'

'Me?' Skye feigned a laugh.

'You are married?'

'No,' she said, readjusting her grip on the handle of the basket. 'Not married.'

Cora and Klodi exchanged a look.

'You came here by yourself?' the woman clarified, to which Skye reluctantly agreed. Her skin was beginning to prickle, but the two of them had her penned. To get into the aisle behind and continue her grocery shopping, she would need one of them, at least, to step out of her way.

'I should really—' she began, only to be interrupted by the arrival of another customer. Skye had a few seconds with which to register the unruly mass of tawny curls, stacks of bracelets and bright-pink harem pants, before the woman bowled across and grabbed her by the hand.

'Please tell me you speak English?' she said in a broad Australian accent. Then, when Skye said she did, 'Thank God for that. I've asked about twenty people between the boat and here, and they all looked at me as if I was talking in bloody Liki.'

Klodi started to say something, but it was impossible for him to get a word in. The woman had launched into an animated story about 'the bloody ferry crossing', how she'd had to leave her luggage down at the port because there were 'no bloody taxis' and how the woman she'd collected her key from had been 'worse than bloody useless' at giving her directions.

'Apparently my new digs are at the top of a place called Ano Meria, but I've got no clue where that is, or even if I'm pronouncing it right, and my phone's no bloody help,' she went on, glaring at the mobile in her hand.

'There's no signal.' Skye held up her own phone. 'I've had the same problem, but you are in the right place. This is Ano Meria.'

Klodi and Cora had melted away, he to resume the restocking of figs, and she to the counter, where she propped herself on a stool. The woman moved past Skye and slid open the door of the freezer, extracting a bag of ice and holding it against her chest.

'That's better,' she said with a sigh. 'It's hot enough to sizzle steaks on the road out there. I thought I was going to pass out walking all the way up here – forty-four sure isn't twenty-four, if you know what I mean. There was a likely chance you'd have found me in a ditch, half-eaten by mountain dogs.'

'I don't think they have those here,' Skye mused.

The woman laughed. 'Well, that's something to be cheery about, I guess. I'm Joy, by the way.'

'Skye.'

'Good to meet you, Skye. Now, I don't suppose you happen to know where I could find a load of houses that have just been given away for less than two dollars, do you?'

5

It was late morning by the time Skye and her new neighbour made their way back up the hill from the village. Once it had been established that Joy was also taking ownership of a lottery house, Klodi and Cora had been effusive in their welcome, insisting the two women join them for iced coffee in the garden, before pressing gifts of fresh herbs, ripe limes and a jar each of Cora's homemade pasteli into their hands.

'I can't get over the view,' Joy exclaimed. At numerous points along the pathway, she had stopped to take it in, a hand raised to shield her eyes from the sun. The sea that had been quiet that morning was agitated by light into a blur of movement, its surface a treasure chest of sparkles. 'As soon as the rest of my stuff arrives, I'll have a go at painting it.'

'You're an artist?' Skye said, and Joy pulled a face.

'So it says on my tax return, but it's been a while since I produced anything worth a bloody second look. What do you do?'

'Teach,' Sky said, 'or did, until this whole moving to a tiny Greek island thing happened.'

'When I told my folks I was moving here, my dad told me I must be ambo.'

'Ambo?'

'As in ambulance. He reckons I need one, to cart me off to wherever it is they take the crazies. But I don't know, my friends were all for it. I have quite a few Greek pals back in Sydney, and they told me I'd love it over here. Bit of P and Q, find my mojo again, you know.'

Skye nodded.

'I think I do know,' she said.

Joy's house was one of the smaller single-storey dwellings, though she had the benefit of a long rear garden, complete with stone-walled hut that she immediately earmarked as a studio. The interior was structurally sound, though the walls were in dire need of repainting, a task that did not daunt Joy in the slightest. She was also delighted to discover that the crate of furniture she'd shipped across had arrived before she had. Skye helped her unload a decorative patio table and two foldout chairs, a tightly strapped mattress and a stack of wooden planks that Joy would reassemble into a futon.

'I really must order a few bits,' Skye said, thinking forlornly of her deflated airbed.

'Share with me, if you like,' Joy offered, 'though if you do, bring your earplugs. I snore louder than those drills they use to break up the highway, or so my husband used to tell me.'

Skye paused in the process of unboxing cushions.

'You're married?'

Joy looked away.

'Was,' she said, 'until the old bastard went and died on me.'

'I'm so sorry,' Skye began, but Joy waved her away.

'It's stupid,' she said. 'Every day that I knew him, I'd be like, "Bobby Monroe, if you don't put your dishes in the sink, or your towels on the hook, or your dirty kecks in the hamper, I'll bloody kill you." I couldn't believe it when he went and called my bluff. I still don't believe it, a lot of the time.'

She fell abruptly silent, and Skye waited, paralysed by indecision, torn between wanting to offer her neighbour a hug, and wanting to run away. In the end, Joy got up and left the room, and a moment later, Skye followed her, out through the back bedroom onto the sunlit patio beyond. Joy's head was down, but her eyes were dry.

'I told him,' she said. ' "We're in our mid-forties, Bobs, it's time to stop pretending you can surf." He wasn't very good even in his twenties, and it only takes one slip-up, one bang on the bonce. He was there, and then he wasn't, and I was supposed to just carry on.'

'You have,' Skye said, gentle but firm. 'You are.'

Joy nodded slowly, then turned to face her. 'Have you ever been married?'

Skye hesitated, then shook her head.

'Smart cookie,' Joy drawled, and then, with more humour, 'Hey, do you think they gave all these houses away to single women? Maybe there's an excess of unmarried Greek men on Folegandros and the locals have had enough of them jackbooting around, going after other fellas' wives?'

'I'd much rather live surrounded by women than men,' Skye said, and Joy laughed.

'I'll raise a beer to that – speaking of which, do you fancy one?'

It was too early, and too hot, and she had too much to do, but Skye was in a 'what the hell' mood. Joy had got as far as unearthing a bottle opener from one of her many boxes when they heard the roar of an approaching engine and went out through the front door to investigate. A pick-up truck was lumbering into view, its bed piled high with an assortment of items including, Skye saw, with a rush of pleasure, a fridge-freezer and small oven.

'*Geia sou*, ladies,' Andreas called through the driver's-side window.

'Oh wow, he's brought up my luggage,' Joy crowed. 'You know this guy?'

'Barely,' Skye said, as the truck came to a groaning stop outside her house. The passenger door was flung open, and a man hopped out and went straight around to lower the tailgate.

'*Ela*, Stamati,' Andreas said, beckoning urgently to his companion as Skye and Joy walked over to join them. 'Come and meet our new friends.'

Stamatis, who Skye guessed to be in his late teens or early twenties, nodded briefly at the two women, grunted out a 'Hello', then fished a vape from the pocket of his shorts and began to suck on it. Andreas rolled his eyes theatrically.

'My apprentice,' he explained, 'and the younger brother of my best friend.'

He was wearing the same belt and boots as the previous day, though the jeans looked smarter and the shirt ironed. Skye thanked him for the basket of food and wine.

'I was worried that you might starve,' he said. 'I must have food every few hours, like a baby.'

'You and me both,' Joy agreed, going on to introduce herself. As Skye had privately predicted, Andreas knew not only what the artist's name was, but had also gone to the trouble of looking her up online.

'I have seen your paintings,' he said. 'They are beautiful.'

A bead of colour appeared on each of Joy's cheeks that was every bit as bright pink as her trousers. It was the first time Skye had witnessed her be at a loss for something to say and felt a smile begin to tug at her lips.

'OK.' Andreas clapped his hands together. 'Now, Stamatis and I, we will bring inside the appliances, and then I will come back for the rest.'

'I can manage these.' Joy was already reaching for one of three large suitcases, and Stamatis hurried forward to help. Left alone, Andreas turned to Skye.

'How was your first night on Folegandros?' he asked.

'Fine,' she replied, 'although my bed deflated.'

Andreas's brows shot so far upwards that she laughed.

'If you think that's bad, wait until you see the state of my walls.'

As it soon transpired, there was nothing about the house that Andreas did not already know, having spent weeks inside prior to her arrival, laying cables and digging trenches for pipes. Once satisfied that the fridge and oven were in place and fully functional, he joined her in the back garden, where Skye had escaped to while the two men worked.

'There is a lot of space,' he mused. 'Perhaps you would like to have a plunge pool.'

'A what?'

'Many of the villas and apartments in Chora have one of these things. A place to cool off at the end of a long day.'

'I think I'm all right for a plunge pool.' She eyed him sideways. 'At least for now.'

'Or,' he went on, seemingly unperturbed, 'perhaps an extension along the wall there, a place for guests to sleep when they come to visit.'

'I'm not planning on many of those,' Skye told him.

'*Ela*, surely your friends from England will come to see your new home?'

'Nope.'

'Your family?'

Again, she shook her head.

'Are you on the run from the law?' he asked, his tone jovial. 'A fugitive.'

A rush of heat washed over Skye.

'That's right,' she said lightly. 'I'm one of England's most wanted criminals.'

He laughed good-naturedly, and they both turned as Joy came out into the garden.

'There you are,' she said. 'Been having a pokey around the place, I hope you don't mind?'

'You won't have been the first,' Skye said, with a pointed look at Andreas. 'We were just discussing the merits – or not – of building a pool out here.'

'A pool?' Joy brushed a sweep of frizzy curls off one shoulder and fanned her face with a hand. 'Hadn't you better see to the bloody floors first?'

'Ah, yes,' Andreas said, reanimated by the mention of potential construction. 'I have some things I must do this afternoon, some materials to collect, but perhaps I could come back in the morning and together we can make a plan?'

Skye looked past him, up at the windows with their broken shutters hanging loose, the whitewashed walls stained and the roof peppered with gaps where tiles had long since been taken by the wind and by the passing of time. She thought of the money she had, the contract she had signed agreeing to restore the house to traditional standards. Like her, it needed patching up, rebuilding, a second chance at a better future.

'What do you think?' Andreas asked hesitantly, as Joy picked her way over the cascade of stones below the wall.

'I think,' Skye said slowly, her gaze sliding back to meet his, 'that tomorrow morning would be perfect.'

6

They began in the front yard, Skye clutching a chipped mug of coffee that was doing little to temper her headache – a result of the three beers pressed on her by Joy the previous evening. Returning home from her new neighbour's house long after dark, Skye had attempted to prepare a meal of aubergine pasta using the single burnt frying pan donated to her by Andreas and had not been successful in her efforts. Eventually, she'd had no choice but to gnaw on the remaining chunk of bread, which had become so tough that even soaking it in olive oil made little difference to the texture.

The morning was bright, luminously so, with a lively wind that twitched through the coarse patches of grass and flattened the damp strands of Andreas's hair. He was in his overalls and boots, the former unbuttoned to reveal a paint-flecked T-shirt bearing some kind of logo. Skye squinted at it through her sunglasses, but all she could make out was a fish.

'Is there something on me?' Andreas asked, his chin squashing against his chest as he attempted to look down.

'No,' she said. 'Sorry, I was—Ignore me.'

'It is early for mosquitoes, but sometimes they will hunt during the day, if they are hungry enough,' he said, saying the last part with a flourish of gleeful menace.

Skye, who had woken to find three new bites on her left ankle, frowned as she sipped her coffee.

'I hate them,' she said.

'*Ela*,' Andreas replied, 'they are only doing what they must do to survive.'

That, at least, she could relate to.

'I was going to ask you about this,' she said, gesturing to a large, white concrete block that was situated not far from her boundary wall.

'Ah, yes.' Andreas moved towards it. 'This is protecting your power cables. Each of the houses has one. Without them, there would be no electricity.'

'Did you put them in?' she asked, but he shook his head.

'This is not my area of expertise. The power and the water were done by a separate company hired by the municipality. Stamatis and me, we helped to dig the trenches for the pipes and removed some of the old materials, then we installed the bathrooms.'

'All of them?'

'In five of the houses, *nai*. It was a big job, because at the time of the war, when the homes here were abandoned, the facilities inside were very basic.'

'I did wonder why the bathroom was so neatly finished,' Skye said.

Andreas brushed a fly off her arm.

'There was not much of a budget given to us,' he said. 'We did the best that we could, but if you wanted to change anything...'

'No,' she assured him. 'I don't mind the plain white at all, and Joy was thrilled with hers. She has grand plans to paint motifs on the tiles.'

Her coffee had cooled, the milk leaving an oily sheen across its surface. Skye tossed what was left in her cup across the ground, watching as the liquid seeped through the dry earth.

'I suppose we'd better do the inside next,' she said. 'I've started making a list, but—' She paused as Andreas produced a slim notebook from the pocket of his overalls, and the stub of a pencil from behind one ear. 'It looks as if you had the same idea?'

He showed Skye the page, but the scribbled words were Greek, and thus indecipherable to her.

'Do either of those things say "new floorboards" or "replastering"?' she asked.

Andreas chuckled. 'Unfortunately, yes, they do.'

When they reached the front door, Skye once again had to shoulder it open.

'I can fix this for you today,' Andreas said, running a hand around the wooden edges, which were warped and misshapen. 'I have the tools in my truck.'

'I thought I might have a go at scraping the rest of the paint off,' Skye told him as a confetti-toss of blue flakes floated down onto the floor. 'Although maybe I should concentrate on the bigger stuff first.'

'I think it is better to wait,' he agreed. 'When the

replastering work is done on the outside of the house, there will be a lot of dust, a lot of mess.'

The stone floor of her main living area was not, according to Andreas, in a bad state, considering its age. When Skye tentatively asked how much it would cost to lay terracotta tiles throughout, he tapped his pencil against the edge of his notepad, murmuring sums under his breath.

'The space inside is around thirty square metres, so with materials and labour, it would not be too much, perhaps one thousand, or twelve hundred euros.'

'That seems reasonable,' she said. 'What about upstairs? I'd ideally like to redo both bedrooms and the attic.'

'Wood or tile?' he asked.

'Wood,' Skye replied, then, seeing his forehead crease into a frown, 'Is that not the best option?'

'It is the most expensive option. You can get some cheaper types of boarding, but it is better to use oak or pine, something strong and durable.'

Skye mulled this over as they continued through the house, listening as Andreas explained about limestone plastering, woodworm and the fortunate lack of subsidence.

'Many of the buildings on Folegandros become damaged by earthquakes,' he told her. 'You are lucky to have won a house with good foundations.'

'Earthquakes?' Skye repeated faintly, and Andreas turned to her.

'Do not worry. It is rare to feel more than a little

shaking. As soon as you realise it is happening, it will have ended.'

As if in reply, a robust gust of wind buffeted the house, slamming back the shutters and making the windows rattle. Skye was becoming slowly accustomed to the constant sound of it, sometimes a whisper, occasionally a roar. It may have been a quiet island, though Folegandros was not a silent one.

'Where do you live?' she asked, as they moved from the small kitchen towards the stairs. It was a bold question, though given how well-acquainted he was with her own living arrangements, it felt fair, and Andreas did not seem to mind.

'Karavostasis,' he said. 'I prefer to be near the water, away from so much wind.'

'That's where the main port is,' Skye said, and he nodded.

'I do not have a garden. Instead, I have a beach.'

'And have you always lived there?'

'No,' he said, 'not always. I grew up in Athens and lived there until I was twenty-one, so I have been here now for fourteen years, although I travel often for work, over to the other islands or back to the mainland.'

Skye did the maths. He was thirty-five – a year older than she was.

'Why Folegandros?' she asked, as they reached the landing.

A fleeting smile passed across his face. 'My *giagia* – that is the Greek word for grandmother – she was born here. When I was a young boy, she would tell me stories about the island, describe it to me. As soon as I was old enough to travel by myself, I came here to see it, and after that it became . . . how do I say this?' He put a hand to his chest. 'It became a part of me, and I a part of it.'

'And your grandmother?' she pressed, as they went into the room she'd been sleeping in, with its desultory airbed and open suitcase. 'Does she live here too?'

Andreas appeared momentarily stricken. 'No,' he said, shaking his head. 'She has not been back to the island since she was very young, not once.'

Skye wanted to ask more, but Andreas had become distracted. He knelt to examine the split wooden boards, applying pressure that was answered with creaks and groans.

'Rotten,' he said, confirming what she had been expecting to hear. 'We will need to rip all these out and begin again.'

It was the same in the second, smaller upstairs room, though Andreas surprised her when they climbed the ladder to the attic.

'The floor here is OK,' he said, bouncing on the balls of his feet. 'There are some places on the roof that will require attention, but we can do that from the outside.'

Skye stepped cautiously round to where she'd discovered the 'K' engraving and beckoned for him to join her.

'Do you know anything about the family who used to live here?' she asked.

Andreas steadied himself on the boards.

'No,' he said, 'but there may be a way to find out. In

Greece, it is usual for the Church to hold such records. If you want, I can make a visit to the one here, in Ano Meria, and speak to the priest?'

Skye could tell from his rapt expression that he was intrigued; drawn in, as she was, by the lure of a mystery.

'There is also a Greek National Archive,' he went on. 'But the office is on the mainland, in Athens.'

Leaving the island was not an option. Skye closed her eyes briefly as disappointment flared.

'Don't worry,' she said. 'I wouldn't want to trouble anyone, least of all you. Maybe the question of who this "K" person is, or was, is one mystery that isn't meant to be solved.'

Andreas did not look convinced.

'Somebody, somewhere, will know the truth,' he said. 'All we must do, is locate the right person.'

7

August 1940

Katerina told herself not to fall in love with Stefanos, but it was like telling the sun not to rise. And as that same sun was coaxed each evening to the horizon, so she was drawn to him, hopelessly and irretrievably.

It had soon transpired that he was the cousin of her *kounia-dos*, Michalis, come from Ikaria, he said, in search of work, though he could not settle to anything. Stefanos did not want to fish, or tend to the animals, or be shut away in a hot bakery – all he wanted, or needed, to do, was spend time with her, his 'Katsi-kaki', read his political books and essays, and indulge in lively debates with the exiled brothers, Zephyr and Atlas, who lived not far away in the village. Each night, Katerina would wait until she heard the low grumble of Baba's snores before stealing silently from the house, up to where Stefanos was waiting, the orange bud of his lit cigarette guiding her across the mountain. Together, they would sit, listening to the roaring sea, talking, confiding, laughing. She longed for him to touch her but feared it also, aware of her body in new and thrilling ways, alert to even the merest contact – a brush of his knuckles, the sweet, tobacco taste of his breath, his fingers grazing hers when they saw one another at church. Nobody could know – of that, Katerina was adamant. If Baba were to get as much as an inkling, he would lock her up. She might have reached marrying age, but there were ways of doing such things, rules that must be adhered to, and Stefanos had given her no assurances. For all she knew, he saw her as a little sister, someone to whom he felt affection, but nothing more. At twenty-one, he was only three years older than her, though he knew so much, had seen and experienced so much more than she. How could she hope to impress him, when he was a competent man, and she a sheltered farm girl?

On the evening that marked one month since they had met, Katerina went earlier than usual to their meeting place below the ridge. Her parents were in Thira, gone to visit Baba's *giagia*, who was ninety-seven and not expected to last another winter. Leni had wanted to go with them, but Michalis would not allow it.

'Why can't the stupid fool cook his own meals for once?' Katerina had fumed, only to be shushed by her elder sibling.

'Michalis works hard, *agapi mou*, it is up to me to look after him.'

It was absurd, this talk of looking after. Katerina had long watched her mother do it, and now she must endure the fate of her sister following the same path. Stefanos would never expect such coddling – he told her often that her life was her own, to live as she pleased, and that the old traditions were anchoring them in the past.

'Greece is a great ship, Kat, but I fear it is doomed to be moored forever in place, while the rest of the world moves forwards without us.'

Katerina sat down on the grassy slope and stretched her legs out in front of her. The wind had quietened to a rare whisper, for once content not to tug and claw, though she could feel the weight of rain in the air. Through the myriad hues of a burning sunset, storm clouds were gathering. She watched, and she waited.

When the night finally came, it brought with it Stefanos, a sauntering figure trailing smoke and dust.

'*Kalispera*,' Katerina said, nonchalant even as her heart began to beat twice as loud.

'*Ti canis?*' he responded, easing down next to her. 'How are you?'

'You missed the sunset,' she told him. 'It was a good one.'

Stefanos took a long drag of his cigarette.

'I was talking. Time, it vanished from me.'

'Talking to the brothers?' she said, as he blew several smoke rings into the air above them. Stefanos glanced towards her.

'Zephyr received news from the mainland,' he said. 'There are rumours about an invasion.'

He spoke so casually, as if the two of them were discussing the plot of a play.

'An invasion where?' she asked. 'By whom?'

The cigarette crackled as he inhaled.

'Into Greece, by the Italians. Mussolini thinks he can annexe us. He will hitch himself like donkey shit to the tread of Hitler's boots, but Metaxas is not a dog. He will not roll over and let the fat Italian dictator stick a knife between his ribs.'

Katerina's mouth had gone dry. 'What will happen?' she asked faintly.

Stefanos sniffed. 'There will be a battle.'

'Not here?'

He turned to look at her. '*Ochi*, Katsikaki, not here. In the north, far away from here.'

'If they tried to come here, I would fight them,' she said, sitting up straighter, pushing out her chest. 'I will kill them if they dare it.'

She fell abruptly silent as Stefanos touched a finger to her lips.

'Hush,' he said softly. 'It will not come to that.'

'You think I am too weak,' she challenged. 'That I don't mean it, that I'm nothing more than a silly girl.'

Stefanos began to laugh softly, shaking his head as he ground out the cigarette. Katerina had picked up one of the stubs once, when his attention was elsewhere, put it in a box with other small keepsakes; animal bones and shells she had picked up along the shoreline.

'You are not weak, Katsikaki,' he said, 'and you are not a fool. That is why, if war ever does come to this place, you must use your head. Not your body, but your mind – do you understand?'

'You said it would not come to—'

'Do you understand?' he persisted, all trace of

sanguinity gone. Katerina glared at him, and then, having withered under the intensity of his gaze, she nodded. Stefanos returned the gesture, then set about constructing a second cigarette, removing each component from the small leather pouch he kept in his trouser pocket.

'You are angry,' he said, to which she sighed. 'I do not say these things to belittle you, Kat, it is because I want you to stay safe. If anything were to happen—' He paused, bringing the rolling paper up to wet it against his lips. Katerina felt a stab of envy; she was jealous of the cigarette, jealous of the earth he sat on, of the clothes he wore.

'There is a war,' she reminded him bitterly. 'People all across the world are being killed – what does it matter so much about me?'

Stefanos took out his matches, struck one on a nearby rock. The flame burned intensely white as it flared, the light flashing in his eyes. Katerina's hair had been braided since the morning, and in her agitation, she began to yank out the thin strips of cloth holding each one in place. Her long dark curls fell loose around her shoulders. Leni had taught her to rub olive oil through the ends to make it shine, though Katerina had never been fond of the scent. It reminded her too acutely of Baba, and of her mama, the constraint on her life that each represented. When she looked again at Stefanos, he was staring at her, the cigarette burning away between his fingers. Bending towards her, he half-closed his eyes, breathing her in.

'Harvest,' he murmured, a smile playing around his lips.

Katerina looked stubbornly towards the horizon, saw the scatter of clouds bloom with a sudden flash of light. Nature was waging a war of its own to match that of the planet's inhabitants and would continue to do so long after the conflict came to an end. Why must these men – for it was always the men – seek to destroy one another in the pursuit of power, or because of a difference in opinion? In the end, they would all turn back to ash, and the world would swallow them whole.

'Katsikaki. Kat?'

She turned at the name.

Stefanos reached across and gently stroked a curl from her cheek.

'I want you to stay safe,' he said again. 'To stay exactly as you are, for always.'

She scoffed, making his brow crease into a frown.

'Nobody stays the same, Stefanos. We all must change, life insists upon it.'

In one swift movement, he had taken her hands in his. Katerina gasped as he squeezed her fingers.

'Promise me,' he said, urgency in his voice. 'Promise that whatever happens, you will not let that fire inside you go out.'

'It is not up to me,' she said, barely daring to whisper. 'You are the one who lit this fire.'

Stefanos drew in a breath, and then, with infinite tenderness, slid his hands up until they were cupping her cheeks. Katerina wanted to close her eyes, but she made herself look at him – really look at him, the thud of her heart loud in her ears. For a moment, she thought that he would laugh, make some joke as he always did, but instead, Stefanos moved closer.

The kiss, when it finally came, was accompanied by the first rumblings of thunder.

8

※

Skye and Andreas travelled the five kilometres from Ano Meria to Chora in his truck, parking on the boundary of the elevated village before setting off through its labyrinthine streets.

'You cannot spend one more night in this house without some plates and glasses,' he'd said, once the two of them had finished their renovation to-do list. 'There is a place we can go that sells both.'

She had not been able to argue with that, though Skye required more than crockery – she was also in urgent need of furniture, linens, lamps, cushions, a washing basket, clothes hangers and additional towels. She pictured all the items she'd left behind in England, the image of each coloured by the frustration she felt. As such, she said little, content to listen as Andreas talked. Chora, he told her, in the precise, measured way he had of speaking English, was one of the oldest medieval towns in the Cyclades, with the fortress at its top dating from the thirteenth century. It did not surprise Skye to discover that of all the villages on Folegandros, this was the one most popular with visiting tourists, and its guests were catered for by a number of cafés, bars and restaurants, as well as souvenir shops and boutiques.

'How do you like it?' he asked, as they sidestepped an old woman shrouded in black.

Skye stared around at the pristine whitewashed houses, at red chrysanthemums in clay pots and flat slate tiles baked hard by the ever-present sun.

'It's beautiful,' she said, 'but I prefer Ano Meria.'

'I agree,' he said. 'Chora is a place to visit, to take photographs, not a place to live.'

The wind dropped away as they traversed a row of modest, step-fronted houses, each one snugly pressed against the next. Built within the walls of what had once been a castle – or *'kastro'*, as Andreas referred to it – she imagined none had been altered much in the intervening years, at least not structurally. Folegandros was a place where tradition mattered, its preservation a point of pride to its people. This much had been made apparent to her in the information bundle she'd received upon securing the house.

Andreas led the way as they continued on, winding through lanes that tapered into evermore slender channels. Twice she paused to allow a cat to prowl past, and both she and Andreas had to stoop through low archways in order not to bang their heads. When they emerged onto a wide, walled viewing platform, she gazed out at the sea below; endless, fathomless, a moat between what had been, and what was to come.

'Do you see that building, there, at the top of the mountain?' Andreas asked.

Skye tore her eyes from the water.

'I can see it from my attic window,' she said, admiring the domed roof and dazzlingly white walls.

'The Church of Panagia,' he said reverently. 'There is an old story, a myth, that in 1790, a band of Algerian pirates came to Folegandros, and the local people went up to Panagia and asked the icon of the Virgin Mary inside to save them. They believed all was lost, but then, a great and powerful wind came across the sea and sank the boats. The pirates drowned, and the people of the island were spared. Many still go there today, to thank the lady for her protection.'

Skye was silent for a few beats.

'That's quite a story,' she said. 'Do you think there's any truth to it?'

Andreas's hand went to the silver cross he wore around his neck.

'I do not know for certain, but I do trust that this island is a safe place,' he said. 'Nothing bad happens here.'

Skye admired his optimism, but she couldn't quite believe him – though she wanted to. She wished it could be that simple: a safe haven sought and found.

Chora drew them back into its tangle of slate-paved lanes, through tiny squares where old men sat at tables beneath the plane trees, a backgammon board between them, pipe smoke swirling into the air. Skye found herself bombarded by colour – flashes of magenta bougainvillea, the throbbing blue of doors and shutters, a bright-red ball kicked from one child to another. She heard the distant bray of a donkey, picked up scents of rosemary, basil and grilled fish, heard the melodic *tok-tok* of windchimes, a selection of which were hanging from a display outside a small gift shop.

Andreas came to a stop.

'This place is very nice,' he told her, as Skye peered in through the open doorway. 'It is called Giant's Workshop, because there is a room at the back where the owner makes furniture, some gifts, things like this.'

'I like these,' she said, fingering a stack of wooden fish that were piled in a nearby basket, each one hand-painted and stencilled with patterns. 'I could hang some in my bathroom.'

Scooping up four in various shades, she made her way inside, where shelves groaned under the weight of ornaments, trinkets and Folegandros-branded souvenirs. There were model sailboats, a musical merry-go-round, spinning tops and pull-along toys. In addition to the woodwork offerings, there was a display of ceramic mugs, plates and serving bowls, many of which bore the image of an octopus, sardine, or other sea-dwelling creature. Skye chose a pair of dinner and side plates, plus one large serving platter with a single pink fish design. Andreas was at the till, talking to a man of around fifty with excessively hairy forearms, who smiled across at Skye as she stacked her crockery in her arms.

'I want to buy everything,' she said as she joined them, and the man's smile grew broader. 'Can I leave these here while I keep looking?'

He inclined his head.

'*Parakaló.*'

'If you decide to buy any furniture second hand,'

Andreas said, as the two of them moved towards an arrangement of birdhouses, 'the items can be restored here using the traditional methods and tools.'

'It sounds as if he has you on the payroll,' she remarked, to which Andreas laughed.

'*Ela*, no. It is nice to have a few pieces like this – a chair, perhaps a small table – then the rest, you can order in flat-pack boxes.'

Her dad had once made a similar suggestion, not long after Skye moved into her first flat. There was limited space inside, and she had limited funds with which to furnish it.

'Think about what you use most and go from there,' Cosmo MacKinnon had said. And she had. She splurged on a solid-oak bedframe and sturdy chest of drawers, but went budget-friendly with IKEA bookcases and plant stands from Home Bargains. The next place she lived came furnished, much of it built-in or made from glass and metal: cold, characterless pieces that she would never have chosen herself.

Now, she would never have to again.

Skye reached up and unhooked a wooden-framed mirror from the wall. She looked past her own reflection and caught sight of Andreas – his hair a stark black against her blond, his sun-warmed skin a contrast to her pale, freckled complexion. For the briefest moment, their eyes met, and in his she glimpsed something – a flicker of concern, perhaps, or just curiosity, as if she were a puzzle he was trying to solve.

She cleared her throat and lowered the mirror,

carrying it – and two clay mugs – back to where she'd left her stack of plates. The man at the till packaged each item with meticulous care, sealing bubble wrap with strips of tape and layering tissue paper around her wooden fish. As she tucked away her change, Andreas set one of the birdhouses gently on the counter.

'Do you like this one?' he asked.

The small wooden structure had a roof made from assorted chunks of driftwood, and the front was painted with olive leaves and flowers.

'It's adorable,' she said. 'Is it for you?'

Andreas huffed with laughter. '*Ela*, not for me – for you.'

'Me?'

'I have already four,' he said, exchanging a look with the shop owner, who grinned.

'I'll buy it then,' Skye replied, but as she reached for it, Andreas swept it out of her grasp.

'It is a gift,' he protested.

Another gift. From the man who had brought her food, wine, and an admittedly awful frying pan – all essentials. This, though, was different: a gift given not out of sympathy but a desire to please. She wasn't sure how she felt about that.

Skye was about to argue when her phone vibrated. Stepping back, she fished it from her bag, her heart sinking as she saw the screen.

A message, from *him*, three simple words that called a halt to the spinning of her world.

Where are you?

9

Skye stared at her phone.

One bar of signal, that was all it had taken to drive a stake of dread through her heart. He was always going to reach out, to demand an explanation, but the silence of the past few days had allowed her to hope.

'Is everything OK?' Andreas asked as Skye shoved the phone back into her pocket. 'Has something happened?'

'No, nothing,' she said, her teeth clenched as she hefted her bag of purchases.

'*Ela*, let me—'

She stepped away, making for the exit, the bubble-wrapped mirror awkwardly pressed to her side. He followed, the birdhouse left forgotten on the counter behind them, and didn't object when she suggested they head back to the truck.

The interior was baking hot, and having started the engine, Andreas promptly switched on the air-conditioning.

'Have you decided yet what to do about furniture?' he asked, turning in his seat as he reversed out from their parking spot. When Skye didn't answer, he glanced across at her.

'There are good stores in Santorini, more in Paros, and many, of course, in Athens. You can pay for the delivery or travel across on the ferry to collect things yourself.'

Skye was only half-listening, and moments later, found herself apologising for having ignored him.

'You say sorry a lot,' he observed.

'Do I?'

'This is not a very Greek behaviour.'

'Oh,' she said distractedly. 'Sorry.'

Andreas groaned. '*Ela re*,' he muttered in mock despair, shaking his head over the steering wheel. Skye tried to focus on the view, but the vast sweep of sea no longer felt like a security blanket, the desolate land that flanked the highway an empty surface from which she could easily be snatched. Shifting in her seat, she took out her phone and once again read the text.

Where are you?

There was no way of knowing when it had been sent, not without opening it properly – and doing so would alert the sender.

'Pantelis's taverna has Wi-Fi,' Andreas said. 'If you want to stop to send a message?'

'No need.' Skye's tone was too shrill. 'It's fine.'

As they reached the hillside in Ano Meria, she was ready and leapt out as soon as Andreas applied the handbrake. The scene was lively. Two other trucks were parked outside the large house, one a gleaming Toyota that looked fresh off the forecourt, the other a dented wreck. A flustered-looking man with sand-coloured hair was struggling beneath the weight of a potted orange tree. Andreas hurried forward and grasped one side of it. Skye could tell the newcomer was British from the grateful 'Thank you' he issued, though the woman who emerged through the front door moments later, svelte in form-fitting gym gear, greeted her with a cheerful 'Hey' in a distinct American accent.

'I'm Victoria,' she said, as she and Skye did the strange dance of whether to shake hands or kiss cheeks. In the end, they did neither, though Victoria did not once stop smiling. Having learned Skye's name, she enthused that it was 'so pretty', adding, 'I have an aunt named Star.'

'We have a Joy here, too,' Skye told her, and Victoria nodded with enthusiasm.

'Yeah, we met her already. She's just over helping the other guy – Theo, I think he said his name was, has his kid with him, little boy, doesn't say a lot.'

Skye craned her neck and saw a stack of boxes piled up outside one of the shabbier, single-storey dwellings, a battered red jeep parked nearby. Andreas and the sandy-haired man had deposited the tree and were now lowering a static exercise bike from the rear of the newer truck.

'That's my husband, Adam,' Victoria said. 'He's English, same as you, but we live in the States – or did, I guess.' She looked around, ponytail swinging. 'I didn't expect it to be so . . .'

'Quiet?' Skye suggested.

'Everywhere is quiet after New York,' Victoria replied. 'But it's more than that. It's not so much silent as forgotten, you know? Like a closet nobody's opened for a long time. It has that aura about it.' As she spoke, she rubbed the top of her arms. 'God, listen to me being all spooked, talking about auras as if I know anything about them.'

'You're not a psychic then?' Skye said, and Victoria laughed.

'Try fitness instructor, although I doubt there are many gyms in this place.'

Skye had to agree. But who wanted to run on a treadmill when you could swim in the Aegean Sea?

'Adam's a lawyer,' Victoria went on, flinching as a large insect hovered close to her nose. 'He's on a short sabbatical for now, but eventually he'll need to set up remotely. The lady we collected our key from a short while ago said there's no broadband up here. I thought Adam was going to faint, right there on her office floor.'

'Is it just the two of you?' Skye asked.

Victoria appeared to droop a fraction.

'Yeah,' she said with reluctance. 'Just the two of us.'

They went to offer the two men some assistance, and Skye pushed all thoughts of the text message to the back of her mind as she ferried possessions into the big house. Despite her claim of having 'packed light', Victoria seemed to have brought an inordinate amount of clothing and cheerfully told Skye that her heaviest case was 'literally just cosmetics'. Adam, whose shirt was wringing with sweat, tripped over carrying a crate of white wine into the kitchen and promptly cut his hand open on the broken glass.

'I have no idea where the first-aid kit is,' Victoria wailed, only for Andreas to magic one up from the glove compartment of his truck.

'That bloke's a bloody marvel,' Joy remarked. She had rolled up with a welcome six-pack of Mythos and was busy flicking through a cardboard box of framed pictures. 'Who's the photographer, do you reckon?' she asked Skye. 'Her or him?'

Skye, who had seen Adam cradling a camera bag on one of her trips out to the car, felt confident enough to make an educated guess.

'Whoever it is, they have a good eye,' Joy said, extracting an image of the Manhattan Bridge and holding it up. 'It's real tricky to get a fresh angle of a structure this well known.'

'I like all those old photos of New York,' Skye said. 'Seeing how people lived, what they wore, how they were day to day.'

'You're more interested in faces than landscapes?' Joy said. 'That's fair enough. Hey, do you reckon there are any old photos of this place, you know, from back in the days before the war?'

'There must be,' Skye reasoned. 'Even if the people living here didn't have access to a camera, there would have been visitors – European tourists if nobody else. There are plenty of photos taken in and around Athens, and loads of Corfu, too, both before and after the occupation.'

'Greece was occupied?' Joy asked.

'Yep. The Italians were here, along with the Germans and the Bulgarians,' Skye said, casting her mind back to her university textbooks. 'I think I'm right in saying that Folegandros was one of the islands that the Italians took, until the country surrendered in 1943. After that, the Germans moved in, though by then, of course, things were beginning to unravel for the Axis.'

Joy slotted the framed photograph back into the box.

'I wonder if any of those Nazi drongos took over one of our houses,' she said.

Skye grimaced. 'There would've been fewer soldiers here than on the mainland,' she said. 'But there's always a chance. Some of the things that happened in Greece were appalling. I read that—'

'Don't tell me.' Joy slapped her hands over her ears. 'My imagination is bloody bad enough.'

Victoria came out through the kitchen doorway and smiled briefly at them before heading for the stairs.

'Your hubby all right?' Joy called, just as Andreas emerged, followed closely by Adam. There were spots of red on the front of his shirt, a wad of plasters around one finger.

'Apologies for all the fuss,' he said, looking faintly embarrassed. 'The trouble with everything being so white around here is that it shows up the blood far more dramatically.'

'I think I've got some bicarb of soda under my sink,' Joy said. 'I'll go and fetch it.'

'Hey, guys,' Victoria's voice called from above.

'You're not going to believe it, but I have signal up here.'

Adam almost stumbled in his haste to join her, but Skye went straight for the front door, keen to escape far beyond the reach of any signal. Why hadn't she just turned the damn thing off – or better yet, thrown it overboard from the ferry on her way across from Piraeus? Fully intending to take if not the second then definitely the first option, she ran along the stony path outside only to freeze as she felt it.

The vibration of a ringing phone against her side.

10

It was her mother.

Skye breathed out, swore, then answered.

'Finally. Where on earth are you?'

'Hi, Mum.'

The line was faint. Skye pressed the handset closer to her ear, listening to the volley of tuts that followed.

'Glad to hear you're alive,' her mother said sarcastically. 'I've only called you, oh, eight times in the past two days.'

'Sorry.' Skye waved limply at Joy, who was back with a selection of cleaning products, including – rather alarmingly – a bottle of turps. 'I meant to check in, I've just been busy.'

'Busy?' her mother said. 'Busy where? Doing what? Are you abroad, the ringtone sounded strange?'

Skye made a murmur of disagreement that was quickly interrupted.

'I know you're not with Sal, I've already spoken to her.'

'You called Sal?'

'Well, you weren't picking up. I thought if you'd run

off anywhere, it would be to her. Wouldn't exactly be the first time.'

'What did she say?' Skye asked, to which her mother sighed.

'That she had no idea where you were, although I got the distinct impression she was lying to me. Lies are like rotten eggs – they always leave a bad smell.'

She should not have answered the phone. Cassandra MacKinnon, corporate lawyer, business owner and breaker of the world's balls was not accustomed to being ignored. Now that the worry over her daughter's safety was gone, Skye guessed her mother would go in on the attack.

'I've told you time and time again,' she said, 'running away from your problems never solves them.'

What was it Skye's father had once said? 'Your mum is full of so much fire that she could easily have earned herself a walk-on part in *Game of Thrones*.'

The phone was hot against her ear.

'I know you lost your job, but so have a lot of people, and not all of them upped and fled the country as a result.'

'It's got nothing to do with that,' Skye said truthfully, moving to one side as Andreas appeared. Seeing her on the phone, he raised a questioning brow, and she flashed a smile, watching as he crossed to the truck and lifted down another box. This one had *Adam's office* written on the side, and several cables trailing from a rip at the bottom.

'Listen, Mum, this isn't really a good time—'

'Are you going to be back by the tenth?' she said tersely, and for a moment, Skye was lost.

'The tenth?'

'Yes, of June, as in six days from now. It's Jonathan's sixtieth. Don't tell me you've forgotten.'

Skye said nothing.

'For goodness' sake. The table plan is done. You RSVP'd a yes.'

Had she? Skye cast her mind back, tried to recall an invite arriving.

'And are you getting him the cufflinks, or the silk tie? Please stick to the list I sent over, you know how particular he is when it comes to gifts.'

Skye could feel a heat rising through her that had nothing to do with the soaring afternoon temperatures. Jonathan, her mother's partner – Cassandra abhorred the term 'boyfriend' – was a priggish bore of a man with an ego the size of Belgium. It had been loathe at first sight for each of them, and matters had not much improved since. Skye's phone buzzed with a notification, and checking the screen, she saw that another message had come through, this time from her friend Sal.

Your mum is on the hunt, she had written. *Call me when you can. Love u.*

Too late, Skye realised her error. By reading Sal's text, she had shown herself to be online.

'Shit,' she muttered, fumbling in her belated attempt to change the settings.

'Charming,' her mother barked.

Victoria came out through the open front door.

'Oh, great,' she said to Skye, 'you're still here. We thought we'd all wander down to the taverna – lunch on us, to say thanks for helping out.'

Skye clamped her hand over the phone, nodding furiously.

'Are you still there?' Her mother sounded disjointed, as if she was underwater. 'The line is breaking up.'

'I really have to go,' Skye said, her tone rising as Adam, Andreas and Joy filed out into the yard. 'Sorry about the dinner. I'll explain everything when I can, OK?'

'No,' her mother said imperiously. 'It is not OK. Tell me where you are.'

Joy paused by the path.

'You coming, chook?' she asked. Skye gave her a thumbs up, trying to communicate through gesture alone that they should all go ahead without her, that she would catch them up. Tears were beginning to threaten; her neck and face were hot, hands clammy.

'I can't,' she whispered into the phone.

'Can't? Can't what?'

'Tell you where I am,' Skye said. 'I'm sorry, Mum, but I can't.'

'Are you in trouble? Is someone holding you against your will?'

'No, Mum – I'm fine. I'm safe. I just needed to get away.'

'Oh.' She let out an arduous sigh. 'Have you and Martyn fallen out again?'

Martyn.

At the mention of his name, Skye went cold. Bile rose in her throat as she croaked out a faint 'No.'

'I'm happy to call him, if you want,' her mother went on. 'I'm a proficient mediator. Did it enough times when I was working my way through the divorce court ranks.'

'No.' Skye practically shouted the word. 'Please, Mum. Leave it to me to sort out.'

Cassandra MacKinnon launched into another tirade, but her words were breaking up. Skye moved away from Adam and Victoria's house, passing her cracked front door and heading up the hillside beyond, where she slipped, scrabbled, and almost fell to her knees. The signal was lost, her connection to her mother severed, and through her ragged breaths, Skye tapped at the screen, blocking first Cassandra's number and then Martyn's. Only then was she able to breathe normally again, though her dash up the stony slope had left her chest burning. She had done it again, the thing her mother had so callously accused her of doing whenever life became tough. But this time, Skye had not run away out of selfishness, she had run out of necessity.

Mindlessly, she continued to climb, over tufts of grass and sand-blasted hulks of rock. The sun beat down against her shoulders, dappling sweat across her neck and back. There was nobody in sight, though she felt pursued. She saw a narrow ridge a short distance ahead, and half-fell to the ground below it, blinking away dust as an image of the village and sea beyond swam into view. She saw the roof of her house with its missing tiles, the glint of a faraway attic window, the pale walls and chipped blue paint. Her phone was still in her hand, and for several still minutes, she contemplated hurling it as hard as she could down the mountainside. What was it, in the end, if not a portal to the past?

Skye shut her eyes as a memory swirled, the image tarnished by shame. She pressed the heels of her hands against her temples, a scream building that she released through gritted teeth. She could hear him now, the ominous tone of the quietly furious, his mouth set as he crouched beside her, a cup and spoon in hand.

'Behave like a baby, and I'll treat you like a baby.'

Skye shied away now as she had then, a whimper escaping as she once more felt the hard edge of the spoon against her lips, the cold smear of pureed food on her chin, the mocking taunt of 'Open wide'. The trembling began, every part of her quivering. Skye curled into a ball, dropped her head onto her knees, and began to weep.

11

Skye did not join the others at the taverna.

She stayed where she was, in the dirt – staring but not seeing, listening but not hearing, thinking while trying her hardest *not* to remember. There was a distance between her and Martyn now, but she couldn't rid him from her mind, couldn't silence the sense that he was coming for her. His message – three words that would seem innocuous to most people – represented the firing of a starting pistol. Martyn Lockhart was on the hunt, and he wouldn't stop until he found her.

Aware of movement on the slope below, Skye looked down and saw the ginger cat, Tigri, making his way towards her, delicate paws sidestepping stones and tufts of grass.

'*Geia sou*,' she said. The Greek language sounded strange in her voice, though she supposed it would become less so with more effort. Tigri responded by nuzzling his soft head against her ankle. He wore no collar, yet appeared well fed and healthy, his eyes bright and fur clean.

'Hungry?' she asked, scratching under his chin. 'Me too. Come on then.'

When she stood and headed back the way she'd come, the cat followed, lagging at first then bounding ahead as they neared the houses. There was another pick-up truck parked at an angle outside the cottage next door to Joy's. It had a UK licence plate and a sticker on the bumper that read: *Sorry for driving so close in front of you.* As Skye approached, a crash rang out from inside the house, followed by a shout of frustration. The door flew open and a petite young woman burst into the yard, chased by another – a head taller though seemingly younger. Both had the same fiery red hair.

'How can someone so small be so bloody clumsy?' the taller woman raged, in a strong Bristolian accent. Then, noticing Skye, 'Oh, hello there.'

'Hi,' Skye said. The shorter women smiled with faint embarrassment.

'Sorry about all the yelling,' she said. 'I dropped a vase – but it wasn't *my* fault,' she added, turning to her pursuer. 'I tripped over Bruno.'

'I told you to leave him in the truck.' The other woman sighed and wiped her hands on the front of her dungarees. 'Bruno is our almost-blind basset hound,' she told Skye. 'No one knows how old he is in dog years, but I reckon he must be at least a hundred by human standards.'

'Rude,' the other woman intoned. 'Bruno isn't a day over ninety.'

Right on cue, a large, droopy-eared dog lolloped out of the house and walked straight into a stack of clay pots. Tigri, who had sprung up onto the mottled stone wall that surrounded the property, hissed in disgust.

'Oh, how gorgeous.' The first woman shot forward, bending so she could peer at the cat's face. 'Nice moggy,' she said. 'Is he yours?'

'Not mine, no.' Skye matched her smile. 'I think he might belong to the village collectively – he certainly seems to behave as if he does.'

'That's cats for you,' the woman said. 'I'm Mia, by the way. And that crosspatch over there is my younger sister, Dusty.'

'Younger but wiser,' Dusty called across, and Mia rolled her eyes theatrically.

'Is it just the two of you?' Skye asked, once she'd introduced herself. Dusty glanced up from where she'd bent to tie her laces. She wore the same thick-soled boots as Andreas.

'There's a third sister,' she said. 'Louisa, she's the eldest. I think she went off in search of a shop, though I have to admit, I wasn't really paying much attention to what she said.'

Bruno gave up trying to find his way back indoors and lay down across the front step, stubby tail flicking away flies.

'Of all the places . . .' Dusty sighed, readjusting her baseball cap over an untidy bun.

'Do you want to see our house?' Mia offered. 'It's a bit of a shell, but there's running water and electricity, which, apparently, we should feel thankful for.'

'The listing said derelict,' Dusty reminded her. 'I'm thankful we have a roof.'

They took it in turns to step over Bruno – who'd rolled onto his back and was snoring loudly, all four paws dangling in mid-air – and went through into an open-plan room cluttered with half-open boxes, suitcases and three tightly knotted binbags.

'Duvets,' Mia said, prodding one with her foot. 'Not that we'll need them, if it stays this hot.'

'I've been sleeping under a pashmina,' Skye said, deciding not to mention the hated airbed.

Dusty had marched over to the far wall, to where a livid crack ran across the plaster.

'What in the crumble-stiltskin?' she said with a groan.

Mia pulled a face and ushered Skye through into the kitchen, which was even more compact than her own. The sisters had only a small fridge and microwave, and, aside from a single rickety chair, no furniture to speak of.

'I'd offer you something to drink,' Mia said, 'but we have no teabags, coffee, milk or sugar, and I've no idea which box the mugs are in.'

Skye's stomach growled, the sound embarrassingly loud.

'I can stretch to a chocolate digestive, though?' Mia went on. 'I'm sure there was a half-finished packet somewhere around here, unless Dusty ate them. She eats like most people breathe,' she added, and Skye laughed as an indignant 'Oi' filtered through from the other room.

'The bathroom is in there' – Mia indicated a second door – 'but that's it. The only other space we have is at the far end of the garden, and that's just a hut full of broken pots and a few old tools. Dusty has grand plans for the place, of course, but for a while, it looks like we'll be bunking down on the floor, all three of us sharing one room again, like we did as kids.'

'You don't sound too thrilled by the prospect,' Skye observed, and Mia shrugged.

'Needs must. At least I can use Bruno as a pillow.'

'Is he your dog then?'

Mia ran a finger along the wall, watching as a shoal of plaster cascaded to the floor. She wrinkled her nose, then turned to Skye.

'Officially, he belongs to all of us, but I've looked after him the most since my mum passed away. Bruno and me, we have a bond.'

Touched by Mia's obvious sorrow, Skye searched for something to say, the silence that stretched broken by another loud groan from Dusty.

'I could park a quad bike in this crevasse,' she muttered, before calling through, 'This whole interior will need to be replastered.'

'Don't pretend you're not glad about it,' Mia called back. Then, to Skye, she added, 'Dusty works in construction, hence all the tools, and the grand plans.'

'And you?'

'I'm a vet,' she said, with a certain amount of pride. 'Newly qualified. I don't suppose you know if there's a clinic on the island?'

'Sorry, no.' Skye thought for a moment. 'Though if there is one, it'll most likely be in Chora.'

Mia nodded, looking thoughtful. 'I hope you're right,' she said. 'Moving here wasn't even my idea. It wasn't—Never mind.'

'It wasn't what?' Skye said, but Mia had stepped away and was peering into the other room.

'Did you hear that?' she said. 'I think there's someone outside.'

It was Andreas, accompanied by the eldest sister, Louisa, who was tall and willowy with a Rapunzel sweep of red curls. Both were holding bulging carrier bags.

'I might have overdone it,' Louisa said, lowering her cargo of groceries to the floor. 'There were so many delicious-looking things, all so fresh, and the nice man at the shop insisted I take a bottle of ouzo on the house.'

'I'm starved,' Dusty said, bending to root through the nearest bag. Having extracted a packet of Lays oregano crisps, she tore them open and began to crunch noisily. Bruno the basset hound, having been roused from his doorstep slumber by the whiff of food, heaved himself onto all four paws and shambled towards them.

'Not a chance,' Dusty scolded, when he pressed his snout against her leg. Mia threw her sister a scathing look before digging in the pocket of her shorts.

'Here,' she said, tossing the dog a treat. 'Good boy.'

'This is Andreas,' Louisa said, turning pink as the man in question smiled around at them. 'He saw me struggling up the hill and offered to help.'

'It was my pleasure,' he said. 'I am always at the service of a lady in need.'

Dusty choked on a mouthful of crisps, and Mia shot back with a yelp as crumbs sprayed out in all directions. It was clear that nobody was going to introduce Skye to Louisa, so this she did herself, pointing across the hillside to indicate which house was hers.

'You are the final arrivals,' Andreas told them. 'The last lottery winners on Folegandros.'

'That can't be right,' Skye said. 'What about the sixth person? There's still one property yet to be claimed.'

Andreas rubbed a hand across his jaw. *'Nai,'* he said, sounding thoughtful. 'There is another empty house here, but I do not think it belongs to the municipality. There must be some other situation.'

'Another owner?'

He shrugged. 'Perhaps so.'

The five of them stared across at the abandoned property, with its crumbling outer walls and collapsed roof. There were only two windows at the front, and each had been boarded up with thick planks of wood, hammered in place from the inside.

'Whoever's it is, they're going to have a hell of a job on their hands,' Dusty mused. She had finished the first packet of crisps and was now polishing an apple on the trouser leg of her dungarees. 'Roofs don't come cheap.'

'Your own foundations are some of the best,' Andreas informed her. 'I did not have to do much to make the house secure.'

'The new supporting structure is your handiwork?' Dusty asked, and he nodded. 'Oh. Well, I'm not sure I would've done it like that, but I guess it'll do the job until I get around to replacing it.'

The genial smile fell from Andreas's face. 'You do not think it is good enough?'

Dusty bit into her apple and chewed for a few seconds before replying. 'I'm sure it's sturdy, it's just a bit . . . unsightly.'

'It is traditional,' he said firmly, as a still-blushing Louisa took the carrier bags from his hands. Andreas folded his arms across his chest. He looked seriously unimpressed. Skye met Mia's eye, both women suppressing the urge to grin.

'Greeks have been constructing their houses this way for hundreds of years, and here on Folegandros, we build strong homes, those that can withstand the wind, the rain, and the earthquakes.'

Dusty began to twist the stalk off her apple, reciting the alphabet as she went. '. . . G, H, I, J—oh, J. Who do I know whose name begins with J?'

'You'll know your new neighbour Joy soon,' Skye said.

Dusty screwed up her features. 'Wrong sex, but never mind,' she said, and having thrown the apple core as far as she could into the surrounding undergrowth, she headed back into the house.

'Sorry about that,' Mia said to Andreas. 'She doesn't mean to be rude, she just likes to do everything her own way. Having the job she does can be tough – there's still a lot of sexism in the construction industry, at least in the UK,' she hastened.

'*Entáxei*,' he muttered. 'It is OK.'

Bruno sniffed at Mia's pocket in search of more treats, and Andreas crouched briefly to pat him. Tigri, meanwhile, remained on the wall, washing his bottom and feigning indifference.

'I should let you get on,' Skye said. 'Unpack and settle in. You know where I am if you need anything.'

Mia smiled gratefully, but Andreas continued to frown.

'I am not sexist,' he told her, 'but I am right to be worried. Things here, they must be done a special way, to a standard that is very particular for this island. I'm not saying that it must be me who does the work, but it is important that you use the right materials and processes.'

'Dusty knows her stuff,' Mia assured him. 'I'm sure she'll do everything by the book.'

'She must.' Andreas's expression was stern, his tone no-nonsense. 'To do it any other way would place all of you in a lot of danger.'

12

September 1940

They went by boat to the cave, Stefanos pulling the oars while Katerina took charge of the rudder, steering their course around the north-eastern coast of the island.

At one time, it had been possible to reach Chrysospilia by land, though the carved footholds had long since been eroded by the elements, and Katerina did not want Stefanos to be at risk. She was nimble across the rocky terrain, he less so. Unlike her, he had not grown up on Folegandros, had not spent his childhood scavenging every inch of the land in search of adventure. In truth, Katerina would be placing both of them in danger with this excursion, but she wanted Stefanos to see the places that meant something to her. To know them would help him to know her a little better.

'We can climb up from there,' she said, pointing to a spot below the mouth of the cave, which was situated sixty feet or so above them. Stefanos's gaze trailed up, then he turned to look at her, a question in his dark eyes.

'*Paihnidaki*,' she teased. *Child's play*.

While Stefanos unfurled a rope and fastened the boat to an outcrop of rock, Katerina tucked up her long skirt and strapped the small pack she'd brought across her body, feeling the cool surface of the pot inside as it pressed against her cotton shirt. Atlas had shown her how to blend the mixture using charcoal, reddened dirt and animal fats.

'It has to last for ever,' she'd told him, and her friend had smiled in a way that showed her he understood.

'Do not worry, Flogeros. *Fiery one*. It will.'

The exiled brothers were two of only three souls on the island who knew about her relationship with Stefanos. Leni was the third, though Katerina had only confessed the truth to her sister the previous day, making her promise not to breathe a word to anyone else, not Michalis, and definitely not their parents. Baba and Mama had yet to return from Thira, and miss them though she did, Katerina had benefitted from their absence. Without anyone there to take note of her comings and goings, she had been free to spend as much time as she pleased with the man who had stolen her heart.

'Be careful, *agapi mou*,' Leni had warned. 'He has a target painted on him for trouble, that one.'

Of course her sister would say such a thing. Her own love affair had been predictable, the man she married ordinary, and the life they lived together dull. Leni must be burning with envy that Katerina had found a man such as Stefanos to love. He was everything that the uptight and worrisome Michalis was not – and thank the gods for it.

'I will go ahead,' she said now, stepping over the side of the boat and springing up onto the steep Panagia rock beyond. 'Watch where I put my feet and use the same places.'

'You have never looked more like a little goat,' he called after her as she began to climb. Katerina laughed.

'You are the one who enjoys kissing a goat,' she threw back, and heard him bleat loudly in reply.

Their shared laughter was snatched away by concentration as they each focused on the task at hand. The rock face was sharp and slick, the sea below hurling up great shoals of salty spray that soaked Katerina's clothes and left her hair dripping. Motivated by a desire to escape it, she began to move more quickly, Chrysospilia growing larger with every second that passed. When she finally reached the cavernous entrance, she allowed herself to rest, shuffling round into a sitting position as she waited for Stefanos to join her.

'My God,' he said, through breaths that were coming fast and ragged. '*Paihnidaki?* I do not think so, Katsikaki. Are you trying to kill me, is that it?'

Katerina bent and kissed the top of his head.

'If that is what I wanted to do,' she said, 'then I would have done it a long time ago, perhaps while you were sleeping.'

Stefanos pushed himself up from where he'd collapsed, panting, against the stone floor.

'You would steal into my bedroom in the dead of night?' he said. 'I think I would enjoy that.'

His eyes lingered on hers, and she held his gaze for a moment, toying with him before getting to her feet.

'*Ela*,' she said, reaching a hand down to him. 'Come and see my cave.'

They began by circuiting the first chamber, Katerina talking as they went, explaining about the artefacts that had been discovered inside, the Roman cistern, broken shards of pottery, piles of shells and the skeletal remains that were thought to have belonged to Greeks who had entered the cave to hide from pirates, only to become stranded. The second chamber was at the end of a narrow corridor, and she took Stefanos's hand as they entered it, felt the tightening of his fingers around hers as he stared at the stalactites.

'This is what I believe the moon to look like,' he said. 'These formations, they do not seem as if they are part of our world.'

The leather pouch he kept in his pocket had somehow remained dry on the climb up from the boat, and taking out a match, Stefanos struck it. The stalactites shone gold and red. Katerina knew from Baba's teachings that it was the iron oxide that gave each its colour.

'Here,' she said, taking his arm, 'bring the flame to the wall.'

Stefanos's mouth fell open as a series of names appeared in the pool of flickering light.

'Who painted these?' he asked, drawing his arm up and around. More names and places were etched not only on the cave walls, but across the ceiling, a beautiful jumble of letters and marks. Katerina thought of the single 'K' she had carved in the attic and shook her head. How futile that seemed when compared to this.

'They have always been here,' she told him. 'Baba says they are the names of young people who came here to worship Artemis and Apollo, perhaps as long ago as the fourth century before Christ.'

'Over two thousand years ago?' Stefanos's eyes bulged. 'And they are still here, not washed away.'

'Remembered for always,' she said, her throat tight with emotion. It had always moved her, this place. The whisper of the waves could so easily have been the murmurings of the past, voices of those who had deemed this island special. Katerina slipped her bag from her shoulders and opened it, taking out the pot and small brush. There was an empty space on the wall, not far from where they'd come through from the first chamber, and it was here that she began to paint her name. Only when she had finished, did she turn to Stefanos.

'Now you,' she said, and he nodded, striking a second match and passing it across to her. The flame danced, throwing warped shadows, though she held it as still as she could. He had a steadier hand than she and finished his inscription more quickly. Afterwards they stood, shoulder to shoulder, admiring their work.

'I need to tell you something.'

Katerina stiffened. 'Tell me what?'

Stefanos sighed, and taking her hands, turned her to face him. 'I have to leave.'

Time slowed, paused, stood still.

'Leave?'

'The war is coming closer,' he said. 'I hear the thud of the enemy's boots.'

'It is not our war,' she hissed. 'It is their war.'

'*Ochi*, Katsikaki, it will become Greece's war soon enough. The people will resist, and I must be there to fight alongside them.'

'Why?' she insisted. 'Why does it have to be you? Why not every other man in Greece before you?'

He attempted to draw her closer, but she pulled away.

'Why?' she said again, her nose stinging, eyes burning.

'You would have me be a coward?' he said. 'Hide beneath your skirts while the Axis powers trample across my country, kill my people.'

'It is not brave to die for nothing,' she told him, furious now, with him but also with herself, for not having prepared a better argument.

'I will not die,' he said, urgent now. 'But if I did, it would be for freedom, for the most important thing of all.'

'Then I will come with you,' she began, but he shook his head. 'Why is it acceptable for you to go, but not for me? I am strong like you, I am braver than you think, Stefanos. And I love my country. I love Greece.'

'You are strong,' he said, lowering his head to hers. 'You are strong and brave and patriotic – it is why I love you.'

Katerina's head jerked backwards.

'You—you love me?'

'*Ela re.*' He slid his hands to her waist. 'Of course I love you.'

'Then stay,' she pleaded. 'There is nothing more important than love, not even freedom.'

When he said nothing, Katerina felt her body sag with despair. How could she survive without him? What would she do if the worst were to happen?

'When?' she asked, barely daring to hear his answer.

Stefanos drew her close against him. 'Soon,' he said. 'I will go with Michalis to Athens, and from there to the north.'

'Michalis?' Katerina's blood turned to stone. 'Your cousin Michalis, my brother-in-law is going with you?'

'*Nai.*'

'But he is a—How can he? I don't understand.'

'He is not so different to me,' Stefanos said. 'He wants to play his part in this war, as his father did, twenty-five years before him.'

'Leni will be broken by this,' Katerina said. 'She will blame you.'

'I know,' he said simply. 'And I am sorry for it.'

'I cannot leave her, not when Baba and Mama are away. But after they return, I will come to find you. I will fight alongside you and—'

Her next words were taken by his kiss, and for a moment, as she melted away on the tide of sensation, Katerina believed that she had won, that he would stay, that they would remain together, here on Folegandros, and be happy.

Stefanos released her, his lips coming to rest against hers.

'I will write to you,' he said. 'Tell you what is happening.'

'When will you come back?'

'As soon as I can.'

'I will worry,' she told him. 'Even as I sleep.'

He kissed her again, over and over, not only her lips but her cheeks and throat, the soft dip behind each ear, the closed lid of her eyes as she fought to hold back the tears.

'Do not worry,' he said. 'Fears are like oil on the water of your dreams, Katsikaki – they will always rise to the top, if you let them.'

'What should I do to stop them?' she asked, clinging to him.

'Do as the people who came to this cave did, when they wrote their names on its walls. Do as we did, when we added our own.'

There was no need to ask him what he meant, because Katerina already knew the answer.

All she needed to do was believe.

13

If Skye had to choose one word to sum up her first week on Folegandros, it wouldn't have been something idyllic, such as 'peaceful' or 'sun-soaked', but rather 'chaotic'. Despite the gentle pulse ticking over at the heart of the island, life for its newest residents was anything but serene. When she opened her eyes each morning, the patched airbed lumpy beneath her, Skye was met not with birdsong and the purring breeze, but growling engines, a whirring cement mixer and the thud of Andreas's heavy fist against her front door.

His was the first face she saw, he the first person she spoke to and, more often than not, the last, too. Good morning: *kalimera*; and goodnight: *kalinychta*, were among the first entries on her slowly growing list of Greek words.

As promised, Andreas had designated her house a priority, and in the days since their drive out to Chora, he had fitted steel support beams in the attic and stripped one bedroom of rotten floorboards. For the past two nights, Skye had bunked down in the main living area, but that, too, was about to become off-limits. The downstairs floors had to be levelled before the terracotta tiles could be laid – a process that involved spreading fresh cement.

'It will take around forty-eight hours to dry,' he told her. They had stepped outside to escape the noise of Stamatis's hammering, though Skye could still hear it, low and monotonous.

'Does that mean I won't be able to get in or out?' she asked. Andreas rubbed his chin in the way he always did when turning a problem over in his mind.

'We can set planks across from the front door to the stairs,' he said. 'But it is better if you stay somewhere else for a few nights. There are some nice hotels in Chora and—'

'I don't want to stay in a hotel,' she said. Hotels meant credit cards and names kept on file. 'I'll just be very careful not to step on the floor.'

'It is your decision, of course.' He paused, jaw shifting as if working against him. There was plaster dust in his hair, a crease deepening between his brows. 'Although' – she'd known there would be a caveat – 'if there is any damage, we will need to begin again.'

Just then, Joy's halo of copper curls appeared around the side of Andreas's truck, framing a smile that widened when she caught sight of them.

'G'day,' she said, long red skirt swirling as she made her way over. 'How are we doing today, folks?'

Andreas got in before Skye had the chance.

'We were in the middle of discussing the problem of Skye's floor,' he said, going on to explain briefly about the wet cement, and her reluctance to stay elsewhere while it dried.

'Don't waste your money on a hotel,' Joy said to Skye. 'You can bunk up with me.'

'Bravo.' Andreas gave a short nod, as if that settled the matter. 'The perfect solution.'

'Are you sure?' Skye turned to her neighbour. 'I wouldn't want to get in your way.'

'Very sure,' Joy said, bracelets jangling as she swatted at a fly. 'Feel free to stay as long as you like.'

Stamatis appeared at the open bedroom window above them and called down to Andreas.

'*Nai.*' He turned to Skye. '*Perimene.*'

This word, she had quickly learned, meant 'wait'. Andreas threw it out often, seemingly to prevent her from straying too far away. He might have been in charge of the renovation, but she was still the boss – another fact he frequently reminded her of.

'*Ela*, you are the one who is paying the wages, and you must be stern with the men as they come and go, tell them what you want, and if you see them being lazy, you must shout at them. They will not respect you if you are too nice.'

It was good advice, in theory. Skye could easily have issued instructions to a classroom of children, but a handful of strange men, whose language she did not speak, was beyond her capabilities. The previous day, she'd cautiously asked Stamatis if there was any chance of saving the original wooden shutters. He had stared at her blankly, then wordlessly tossed the remnants over her shoulder onto the scrap pile. Skye had waited until nightfall to sneak out and retrieve them, though she had no idea how to begin repairing them. Her dad had been the artistic one, and he was no longer there to ask. It caught her off-guard, the grief short and sharp, as if she'd plunged into freezing water. A tight ache pulled taut behind her lungs, and she swallowed, blinking hard.

'You all right there, chook?' Joy's concerned face swam into view. Andreas had already moved away, she could hear his voice filtering out through the open window.

'Sorry.' Skye forced herself to focus. 'Drifted off for a second there.'

'It's this heat,' Joy said, fanning her face with her hands. 'God only knows how Dusty spends all day working in it. Have you seen what she's building over in the girls' backyard?'

'I haven't been over since they moved in,' Skye admitted. 'It's been a hectic few days.'

'You're not wrong,' Joy agreed. 'Dusty's been out there all hours, digging over the ground, creating this long patch from the back of the old hut to the house. It's going to be an extension eventually – and a fancy one at that. All glass doors and underfloor heating.'

'That sounds ... modern,' Skye said. 'Aren't we supposed to complement the local aesthetic?'

'That's what I said,' Joy replied. 'But apparently, she had the planning permission signed off before they even arrived.'

'And she's doing it all herself?'

'Seems to be.' Joy leaned in conspiratorially. 'Mini

Mia's been doing her best to help, but the poor kid gets yelled at so often. Dusty's a doer, that's for sure, but woe betide anyone who gets in that girl's way.'

They both turned at the sound of Andreas thundering back down the stairs.

'I have to go,' he said as he reached them. 'Stamatis will remove the floorboards from the second bedroom, so there will be a lot of noise, a lot of dust. Later, we will begin downstairs.'

'Hot date, is it?' Joy drawled. Andreas frowned, momentarily confused.

'Ah.' He grinned. 'Yes, a hot date with a man named Fotis, who sells rubber insulation panels.'

He wiggled his brows suggestively, making both women laugh.

'See you later, OK?' He looked directly at Skye.

'OK,' she said.

The truck engine fired and almost immediately a loud banging began above. Joy glanced at Skye.

'Is he always like that?' she asked, as the two of them started across the hillside.

'Who?'

'Andreas. I don't know, he seems so concerned about you. He's always checking in, telling you where he'll be, making sure you're all right.'

'Is he?' Skye was careful to keep her tone neutral. 'I hadn't noticed.'

'I reckon someone might have a little crush . . .'

Skye gave a half-smile. 'I hope you don't mean me?'

'Not you, him. What's his story anyway – is he married?'

'I wouldn't know.'

'He doesn't wear a wedding ring, does he? But then, maybe Greeks don't.'

'They do,' Skye told her. 'On their right hand.'

'Well, there you go then. Single and ready to mingle – and you could do a lot worse,' she went on, opening her front door. 'Andreas is pretty lush, and I'm not the only one who thinks so.'

'Oh?'

'Yeah,' she said, leading Skye through into the kitchen. 'Haven't you noticed Louisa having a good old gawp? That's one smitten kitten, if you ask me. You want a tea?'

She held up two boxes, one of peppermint and the other ironwort.

'Mint is great, thanks.'

Joy filled the kettle and readied two cups.

'Would you, though?' she asked, and Skye turned from where she'd been admiring a framed print of anatomical fruit. Joy had several – a lemon, a fig, and one that depicted red cherries.

'Would I what?'

'Go out with Andreas, if he asked you.'

'He's not going to do that.'

'But if he did,' she badgered. 'Would you?'

'The kettle's almost boiled,' Skye said.

'So, that's a yes then?'

'That's not a yes.'

'But it's not a no either, is it?'

Skye laughed helplessly.

'Stop,' she pleaded. 'Andreas is great, and yes,

he's also attractive, but I'm not interested in dating him, or anyone else for that matter. You can quote me on that.'

'I may well,' Joy said, 'the next time Ms Mentionitus next door brings him up in convo.'

'You mean Louisa?' Skye blew on the tea Joy passed across. 'Isn't she a bit young for him?'

'She's twenty-five, and I reckon he can't be much over forty.'

'Thirty-five.'

'There you go then. Ten years is nothing, especially when it comes to men. Most of them would jump at the chance to hook up with a— Oh, hey Theo.'

Skye turned as Joy's other neighbour strolled into the kitchen. Stocky and square-jawed, with dark stubble and thick-framed glasses, Theo had the air of someone more comfortable observing than being observed. He was a writer, born in Greece but raised in England – details Joy had managed to dig up with no small effort, as she'd confessed to Skye, 'not from want of trying'.

'Apologies,' he said now, looking from one to the other. 'The door was open and I—'

'Not a bother, mate. You remember Skye, don't you?'

'Yes.' He flashed her a hesitant smile. 'Hello again.'

'Tea?' Joy offered, but Theo declined.

'I have a favour to ask,' he said. 'I was wondering if you could perhaps watch George for me tomorrow. I have a Zoom meeting with my editor and—'

'Say no more,' Joy said. 'Send him over whenever suits.'

Theo rubbed the back of his neck, eyes flicking towards the floor.

'I'd keep him with me,' he said, 'but he doesn't like the taverna, and that's the only place nearby with reliable Wi-Fi. It gets so loud in there, and George is— He doesn't like it.'

'Poor little mite.' Joy sipped her tea. 'How's he coping with all the building work that's been going on?'

Theo grimaced.

'Not that well. He has his noise-cancelling headphones, but when he uses those, it's hard to help him with his schoolwork, and I have this deadline looming . . .'

He trailed off, bottom lip drooping miserably. Skye put down her mug.

'Is George a SEN child?' she asked gently.

Theo looked up, nodded.

'I might be able to help you,' she said. 'I was a teacher in my former life, and I have some experience of working one-to-one with children like George. If you'd like, I could sit with him for a few hours on weekdays. It doesn't have to be here, we can find somewhere quieter.'

'You'd do that for him – for us?'

'I'd honestly love to,' Skye said. 'But only if George agrees. It can be his decision.'

'Thank you.' Theo's shoulders dropped a fraction, as if a weight had been lifted. 'So much. I'll go and tell him. This is . . . Thank you.'

'Sweet fella,' Joy observed, as Theo hurried from the house. 'It's good of you to help out.'

'It's not an entirely selfless act,' Skye said, her voice quiet but firm. 'Teaching wasn't something I chose to give up.'

It was the first crack she'd allowed to show, and Joy caught it, though for reasons unknown, she chose not to probe further. Instead, she offered a simple, if not entirely untrue, assumption.

'You miss it, don't you?'

Skye was silent for a beat, and when she finally spoke, the words were heavier than she expected.

'Honestly? Teaching is the only thing I miss about my old life.'

14

A quiet tug-of-war played within Skye.

The readiness with which she had volunteered to start teaching again had taken her by surprise, the surge of enthusiasm vanishing as quickly as it had arrived. It wasn't that she lacked faith in her own ability, more that she wasn't sure how it would feel to slip back into the role. Being made redundant from her last teaching position had been a pivotal moment in her life, one that had spiralled downward in a way she did not anticipate. The suddenness of it still unsettled her. One day, she'd had structure, purpose, and a roomful of eager faces, the next, it was all gone. The work she'd poured in and the relationships she'd built had all evaporated with nothing more than a polite handshake and sympathetic smile as they showed her the door.

While the desire to teach again was undeniable, her uncertainty lingered. Was she really prepared to risk being pulled back into a past she thought she'd left behind? Skye could not answer that, not yet. But she did know one thing for certain: she wasn't prepared to go back on the promise she'd made to Theo and George. That mattered more than anything else.

Her pensive mood continued into an afternoon that crackled with heat. Skye left a bikini-clad Joy stretched out on a towel in her garden, her red skirt removed and rolled into a makeshift pillow, and made her way back across the hillside to collect what she needed for the night.

Andreas's truck was blocking her path, and Skye manoeuvred around it, doing her best not to get dust on her shorts. The windows were down, and peering into the cab, she saw a folded newspaper, several tins of white paint, and a large plastic bottle filled with some kind of oil. Hanging from the rear-view mirror was a blue-glass evil eye pendant on a gold chain. She'd noticed it before, during their drive to Chora, and it made her wonder about his superstitions, and how they aligned with his beliefs.

'*Geia sou*,' she said in passing to Stamatis, who was leaning against the outer wall of the house, vaping and scrolling on his phone. Not far in front of him, the cement mixer churned. Skye went inside and found Andreas standing in the far corner of the main living area, his head cocked to one side.

'Ah,' he said. 'Good.'

'Did you find another crack?' she asked, moving in beside him.

Andreas pointed towards the wall where the old fireplace had once stood. Its semicircular opening had been haphazardly bricked up with stones of all shapes and sizes.

'This is very ugly,' Andreas said, without a trace of humour or irony.

'It is,' Skye agreed solemnly, suppressing a smile.

'I have not been up onto the roof yet to check the, er, flume, but if you want to use the fireplace, then we must remove all of this' – he whirled a hand around in mid-air – 'stupid stuff. Do you want a fireplace?'

Skye thought for a moment. He'd already convinced her to install air-conditioning units in several rooms, and these would provide heat in the colder months, yet there was something irresistibly comforting about the idea of a log burner.

'I think I do,' she told him. 'I don't know if I'll ever use it, but I'd like to have the option.'

'Bravo,' he appraised. Then, as was customary, '*Perimene.*'

He went out to the truck, returning moments later with a set of overalls on over his jeans and shirt and two sets of plastic goggles – one of which he passed to Skye.

'Put these on,' he said, weighing a large mallet in his other hand, 'and be sure to stand back.'

The first strike sent cracks spidering through the surrounding plaster, the second brought down a cascade of stones and rubble. Skye coughed, quickly covering her mouth. Tightening his grip on the mallet, Andreas crouched to adjust his angle before winding up for another swing. More bricks tumbled, followed by lumps of blackened clay, and the mummified body of a long-dead mouse. Shuddering, Skye fetched a dustpan and brush from the kitchen.

When she returned, Andreas was crouched low,

peering through his dirty goggles into the empty space he'd created.

'There is something here,' he said, half-turning towards her. 'Can I use this?'

Skye gave him the brush and Andreas used the handle end to poke up inside the chimney, just above where the curved hood of the fireplace met the shaft. A moment later, there was a soft thud as something landed on the pile of rubble.

'It's not another dead rodent, is it?' she asked, tiptoeing forward with trepidation.

Andreas lifted the object and examined it for a moment, blowing hard across the surface to clear away the dust. Whatever it was appeared to be shrouded in some kind of hessian sack.

'Shall I open it?' he asked, glancing up at her. Skye pulled down her goggles, her thoughts already racing.

'I guess so,' she replied, her mind spinning with possibilities. As a child, she had spent hours digging through the garden, imagining ancient treasures hidden beneath the soil, in search of ancient pottery. She'd joined her dad on metal-detecting excursions, scoured beaches for hidden sea glass, driven by the need to discover something new. It was a passion that had never quite left her.

Andreas began to unwrap the package, peeling off the hessian one layer at a time until it fell away completely. Skye gasped when she saw what it had been shielding – a stack of envelopes, tightly bound with twine, the topmost bearing a name neatly written in faded ink.

'Is it in Greek?' she asked. 'Can you read it? What does it say?'

Andreas stood from where he'd been kneeling and crossed to the open doorway, Skye close at his heel. The sunlight made the words clearer, though she still couldn't make sense of the characters – except for one. A bold unmistakeable 'K', exactly the same as the one carved in her attic.

15

The letter was addressed to Katerina Sideris.

Katerina.

Skye repeated the name several times, copying the way Andreas sounded the 'e' as an 'a', and adding emphasis to the vowels as he did.

'Sideris means someone who is made from iron,' he told her. 'The same as this island. Folegandros is the iron isle of the Cyclades.'

'So, we can assume she was from here, this Katerina?'

'Perhaps.' Andreas fingered the envelope. 'I have heard this name before, but not very many times.'

'Who's it from?' she persisted, leaning over until her forehead was almost touching his. 'Does it say?'

'I will need to open it,' Andreas said, glancing up so that their eyes met. He, too, had taken off his goggles, though a pink outline remained. There were specks of masonry in his beard, a smear of black on his cheek. 'Do you mind?'

'Of course I don't,' she said. 'I'm dying to know more.'

He began by unfastening the twine, being careful not to drop any of the letters. At a glance, Skye estimated that there must be at least twenty in the stack, perhaps more. A discovery that, as far as she was concerned, felt like winning the lottery for a second time.

Andreas removed two sheets of paper, each of which were thin and yellowed with age. The writing was small and cursive, the lines of text squeezed together. Its author had left barely enough room for punctuation, and splodges of ink dotted the margins.

'Is there a date?' she asked, and he nodded, sliding a finger up to the top corner of the first page. There were no numbers that Skye could see, only three symbols – 'M', an 'O' with a line through its centre, and an upright triangle.

'Nineteen forty,' Andreas said. 'It is dated from the thirtieth day of October.'

Skye scoured her memories, trying to recall what she remembered about the Second World War in Greece. She was sure something important had happened at the end of that month, but the answer remained stubbornly out of reach. Andreas had continued to read, his mouth working silently as he skimmed over the words. Several times he paused, bringing the paper closer, squinting to make out what was written, while beside him, Skye fizzed with barely tempered anticipation.

Andreas lowered the letter and blew air into his cheeks.

'What is it?' she asked. 'What does it say? Who's it from?'

'A man,' he said. 'He signs at the bottom with only one letter, a sigma, which is an "S".'

'How do you know it's a man?'

Andreas tapped the letter with a finger. 'Because he talks about fighting.'

'But women fought in the war, too, didn't they?'

'Yes,' he agreed, 'but not at the beginning. That all happened later, during the resistance.'

'I clearly need to brush up on my history.'

Andreas gestured once again to the letter. 'This man, he was in love with Katerina.'

'It's a love letter?' Skye felt a twinge in her chest.

'*Nai*,' he said softly. 'But I don't believe they were married, not when this letter was written. There is a lot of' – he paused – 'passion.' Skye wasn't sure if she was imagining it, but it seemed to her as if Andreas was blushing slightly.

'Will you read it out to me?' she asked.

His mouth fell open, then closed again as he pressed his lips into a thin line. A cloud of vape announced the arrival of Stamatis from around the side of the house. He glanced from the expression on his boss's face to the letter in Andreas's hands, and then to Skye, who quickly explained what they'd found in the fireplace. Stamatis smirked at the mention of a 'love letter' and leaned in, trying to read it upside down.

'*Ela re*,' Andreas grumbled, folding the papers and tucking them back into the envelope. 'Break time is over.'

Stamatis gave a long-suffering sigh, but didn't argue, heading back inside just as Joy, a sarong knotted over her bikini, emerged at the boundary wall.

'There you are,' she called. 'I was starting to think I'd been stood up.'

'As if I would,' Skye protested. 'I was about to head back to yours.'

'Wait until you see what the girls have found,' she said, which piqued Andreas's interest.

'Found where?' he asked. 'In the house?'

'Out back,' Joy told them. 'Dusty was turning over some more earth out there when her shovel hit something. It's pretty cool actually, reckon it's an antique.'

Skye did not need to hear more, she was already moving, hurrying across the dry ground with Andreas at her side. When they reached the truck, he slid the bundle of letters into the glove compartment, then rolled up the windows and locked the doors.

'They will be safe in there,' he said. Skye offered him a grateful smile and fell into step beside him as they followed Joy to the sisters' house. A small crowd was gathered outside. Victoria and Adam – bizarrely dressed in swimming trunks and flip-flops below, with a shirt and tie on top – as well as Louisa, and Cora from the village shop, who had her two young children in tow. A harried-looking Theo was mid-apology, assuring her that George would like to play with Iris and Ajax another day.

'I'm afraid his social battery has run dry,' he said.

Cora nodded sympathetically as the younger Ajax broke away to pet Bruno, his face brightening at the sight of Mia approaching with a box of ice lollies.

'We heard you have found something,' Andreas prompted, and Louisa, whose dress and bare legs were caked in dry mud, turned as red as her long hair.

'Dusty did,' she said, shifting awkwardly. 'She's still out back.'

He stalked away and Skye followed, into the living area where three camp beds were set up in a row along one wall, and out through the kitchen to the garden beyond.

'Told you she'd been busy,' Joy said, jogging up behind them.

The once flat expanse of ground had been almost completely dug over, and there were separate piles of stone, mud and other detritus such as wire, broken clay pots and larger rocks. Dusty had somehow sourced a cement mixer and a vast bag of sand, and there were numerous white sacks in a heap next to a mound of wooden planks.

Andreas ran a hand through his hair. He was still wearing the overalls he'd put on to demolish the fireplace, and sweat was beginning to dapple across his forehead. The peak heat of the day was allegedly the middle part, though Skye consistently found that this hour, between four and five p.m., was hotter, when the wind dropped off and the air grew still and heavy.

Dusty emerged from the hut at the far end of the garden and raised a hand in greeting. Clad in board shorts and a crop top, she was sporting two sunburnt shoulders, and her pale shins were dotted with plasters.

'Bites,' she explained, in answer to Skye's enquiring glance. 'The mozzies can't seem to get enough of me.'

'You should burn a citronella candle in the evenings,' Andreas said, to which she tutted.

'Tried that, to no avail, and I practically bathe in DEET. I wouldn't mind if all of us were equally afflicted, but for some reason they don't seem to go after my sisters.'

'I heard that it's something to do with all the Marmite we eat,' Mia interrupted. She had come out to join them, Victoria and Adam in tow. 'It's packed with B1, and apparently they hate it.'

'Is Marmite the black gooey stuff that tastes like the bottom of a beer barrel?' Victora wrinkled her nose. 'Gross.'

'She's banned me from eating it,' Adam lamented. 'I'm not even allowed a jar in the house.'

Skye, who'd always been able to take Marmite or leave it, turned back to Dusty.

'We heard you'd found something?'

'News really travels fast around here,' she remarked drily. 'I'll go and get it – one sec.'

Andreas, meanwhile, was asking Adam about his absent trousers – 'Did you leave them on the beach?' – which promptly sent Mia into a fit of giggles.

'I've had a day of meetings,' he explained, 'but as they're all done online, only the top half of me needs to look presentable.'

'Do you have Wi-Fi at the house now, then?' Mia asked, suddenly hopeful, but Adam pulled a face.

'Not yet. The engineer can't get here until June eighteenth, so a week on Wednesday. I've been working out of the taverna most days, drinking every last coffee bean Pantelis has in stock.'

Dusty was coming back towards them, a long,

slender object balanced carefully in her hands. As she came closer, Skye saw it resembled some kind of leather-bound tube.

'Cool, right?' Joy said.

'Erm . . .' Skye havered. 'I'm not actually sure what it is I'm looking at.'

'I didn't either at first,' Dusty said. 'Almost took my hand off fishing it out of the dirt.'

She gripped the narrower end and gave it a gentle tug, releasing a slim, curved blade from what Skye now realised was a scabbard.

'Ah.' Andreas leaned in. 'Can I hold it?'

Dusty slid the pieces back together before handing it to him, and Andreas stepped back a few paces before drawing the sword out fully, angling it to catch the light. Skye caught a glimpse of an intricate pattern, stencilled into the silver.

'It is a sabre,' Andreas said, as Adam approached him for a closer look. 'I think, perhaps, it is Ottoman.'

'Valuable?' Dusty asked.

'Maybe one thousand euros, maybe a lot more.' He shrugged. 'You will have to find an expert to examine it, somebody who specialises in these kinds of things.'

'And this was just buried here, in your garden?' Adam marvelled. 'Hear that, Vic? Maybe we should take Andreas's advice and get him to dig that plunge pool after all. Who knows what we might unearth.'

Skye smiled wryly. What was it with Andreas and his obsession with plunge pools?

'Is that rust all around the top, do you reckon?' Joy asked.

Dusty licked a finger and rubbed at the stain. 'Not clay or soil,' she said. 'Whatever it is, isn't budging.'

'You probably shouldn't lick it,' Mia advised.

Andreas scraped at the same patch with his thumbnail. 'It could be rust,' he allowed, 'or perhaps blood.'

'Blood?' Victoria exclaimed, scurrying sideways as Dusty spat onto the ground.

'Told you not to lick it,' Mia drawled.

'You really think it could be blood?' Skye asked Andreas, and he nodded, deep-set eyes serious.

'Consider what it is,' he said, 'and why somebody would choose to bury it.'

They all fell silent at that.

Skye looked again at the sabre.

An antique blade, buried below ground; a bundle of letters, sealed behind stone. Six houses, abandoned since the war, with nothing and nobody to tell them why. There were secrets here. Secrets that someone had gone to great lengths to hide.

A prickle ran up the back of Skye's neck.

The past, it seemed, had begun to reawaken.

16

It was Joy's suggestion that they decamp to her house for an impromptu party of sorts. She was 'bloody proud' of the barbecue she'd built out back and wanted an excuse to use it.

'You fellas go and get some chicken for souvlaki,' she told Andreas and Adam. 'Me and the girls will throw together some salad, not that there's room to throw much of anything in my kitchen.'

Mia followed Skye, Victoria and Joy next door, while Louisa and Dusty stayed behind to wash off the day's dirt.

'How did you get out of the excavating?' Joy asked. Mia threw her a mischievous grin.

'I promised I'd muck in after walking Bruno, but once we'd got all the way down to the beach, neither of us felt much like moving again, did we, Brunes?'

The dog, who had dutifully accompanied his mistress across to Joy's and was now splayed out on her kitchen floor, wagged his tail by way of reply.

'He's a regular little shadow of yours, isn't he?' Victoria observed, tossing her hair over one shoulder. The galley kitchen was so narrow that the tip of her ponytail hit Skye in the eye. 'Adam thinks we should adopt one, but I don't know.'

'Oh, you should,' Mia enthused. 'As a vet, I'm not supposed to have favourites when it comes to animals, but dogs really are in a different league – and you go off on hikes a lot, don't you? A dog would be great company.'

'Who says I want company?' Victoria said mildly. 'Hiking is when I do my thinking – it's my timeout from reality.'

Skye took three red peppers from the fridge and cast around for a chopping board.

'I'm terrible at spending time by myself,' Mia went on. 'Dusty's always been a bit of a loner, and Louisa goes along with what everyone else wants, but I prefer company. Human or animal, it doesn't much matter. Shall I go and see if Theo and George want to join us?'

'Good idea,' Joy said, shooing her from the room before turning back to the others. 'She reminds me of a bee, that one. Always buzzing from place to place, person to person.'

Victoria mopped her eyes.

'Jeez,' she said, 'these onions are savage.'

'I can do them,' Skye offered. 'You take over the peppers.'

They switched places, Victoria almost sending a bowl of lemons flying as she squeezed past the table.

'I'm starting to think Andreas might have a point about doing an extension,' Joy mused, as she reached around them to open a drawer. 'If I let the builders in, though, I'll never get any bloody peace and quiet.'

Skye swept the chopped onion on top of the pepper, then tore open a slab of feta. The cheese was slick with moisture, its aroma ripe and salty.

'Do you have any oregano for these tomatoes?' Victoria asked. Joy went outside, returning with a fresh sprig just as Mia burst back into the kitchen, followed by Adam and Andreas. Both were weighed down with an assortment of meats, beers and packets of crisps.

'If you can allow me a space,' Andreas said, extracting a pot of yoghurt from one of the bags, 'then I will prepare my special tzatziki.'

Joy, who'd just prised open a bottle of Mythos on the edge of the sink, moved aside only to trip over a still-slumbering Bruno. 'Bloody hell,' she cried, as beer sprayed up the wall.

Skye caught Andreas's eye.

'No Theo?' Victoria said, as Mia began to spear chunks of raw chicken breast onto a skewer.

'Sadly not,' she said. 'He can't leave George on his own but sent his apologies.'

'Once the smell of the barbecue drifts over the wall, I bet they'll change their minds,' Adam said. He'd swapped his shirt and tie for a plain tee and seemed far more relaxed. Victoria, by contrast, had grown quieter, more reserved. Her earlier remark about not wanting company had stuck with Skye, though the reasons behind it remained unclear. It didn't seem to be about Adam, whose arms were wrapped around his wife, his voice low in her ear, but something else lingered beneath the surface.

Skye wondered if the comment had been a subtle invitation to talk. Had her own guardedness caused her to miss an opening? She attempted to catch the other woman's eye, but Victoria's attention was solely on her husband.

'Finally,' Mia chorused, as Dusty and Louisa appeared in the kitchen doorway. 'Took you long enough.'

'Cinderella here made me wait while she did her make-up,' Dusty said, accepting a beer from Adam.

Louisa cringed with mortification. 'I told you to go ahead without me,' she protested.

'Well, you look lovely,' Joy said. 'Doesn't she, Andreas?'

'Eh?' He paused in the process of grating cucumber and turned around. '*Nai*. Very nice. All you ladies are very beautiful.'

'Kiss ass,' Joy said with a smirk, before heading into the garden.

Skye went after her, clutching the bowl of Greek salad. She couldn't remember the last time she'd been at a gathering like this – three years ago, maybe four? Her dad had loved hosting, but every party he threw was of the laid-back kind; friends turning up with a bottle, pizzas ordered and shared, lanterns lit in the garden and laughter filling the air. Her mother had continued to invite those same acquaintances to the house after he died, but the set-up was more formal. Dinner parties with labelled seating plans, an Ottolenghi recipe painstakingly prepared and matched with expensive wine. Talk at these types of gatherings was muted, dry, political – Skye would sit beside Martyn, saying nothing at all while he sermonised about this subject and that, his hand on her thigh, the pressure just hard enough that she knew not to move, not to speak, not to do anything that might draw attention. Not once, on all those occasions, did her mother notice that anything was wrong.

'You all right, chook?' Joy asked.

Skye started. 'Fine,' she said. Her new most-used word. 'I'm fine.'

Joy transferred the chicken skewers from a tray onto the barbecue.

'You know, if you ever need to talk,' she said, 'about anything, you can talk to me. I know I've got a gob on me the size of a croc's, but I'm not a gossip. You can trust me.'

'Thanks,' Skye said, then, unable to think of anything better to say, she added a 'sorry'.

Joy picked up a set of tongs and made as if to pinch her with them. 'Enough of that,' she said. 'I won't mention it again, I just wanted you to know.'

Skye felt the swell of tears in her throat. The view was different from Joy's garden, the Church of Panagia not visible, its soft pale edges hidden behind the curve of the hillside. But there was still the sea, shimmering in the distance, and above it, a sky so blue that it barely seemed real. Not a cloud in sight, only the honeyed yolk of the sun, moving slowly west.

'Where do you want these?' It was Mia, clutching paper plates and a fistful of cutlery.

'Oh, anywhere,' Joy said, turning a skewer. Adam and Victoria were busy setting up a makeshift bar on the patio table, while Dusty stalked around with a can of mosquito spray, ready to douse any unsuspecting insects. Joy half-turned to face Skye.

'Be a darl and go get me another beer, would you?' she said. 'There's Mythos in the fridge.'

Skye went inside to find Andreas where she'd left him, adding a finishing garnish of mint leaves to his dip. Louisa was next to him, damp red hair trailing down her back, head bowed as if the two were sharing a confidence. When she noticed Skye, her cheeks flared.

'*Ela*.' Andreas dug a teaspoon into the tzatziki and beckoned to her. 'You can be my tester.'

He made as if to handfeed her, but Skye ducked away, assailed by a sudden image of herself, curled up and cowering.

'I can do it,' she said, taking the spoon from him. The tzatziki was tangy and fresh-tasting, with a satisfying punch of garlic.

'What is the Greek word for delicious?' she asked.

Andreas smiled broadly. '*Ypérocho*,' he said, looking down at the cluttered countertop. 'The only problem is how much mess it makes.'

'I can clear all this away,' Louisa said. 'Honestly, it's no bother.'

Andreas hesitated. 'You are sure?'

'I'm very sure.'

Louisa, Skye mused, as she edged past them to reach the fridge, couldn't have looked more smitten. Unfortunately for her, Andreas seemed oblivious. He simply wiped his hands on a tea towel, scooped up the bowl of dip and headed out into the garden without a backward glance.

'Do you want some help?' Skye offered, as Louisa turned on the tap.

'No, don't worry.'

'A beer?'

'Not for me.' Louisa let out a small sigh. 'I don't really drink. My mum, she was ... she drank too much. It made her ill, hard to live with.'

Skye cursed inwardly. 'I'm sorry,' she said. 'That must have been tough.'

'I knew it would catch up with her eventually,' Louisa said, her head down, hands busy. 'Dusty's still angry with her for dying, and I think Mia's in shock. She refuses to talk about it, even to me.'

'Losing a parent is—' Skye stopped abruptly as something untethered inside her.

'It's why we came here,' Louisa went on, sponging yoghurt off a fork. 'Mum's dream was always to live on a Greek island. She told us about Folegandros, said she'd been here a few times during her hippy heyday. When the news about this lottery appeared the day after her funeral, it felt like she was sending us a message. I didn't even tell the other two, I just went ahead and entered, and now, well, here we are.'

She spoke carefully, her voice strained and movements slow, all at once seeming much older than twenty-five. Grief had done that to Skye, too, wrenching her inside out. Even now, years on, it still had the power to dismantle her. No wonder Louisa was drawn to someone like Andreas – steady, capable, kind. As dependable as the steel beams he was adamant on installing in each of their homes.

'Is it helping?' Skye asked. 'Being here on the island, I mean.'

Louisa turned from the sink. 'It's funny,' she said. 'I thought coming here would make me feel closer to Mum, but if anything, I feel further away from her.'

Skye thought about her own grief, how it would never leave her.

'The people we truly love become part of us,' she said. 'It doesn't matter how far we go from where they last were, because they're still here, living quietly in the folds of our hearts.'

Louisa's eyes shone. 'Do you really believe that?'

Skye met her gaze, a small wistful smile tugging at her lips.

'I have to,' she said.

17

The night drew in gradually, a lilac dusk that deepened to claret as the moon slid out among the stars.

Skye wandered to the far end of Joy's garden, a glass of wine in her hand that she'd been nursing for hours, and stared out at the molten sea, its hush barely audible beneath the low hum of voices behind her. Then a new sound, steady footsteps on dry earth. There was no need to turn around, she knew who it was.

Andreas came to a stop a few feet behind her.

'Do you want to be alone?' he asked.

Skye smiled to herself.

'I was just thinking what a shame it is,' she said, 'that nowadays, people tend to spend more time staring down at devices than they do looking out at the world around them. I mean, why gaze at a six-inch screen when you have the whole of the night sky?'

'It is a good question,' he agreed, moving to stand beside her. 'Instead of trying to expand our minds, we are allowing them to shrink, be muddled by nonsense.'

'You can see so many more stars here than in England,' she went on. 'My dad taught me the basic constellations, but I can't remember a single occasion since childhood when I've had time to stand still and simply take them all in. It's overwhelming, to have visibility this good. In England, there's so much light pollution – especially in London.'

She stalled for a moment, cursing herself inwardly for allowing this nugget of information to slip out, though if Andreas had registered the revelation, he didn't remark on it. He was still gazing upward, chin raised and shoulders rounded.

'It was the Greeks who gave most of the stars their names,' he said. 'Do you think it was because they were curious, or because they laid around on their backs a lot?'

Skye raised an amused brow. 'Shall we be generous and say both?'

He gave her a sidelong look. 'You are already starting to think like a Greek.'

'What can I say?' she replied. 'I'm a good student.'

'The best teachers always are.'

They both turned as a shriek rang out, just in time to see Victoria picking herself up from where a chair had deposited her on the ground. Skye laughed, unable to help herself. Of all the guests, Victoria had been the most enthusiastic at the makeshift bar, and Adam's repeated attempts to discourage her had so far proven unsuccessful.

'Someone is going to wake up with a sore head tomorrow,' Andreas remarked.

'And a sore bum, by the looks of things,' Skye said. 'But I think we can let her off. It is a party, after all.'

Andreas pulled a face.

'What?' she demanded.

'This is a small gathering,' he said gravely. 'Not a party.'

'This is plenty party enough for me.'

'*Ela*, there is no music, no dancing.'

As if on cue, Victoria started singing, loudly and with little adherence to any kind of melody. Andreas winced, shaking his head as Bruno began to howl along.

'The dead will begin to wake up soon,' he said.

Skye felt the featherlight brush of a shiver run up her spine.

'I think we might've already woken them,' she said. 'Someone buried that sabre for a reason, and they might not take too kindly to us having dug it up.'

'It was not us.' Andreas folded his arms, drumming his fingers against a bicep. 'And I do not think that even a ghost would scare Dusty. In Greece, we would say that she is *zoriki gomana* – a tough chick.'

'I think she'd appreciate that,' Skye said, raising her voice to be heard over the caterwauling. 'I heard you two squabbling earlier over the best way to pour cement.'

Andreas's brows knitted together. 'I have offered my help, but I cannot force her to accept.'

Skye took a sip of her wine, so warm now that it tasted vinegary. Andreas had refused all offers of alcohol, though he had polished off every scrap of leftover food – including Skye's salad, which he'd deemed '*poly kali*'.

'That means "very good",' Mia had confided. 'Klodi taught me.'

Greeks, indeed, were natural teachers. Skye had gleaned as much through the few interactions she'd had with people in the village, where those she spoke to appeared compelled to impart some nugget or other of wisdom during every conversation. Andreas was chief among them, schooling her on language, local history and cultural quirks. They talked often, though hadn't yet ventured beyond the surface level of friendship. To delve any deeper would invite questions, and Skye had long since raised that drawbridge. She had no intention of revealing more than was absolutely necessary.

'I hope Dusty doesn't lay her foundations down too soon,' she said. 'That sabre was such a fascinating find. If it were me, I'd want to keep digging for more.'

'Perhaps there is more to be found,' Andreas mused. 'Not only in that garden, but in all the houses. Nobody has touched them since the war ended.'

'Apart from you,' she reminded him. 'You were working up here for weeks before we arrived.'

'Correct,' he agreed. 'But it was only after you came that we found something.'

The bundle in her fireplace. Skye had thought about little else since their discovery.

'Did you sneak another look at the letters earlier?' she asked.

Andreas unfolded his arms and rubbed a hand across his jaw. 'No,' he said, his tone pensive. 'It is not my place to do so. They belong to you.'

Skye supposed that they did, though it felt wrong to possess another person's innermost thoughts and feelings, their hopes and dreams, their expressions of love.

'Will you read me the one you opened?' she asked. 'It doesn't have to be tonight, but soon?'

Andreas glanced up, and she followed his gaze, across Orion's belt and the 'W' constellation of the vain queen Cassiopeia, before trailing her eyes down to the Great Bear. The beauty of it, the wonder, made her emotions unravel, as if dropped like a ball of wool. She looked away, back towards the glow of the small house, where the inhabitants of her strange new world were silhouetted in the half-darkness.

'*Ela*,' Andreas said, the softest touch on her elbow. 'Let's go.'

He strode down the garden, and she followed him, aware of multiple sets of eyes on them as they passed the small group.

'Back in a sec,' she called to Joy, ignoring her friend's bemused expression. Outside, they made their way across the dark hillside to the truck, where Skye climbed into the passenger seat. With a soft click, the glove compartment dropped open, revealing the stack of letters nestled inside. Andreas took the top envelope and carefully unfolded its pages.

Skye shifted to face him, one leg curled beneath her, the gearstick nudging her knee. Above them, the evil eye pendant swung gently from its gold chain, no longer blue but dulled by night.

Andreas sat back, cleared his throat, and began to read.

30 October 1940

My dearest K,

Two days ago, as the dawn began to wash clean the sky here along the spine of our country, Italian troops came from Albania to the Greek border and began their attack. The war has come as we feared, but our resistance is stronger than the will of theirs to succeed. There is disorganisation, weakness, and a lack of discipline from their soldiers, while we, alongside the Hellenic Army, crush them as we might a fig between our teeth.

The men here say that Metaxas refused to yield when told to do so by the pig Mussolini, that he shouted for war. Afterwards, men ran into the streets of Athens, the cry of 'ochi' on every street, an echo that chased around the columns of the Acropolis, finding its way into the proud heart of every citizen. It is as I told you – our people will not take the knee, they will not bend, nor will they cower. Our heads are held high, and we will honour their bravery by continuing to fight.

Michalis and I have embedded ourselves with the same unit, each given a uniform and a rifle. We were accepted with the papers that the brothers prepared for us, and as Zephyr and Atlas assured me, there was no demand that we be trained at any camps. 'We are freedom fighters,' I told them, and they put up no argument. When we heard the sound of explosions on the first morning, your brother-in-law began to shake, all over his body, the teeth inside his mouth rattling as though they were pebbles inside a jar. Do not tell your sister this. She must not worry. I will remain close to Michalis, protect him from harm, show him that there is no cause for terror, not from these weak men that try to come. Perhaps I will capture one for you, an Italian to tie up on the hillside with your goats.

I think of you often, my dearest Kat. I imagine that I am stroking your hair, kissing your lips, touching your body in all the forbidden places. I wish that I had a photo of you. Do you have a picture that you could send here to me, so that I might keep it close? There is no way to know yet how long it will take for us to push back our enemies, throw them from the highest peaks of the Pindus mountains so that their bodies shatter against the rock, though I want you to know that I miss you. Every moment. The taste of you, the way my body is ignited when it is beside yours, that fire that spreads between us. It is thoughts such as these that will focus my mind, make me the sharpest, smartest and truest soldier; ensure that I survive, and come home to you.

I must go now, for soon we move once more towards the battle. Write to me, Kat. Give me the company of your words in place of your body, until we see one another again.

S

18

Skye lay on the futon mattress, her world muffled by darkness, and muted by the earplugs lent to her by Joy. Her friend had not been joking about the snoring, and even with a wax barrier in place, Skye could still hear her nasal growl, low and rhythmic, regular as a tide.

But it wasn't this noise that was keeping her awake, it was the letter.

Andreas had read it so exquisitely that she'd begged to hear it a second time, and then a third, delighted not only by the language, but the sentiment. The lonely 'K' carved in her attic was gaining clarity – Kat now had a name, a story, a man who had loved her so intensely that he burned with it.

Martyn had written to Skye for the first few months after they met. Postcards would turn up each week from wherever his work as a pilot had taken him, colourful images of Bali, Los Angeles, Morocco and the Caribbean, each with a cursory few lines scribbled on the back. Sometimes he would jot down a joke, occasionally there would be an observation, but most often, he asked her a question – the same one every time: 'When can I see you again?'

Everyone, from Sal to her mum to the other teachers in the staff room, thought the gesture was romantic, urging her to 'put the poor man out of his misery' and agree to a date. Skye had continued to hold back. Receiving postcards and exchanging the odd text message was all she felt able to offer. She assumed Martyn would grow weary of asking, that her knockbacks would eat away at his ego until pride stepped in and called a halt to the whole charade. But he never did, and, eventually, she had given in.

The thin sheet was suddenly too tight, her heart a trapped bird. Skye got out of bed and slipped from the room, careful not to wake Joy. Her friend was on her back, mouth wide open and russet curls askew, anointed into slumber by alcohol. The party had continued until midnight, after which a yawning Mia had announced that it was way past Bruno's bedtime, and Adam, whom Skye suspected had long been waiting for an excuse to politely depart, fireman-lifted his comatose wife out of the house. Andreas had left at the same time, taking the precious bundle of letters home with him.

'Are you sure you don't want to keep hold of them?' he'd asked, but Skye had been adamant.

'My house is ninety-nine per cent rubble,' she'd reminded him. 'They'll be safer with you.'

Watching him drive away, however, had been a wrench.

She closed Joy's front door behind her, cringing at the clink of the latch, and made her way across the hillside, silent in rubber-soled sandals that she wore with pyjama shorts, her bag clamped to her side. Instead of heading towards her own house, Skye banked left, slowing as she approached Victoria and Adam's front yard. Only then did she switch on her phone.

For the first few seconds, nothing happened, and then the handset began to buzz with activity, notifications falling across the screen like toppled dominoes. Her email inbox was crammed, as were the two messaging apps she used most regularly. There was a slew of news updates, social media prompts and alerts from her banking app. Skye had methodically changed every single one of her passwords in the days running up to her departure from London, before turning off her location services. It had been eye-opening to discover quite how many digital doors were propped open, and how easy it would've been for Martyn to track her down, had she not done her research.

There were no text or WhatsApp messages from either him or her mother, though that was no surprise, given that she'd blocked both numbers. They had each attempted to contact her via email, and Martyn had also reached out on Instagram. A few of her former colleagues had been in touch, asking how and where she was, and there was a flurry of voice notes from Sal. Skye pictured her friend, with her wide smile and seal-bark laugh, nails always painted in different colours because 'I get bored easily, you know that'. She missed her, so very much.

Turning the volume on her phone to its lowest setting, Skye held it close to her ear, and pressed play.

'Hey, it's me. Listen, your mum called again, cross-examined me on your whereabouts. I didn't tell her where you were, but I had to admit that I knew. She sounded really worried – like, genuinely – and I can picture your face as I say that, but she really did. I've been mulling it over and I think you should tell her, not just about the move, but everything. What Martyn did . . . she needs to know so she can help protect you from him, don't you think? Sorry, I know this isn't what you want to hear, but we promised we'd always tell each other the truth, the whole truth and nothing but, didn't we? This is just me doing that, so please don't be cross. Love you, Skittle. Message me back.'

Skye checked the date on the voice note. Sal had sent it six days ago – not twelve hours after Skye had sat up by the ridge and contemplated throwing her phone into the sea. No wonder her mum was worried. Skye had shut her out – blocked her own mother. Self-loathing swirled, a pain growing hard in the back of her throat. She coughed to clear it, raising her hand to mask the sound, and clicked on Sal's next message. This recording was short – less than fifteen seconds in length.

'Pick up your phone, woman. Martyn has been in touch again – he's bombarding me. He says he's going to fly out here if I don't tell him where you are. I'm freaking out here. Call me back.'

Fly out to Australia? Skye felt a loosening in her bladder, the strong need to pee accompanied by a frantically racing heart. She squatted and pressed a hand against the ground, steadying herself. There were two more voice notes, both sent in the past few hours. She didn't want to listen to either, but hadn't she come out here to do just that? Not bury her trepidation in the dirt but confront it. Her mind went to the man described in the letter. Poor Michalis, with his teeth that rattled like pebbles in a jar, waiting on the frontline of a war. This was her war, and it was not fair of her to expect others to fight it.

She stood, took a deep breath, and pressed play for the third time.

'He's here. Martyn. In Sydney. He turned up at the school office about fifteen minutes ago, demanding to see me. Thankfully, Brenda is the last woman who will ever be told what to do by a bloke, so she told him to sling it and tipped me off. Apparently, he's sitting in a hire car opposite the front gates – just sitting there. Jesus. The guy is a proper psycho. I don't know what to do, Skits. I can get out the back way, but he knows where I live. I'm thinking maybe it's better if I go out there now and just speak to him. He can't do much to me in the school yard, not with five-hundred-odd students liable to be peering out through the windows. That's a lot of smart phones right there, and he's too smart to do anything stupid, isn't he? Fuck. I wish you'd pick up.'

A loud bell began to ring in the background of the recording, and the voice note ended abruptly. Skye glanced at her phone. The final message had been sent only moments later and lasted just three seconds.

'Screw this. I'm going out there.'

No. Skye stared at the phone, wide-eyed with horror, her legs beginning to shake. Sal had sent the message two hours ago, and since then, there had been nothing. Images began to assault her, a macabre slideshow of what might be. Had Martyn threatened her, hurt her, coerced or tricked her? Why hadn't Sal updated her? Was her friend locked in his hire car, unable to call for help? Each scenario landed thump-hard against her chest. Skye checked the time – it was almost four a.m., which made it lunchtime in Sydney. She knew what she had to do, though her fingers shook as she scrolled to Sal's number. It rang, and she waited, holding her breath, knuckles white as she gripped the phone. Then, at last, her friend's voice came on the line.

'Skittle?'

'Oh, thank God,' Skye said, letting out a shaky laugh. 'You're OK.'

'Well, I'm a bit freaked out, but yeah, I'm still in one piece.'

'I'm so sorry,' Skye wailed. 'I only just listened to your voice notes. What happened?'

'What happened is I told him.'

Black spots began to swarm. Skye shook her head.

'Told him?' she said faintly. 'Told him what? Not where I am?'

'Of course not that,' Sal replied. 'I told him you were

done, that you weren't coming back, that he should stop trying to find you.'

'I'm guessing he didn't like that much.'

Her friend sighed. 'Not much, no. He did a good job of pretending he wasn't angry, but I could see it – hell, I could feel it. The guy was redder in the face than a barbecued lobster.'

'I'm so sorry,' Skye said again. 'I can't believe he flew all the way out there.'

'Well, he did. Told me he happened to be in the neighbourhood, but there's about as much truth to that as there is to the conspiracy theories about Nicolas Cage being a time traveller.'

'That he's what?'

'Never mind,' she said, her voice stony. 'How are you anyway? How is island life?'

'You're angry with me,' Skye said.

'No. Well, yes, maybe a little. I'm angriest with Martyn, for creating this situation. If he wasn't such a grade-A narcissist . . .'

'I never wanted any of this to rebound on you,' Skye said. 'I knew he'd be apoplectic with rage once he realised that I wasn't coming back, but I didn't expect him to go this far.'

'He thinks of you as one of his possessions,' Sal intoned. 'As if you're a set of cufflinks or one of those awful Mr T-style watches he likes to wear.'

Skye had begun to rock backwards and forwards.

'What else did he say?' she asked.

'That he was worried about you, that he loved you and couldn't understand why you'd left, blah, blah;

that he knew he could make you see sense if only you'd talk to him. He was giving it the hard sell, basically, but he could tell I wasn't impressed. Then he stepped it up a notch, started ranting on about how you'd stolen from him, and how he'd have no choice but to report it to the police. I laughed at that, told him he was talking out of his—well, you know.'

The police.

Skye's ribs felt too tight, her stomach hollow.

'How can he accuse you of stealing, when you've left him the house and everything in it?' Sal went on. 'The bloke's a fantasist.'

'How did you leave things?' Skye's voice was barely a rasp.

'I told him that if he didn't back off, then it would be me calling the police, reporting him for harassment. He took that pretty well, considering, just sort of smiled and said, "You're a good friend to her, Salima," in this really condescending way. Gave me the creeps.'

'And then he, what, just drove off?'

'Not quite.'

Sal said nothing for a few beats. Skye could hear the sounds of a busy school in the background, chattering voices, the bang of a door – echoes of her past, a time when happiness had been more than a glimpse on some far-off horizon.

'He did say one other thing,' Sal said.

Skye went very still.

'What?'

'He said, tell your friend – not Skye, he didn't use your name, but "your friend" – that I know what she did, and that time is ticking. Then he tapped his finger on his wrist. Honestly, it was a bit sinister. I laughed it off to his face, but afterwards, I couldn't stop shaking, not for ages.'

'I'm sorry,' Skye said. Her words redundant, useless, flat.

'I'm the one who should be sorry,' Sal argued. 'I let him sit with us that first night at the Opera House bar, I encouraged you to trust him, talk to him, let him into your life.'

'It's not your fault.'

'No, but I—'

'Sal, please. This isn't on you, and it's not on me either – it's on him.'

The dawn was beginning to show itself, casting the village in a bruised, uncertain light. From somewhere down the hill came the soft, sorrowful bleat of a goat, a sound that seemed to echo the weight in Skye's chest.

'I have to go,' Sal said. 'Will you be OK?'

'Of course.' Skye forced the words out, shaping them into a smile, willing them to be true. But deep in her gut, colder and heavier than fear, two other words had settled.

He knows.

19

The watch Skye took from Martyn was a Rolex Daytona Platinum, its recommended retail price sitting somewhere between sixty-five and seventy-eight thousand pounds.

She had sold it for less.

The man at the Time Vault in London had questioned this, had also wanted to know why speed of sale was such an overriding factor, and Skye had been sure to have her story ready.

'It's an unwanted gift,' she'd told him, as he studied the paperwork. 'My husband and I are using the proceeds to begin our IVF journey, and we don't want to wait.'

'In that case,' he'd said, as he made the transfer into Skye's brand-new account, 'I wish you all the luck.'

She had read somewhere once that in order to lie convincingly, a person should stay as close to the truth as possible. The Rolex had been a gift, though not to her, and it certainly wasn't unwanted, although Martyn had only worn it once. The woman who'd given it to him – a passenger of extreme wealth who claimed to have bought it for her son-in-law only for him to reject it – was nobody special to him, and the timepiece carried no sentimental value. To him, it was simply a prop; to Skye, it represented the possibility for escape.

After ending the call with Sal, she went back to scrolling through her inbox. There were ten emails from Martyn, the most recent of which had arrived while she was still on the phone.

You can run, he'd written in the subject line, adding in the body of the message, ... *but you can't hide for ever.*

Scare tactics – a ploy by him to make her believe he was close to tracking her down. Skye deleted the email, then opened one from her mum, skimming the lines of text through narrowed eyes. Demands and histrionics, further attempts at coercion. Her finger hovered for a second over the trash can symbol, then she relented, firing off a reply saying she was fine, and not to worry.

Back at Joy's, she tiptoed through into the bedroom and retrieved her clothes, dressing in the bathroom and brushing her teeth. It was not yet six a.m., and out on the hillside, all was quiet, the houses blossom pink below a reddening sky. All at once, she was bombarded by a slew of conflicting emotions, as dread fought with relief, and loneliness battled remorse. Movement helped, and so she walked, heading north through the village until she reached the Serfiotiko Beach trail. Skye had yet to hike along it, though Victoria had been several times, as had Joy, and each had been effusive in their praise.

The path was rough and dry, littered with stones that tumbled away beneath her trainers. She managed to maintain a decent pace, spurred on by the unfolding scenery and the promise of sea at her journey's end. The land on either side of the trail was scalloped by terraces, fields that were smudgy green in the emerging daylight. She drew in a breath, tasting nothing but cool stillness on her lips. Had Katerina from her letters taken this same route? Had she stared out across the water, waiting for her lover to return, condemned to live in perpetual fear that he would not? Their love for one another had been fierce and passionate – that much was clear from the words 'S' had chosen to use, from the yearning he expressed with such eloquence. Skye's own experience with love had been lacklustre by comparison, the feelings she had for her first boyfriend Charlie adolescent, those she developed for Martyn grown from a heart too broken by grief to feel much of anything. She'd allowed herself to be carried along by the intensity of his adoration, telling herself that she would catch up, that in time, her love for him would flourish. What a foolish notion that now seemed.

Ahead of her, the trail tapered off, dropping from view over the cliff edge, where it would lead down to the beach beyond. She crested the hill, a surge of pleasure expanding her chest as the glittering carpet of sea came into full and glorious view. With a spontaneous burst of energy, she covered the remaining few yards at a run, sidestepping a stack of pale stones before coming to a stop in the shade of a bristly pine.

On the far side of the shallow cove, two squat buildings sat derelict, framed by tamarisk trees. Military lookouts. Skye wondered if it had been the Greeks who constructed them, or their occupying aggressors. How much of the war had reached these parts, and how many scars had it left on the island?

She turned away from the weather-beaten structures to stare instead at the water, squinting as the tepid sunlight turned the cresting waves diamond bright. There was a small boat not far from the shoreline, seemingly abandoned, but as Skye drew nearer, she saw the top of a dark head emerge from beneath the surface of the water.

The figure heaved himself up over the side, pulling off his snorkel and flicking back his hair. He was tanned and broad-shouldered, instantly familiar. The moment she recognised him, he looked up. Their eyes met. Andreas raised a hand in greeting. Then, without waiting for a response, he dived over the edge of the boat and swam towards her, cutting through the expanse of shimmering blue as gracefully as a minnow. Skye averted her gaze as he stood, but not before admiring the lean lines of his body, the taut stomach and strong thighs, the way he strode boldly across the sharp-edged rocks as if they were sponges.

'*Kalimera*,' he said, as casually as if they'd bumped into one another at the mini market.

'Hi.'

Skye dropped her eyes to his glistening thatch of chest hair, only to hurriedly look away.

'What are you doing here?' she went on, as he

continued to stare. 'I thought you lived at the other end of the island.'

'Ah, yes,' he said. 'That is why I have the boat, so I can go wherever I like.'

'And you like this beach in particular?'

'Serfiotiko Beach is not so crowded. Now that it is the second week of June and we are in the summer season proper, the beaches on other parts of Folegandros are becoming a bit busier. When I am swimming, it is the fish I want to see, not the white legs of tourists.'

His eyes trailed down, and she blushed.

'I've been a bit preoccupied to sunbathe,' she said. 'And anyway, it's very bad for you.'

'The sun is bad?' He threw back his head. 'The sun is life.'

'The sun is wrinkles,' she countered, and Andreas laughed.

'Can I ask you a question?' he said.

'Fire away.'

'Why did you come to live on a Greek island if you do not like the sun?'

Skye fought the urge to smile.

'Nowhere else was offering houses as cheaply. If the lottery had been run in Norway, I happily would've moved there.'

'I am glad that you came here,' he said.

'You are?' Skye tucked a strand of hair behind her ear.

'In the beginning, when the municipality was discussing the possibility, many people here were not sure that it would work. The hippies, they do not mind so much, but some of the older generation were worried. This is a very traditional island, a very Greek island. I was one of the voices that was loudest in your favour, and if you had been bad people . . .'

'It would have reflected badly on you,' she finished, and he nodded.

'*Nai*. But then you came, and everybody was very nice, so it is OK.'

He hadn't asked her what she was doing, here on the beach alone, so early in the day. Skye liked that about him – his ability to be disarmingly direct while simultaneously knowing when not to pry. Somehow, that quiet restraint made her want to open up even more.

'Thanks again for reading me that letter last night,' she said. 'I haven't been able to stop thinking about it.'

Andreas bent and scooped up a flat pebble, turning it over in his hands.

'*Kai ego*,' he murmured. 'Me too.'

Stepping round her, he leaned back and threw the stone across the surface of the water, where it skimmed, bounced, and sank with a satisfying splash.

'I have copied it out for you into English,' he said.

'You have?'

'The one from last night, and I also began a second. I will try to do all of them for you.'

She moved towards him, drawn by an unexpected ache for connection. Her fingers brushed his arm, her touch featherlight, but enough to make him turn, his eyes finding hers with quiet intensity.

'That's so . . . Thank you,' she said.

Andreas looked down at her hastily retreating hand.

'I will bring them to the house later, unless—' He paused, frowning slightly. 'Unless you want to come now to collect them?'

'To your house?' Skye said. 'Right now? But how would I get there?'

Andreas put a hand on her shoulder, turning her until she was facing the sea.

'*Ela*,' he said, skin cool against hers. 'We will go in the boat.'

20

The boat could not be brought all the way into shore, though Andreas towed it close enough that Skye was able to wade most of the way out. It was trickier than it looked, the water tugging at her clothes and the boat rocking unsteadily. After a few failed attempts to climb in on her own, Skye's frustration mounted and she finally gave in, letting him reach out and help her over the side.

'You are light,' he told her, as she sat herself down. 'I have lifted octopuses that were heavier.'

'Well,' she said, wringing out her skirt, 'they do have rather more legs than me.'

Andreas raised the anchor, its chain curling up by Skye's feet like a slumbering viper. There was a T-shirt tossed over the outboard motor, a tatty pair of flip-flops on the floor beside a cool box.

'There are some drinks inside,' he said, opening the lid with his big toe.

Skye helped herself to a can of Diet Coke. The long walk from the village had left her parched, the sun that had been mellow now more fervent. She had no idea of the hour. Her phone was where she had deliberately left it, back at Joy's house, and Andreas was not wearing a watch. Time had once been at the centre of her working day, her eyes going constantly to the clock on the wall of her classroom. Schools were structured by time – registration time, lesson time, break time, home time – and Skye hadn't realised how much of a comfort that schedule was until she no longer had it. Things were different on the island, however. Here, time seemed endless, the days leaking into evenings that were gradually consumed by nights. There was time to think, to pause, to simply be.

'Ready?' Andreas asked, as the motor rattled into life.

Skye gripped the gunwale with her free hand and then they were off, cutting through water so clear that she could see the pattern of light on the rocks below. The boards vibrated beneath her, a roar that grew in volume as they picked up speed, leaving the bay behind and heading out into open sea. The wind whipped around them, and Skye quickly tucked her skirt between her knees, her gaze drawn upwards to the island's towering cliffs. Grey and weathered, their surface tie-dyed with patches of lichen.

Andreas tapped her shoulder, pointing to where the dark shape of a bird was playing chicken with the waves.

'A Levantine shearwater,' he said. 'They like to chase the wind.'

'Do they nest on the island?'

'Not nest,' he said, speaking loudly to be heard over

the engine. 'They have burrows, the same as puffins. It is safer for them.'

'It seems to me as if a lot of things seek safety on Folegandros,' she said.

Andreas readjusted his grip on the tiller, and the boat slowed.

'Can you see that cave up ahead?'

Skye scanned the cliffside and located the jagged shadow of an opening, dark and mysterious against the sunlit rock.

'I see it.'

'That is Chrysospilia,' he told her. 'It is very famous in Folegandros, because inside, there is a chamber, and painted on the walls are many ancient names.'

'How ancient?'

'The fourth century BC.'

'That's astonishing.' Skye turned back to him. 'Have you ever been inside?'

Andreas shrugged half-heartedly. 'Never,' he said. 'If you want to visit, you must have special permission, and it can be dangerous to try. You must go by boat, and only when the sea is very calm. There can be no wind. Once, a long time ago, it was possible to climb down. The people who lived on the island thousands of years ago would come here to Chrysospilia to hide from pirates.'

'Pirates again?' Skye said, recalling what he'd told her about the church above Chora. 'What was it about this island that kept them coming back?'

'Perhaps it was the same for them as it was for me,' he said, sliding his fist back around the tiller. 'I cannot be the only person who believes that Folegandros is special.'

'No,' Skye agreed, smiling to herself. 'I don't think you can.'

It took them a further half-hour to reach the port-hamlet of Karavostasis. The first and only time Skye had seen it was the day she'd arrived on the slow ferry from Athens, mildly alarmed when the vast vessel aborted its mooring several times. She asked Andreas about this as he neatly slipped his own small boat into place along a narrow concrete jetty.

'The wind,' he told her. 'It can make things very difficult, even for the large vessels.'

Karavostasis was certainly exposed to the elements, sitting as it did on the south-eastern tip of the island. Skye had to clamp down her skirt as they walked, passing a flat-roofed building with a rudimentary 'bus station' sign fixed to the wall, and several plastic chairs outside. It was possible to take either the road or the beach, and they chose the latter, Skye pausing to admire a set of blue-painted benches, arranged below the laden branches of a tree. There was far more life here than up in her sleepy village, and every person they encountered seemed to know Andreas. Cheerful cries of *'kalimera'* were exchanged, other words that she did not yet know, though understood to be friendly.

'The only problem with living on a small island,' Andreas confided, 'is that everybody wants to know your business, all of the time. *Ela*,' he called, breaking away from her. An elderly man had shuffled into view ahead of them, a bristly dog trotting along by his side.

'*Geia sou*, Karolo.'

The man squinted towards Andreas from his stooped position, then rattled off a stream of jovial-sounding Greek. They talked for a few minutes, Andreas turning to usher Skye forwards. When he introduced her, the man, Karolos, nodded and smiled.

'I've been trying to convince him to allow me access to his house,' Andreas explained. 'It needs some work, a lot of work.'

Karolos grinned, showing off more gaps than teeth, and began gesticulating over his shoulder. Andreas shook his head in mock despair.

'He says the house has survived many wars and much bad weather, and that it will be here for many more years after we are all dead.'

Skye considered.

'He's probably right,' she said, and Andreas laughed.

'Do not encourage him.'

The dog let out a short, sharp bark, and Skye crouched to stroke its straggly grey head. It looked like every dog and no dog, a classic mongrel blend of hardy breeds, with wise brown eyes, a curled, upright tail and a lolling tongue.

'What's her name?' she asked, and Andreas translated the question.

'Filia,' Karolos said warmly.

'It means "friendship",' Andreas told her. 'A very nice name.'

Skye stood with a smile. 'I'll remember that one.'

Karolos went on his way, though not before Andreas had extracted a promise from the old man that he would at least consider the offer of renovation.

'I am worried about the structure,' he confided to Skye, as they continued along the stony beach. 'Some newer houses have been built very close to his, and the work has damaged the foundations. There are holes in the wall that I can fit my boot through.'

Skye grimaced. 'That sounds even worse than mine.'

'Your house will be perfect,' he said. 'I will make sure of that.'

She followed him to the end of a row of two-storey whitewashed dwellings. Skye wondered how many of the locals would be speculating who she was, and why she was going into Andreas's house. If there was one thing she'd learned during her time on Folegandros, it was that the answer was probably all of them. Not that it mattered. She and Andreas were friends, nothing more.

His house was the neatest she'd seen in Karavostasis. It was gleaming white, with shutters and a balcony rail painted in the palest blue. The end-terrace abode was also larger than its neighbours and had clearly been extended at some point. A pot of herbs sat on each of the four steps that led up to the front door, the peppery sweetness of basil competing with the woodier sage – a scent so synonymous with the island that it could have been its signature.

The small patio at the top was empty save for a mosaic-topped table, two foldable chairs and the familiar bulk of an air-conditioning unit, tucked into a high corner. Andreas slipped his hand beneath a blue-and-white mat and extracted a key.

'I used to carry this with me,' he said, holding it up, 'but I lost it many times. There are about twenty-five of them at the bottom of the sea.'

'Folegandros doesn't strike me as being a hotbed of criminal activity,' she remarked.

'Ah,' he said, as he opened the door, 'you are forgetting about the pirates.'

Skye wasn't sure if she should take off her shoes, though when he kicked off his flip-flops, she followed suit, bending to tug at her laces. Andreas busied himself with opening shutters, and within a few minutes, the wide lounge area was flooded with light. The first thing she saw as she entered the room was a wooden cabinet, mounted on the opposite wall. It was ornately carved, the two doors propped open to show a series of framed paintings hued in gold, the largest of which depicted a grey-haired, bearded man in red and green robes, one hand raised and the other clutching a scroll. Behind the figure was a tilted cross, and around his head, a halo.

Andreas saw her staring and beckoned. 'That is the Holy Apostle Andreas,' he said.

Skye tilted her head, amused in spite of herself. 'Did you name him?'

He laughed at that, his eyes alight. '*Ela*, no! It is me who is named after him. In Greece, we do not celebrate our birthdays in the same way as other people. Instead, we have a name day, and for Andreas, this is

November thirtieth. On that day, we will share some food, perhaps see our friends and family.'

'And these others?' she asked, gesturing to the smaller images inside the cabinet.

'The Holy Family, Christ Pantocrater, and the Ever-Virgin Mary, bought for me by Giagia when I moved to the island.'

'The same Giagia who was born here?' Skye said, remembering.

'*Nai*,' he agreed softly. 'To remind me that God is always close. If you follow the Orthodox religion, it is traditional to have these icons in your home. Giagia is very traditional.' He scratched the back of his neck. 'She tries her hardest to make me the same.'

'Are you trying to tell me you're a rebel?' Skye asked.

Andreas flashed her a roguish grin. 'The worst.'

'I'd argue that serious rebels are too busy rebelling to keep their house this tidy,' she said, casting an eye over the immaculate cream sofas, shiny flatscreen television and polished-wood coffee table. A row of books was stacked on a low shelf, and she crossed the room and slid one out, charmed to find that it was an encyclopaedia of birds.

Andreas disappeared through a side door. A moment later came the bubble of a kettle, the soft clunk of cups and clinking of a spoon. When he returned, it was with coffee and a slice of cake.

'Honey,' he said, 'from the bakery. A rebel does not have time to cook.'

She started to protest, but he pressed the plate towards her.

'Real Greeks eat, remember?'

'Aren't you going to have any?'

Andreas tugged off his T-shirt, the silver cross he always wore slipping down into the dark forest of chest hair.

'I ate two slices already in the kitchen,' he confessed. 'But now, I must have a shower.'

'Before you go,' she said, and he turned at the bottom of the stairs, 'can I have another look at the letters, maybe read the one you copied out for me?'

'*Ela*, of course.' He pointed behind her at the bookshelf. 'Pull those out, and you will find the letters hidden behind them.'

'You hid them? Why?'

Andreas met her gaze.

'To keep them safe,' he said.

Skye ate her cake, waiting for the sound of running water before she moved. Carefully, she retrieved the bundle, set her empty plate and coffee on the table, then sat down. Her fingers hovered briefly as she stared down at the letters, giving herself a moment with which to shut out the present. The past was right there, in her hands, and she was ready to lose herself in its mystery once more.

21

December 1940

Winter had come to her island.

Katerina stood in the doorway that led through into the bakery kitchen, watching as Leni prepared a batch of spanakopita. She could hear the rain as it pummelled the windows and walls, blown in by a wind so furious, it was as if the earth-shaker Poseidon had sent it.

'Why doesn't he write?'

Leni paused, her hands damp from rolling out the boiled spinach. It was not the first time Katerina had asked this question, and she could see that the subject was grating on her sister.

'They are busy, *agapi mou*.'

She scoffed. 'Too busy to scribble a few lines, tell us that they are alive?'

It had been weeks since her last communication from Stefanos, though he, at least, had written to her. Michalis had sent not one word to his wife, and Leni must care – she must be angry with him, though she would never admit it. Katerina had not told her what she knew of Michalis – what would be the point? Becoming aware that her husband shook from fear when faced with battle would only cause her sister to suffer. All this waiting they were required to do was pain enough.

'I am sure that they would write to us if they could,' Leni said. 'Now, come here and help me with the pastries.'

Katerina dragged her feet. She did not like baking. Food, for her, was fuel, nothing more.

'Why do you put raisins inside?' she asked grumpily. 'It is not a cake.'

'For energy,' Leni said, 'and also for sweetness. It is the sugar that makes the flavour of the cheese come to life.'

Her sister's fingers moved with practised ease, sprinkling freshly chopped dill into her bowl before cracking in three eggs. Katerina waited to be told before splashing in olive oil, while Leni added a pinch of cinnamon.

'Stir,' she said, passing Katerina a wooden spoon stained black from the grill.

Katerina obeyed, brooding in silent contemplation as Leni turned her attention to the phyllo pastry that was cooling between dry cloths. Each individual sheet must be paper-thin, though thick enough not to tear. It was a delicate balance, one that Katerina had no patience for, nor could imagine having. If she and Stefanos were ever to marry, he would have to survive on lemons, figs and goat milk – anything more elaborate was out of the question.

'Do you think that Mama and Baba will come home soon?' she asked.

Leni looked up, eyes dark below the headscarf she wore, the shadows beneath them darker still. 'Why do you ask me so many questions? I do not know the answers any better than you do.'

'It has been a long time,' Katerina said, though her observation was both unneeded and unwanted. 'The sea will be too rough for them now until the spring.'

'Perhaps.' Leni took the bowl from her and began to layer the mixture into a wide, clay dish. Katerina sat on the edge of the table only to leap off as Leni scolded her.

'If you are bored,' she said, 'there is plenty of work to be done at the house. Why don't you write your own letter to Stefanos?'

'Another letter? I have sent one already today. I told him about the weather, and the goats, and about the teenager Kostas breaking his arm – it is all nonsense, a noise. He is fighting, and me?' She huffed. 'I am doing nothing, nothing to help our people.'

'*Ela re, agapi mou.*' Leni sighed. 'After the war, the men will want to come back to their homes. We must be here to welcome them, we must keep everything as it is, look after the animals, and the crops, and the trees. They are fighting for Greece, but there will be no Greece unless we look after it. That is our job in this war.'

She smoothed out the final square of pastry and rubbed her hands together. Katerina watched as a dusting of flour fell to the ground.

'Stefanos says that men and women are equal.' The words felt like a deliberate provocation, though she craved the satisfaction of having said them. 'If they can fight, why can't we?'

Leni turned away, her tray of spanakopita balanced in her hands. 'Open the oven,' she said.

With great reluctance, muttering under her breath, Katerina did as she'd been asked, standing back as Leni eased the pastries through the semicircular opening. Her sister was not going to nibble at the bait, a fact she made clear a few moments later by leaving the room. Katerina followed her through into the shop, ready to launch her next argument until she saw that they had a customer. Dafni stood by the counter, her scarf knotted tightly beneath her chin. She and her husband Giorgos were in their seventies, though time had done little to dull the energy of either one. Katerina often saw them outside their hillside home, tending plants or trimming trees – never idling like Baba, but busy, active, full of purpose.

'Ah,' she said, dripping rainwater onto the tiles, 'what is this? Two Sideris sisters – what a piece of luck.'

Dafni, reflected Katerina, always seemed to be on the verge of laughter, though she'd never once shared what amused her. Now, her beady gaze was fixed on the display of Leni's maza loaves, still warm from that morning's baking.

'Giorgos has been on the boat and brought home a big swordfish,' she told them, not without pride. 'There is too much for us alone – why don't you come to eat with us later?'

Katerina perked up. A meal with Dafni and her husband signalled an opportunity to talk about something other than chores, goats and the various merits of raisins.

'Is it true that Giorgos fought in the Great War?' she asked.

Dafni's face immediately fell.

'Yes,' she said hesitantly, 'although he does not like to speak about it.'

'Will he fight in this war?' Katerina went on, ignoring a stern look from Leni.

Dafni bent her head to remove a few coins from her purse.

'He is not young any more,' she said, which was not strictly an answer. 'The army needs young men, strong men.'

'But surely he wants to join them,' Katerina persisted.

'*Ela stamata*,' Leni admonished, wrapping one of the loaves in wax paper but refusing the woman's money. 'Please,' she said, 'take it – an apology for my sister's rudeness.'

'How is it rude to ask a simple question?' Katerina demanded. 'It is a fact that if the line cannot be held, or if the Germans join with the Italians, then all the men will have to go.'

'Stop this,' Leni said, her tone harsh. Katerina stared wide-eyed. Her sister never raised her voice, let alone to shriek at her in this way. Her cheeks had turned bright red, as if it were her, not the spanakopita, that had been cooking over the wood fire.

'All this talk of war,' Leni hissed. 'It is as if you enjoy it, the thought of it. You sound as if you are sick.' She tapped furiously on her forehead. 'There is something wrong with you.'

Dafni no longer looked as if she wanted to laugh. Katerina took a single, defiant breath. 'At least I am not pretending,' she said. 'If the enemy arrives on Folegandros, what will you do, eh? Hide away like a turtle in its shell?'

'*Ela, ela,*' Dafni soothed. 'Do not fight. You are family.'

Katerina threw up her hands, though there was truth to the older woman's words. If Baba could see her now, he would bring his hand hard across her face. Leni had begun to cry silently, her jaw rigid and shoulders hunched.

'I will tell you something I know about war,' Dafni said, darting a warning glance at Katerina when she began to interrupt. '*Ela*, listen to me – you were not born the last time there was a war such as this one. You do not know what it was like for us, those who fought and those who did not. The Giorgos that came back to me was not the same man who left. He has not ever been the same, and I cannot help him. I cannot take away the horrors that he saw, the violence, and the death. War is not glorious, it is barbaric.'

'I do not believe that it is glorious,' Katerina protested, 'only that it is coming. I want to be ready if it does. I want all of us to be ready.'

With a sudden gasp, Leni ran back to the kitchen. Katerina followed, Dafni close behind, all three crying out in dismay as the spanakopita, blackened beyond saving, was pulled from the oven. For a moment, nobody spoke. Smoke trailed up towards the ceiling. Outside, the rain beat steadily against the windows.

Dafni laid a hand on Katerina's arm, her skin as papery thin and fragile as the phyllo pastry smouldering before them.

'There is no way to prepare for war,' she said. 'The only thing you can do is try to survive it.'

22

Three weeks after arriving on Folegandros, Skye experienced her first Greek storm.

The morning had begun in stillness, the mountains standing sharp against a backdrop of clear blue. By the time she had scraped the last of her breakfast from the bowl – yoghurt, fruit and honey having become a quiet ritual – the light had shifted. A wind rose out of nowhere, wild and impatient, rattling what remained of her shutters and sweeping grit across the floor.

Andreas appeared not long after, pausing by the front door with his arms folded and chin tipped to the sky. His hair was damp, the dark curls brushed back but already at the mercy of the wind.

'Are you attempting to have a staring match with those grey clouds?' Skye asked.

Something close to a grin tugged at his mouth.

'Rain in June is not impossible,' he said, 'but it is unusual. Most of the time, we have a lot more at the end of August, and also in the winter.'

'You're forgetting I grew up in England,' she reminded him. 'Rain is part of my DNA.'

Andreas's smile grew. 'If that is true,' he said, 'it means the sun is part of mine.'

The two of them shared many of these playful exchanges and the moment itself did not demand attention. Yet there was something in the way they looked at each other, soft and unhurried, that made it feel like one worth remembering.

'I didn't think I'd see you today,' she said. 'I thought everything was on hold until Pantelis had time to do the plastering?'

A violent gust of wind tore through the house, and Andreas flinched as the back door slammed shut with a crash that echoed through the walls.

'That is true,' he allowed. 'But today, I have brought my potty.'

'Your ... potty?' Skye spluttered out a laugh. 'I know this place is a work in progress, but there is a functioning toilet.'

He stared at her, incomprehension writ large. 'Why would I use a toilet to fill holes in the walls?'

'Oh,' she said, 'you mean putty.'

'*Nai*, potty.'

'What do you call it in Greek?'

'*Stokáki*,' he said.

Skye let her own smile come, small and irrepressible.

'Maybe stick to that in future,' she suggested. 'Less risk of misinterpretation.'

Andreas gave a faint shake of his head, as if amused but slightly resigned.

'Do you want to help me?' he asked. 'It is a messy job, but quite satisfying.'

'I can't,' Skye said. 'It's Monday, and Mondays and Wednesdays are my teaching days, remember?'

'*Nai*, of course,' he said. 'And how is the boy Patarakis getting along?'

'George? Very well. Now that the initial adjustment has eased, I think he's starting to really enjoy living here. I've discovered that he finds it easier to concentrate when we're outside, walking and talking, rather than sitting together at a desk. I was actually planning to head down to the beach today, but perhaps that's unwise?'

She glanced up towards the sky, the clouds congregating in bruised layers, their dark underbellies threatening to spill.

'I think it is better to stay indoors today,' Andreas agreed, briefly touching her arm. 'Teach him some Greek history.'

Skye lingered inside the door, watching as he pulled a tub of '*potty*' from the back of the truck. Andreas was right, history made sense. Teaching it wouldn't just provide George with some background about his new home, it might deepen her own understanding, too. The thought sparked something, and she dashed up the stairs, returning moments later to find Andreas unfolding a dust sheet. Like her, he was protective of the terracotta floor tiles they had laid together the previous week – a task that had offered a welcome distraction to all the things she was trying not to think about. Martyn's emails had stopped, though the silence was, in its own way, more unsettling. Her insomnia had worsened since leaving London, and even when sleep came, it was fragile. The slightest noise would jolt her awake, adrenaline surging and nerves shred, leaving her twitchy and irritable.

'Sorry I can't stay and help,' she said, grabbing her bag and making for the door.

'*Ela*, it is OK. This is my happy place, and now, you must go and be in yours.'

It was uncanny, the way his words always found their mark. Language, to Andreas, was a tool too, wielded with the same gentle precision as his hammers and drills.

There was a spring in Skye's step as she crossed to house number three. She raised her hand to knock but the door was swung open.

'Hi,' George said, in a sullen sort of voice. 'Dad's on the phone, like always.'

'Ah,' she said. There had been much celebration the previous Wednesday when their hillside homes were finally connected to the internet. Theo and Adam no longer had to trek down to the taverna to work, and Victoria was already planning online yoga sessions, just as soon as their garden had been suitably landscaped. For Skye, it made little difference, though she had bought a new SIM card for her phone and was using it to check in regularly with Sal. Her friend repeatedly urged her to find someone on the island that she could open up to, but she wasn't ready. Not yet.

'I thought we'd stay here today,' she told George. 'Andreas says it's going to rain soon.'

The boy fiddled with his headphones, his 'all right' of reply coursing out on a sigh. Skye followed him inside. The layout mirrored Joy's next door, though with an extra bedroom for George, and a tiny office Theo had created in an alcove behind the old fireplace. The walls and ceilings still needed plaster and paint, and aside from several overstuffed bookcases, the furnishings were minimal. One low table displayed George's creations – air-dry clay animals, mosaic tiles, and painted shells he and Skye had collected from Livadaki beach. The boy was like many nine-year-olds – rambunctious, physical, easily distracted – but also capable of sitting quietly with a task. She had learned that if she hit upon a subject that interested him, he would respond with studied enthusiasm.

'I brought something exciting to show you today,' she said, mouthing a silent greeting to Theo as he leaned out from his alcove. George slumped down on the shabby sofa and began to pick at a scab on his knee.

Drawing a sheath of papers from her bag, Skye spread them across the seat. It was the first letter from the bundle, not Andreas's translated version but the original, age-stained and blotted with ink. George leaned over, scanning the words through his thick, smeared glasses.

'It's in Greek,' he said, looking up. 'Who wrote it?'

'I don't know for sure,' she admitted. 'Though it was probably a man, and his name began with an S.'

George thought for a moment.

'Stamatis's name starts with an S,' he said. 'Maybe it was him.'

'He might well have been called Stamatis,' she said, 'but whoever wrote this did so in 1940.'

George tilted his head, curiosity catching hold. 'Where did you get it?' he asked.

'Well now,' Skye began, 'that's where the story gets really interesting, because—'

'Sorry, sorry.' Theo's chair had fallen to the floor and he was hurrying towards them. 'I heard what you said and—Is this the letter Joy told me about? Can I see?'

Skye passed him the pages, which he read silently.

'This is quite a find,' he said. 'I like the way he writes, this man.'

George began to tap the arm of the sofa. 'Will you read it out, Dad?'

Theo drew in a short breath.

'Please!'

'OK,' he said, sitting cross-legged on the threadbare rug. He read almost all of it, leaving out the parts that Skye agreed might be a little hot for younger ears to handle.

'There are lots more,' she told them. 'I found a whole bundle, hidden inside my chimney.'

'Whoa!' George exclaimed. 'Like that sword thing Dusty showed me?'

'That was in her garden, but both are buried treasure if you ask me.'

Theo reached across and stilled his son's tapping fingers.

162

'If you bring the other letters here, I can translate them for you,' he offered.

'That's kind of you, but I think Andreas wants to do it.'

'Isn't he very busy?'

George swung a leg, narrowly missing his dad's kneecap.

'You're always busy too,' he said mutinously. 'I heard you on your laptop last night, crashing on the keyboard. It was going on for ages, I couldn't even sleep.'

Theo blinked, as if something had dimmed inside him.

'It's a tricky edit,' he said, glancing at Skye. 'You change one thing, and it's like a domino's been knocked over in the novel. I'm so close to the end now, and then' – he turned to his son – 'I promise I'll have more free time.'

George resumed his slump, bottom lip protruding. 'When's Mum coming?' he asked.

Skye began to fold away the letter. She could almost feel the heat of Theo's discomfort.

'I've told her where we are,' he said. 'Whether she comes or not is up to her.'

George tore off what was left of the scab, blood blooming.

'Maybe she can't afford the plane ticket,' he said hotly. 'Or she might be scared of flying – you don't know.'

'I wish that were the case,' Theo began, but George had gone past the point of calm discussion. He began flicking together his thumb and second fingers, his body hunched over. Skye put a gentle hand on his shoulder.

'Why don't you go and get your pens, George, and we'll do some sketching?'

He shook his head, the flicking becoming more insistent.

'Come on, mate,' Theo began, only to be interrupted by a loud rumble of thunder. Skye jumped, though the noise steadied George. He stopped stimming and crossed to the window.

'I saw lightning,' he said. 'Do you think it was like this in the war, when bombs were going off all the time and people were being blown up?'

Skye went to join him.

'I think that would've been far scarier,' she said, peering out. The sky had turned eerily dark, the wind whistling as it tore at the earth.

'Dad, what was the biggest explosion ever? Was it from a nuclear bomb?'

'I don't know,' Theo said tiredly. 'Maybe. Why don't you go and look it up on the iPad?'

'But it's not my screentime.'

'I'll make an exception,' Theo said. 'Off you go.'

George scampered off as if the disagreement with his dad had never happened. Theo waited until his bedroom door closed, then turned to Skye.

'Sorry you had to hear that,' he said. 'The situation with my ex-wife is complicated.'

'Say no more,' she said, but Theo wasn't finished.

'We broke up a long time ago,' he said, sitting in the space that George had vacated, his elbows on his knees. 'Everyone said we got married too young, but when you're twenty, you don't listen to anyone. George wasn't planned, and Deirdre, that's my ex, didn't enjoy being pregnant. They say women bloom, but it was the opposite for her, and when George was born, she struggled to bond with him. I did what I could, took her to the doctor, and then another doctor.' He sighed. 'Somehow, we made it through the first few years as a family, but it was as if a part of her wasn't there. The day after George's fourth birthday, she told me she'd met someone else and wanted to leave. I thought at first that she'd want to keep George with her, but I was wrong about that.'

'I'm so sorry,' Skye said.

Theo pulled a 'what can you do?' expression.

'Deirdre went from seeing him every weekend, to every other weekend, and then slowly, the visits dropped off. There was always an excuse, and suddenly, six months had passed with no contact, not even a phone call. My friends told me I should go down the legal route, but I didn't want that, not for any of us. The final straw came when she missed his birthday in October. I was so angry.' He shook his head. 'I left George with a friend and went to confront her, but when I knocked on her door, a stranger answered, told me they'd bought the house from her months before. There was no forwarding address, and she didn't answer my calls or emails.'

Skye's skin turned clammy, her breath catching in her throat. Rain had started to fall, hard and steady.

'What about grandparents?' she asked.

'Deirdre's parents were in Ireland, and they were never close. The only time we took George to see them it ended in disaster, so we never went back.' He stared glumly at his hands. 'My parents still live in Athens, but they didn't know where she'd gone, nobody seemed to know anything – until this one day. I got a message on Facebook, of all places, from a friend of hers. She said she felt sorry for me and told me where I could find Deirdre.'

'And did you?'

Theo's eyes briefly closed.

'Eventually, yes. Sometimes, I wish I hadn't. I don't want George to ever know what she said. I haven't lied to him, though, except by omission. Deirdre does know where we are.'

'Do you think she'll ever come here?' Skye asked.

'Honestly?' he said. 'No, I don't think she will.'

His words anchored them for a few moments in silence, the only sound the persistent rain. Theo removed his glasses and rubbed his eyes.

'I really would like to translate the rest of the letters for you,' he said. 'My way of saying thank you for helping George, for caring about him.'

'You don't need to thank me.'

'No, but I want to,' he said. 'Maybe we can start a project once this edit is done, do some proper research into the people who lived here before us, build up an archive of letters, photos, artefacts.'

Thunder cracked across the hillside, loud enough to make Skye step back from the window.

'There are bound to be more things out there,' Theo said, his tone thoughtful. 'Waiting to be found.'

Skye nodded, a thrill rising in her chest. 'I can't wait to see what this mysterious little village turns up next.'

Outside, the storm rolled on, and somewhere beneath it, the past stirred, patient yet unresolved, waiting to surface once more.

23

When Skye returned home several hours later, it was still raining; great sheets of water that seemed to blow in from every direction. She clutched her bag to her side and ran, slipping on the wet earth and almost falling in her haste to reach shelter.

There was no sign of the truck or Andreas, though she could see from the glistening patches of putty on the walls that he'd been hard at work during her absence. The downstairs area had been transformed over the past few weeks. Skye took a moment to admire the smooth curves of her new fireplace, the stacked seating area that wrapped around the room, and Andreas's beautiful wood-panelled ceiling, reinforced by steel supports. Stamatis had laid rubber panels beneath the floors upstairs to minimise sound and trap heat, while up in the attic, boards had been hammered into place. She no longer had to hop across the joists in order to reach the window. It was still her favourite spot, the place she retreated to whenever thoughts of Katerina crept in. Skye didn't believe in ghosts, not in the spectral sense, though she couldn't dismiss the idea of energy, that invisible trace a person leaves behind. The notion that death was merely a full stop struck her as not only cruel, but insufficient. Her dad had gone, yes, but something of him remained, threaded through her in ways she could not explain. And now Katerina, too, existed in that quietly persistent way: not seen, but felt.

In the bedroom, she peeled off her dress and hung it up to dry before rooting dejectedly through her open suitcase. She'd finally got around to ordering a chest of drawers, wardrobe and a bedframe and mattress, all of which were due to arrive before the weekend – and not a moment too soon. Skye was well aware that she also needed to buy a sofa and chairs, rugs for every room, as well as a desk and bookcases. She was also keenly aware of her rapidly depleting funds. The proceeds from the Rolex would cover the renovations and her own living costs for the first year or so, but after that, she would need a steady income.

The downpour still hadn't let up. Rain pummelled the roof as Skye pulled on a shirt and shorts, the fabric clinging to her damp skin. She was halfway to the kitchen, her mind on coffee and maybe some lunch, when a sharp knock split the air.

'Bloody hell,' was how Joy greeted her. 'It's wetter than a sea lion's flipper out there.'

'Come inside,' Skye said. 'I was just about to put the kettle on.'

'Got anything stronger than tea?' Joy asked, shaking out her umbrella and leaning it against the wall, where it promptly began to drip a small puddle across the tiles. She wore a tie-dye maxi dress in swirls of purple and green, her mass of frizzy hair pinned up in a loose, slightly lopsided bun, and her bronzed arms were flecked with what looked like paint.

Knowing Joy, it could just as easily have been part of the outfit.

'I don't think I do,' Skye said, smiling an apology. 'But there is some honey cake.'

Ever since Andreas had given her a slice, she'd been addicted.

'Sophia's honey cake?' Joy said.

Sophia was the owner of the village bakery – a wily, sparkly-eyed woman in her seventies, who was forever telling Skye that she was *'toso omorfi'* – *so beautiful*.

'Naturally,' Skye said now, leading Joy towards the kitchen, 'although one of these days, I might have a go at making one myself.'

'Least you've got an oven. You know the girls are still getting by with only a microwave? Dusty's so set on finishing the extension that she's ignoring all the other rooms in the house. I told her she should let Andreas and his crew help out, but she won't have it. She's started some Instagram account now. I've seen her out in the garden filming "day in the life of a Greek renovation" videos.'

'Sounds like a nice idea,' Skye said. She had disabled her own social media accounts before coming to Folegandros, though she'd taken plenty of before-and-after pictures of the house at Sal's request. Her friend had promised to try and visit at the end of September, once the third Australian school term broke, which meant Skye had plenty of time to finish the place.

'Did I tell you that Mini Mia's started working at the vet clinic?' Joy went on. 'Only for two days a week, but she's loving it so far.'

'Has Louisa had any luck?' Skye asked. 'I know she was looking for something.'

Joy accepted a mug of coffee, turning it so she could drink from the non-chipped side. Despite buying new crockery, Skye remained attached to the items donated by Andreas. Her own mug had a faded map of the island on one side, and *I don't need therapy, I just need a trip to Folegandros* printed on the other.

'Nothing yet,' Joy said, 'although she has been looking after little Iris and Ajax now and then. Cora and Klodi are so tied up with running the mini market, especially now there are more tourists here.'

'Don't most people stay in Chora?' Skye asked. The idea of strangers traipsing through Ano Meria made her uneasy.

'Yeah,' Joy said, 'but more and more of them are starting to discover this place. Pantelis had a full house for lunch last week at the taverna.'

That explained his inability to make time for her external plastering.

'Maybe Louisa should work for him,' Skye suggested.

Joy lowered her mug. 'Bloody good idea that, although I think she'd rather be employed by Andreas, if you know what I mean?'

Skye avoided having to reply by turning away to slice the cake.

'I haven't told you my news, have I?' Joy continued.

'News?'

'Yeah, I met this fella from the Netherlands down at the beach the other day. He runs a gallery in Chora. Sander, his name is. Anyway, we got to chatting, and he's offered me a slot, says they do a good trade, especially during the summer months. If I can get a few pieces done over the next few weeks, he reckons he can sell them through July and August.'

'That's brilliant,' Skye enthused, passing her a plate. 'What are you going to paint?'

'Well . . .' Joy took a bite of the cake and her eyes rolled back theatrically. 'Christ, that's good. Yeah, anyway, that's actually why I popped round. I was hoping you'd let me paint you.'

'Me?' Skye said. 'Why me?'

'Don't look so surprised, you're bloody gorgeous, what with all that blond hair and delicate bone structure. My plan is to do a Greek gods and goddesses series, only modernised, put the old Monroe twist on them, you know. I want you to be my Aphrodite.'

'But I'm not Greek.'

'You're not a goddess, either, but since when has reality stood in the way of artistic creation?'

Skye put her plate in the sink.

'Wasn't Aphrodite traditionally depicted naked?' she said.

'Well, you're welcome to do it in the nuddy if you like,' Joy began.

'No! God, no.'

Joy let out a chuckle. 'Don't worry,' she said. 'There won't be any nudity, and I won't ask you to wear anything silly. I know I kid around a lot, but when it comes to art, I'm deadly serious.'

'I don't know.' Skye's fingers curled around each other. 'Can I think about it?'

'Sure.' Joy began rinsing out her empty mug, before adding lightly, 'Done thinking yet?'

Skye was, in fact, thinking about her dad. He'd have loved Joy.

Though he'd worked with clay, Cosmo MacKinnon had always been drawn to paintings – portraits in particular. He used to call them 'maps of the soul'. She knew what he would've said, had he been there to say it, and yet . . .

'I'm just not sure,' she told Joy. 'Can you start with someone else? What about Victoria?'

'Maybe.' Joy didn't seem overly enthused. 'I guess I could pop round and ask her, once it stops bloody raining.'

They both paused to listen. Skye eased open the back door to see the faintest glimpse of blue between the clouds.

'It's stopped,' she called, and Joy joined her.

'You never get used to it, do you?' she murmured. 'The view out here, all that sky and mountain and sea. Victoria said it makes her feel small, but it's the opposite for me. I felt small at home, just another cog in a city full of moving parts. Now don't get me wrong, Sydney isn't all bad. We have parks and the harbour, but there's still a claustrophobic element. I reckon it's unavoidable when you cram that many folk together. When I still had Bobby, it was all right, you know? I was in my bubble. But afterwards ... well, death has a way of bringing everything into sharp relief, doesn't it?'

The sun had yet to reappear, though Skye could feel the warmth of it.

'I went to Sydney, a year after my dad died,' she said. 'I didn't want to be at home on the anniversary, and my oldest friend lives there. I walked around that place all day every day for two weeks on my own, while Sal – that's my friend – was at work. I don't think I've ever felt more invisible. That's not to say Sydney is unfriendly,' she added, as Joy's lips tightened a fraction, 'just that it was easy to get lost in; become one of the cogs.'

'Nobody enjoys feeling invisible,' Joy said.

Skye stared beyond the boundaries of her garden, her eyes tracing the roughly hewn pathway that led up to the ridge.

'I didn't used to,' she said, the words catching somewhere in her chest. 'Dad always told me I was his compass point, the pin keeping his life on course. Soppy old fool.' She shook her head. 'It's no wonder, really.'

'No wonder what?' Joy asked. Her voice had softened, the usual teasing edged out by something gentler.

She could tell her. About Martyn. About all of it.

Skye drew in a breath only to let it go as Tigri sprang

up onto the wall, mewing indignantly. The cat was no doubt outraged by the puddle-strewn route he'd be forced to take to reach her.

'I'd better go and get him,' she said, slipping her feet into flip-flops.

'Mind your step,' Joy called after her. 'Looks as if more of that wall's fallen in there.'

All the stones Skye had spent weeks carefully resetting had collapsed back into the mud, dragging more with them. A shallow cavity gaped beneath where the largest rocks had stood. As she stepped closer, something caught her eye, half-hidden in the dark hollow.

'In a minute,' she murmured to Tigri, who had stalked along the wall to meet her. Skye shifted her weight then crouched, trying to see more clearly.

'You found something?' Joy asked, picking her way across on bare feet.

'I'm not sure. There are stones in the way – hang on.'

The first one she lifted was wet and slithered from her hands.

'Careful,' Joy said, scooping up her dress to avoid being splattered with mud.

Skye shifted three more stones, each one landing with a thud as she flung it aside. The last was lodged deep, wedged between the crumbling edge of the wall and the gnarled roots of the lemon tree. She crouched lower, braced her knees, and, with a groan of effort, worked it free.

At that moment, the sun broke through, spilling

wide shafts of light across the hillside. Puddles shimmered, and crystal droplets shook loose from the branches overhead.

In the hollow below where Skye and Joy stood frozen, a collection of tiny bones lay gleaming in the earth.

24

'Are they human?'

Skye had directed her question to Andreas, but it was Mia who answered. Joy had called on the middle Harkin sister, arguing that their resident vet was the closest thing they had to an expert.

'Some look as though they definitely aren't,' Mia said thoughtfully, 'but I can't be sure. A few are quite dense, which makes me lean towards animal. The only way to be certain is to have them measured and tested.'

'I'm not sure we should even touch them,' Skye said. 'Whoever buried them would probably hate the idea of us having dug them up.'

'You didn't,' Joy pointed out. 'It was the storm.'

Andreas, who'd arrived of his own accord to deliver a set of paint samples, was bending over the exposed grave, hands on his knees and a stoic expression on his face.

'The bones are on your property,' he said, turning to Skye. 'I think it is only right that you decide the next steps. We can fill in the hole, no problem, or I can ask someone from the police authority in Chora to collect the remains and conduct some tests.'

'You think we should call the police?'

'I think that we can, but also, we do not have to. *Ela*, it is your decision.'

Joy stepped gingerly over a puddle. 'I guess it comes down to whether you want to know, or if you're happy to let sleeping bones lie,' she said. 'If it was me, I know what I'd do.'

Skye looked at her with quiet interest.

'I'd want to know,' her friend confirmed.

'Hey, guys.'

They all spun round to see Victoria approaching from the side of the house, immaculate in lilac leggings and matching crop top, her hair pulled back in a swinging ponytail. Adam trailed a few paces behind, looking sunburnt and slightly dishevelled in a crumpled shirt.

'We saw you out of our bedroom window,' she said. 'Figured you'd found something.'

Andreas moved aside so they could peer down into the hole.

'Oh my God,' Victoria gasped. 'Are those—Is that part of a skeleton?'

Adam crouched, only to slip. He pitched forwards, both palms splaying in the mud.

'You klutz,' Victoria chided.

'I'll go and wash up.' Adam bounced back onto his feet. 'Get my camera while I'm at it. May as well get a photo of these – that's if it's OK with you, Skye?'

'No worries,' she said distractedly.

'I wonder if there is any kind of grave marker?' Joy mused. 'If these are human bones, surely whoever it was would've had a monument of some sort?'

Andreas turned over one of the fallen stones with the toe of his boot.

'Most of these were part of the wall,' Skye said, 'but you're right, we should have a look.'

She, Mia and Andreas moved among the stones, checking each one for a name or date, but none showed any sign of an engraving.

'A secret grave then,' Victoria said in awe. 'Maybe the bloodstain on that sabre Dusty found belonged to whoever is buried here?'

'Or whatever,' Mia cut in. 'It could easily be animal.'

'A sacrificial lamb,' Victoria cried. 'Or a chicken!'

Mia frowned. 'They're definitely not bird bones – that I can say for certain.'

Adam returned with his camera, and they all moved to allow him space. Skye's fingers toyed with a fraying thread on her shorts, as if the right decision might unravel with it.

'You look troubled,' Andreas said, coming to stand beside her with his back to the others.

'I am,' she concurred.

'What is the thing that is worrying you the most?'

Where to start . . . ?

'I don't want to do anything disrespectful,' she said. 'Do you think the locals would be angry with me if I did agree to have the bones examined by an expert?'

Andreas gave her question proper consideration.

'No,' he said after a beat. 'Greeks, we are nosy. It is in our nature.'

'What would you do?' she asked.

'For me, the knowledge always wins. If it happens

that the bones are human, there is no reason why they cannot be buried again in the right way.'

'You mean these weren't?'

A series of lines dappled his forehead. 'There is no casket,' he said. 'No sign of anything wooden inside the soil.'

'So, they most likely aren't human then?'

The shutter of Adam's camera clicked. Skye glanced up, only to recoil slightly at the flash.

'Most likely,' Andreas agreed. 'However ...' He paused to retrieve his phone from his jeans pocket and activated the compass function. 'Ah, it is as I thought.'

'What is?' she said, standing on tiptoes so she could see the screen.

'In Greece, it is customary to bury the dead facing east.'

A shiver passed through Skye.

'And that grave is facing ...'

'East,' he confirmed.

They looked at each other.

'Will you call them for me?' she said. 'The police, I mean.'

Andreas brushed his fingers lightly against her arm. '*Nai*,' he said. 'I will do it now.'

She watched him stride away with his phone to his ear, heavy workmen's boots sinking into the rain-softened earth. He'd been her first thought upon discovering the bones, and somehow, he'd appeared before she could even call, the familiar purr of his truck's engine easing the knot of tension she hadn't realised was there.

'Have you two developed some sort of psychic connection?' Joy had joked, at which Skye had laughed a little too hard.

Adam had finished his impromptu photo shoot and was now squinting down at the screen of his digital camera, scrolling through the images he'd taken. He should really go into the shade, Skye thought, wincing at the sight of his burned cheeks and forehead.

Victoria clearly agreed.

'Your pink bits are turning purple,' she chided, steering him towards home. 'We'll catch up with you guys later.'

They both waved to Andreas as they passed, but he was too intent on his conversation to notice.

'He on the phone to the cops?' Joy asked Skye. Mia had returned to the hole and was on her haunches, peering at the bones.

'I thought it made sense to know for sure what we're dealing with,' Skye said. 'Though it still makes me feel uneasy, the idea of removing them.'

'You're a history buff, aren't you?'

'You could say that.'

'Well, then.' Joy tipped her head to one side. 'If every archaeologist who stumbled across a pile of bones simply upped and left them there, we'd have huge gaps in our understanding of the past. Hell, we wouldn't even know what dinosaurs were.'

'That reminds me of a joke I know,' Mia said, turning to face them. 'What do you call a blind dinosaur?'

Joy grinned. 'Go on then.'

'A Do You Think He-Saurus.'

'Bloody brilliant,' Joy crowed.

'What is so funny?' Andreas asked, coming towards them. Skye wasn't sure if he'd understand the joke, but having furrowed his brow for a moment or two, he smiled.

'Very good,' he appraised. 'Very clever.'

'What did the police say?' Skye asked.

'That they will come to remove the bones later today, or perhaps tomorrow. Do you have some cover or something?'

'I've got an old sheet of tarp over at mine,' Joy said.

'Do you think we should tell the police about the sabre, too?' Mia asked. 'Dusty hasn't done anything with it yet, as far as I know.'

Skye glanced at Andreas, who shrugged.

'It can't hurt to show them,' she said. 'Then they can decide if they want to take it away for testing.'

'Good idea.' Mia bounced upright. 'I'll go and get it now. You coming, Joy?'

Skye and Andreas remained where they were, watching the others walk away. The sun, having been upstaged by the storm, was now reclaiming the sky, beating down with the fierce urgency of a drum. Moisture hung heavy in the air, disturbed only by a nervous wind, while the ground beneath them seemed to crackle in the rapid dry of the heat.

Skye shielded her eyes with a hand.

'I've been thinking,' she said, 'about the letters we found. Do you think it's possible there's anything in them that would give us some clue about this grave? Have you managed to read any more of them or . . .'

Andreas rubbed the back of his neck, offering her a sheepish smile.

'Not all of them,' he admitted. 'However, I have translated one more for you. I did it today, while I was trapped at home during the storm.'

He slid a hand into the back pocket of his jeans and took out two folded sheets of lined paper.

Skye felt a lift in her chest, light and sudden.

'This one is different,' Andreas said.

Was she imagining it, or was there a note of warning in his tone?

'Different how?'

'You will see,' he said, pushing the pages towards her.

Skye's gaze flickered once more to the open grave. Here it was again: death. Not a memory, but a marker on the path ahead. If she wanted the truth about the past, she had to follow it. The letter trembled slightly in her grip, the first step into what waited ahead.

25

29 March 1941

Dearest Kat,

It has been a long time since I wrote to you, and I am sorry for that. I know you must of course be angry with me, and disappointed. I received six letters from you, all on one day, and words alone cannot express how much it meant to read them. It is funny, Katsikaki, that the way you write is also the way that you speak, and while I hold your letters, it is possible for me to pretend, if only for a few hours, that you are here with me. That is the greatest gift.

The reason I have not written sooner is a simple one, though it is hard for me to confess it. Things have happened here, Kat, many things that cannot be forgotten, and perhaps not ever forgiven. Michalis tells me that if God put us on this path, then He must also be willing to understand the reasons for such violence. Men have died at my hand; men that were not so different to me; young and brave and righteous. They sought to steal my country, and for that, I stole their lives from them. My fellow soldiers compare such barbarity to sums on a blackboard, but life and death is not so simple; it is not two plus two equals four, it is only zero, nothing, emptiness. I fear that there will be a day of great reckoning for us all, but the gate has been opened now, and nobody can close it. We must stay, and we must fight, and many more people will be killed.

The line here is held, but we are tired. The mood is one of trepidation, for we know that Mussolini is as tenacious as a mosquito. He will hover, waiting for the right time to strike, and then he will come with the fury of the Nazi power behind him. The men speak of it often, whispers pass between the battalions, the echoes of marching boots following us to our dreamless beds. I do not sleep, Kat. The darkness I hold inside is total.

War will not end here, in the shadow of these mountains stained by blood. You must prepare, Kat. Ration your food, build shelter in a place that cannot be found, collect anything that can be used as a weapon, remove bricks from your walls and hide your treasures inside. The brothers, Atlas and Zephyr, will be able to help you. Show this letter to them, make them understand what is coming. Both men are fighters, and they will teach you, if you ask them. I know that you are defiant, but you must also be smart. Do not allow your anger to make you reckless. Think only of survival, do whatever you must to remain safe.

I wanted more than anything to shield you from the horror of who I have become, but to do so would be to lie to you, and that, I could never do. We are one soul, my fierce girl. We are each other's conscience, each other's pain.

I love you, I love you, I love you.
S

26

Skye assumed that one or two police officers would arrive, collect the bones with minimal fuss, and be on their way soon afterwards. What she didn't expect was for an industrial digger to roll up with them, along with a crowd of local residents.

'How does everyone know already?' she asked Andreas, scooting out of the way as three heavy-set men in navy uniforms stomped past her through the mud.

'A lot of very big mouths on a very small island,' he said, ever the pragmatist. 'As soon as one person discovers something, it is certain he will tell three more.'

'Is it really necessary for them to excavate the entire garden?' she added, as the teeth of the digger broke through the top layer of earth. 'And with that bloody thing? If there are any more bones down there, they'll end up as dust.'

'I will ask them to be careful,' Andreas said.

He moved away just as Adam emerged through the gap in the wall, camera already raised. This time, he didn't stop to ask for permission. Victoria followed, a stout man in glasses at her side. Skye had never seen him before, and the prickle along her spine was immediate.

'There are so many people out front,' Victoria said, as Skye joined them in the shade of the lemon tree. 'I hope you don't mind us sneaking in like this.'

'I don't think we've met,' Skye said, addressing the newcomer.

'We haven't,' he agreed. 'Are you the homeowner?'

He spoke with a clipped British accent and had a pinkish complexion, his round, slightly puffy face giving little away. The linen shirt he wore pulled tight over a protuberant belly. If Skye had to guess, she'd place him in his late forties, though he could've been anywhere between thirty and fifty.

'I am,' she said warily.

'Beautiful spot you have up here.'

'Thanks, I like it.'

'Vicky here was just telling me about your lottery wins. That's what I call a stroke of luck.'

Victoria turned from where she'd been openly staring at one of the more attractive officers.

'We're honestly still pinching ourselves,' she enthused. 'Every day, I find a new reason to love this little rock.'

'What brings you to the island?' Skye asked, though she really wanted to know what he was doing in *her* garden.

'I'm here writing a travel piece for Condé Nast,' he said. 'One of those off-the-beaten-track-type features, though it appears I've stumbled across something rather more newsworthy. A one-euro lottery home with bones buried in the back garden as a kicker! It basically writes itself.'

Skye felt a hammering behind her ribs, too fast and too jagged.

'We don't know that it's anything more than someone's pet,' she said, punctuating her words with a forced-sounding laugh. 'A dog or cat maybe. That's the most likely scenario.'

The man narrowed his eyes. 'Rather a lot of fuss for a pet,' he said evenly, as the digger turned over more clumps of earth. 'And am I right in thinking these houses were abandoned during World War Two?'

'Sure were,' Victoria said. 'You should've seen the state of this place a few weeks ago. Skye's had to gut the whole thing and start over, haven't you?'

'It wasn't quite that bad,' she protested. 'Our local contractor, Andreas over there' – she gestured wildly, hoping he would see and come to her aid – 'he did a lot of modernisation before any of us showed up.'

'But nobody had actually lived in them, correct? So, whatever it is that you've got buried in your yard here, must have been in the ground since the war, if not long before that. This could be the prologue to a decades-old murder mystery.'

Skye opened her mouth and closed it again.

'Do you know much about the previous occupants?' he persisted.

'Well,' Victoria began, 'she did find some—'

'No,' Skye cut in. 'I don't know anything.'

Victoria gave her a curious look.

'Putting a story out could help you learn more,'

the journalist went on, unfazed by Skye's abruptness. 'In situations like these, it's not uncommon for someone to see the article and come forward with new information.'

Skye said nothing.

'I'd only need a few words. I could do the interview right now, if you're up for it. Strike while the iron's hot, as they say.'

'Now isn't a good time,' she told him.

'Tomorrow, then?'

'I can't do that either.'

'The following day?'

'I have plans.'

Victoria had begun to play with the ends of her glossy ponytail, gaze flicking between them as if she were watching a particularly uncomfortable tennis match.

'When would suit you then?' he asked, smile unfaltering.

'I'm sorry.' Skye shook her head. 'I'm not—That is to say, I can't—If you'll excuse me.'

Before he could press her further, Skye had turned and hurried away, slipping through the gap in the wall and past the onlookers towards the village. She shouldn't have run, not when the police were still there, though Skye couldn't imagine any of the officers caring much about her absence. None of them had done more than grunt at her, preferring to speak only to Andreas. Bloody men, she thought, with unusual savagery. Bloody, bloody men.

When she reached the taverna, Skye paused. Pantelis

must have closed on account of the storm. The usually cluttered courtyard had been cleared of furniture, and shutters were pulled down over both doors. He was probably part of the crowd outside her house. She had spotted Klodi as she fled past, his son Ajax sitting up on his shoulders. They all wanted front row seats to the show, while that journalist, whatever his name was, appeared intent on writing its script. What had Victoria been thinking, inviting him in like that? What more would she tell him? For a moment, Skye teetered on the edge of going back. The rush of adrenaline that had driven her had now evaporated, leaving her feeling hollow, unsteady, and thoroughly foolish.

The bakery was not much further. She would buy herself some spanakopita and find an isolated spot in one of the orchards; sit beneath a tree until the coast was clear.

There was a bell above the door that tinkled as she went inside.

'*Geia sou*,' a voice called, and a moment later, the diminutive form of Sophia emerged from the back room. When she saw her customer, she beamed.

'*Omorfo koritsi. Ti canis?* How are you?'

Skye approached the counter. 'OK,' she said, before cautiously trying the Greek word. '*Entaxei*.'

'Bravo, bravo,' the woman said, adjusting her dark-blue headscarf. 'It is very quiet today, not very many people.'

'Most of the village is at my house,' Skye said, explaining about the bones.

Sophia's expression merged from one of polite

interest to clear concern. She reached for the rosary beads coiled beside the till, murmuring what sounded like a prayer as her fingers closed around them.

'Oh, I'm sorry if I've upset you,' Skye began, but the older woman shook her head.

'*Ochi, ochi*,' she said. 'I was thinking only of the past.'

'Do you know much about it?' Skye asked. 'Nobody seems to have any idea why the houses were abandoned.'

There was a soft clunk as the rosary beads dropped onto the counter. Sophia's hands were delicate, the skin nearly translucent, with brown spots scattered among pale-blue veins.

'My father,' she said, 'he lived for a time, up on that hillside.'

'Your father?' Skye leaned in, her mind racing ahead. 'When was this?'

'Before the war began,' Sophia replied, with a small smile. 'He was a . . . *exoria*. Ah, political . . .'

'You mean a political exile?' Skye said.

Sophia nodded quickly. '*Nai, nai* – exile. When the occupation began, it was not safe for him, not safe for a great number of Greeks, and so he had to go.' She raised her arm and made a sweeping gesture. 'A long time after the war had ended, he returned to the island with my mother, and found the houses empty, his friends and neighbours, all of them gone.'

'Did he ever see any of them again?' Skye asked.

'*Ochi*.' She lowered her eyes.

'And he never found out what happened to them, where they all went?'

The older woman let out a sigh that was tinged with sadness.

'This, I do not know,' she said. 'Talking about the war, it made my father very angry. He did not like to remember it.'

'Is he still . . . ?' Skye trailed off. She had been stirred by the possibility of having a conversation with someone who'd lived in one of the houses and could recall their neighbours by name, perhaps even have photographs of them, though of course, this was unlikely. 'He's not still here on the island,' she said tentatively.

Sophia laid a hand against her breastbone, her gaze drifting far away.

'*Efyge*,' she murmured, her voice quiet but heavy. She shook her head slowly. 'He left long ago.'

27

In the week following the storm, Skye tried not to dwell on her encounter with the journalist. There was no story, not really, not until the bones had been tested, and that would take at least another fourteen days.

'Often, when a Greek tells you it will be two weeks, you must add another six,' Andreas had joked. Skye was conflicted. Part of her longed to know the truth, though another, more cautious part, was fearful of what could happen if her small house drew any more attention.

With most of the structural work now complete, the only major tasks left were plastering the exterior, decorating the interior, and tackling the garden, which still looked as if a herd of bison had trampled through it. Certainly, it constituted more than enough distraction from the dread that kept running its icy fingers along her spine.

Sunday rolled around. It was almost the end of June, and the persistent wind felt hairdryer hot as it chased in through the open windows. Skye had made the mistake of checking her emails while drinking her morning frappé. Her mother had been in touch again, insistent as ever, wanting answers about her disappearance, the length of her supposed sabbatical, and when exactly this 'performance' would come to an end. As she had with every other message, Skye replied that she was fine, and not to worry, fully aware that her deliberate vagueness would only deepen Cassandra MacKinnon's simmering displeasure.

She was in the process of sprinkling cat treats across the front doorstep for Tigri when the familiar shape of Joy came into view over the wall. Her friend was in head-to-toe turquoise, from her mirrored bandana right down to her bejewelled sandals, and was sucking on a white ice lolly.

'Made it myself,' she said, offering Skye a lick that she declined with a laugh. 'Mojito flavour, heavy on the tequila. Probably a bit too heavy, truth be told, but you know me.'

Tigri padded over, purring as he crunched through his Dreamies. Skye stared down at him, moony-eyed.

'You're soft on that moggy,' Joy observed.

'I always wanted a cat,' Skye said. 'I couldn't growing up, because my dad was allergic, then later, when I lived alone, I didn't think it would be fair. I was out so much, at work and whatnot, and then there's the worry that they'll get into the road, be hit by a car or stolen by a catnapper.'

'Catnapping is what I do most afternoons here,' Joy said lightly. 'Lay me on a beach towel and I'll be snoring inside five minutes.'

The two of them went inside, Joy slipping her ice-lolly stick into Skye's kitchen bin.

'I was thinking of digging some beds out there,' Skye said, motioning towards the back door. 'But it's so hot.'

Joy cast an eye around the small room. 'No offence,' she said, 'but shouldn't you focus on the indoors first?'

'I have paint charts,' Skye said lamely. 'And I built the flatpack wardrobe and bed without any help.'

'You need a sofa,' Joy said, folding her arms. 'I don't mind perching on that built-in seating bench, or whatever it is that Andreas calls it, but it's not the most comfortable thing, is it?'

'I bought two cushions,' Skye said, leading Joy back into the main living area. She had picked them up in Chora the previous day, having gone there to buy some worming tablets for Tigri. The cat, she had discovered through conversations with several Ano Meria residents, had long been a stray. Nobody seemed to know how, or exactly when, he had arrived in the village. Skye liked that about the cat; it made him more of a kindred spirit.

Joy reached for a cushion. Both were patterned with a blue-and-white evil eye, framed by panels of coral and gold, the details picked out in soft velvet tufts.

'Love these,' she appraised, starting to rummage through her straw bag, 'and it's funny that you chose these colours, because . . .'

Skye's mouth fell open as Joy handed her a framed seaweed print, the blotted-ink design daubed in dusky pink.

'Is this for me?'

'I did a whole series and thought you might like one,' Joy said.

'I should pay you,' Skye began, only to be summarily cut off.

'Don't be daft. It's a gift. It'll look lovely up on the wall over there. You can use it, and these cushions, to come up with a colour palette for the house.'

'You don't think I should leave it all white then?' Skye said. 'Andreas says it's more traditional to—'

'Andreas isn't the one living here,' Joy said. 'Your house, your decision what colour to paint it. If you're worried about going all-out, just do a feature wall, or paint yourself an archway behind the bed. Have fun with it, experiment a bit. It's only bloody paint after all, you can always go back to boring white if you change your mind.'

'The last place I lived in, everything was white,' Skye told her. 'White walls, white carpets, white tiles in the bathroom.'

'Where were you living, a bloody hospital?' Joy crowed.

Sky laughed in spite of herself. 'Try prison,' she said drily. Then, when Joy's smile immediately fell into a frown, quickly added, 'Will you help me look through some paint charts, then?'

With Joy by her side, decision-making turned out to be surprisingly productive. By midday, Skye had chosen her interior palette. Joy had explained the colour wheel, how to find complementary hues, and cheered the idea of an off-peach bedroom filled with plants, simple artwork, and pared-back linen.

'I don't know about you,' Joy said, as Skye moved from wall to wall with the seaweed print, 'but I'm hungrier than a saltwater croc. How about we treat ourselves at the taverna?'

'Could do,' Skye said, giving up and propping the picture on the stairs, 'or I could make us something. I've been meaning to attempt matsata.'

'Is that the flat pasta stuff?'

'A Folegandros speciality,' Skye confirmed. 'Andreas says if I want to be a real Greek, I should eat like one.'

There she went again, mentioning him.

'Not to knock you off your perch,' Joy replied, 'but I'm too hungry to wait for you to make pasta from scratch.'

'I'll do it for dinner, then. We can go to the shop now and buy lunch at the same time?'

Joy snatched up her bag. 'Consider my arm twisted,' she said.

Outside, the breeze persisted, sunlight streaking down through high, threadbare clouds. There was little protection from the elements up in their village, which was why every garden was enclosed by stone walls, built there long ago to protect crops and livestock. Far beyond the road, the sea stretched wide and dark, a sweep of blue so breathtaking, it still caught Skye off-guard.

'Do you ever catch yourself thinking this might all be a dream?' she asked Joy. 'I know this is our home now, but that feels absurd somehow. I mean, why us, of all the people that must've entered that lottery, how did we get so lucky?'

Joy smiled rather wistfully. In the light, her eyes looked every bit as green as her outfit.

'I don't question the good stuff,' she said. 'You know I went through it after Bobby. I suppose I see this as my reward. You lost your dad, didn't you? Perhaps this is your peak after that trough?'

'That's a nice idea,' Skye said, reluctant to commit further. 'Or we could be about to wake up in our beds and find that the last year or so never happened.'

'If Bobby was in that bed, I'd go right now,' Joy said.

After that, they fell into a companionable silence, arriving at the mini market ten minutes later to find Cora on her hands and knees outside, chasing down errant postcards.

'The children knocked over the display,' she said, as Skye scooped up several cards bearing the image of a donkey in a sun hat. 'They are bored, so they play. *Ela*, how are you both?'

Before either woman could reply, two child-shaped bullets fired out through the shop door and ran squealing into the road, the eight-year-old Iris pursuing her younger brother, Ajax. Cora clapped her hands furiously, shooing them back inside. Skye and Joy followed.

'They are like monsters,' Cora exclaimed, with an exasperated laugh.

Ajax slid open the lid of the freezer and helped himself to an ice lolly in the shape of a rocket.

'*Ela stamata*,' Cora admonished. 'No more sugar.'

The little boy tore off the wrapper and let it drop to the floor, yelping as his mother made a lunge for him.

Iris, meanwhile, had crept behind the counter, and was now scrolling through Cora's phone. Not wanting to let on that she'd witnessed such mischief, Skye moved down the aisles, putting semolina flour, olive oil and fresh tomatoes into a basket, while Joy perused the bread selection. They met by the fridge and agreed on a block of locally made manouri cheese, which was similar to feta, only less tangy. The mini market had a section at the back for household items, and Skye found a rolling pin for six euros.

'It'll save me having to use a bottle of ouzo to roll out the pasta,' she said to Joy, who was advancing with a bottle of white wine.

'You ladies are making matsata,' Cora said, as she scanned each item.

'Mama.' Iris tugged her mother's arm, her solemn gaze settling on Skye as she murmured in Greek.

'*Ela, agapi mou*, you can ask her yourself.'

'Ask me what?' Skye smiled at the girl, but Iris buried her face against her mother's shoulder.

'She is shy to speak in English,' Cora explained. 'They have only begun it this year at school, and she does not have much chance to practise.'

'I'm shy to speak in Greek, too,' Skye told the girl, which Cora quickly translated. Iris's eyes widened, and then, haltingly, she said, 'You are very pretty.'

'Why, thank you.' Skye jokingly flicked her windswept hair. '*Efcharistó.*'

'*Parakaló*,' Iris replied, and then, looking to her mum for reassurance, she asked, 'A bag?'

'I have one, thank you – and your English is very good. *Poly kala.*'

Ajax sidled up beside Skye, a lolly stick poking out from one side of his mouth.

'*Geia sou,*' she said, crouching to greet him properly. Without warning, Ajax threw himself into her arms, squeezing her so tightly that she almost fell backwards.

'What was that for?' she asked, when he scurried away.

Cora stared after her son in bewilderment.

'He must like you,' she said. 'Whenever his *giagia* comes to visit, she always wants him to sit on her knee, but he refuses. Screams like a baby goat if we make him.'

Iris looked inquisitively up at her mother, and once again, Cora translated what she'd said.

'Soon, it will be the school holiday,' she said with a sigh. 'No peace for me.'

An unexpected lightness surged through Skye. 'I could give her some English lessons,' she said. 'I'm already teaching George two days a week, so she'd have someone other than me to practise with. Ajax can come, too.'

Cora gasped. 'Are you sure?' she said, and when Skye nodded, she ran around from behind the counter to hug her.

'We will pay you,' she said, shaking her head when Skye began to protest. '*Ochi* – of course. We must, and you must take something now, a gift.'

'Really, there's no need to—' The words died on

Skye's lips as Cora hurried out through the open back door, returning a moment later with a bulging bag.

'Klodi caught two octopus this morning,' she said, as Skye and Joy peered down at a tangle of tentacles. 'It's been drying on the line, so the meat will be tender, perfect for your matsata. All you have to do is grill it, then mix it with the tomatoes, some garlic, a little herbs.'

Skye raised the bag, stepping back as water dripped onto the countertop.

'*Perimene*,' Iris said, imitating the word Andreas used so often. She took a newspaper from the rack and peeled off the top few pages.

'Clever girl,' Cora told her warmly, taking the bag and upending its contents.

Skye said nothing.

She didn't hear the octopus being wrapped, or the chatter of Joy, Cora and the children. A low buzzing filled her ears. Words surfaced in fragments, though none she could grasp. Bile burned her throat, the hand she brought up to her mouth trembling as she stared down at the open newspaper.

At the story.

At the photographs.

At herself.

28

'Can I take this?'

Skye's voice was hoarse. She reached for the newspaper, covering the image of herself with a splayed hand.

'Of course,' Cora said, seemingly nonplussed. She must not have seen the article yet, though it could only be a matter of time.

Mumbling incoherently that she'd be in touch about the English lessons, Skye grabbed her bags and stumbled from the shop, Joy following a few moments later.

'Are you all right?' she said, running to keep up.

Skye tried to say yes, but she couldn't force the word past the lump in her throat. Instead she leaned into the wind and continued to walk, back towards the main road, towards home.

A horn sounded and she swung around to see a truck slowing to a crawl. It was Andreas, his elbow resting on the open window, curls blowing around a smile that fell when he saw the look on her face. Skye said nothing; all she could do was stare at him.

'You on your way up the hill?' Joy called, panting slightly as she caught up with them.

'*Nai*,' he said, not taking his eyes off Skye. 'Can I give you a lift?'

Joy pulled open the back door, but Skye remained where she was.

'I'd better not,' she mumbled, holding up a carrier bag. 'There's an octopus in here and it's dripping everywhere.'

'Do you think I care about a bit of water in the truck?' he replied, his tone more teasing.

Skye shrugged.

'*Ela*,' he said, cocking his head. 'Get in.'

Tigri was stretched out in the sun when they pulled up outside. From across the hillside came the faint sound of drilling, thin behind the whistling breeze. Neither matched the thud of Skye's heart, echoing loud in her ears. She was still tightly clasping the newspaper, its print leaving dark smudges across her skin.

'Let me help you,' Andreas said, as she struggled to get her key in the lock. Several pages fell to the ground, and she scrambled to reach them before he did, their foreheads colliding hard.

'Shit,' she muttered, hot tears stinging her eyes.

Andreas stepped back, rubbing the bridge of his nose.

'I'll take this lot in, shall I?' Joy said, giving Skye a curious look as she retrieved the groceries.

'Sorry about your head,' Skye began. Andreas tried for a smile.

'Why are you hiding the newspaper?' he asked.

'I'm not.' Skye shoved the crumpled pages out of sight.

'*Ela*, you are,' he said. 'But it does not matter. I have already seen it. There is another copy in the truck. I was bringing it here to show you.'

'Oh.'

'Oh,' he repeated.

'You've read it?' she asked.

'*Nai*.'

'And? What does it say?'

Joy appeared in the open doorway. 'What does what say?' she prompted.

Skye looked imploringly at Andreas.

'There is a story in the paper,' he said. 'It is about this house.'

'Really?' Joy prised the pages from Skye's fingers and began to smooth them out. 'Have you read it?'

'No,' she snapped. 'How could I? I can't read Greek.'

Joy's eyes widened.

'*Ela*,' Andreas soothed, 'why are you so angry?'

'I'm not angry with you two, I'm just angry that— They've used my picture,' she said, jabbing an accusatory finger at the newspaper. The image was of her and Andreas in the garden, their heads bowed together, both glancing back at whoever had taken the photo. Adam, she recalled furiously. He'd been the one with a camera.

Andreas held out a hand to Joy. 'Can I?' he said.

Skye wondered if he'd been swimming. His hair and the neck of his T-shirt were damp, and he was in shorts rather than his usual jeans.

'I don't think it's fair that they can do that,' she went on. 'Use a photo of someone without their permission.'

Andreas scrutinised the picture more closely.

'It is not such a bad photo,' he said. 'I do not care.'

'That's because you don't—'

Skye fell abruptly silent. She could feel the two of them looking at her, judging her, trying to work her out.

'Shall we go inside?' Joy suggested. 'Maybe Andreas could read it out to us?'

The shutters were yet to be hung, and the lounge area was bathed in brilliant light. Andreas paused to admire a framed photograph Skye had hung earlier that morning – one of the final few she'd had taken with her dad before he died. They were laughing, her face turned towards his, a cake on the table in front of them aglow with burning candles.

'Your house is beginning to look like a home,' he said, as Skye sat down and hugged one of the evil eye cushions against her chest. Joy perched beside her, but Andreas remained standing, the newspaper taut between his large hands. He cleared his throat, took a breath, and began to translate.

'Proto Thema, *29 June 2025*.

'*Bones found in garden of lottery winner's house.*

'*Police were called to a house on the island of Folegandros after bones were discovered in the rear garden of a property in Ano Meria. The shallow grave emerged following the recent storms, which caused part of an old wall to collapse and expose the cavity beneath.* Proto Thema *understands that the site was not marked by a stone, nor were the bones encased in a casket or other covering. A local police officer confirmed, "We were called at 3.45 p.m. to the report that the homeowner had discovered the bones while inspecting her garden for damage. The items were removed and are in the process of being analysed to determine whether the bones are animal or human."*

'A freelance journalist, who happened to be in the village at the time, told Proto Thema *that he spoke with the owner of the house, a Ms Skye MacKinnon, thirty-four, who claimed, "The most likely scenario is that the bones were someone's pet dog or cat."*

'Ms MacKinnon, who heralds from England, secured the formerly derelict house as part of a one-euro lottery scheme run by the municipality of Folegandros in a bid to revive the area. She has spent the past four weeks renovating the property with the help of local contractor Andreas Vithoulkas [both pictured]. The house is one of six at the heart of the scheme, all of which were abandoned in the final days of the Second World War.

'Ms MacKinnon's neighbour, Victoria Beaumont, thirty-seven, admitted that the bones are not the first discovery made by the island's newest residents, and that her husband, Adam Beaumont, a lawyer and keen photographer, had recently bought a metal detector in order to search the grounds of their own property.

'"We believe this is only the beginning," Victoria told the journalist. "Whatever secrets the village has been hiding, we're determined to dig them all up."

'Folegandros was occupied during the war, initially by predominantly Italian forces until their surrender in September 1943, when the Germans attempted to seize control of the Cyclades Islands. Atrocities were commonplace, and in many areas across Greece, entire villages were destroyed, local people executed and houses burned. It is not yet known what occurred on this small hillside plot in Ano Meria, but perhaps the discovery of these bones will prove to be the first clue.'

Andreas lowered the newspaper, his face impassive.

Skye felt as if she'd been turned to stone. Her name. They had not only used her photograph, but her full name, the location of the house, the details about how she'd acquired it.

'*Proto Thema*,' she said faintly. 'Is it a local newspaper or—?'

'*Ochi*,' Andreas said slowly. 'It's one of the most popular Sunday newspapers in all of Greece.'

Skye swallowed. 'Right,' she said. Then, more decisively, 'Right.'

There was only one thought in her mind, and it was persuasive enough to propel her into motion. She reached the stairs and took them two at a time, her trainers scuffing the white-painted boards.

'Where are you going?' Joy called.

Skye ignored her. In her bedroom, she yanked down her case from the top of her wardrobe and threw it onto the bed, grabbing shoes, handfuls of underwear, leggings, shorts and shirts.

Joy and Andreas appeared in the doorway.

'What are you doing?' he asked.

'Packing,' Skye replied.

'Why? Where are you going?'

'Away.'

'Away to where?'

'Just away.'

'Because of the article?' Joy asked.

Skye swore as the zip of her case snagged on an errant sock.

'I can't be here,' she told them. 'Not any more.'

Andreas moved aside as she stormed through into the bathroom, shoving shampoo, toothpaste and tampons into her washbag.

'What's the big deal?' Joy said, as Skye dodged around her. 'Why are you running away? The story will be forgotten in a few days.'

Martyn would've set up a Google alert for all iterations of her name – of that, Skye was certain. It was no longer safe for her to be here.

'Excuse me,' she said to Andreas. He was blocking her path into the bedroom and didn't budge at her request.

'Where will you go?' he asked. 'To another island – the mainland?'

'I don't know yet,' she said. 'I'll get to the port, then I'll decide. Will you drive me?'

She looked up at him, but Andreas was unmoved. 'Only,' he said, 'if you tell me the real reason why.'

Skye's head rocked back with a groan. 'Please,' she begged, close to tears. 'I just need to get out of here.'

Andreas moved to comfort her, only for his phone

to ring. As he reached for it, Skye slipped past, hurling the few toiletries she'd collected into the suitcase. From the landing, his low conversation drifted in, just a few words: *nai*, *entáxei*. By the time he returned, Joy at his side, she had zipped the case and found her passport. The confusion on his face had given way to something graver.

'What is it?' she asked. 'What's happened?'

He stared at her, his gaze unwavering. 'That was the police,' he said.

Skye went very still.

'The tests on the bones have been completed.'

'Already?' Joy said. 'That was quick.'

'And?' Skye said, taking a step towards him. 'Are they animal or human?'

Andreas glanced down at the phone in his hand.

'It is not one or the other,' he said. 'The police found traces of both.'

29

April 1941

The meeting was held in the church.

Katerina walked through the village with Leni, their arms tightly linked together, shawls wrapped around their shoulders. It was early evening, the wind as lively as a dancing child, and the air ripe with the scent of spring herbs. Greece, it seemed, was impervious to the war, though its people no longer had any choice but to face it. Athens had fallen, and soon, the enemy would come.

News of the defeat and subsequent surrender had come in across the wireless, and upon hearing it, Katerina had fled. She ran until her lungs burned, not down to the sea but up to the mountains, where she buried her face in Chrysí's soft flank and wept. Thousands of soldiers had been killed, and many more taken prisoner. Logic told her that Stefanos and Michalis must be among them, though her hope refused to yield. It was enough to countenance the loss of your country, she could not accept the loss of him as well. He had sounded so unlike himself in the last letter she had received. Katerina read it often, taking it out from where she had secreted it beneath her cotton undershirt, and running her finger over his words, his warnings and instructions, his expressions of love and regret. How would she survive this conflict without him?

It was crowded inside the church, and loud with urgent voices. The twin brothers, Atlas and Zephyr, were standing at the front. Both appeared ready for battle, and had rifles strung across their backs. Atlas, the taller of the two, had twisted his long hair into a neat ball, fixing it at the nape of his neck, while Zephyr's trailed loose. Both had grown a heavy moustache that pulled their features downward, and made each man appear far more serious in nature than Katerina knew them to be. As she led her sister towards a seat at the back, Atlas caught her eye and raised a hand of greeting.

The priest swept forward in his dark robes and began to speak, calling the gathered villagers to attention. Murmurs rumbled around the room. People were scared, and they were angry. Katerina said nothing, not even when Leni gripped her hard enough to stop the flow of blood into her fingers. She merely listened, tapping her foot against the hard floor as the men argued with one another. That was the problem with men – they did not know how to listen, how to hear, none seemed able to abide the idea of someone else having an opinion that differed to their own. Some wanted to flee, others to fight, all were craving reassurance, though that had become an impossibility.

'If we sit here like chickens at roost, the soldiers will come and run us through with their bayonets,' shouted their neighbour Constantine.

His son Kostas, who was not yet sixteen, stood up.

'We must meet them at the shoreline and fight,' he declared, raising the fist that wasn't strapped into a sling. The declaration was met with widespread cheering and jeering.

'Madness,' Giorgos growled, grasping his wife Dafni's hand as he got to his feet. 'They will simply aim their machine guns and shoot us one by one from the water, and then who will be here to tend to the land, look after our families?'

'The land will no longer be ours to tend,' Constantine threw back. 'The enemy will take it, and they will rape our women.'

Leni flinched, her grip growing harder. Katerina took a deep breath and got to her feet.

'You talk about us women as if we are not here,' she said, 'as if we are incapable of defending ourselves and our homes.'

Many heads swivelled, the men shocked by her outburst. Zephyr clapped his hands together.

'She is right,' he said, shouting to be heard over the melee. 'If we choose to resist, the women must be permitted to fight alongside us.'

'Come on now, man, this is nonsense,' Giorgos cried.

'It should be a choice,' implored another voice, this time belonging to Constantine's wife, Phaedra. 'A lot of women will not want to face combat, but who are any of us to stop those that do?'

'It is not right,' Giorgos insisted, shaking his head of grey curls.

'Come, it is not the nineteen-twenties,' Katerina said scornfully. 'The world is changing, and we are at war now. Any rules that were set in stone are crumbling away.'

Giorgos shook his fist, remonstrating that if her father were there, she would never dare say such things.

'*Agapi mou*.' Leni tugged on her sleeve. 'Sit down, please.'

Katerina wrenched her arm free.

'We will only survive this war if we work together,' she said, with such passion that even Giorgos fell silent. 'We cannot allow the enemy to make us turn on each other. Greece must come first, before any petty squabbles or grudges. We are all one family in this village, and everyone here has a part to play in what is coming.'

'She is right.'

Katerina swung around, her gasp coinciding with that of Leni, who was already pushing past her, stepping on the feet of those seated around them in her haste to reach the two men who had just strode in through the open church doors.

'Michalis,' she cried, throwing her arms around her husband's neck. 'You are alive. Praise God.'

Katerina continued to stare. She didn't move, could not seem to make her limbs obey her. It was not her brother-in-law who had spoken out in her favour, but his companion. Stefanos was thinner, his clothes torn and eyes hollow, though the fire inside him had not dimmed. Raising his fingers to his lips, he blew her a kiss.

The brothers ran to greet their compadre, slapping his back in delight.

'I was confident that you would return,' Atlas said. 'You are like a cat, my friend.'

Katerina heard a guttural sob and, realising it had come from her, she slapped a hand over her mouth. She felt as she had at the last Easter Festival of Pascha, when she had spirited a bottle of wine from the shared table, her head in a spin and legs unsteady.

He was here; he had come home to her.

Stefanos did not hesitate, his stride bold as he marched forwards and took up position before the iconostasis. With his dark beard and air of authority, he could almost have been a saint himself. Katerina's chest swelled with pride.

'I have seen the enemy,' Stefanos said, his tone solemn. 'I know what is coming for us, and what they will do if we make any mistakes. My cousin and I' – he gestured towards Michalis – 'we barely escaped with our lives. The Italians were battered by our earlier victory, and a soldier whose pride is damaged can be a fierce adversary. Once the German forces were organised, we could not hold them back any longer. It was carnage.' He closed his eyes briefly. 'We lost a lot of good men.'

Constantine stood. 'How did you get away?' he asked, his suspicion clear. 'Why did you two escape with your lives when so many others did not?'

'Because we did not follow orders,' Stefanos said plainly, glowering at the man as if daring him to pass judgement. 'We used false papers to join the army, so when it was time to retreat, we did not wait around to be told.'

'Cowards,' Giorgos muttered under his breath, though not so quietly that Stefanos missed it.

'What did you say, old man?'

'Deserters,' he said, more loudly this time. Katerina was sure that if they had not been inside the church, he would have spat on the ground.

Stefanos narrowed his eyes.

'You can think what you want about me,' he said. 'All of you are free to do this, but none of you were there. There is no glory in dying at the wrong time, not when you have things you must do' – his eyes strayed towards Katerina – 'people you must protect. That was not a battle we could win, but we can win the next one, and the one after that. We must work together.'

The debate continued until long after the light had drained from the sky. Katerina watched the flickering candles, Leni's head on her shoulder as they sat side by side, watching as the men they loved tussled for dominancy. The women began to leave; children would be at home wanting to eat, chores must be done, fears suppressed. Dafni paused as she reached them, and an understanding of sorts passed between the three. They would look after each other, whatever else happened.

The priest was the one to finally call a halt to the meeting, though Stefanos hung back with the brothers as each of the men filed out. Katerina waited until Leni and Michalis had gone, then she slipped out into the star-speckled night to wait for her lover. The walls of the church were chalk-white in the glow of a yawning moon, its benign smile so at odds with the troubles they faced. She wanted to feel strong but could not prevent the tide of fear from rising, even now, with her most primal of prayers answered. One man could not stop the onset of war; love could not conquer an army.

'Kat.' His voice, low and tender. She shivered but did not turn, her heart beating irregularly, plucked strings of a *bouzouki*. He touched her hair, and she drew in a breath, felt his own on the back on her neck, hot and steady.

'You came back,' she said.

'Yes.' He moved closer, his hands now on her waist. Katerina sank back against him and closed her eyes. A single tear rolled across her cheek, and Stefanos caught it, pulling her round and rubbing his thumbs over her face, examining her, gazing at her, then kissing her, all the while murmuring against her lips, telling her how much he had missed her.

She wanted to bite him, to tear at his hair, to shout and scream, though it was easier to push aside those more complicated emotions and simply be. He tasted of tobacco, and of the sea, the skin on his hands calloused and rough with scars. Beaten, but not broken as he had led her to believe in his letter.

'How long do we have until they come?' she asked, feeling him sag against her.

'Maybe a week, perhaps less.'

'Will you stay?'

Stefanos sighed.

'Come,' he said, taking her hand in his and leading her away from the church. 'I brought somebody back to the island with me, and now, the time has come for you to meet her.'

30

Skye stared at Andreas.

'Traces of both?' she said. 'Human and animal bones, buried in the same grave?'

'That is what the police said.'

Skye let go of her suitcase, and it rolled several inches forward on its wheels.

'Did they say anything else?' Joy asked. 'Do they know when whoever it was might've died, or how?'

Andreas shook his head slowly. 'They didn't tell me much more. It is not my house, and so . . .' He spread his hands wide. 'I think perhaps they will come to visit Skye, once they have completed a full report.'

'Right,' she said, still not moving.

'However, they will not be able to do that if you have left the island,' he pointed out.

Human remains.

Skye's mind kept circling back to the inescapable truth: someone had been laid to rest here, in her grounds. An unmarked grave she could have filled in quietly, without drawing attention and exposing herself to scrutiny. The instinct she'd felt when she first saw the bones had been right. She shouldn't have allowed the others to sway her.

'I still need to leave,' she said.

Andreas began to rub the back of his neck, his T-shirt rising up to reveal an inch of stomach.

'That is up to you,' he said, but Joy made a small noise of protest. 'I can look after the house while you're away,' he went on, 'and when you come back—'

'I'm not sure if I will come back.'

Joy came into the room, her arms raised in offer of a hug. Skye dropped her chin.

'It is Sunday,' Andreas said. 'There are no more ferries today. I think the first one tomorrow is at eleven-thirty, perhaps later.'

Skye considered this. 'You mean there are none leaving or none arriving?'

'Both,' he confirmed. 'If any more boats come today, it would be only the private charters.'

Skye felt the tension slip slowly from her body. Joy had gone very quiet, her arms now folded in front of her, while Andreas continued to frown.

'I don't want to leave,' she said, the words a whispered rush. This was *her* home, *her* bare walls waiting to be painted, *her* view of the mountains, and of the sea beyond.

Joy was beside her in an instant, bracelets tumbling across her wrists as she reached out to grasp Skye's hand.

'You don't have to leave, you silly chook,' she said. 'Whatever's going on in that head of yours, we can work it out. Nothing is worth leaving for, especially not a dream come true.'

'But I can't stay,' she said, her voice thin. 'You don't understand.'

'No, I don't,' Joy agreed. 'But the best thing you can do is tell us. I can see that you're scared,' she added, 'and that's a worry.'

Skye glanced at Andreas, something in her chest catching, a leaf caught on a current of air.

'Fear builds higher walls than whatever it is waiting on the other side,' he said. 'Can I?'

When Skye said nothing, he moved past her and sat on the edge of the bed.

'I had a brother once,' he said, without looking up. 'Sotiris. He was younger than me, and one of those people for whom everything in life comes very easily. He always had many friends, a lot of girlfriends' – he huffed out a laugh – 'and was very successful in his studies. The plan was that he would go to England and study medicine. He had passed the exams, my parents had saved enough money, and before he was due to leave, we decided to have one last holiday together, the four of us.'

Joy crossed the room and sat beside Andreas, but Skye didn't move. Her feet felt leaden.

'Sotiris,' she said, wanting to say his name. Andreas's hands tightened briefly into fists.

'We went to Corfu,' he said. 'There is a small island, Vido, close to the town, and boats to take people across. My brother wanted to swim. He was like a fish, always in the water, and we did not worry about him. I went with my parents on the boat, and we waited together on the beach.'

He stared into the middle distance as he spoke. Skye wondered if he was still, even now, watching for his brother.

'By the time we realised something was wrong, it was too late. The sea had taken him, and it took the heart of my family with it.'

'Oh, you poor love,' Joy said.

Skye took a long steadying breath.

'I don't tell very many people this story,' he went on. 'I think, sometimes, that it is too much. Nobody wants to be around sadness, they do not want to be marked by it.'

The look on his face tugged at something in her.

'I don't feel that way,' she said, her voice softer than before, the edges less sharp. 'I think it's nice to talk about the people we've lost, otherwise you risk allowing their memory to fade. My dad died four years ago now, and my mum still refuses to talk about him. Well, unless she's saying something critical.'

Andreas looked grim. 'Your mother is angry?'

'That about sums it up,' Skye agreed. 'Angry with him, angry with me, angry at life.'

'But you are not?'

'I was.' The admission felt heavy, and Skye hesitated for a moment before continuing. 'I found the anger helpful in the beginning. Anger is a force, it got me out of bed in the morning, made me want to move, to do things, go to work, clean my flat, feed myself – but once that drained out of me, and the sorrow took over . . .' She grimaced. 'That was when things became more difficult. I understand why my mum can't let go of the anger, but that doesn't make being around her any easier.'

'I was angry with Bobby, too,' Joy said. She'd been sitting so quietly that Skye had almost forgotten she was in the room. 'So damn angry that he'd gone and done something as bloody stupid as get himself killed. Coming out here was part of me addressing that anger, you know?'

Skye's body ached with the weight of her sympathy – for Joy, for Andreas, and for herself. They had all experienced the sudden loss of a loved one, though unlike her, the other two had not allowed their grief to muddle them into making a terrible decision. Her gaze trailed towards Andreas. He had tipped his head back and was staring unblinkingly at the ceiling.

'The rage that you both describe,' he said. 'I felt it also, after Sotiris. But when it comes to death, you have to find a way to make a sort of peace with it.' Andreas lowered his chin and their eyes met. 'If you do not, it will eat you alive.'

Skye went still as an image of Martyn surfaced, his jaw tight, a muscle twitching with tension. She'd forgiven his rage-fuelled outbursts more times than she could count, telling herself that he only lost control because of his own grief.

'I do not speak about Sotiris to many people,' Andreas said, looking between the two women. 'Only to friends, and we are friends, I think?'

'Of course we are,' Joy said.

They both turned to Skye.

'We are,' she agreed.

'The thing that is causing you to be afraid,' he said, 'you can tell us.'

'You can,' Joy agreed, nodding along, but Skye's throat had gone dry. Logic told her that she could trust Andreas, though that same voice of reason had led her towards Martyn.

'No,' she said, the word hoarse. 'I can't, I—'

Two deep grooves appeared between Andreas's brows. He was hurt. She was hurting him. All at once, Skye felt suffused by anger. It crashed over her in a great wave that brought her arms up, her fingers into her hair.

Joy got to her feet. 'Do you want us to leave you alone?' she asked.

Skye shook her head. 'Not you,' she said, her tone flat, defeated. 'You can stay.'

An uncomfortable silence was broken only by the low hum of the wind. Skye did not want to look at Andreas. She turned to the window, clouds blurring past like thoughts she couldn't hold on to, waiting until she heard the creak of bed springs, the sigh of surrender, the soft click as he closed the bedroom door behind him.

'His name is Martyn,' she said, without moving.

'OK.' Joy's voice was honey. 'Who is he?'

Skye half-turned, forcing herself to breathe steadily. 'He's someone I was close to, someone I—'

Why was it so difficult to say the word?

'Your boyfriend?' Joy asked, though she sounded uncertain, almost as if she wanted Skye to contradict her.

If only it were that simple.

'No,' she said, 'not a boyfriend. Martyn is my husband.'

31

A whirlwind.

That was the word people used, and it fitted. Skye's romance with Martyn had torn through her life, upending everything she'd carefully built until it was changed beyond all recognition; until *she* had changed beyond all recognition.

'Find someone who loves you more than you love yourself,' was what her dad had always said and, in the beginning, Skye believed she'd found that in Martyn. Nothing ever seemed to be too much trouble for him where she was concerned. He was thoughtful and attentive, stocking his bathroom with the moisturiser and shampoo she used, swapping his washing capsules to the non-bio kind so the bedsheets wouldn't irritate her sensitive skin, and generally making sure that she was comfortable, considered, and coddled in a way she hadn't been before. Nobody, she reasoned, would go to so much trouble for someone they didn't love, and although things moved quickly, the acceleration of their relationship didn't ring alarm bells. The one time she'd joked about 'playing it cool', Martyn had merely pulled a face. He had already told her about his sister – the skiing accident four years previously that had claimed her life – so when he said, 'When you know, you know. What's the sense in wasting time?', it had made a strange kind of sense.

Three months to the day after their first official London date, Martyn asked her to move in with him. His house in Epsom was bigger, and more conveniently located for both their respective places of work – plus, he said, it was only a temporary solution. Eventually, they'd buy a far larger place together. Skye was reluctant to sell her little flat, with its artworks and trinkets and memories of her dad, but he wore her down with promises, love a currency that he doled out as readily as pennies into a fountain. The day she parked her hired removal truck on his driveway, Martyn got down on one knee and presented her with a diamond ring.

'You're the only one I want,' he said. 'For ever.'

Skye had come so far already – how could she say anything other than yes?

'I don't want to wait,' he demurred, when she tentatively pushed back against the idea of a 'quickie wedding' at the local registry office. Skye had always imagined a marquee, a live band, dancing and games and a multi-tiered cake, though Martyn made her see things differently.

'We'd only be sad all day,' he told her. 'No dad there to give you away, no little sister to make fun of me in a speech. Obviously, I'll agree with whatever you want, but doesn't it make more sense to do something just for us?'

The power of his persuasion had won, the pattern of their relationship spooling out in the same way it always had. She didn't need to unpack all her belongings, simply store them until they found their 'forever home'; it was silly to pay insurance on two cars, when she could just as easily be added as an extra driver on his; Scotland would've been nice for their honeymoon, but he'd already gone ahead and booked the Maldives.

It was not in Skye's nature to provoke, nor did she want to cause unnecessary upset, or appear ungrateful. It was easier to go along with his suggestions, and after a while, the balance of control tipped solely over to his side. He was in charge of the food shopping, the bill paying, their weekend plans and trips away; he chose the restaurants they ate at, which radio station they listened to, and what they watched on television. No request was unreasonable, each stipulation presented to Skye as being in her best interests, not his. Soon, he was dictating her wardrobe, her make-up style, how she did her hair, and her reading choices. The pacey psychological thrillers she loved were dropped off at Oxfam, replaced by a stack of Booker-nominated tomes, cloth-bound classics, and biographies of the powerful businessmen Martyn admired.

Their first notable argument occurred one Friday evening in the run-up to their second Christmas as a couple. Skye had finished her final pile of marking for the year and was rewarding herself with a bath and an illicit copy of a real-life magazine, featuring such stories as 'I married my ghost' and 'How I dropped three dress sizes doing headstands'. Such a tawdry publication would've been condemned to the bin by Martyn, but he was away, flying a group of rich property developers back to the Middle East.

Submerged beneath lavender-scented bubbles, a rare glass of red wine propped beside the taps, Skye was relaxed enough not to be unduly concerned when she heard the sound of a key in the lock downstairs.

'Is that you?' she called, picturing her husband slipping off his shoes, hanging up his coat and scarf, putting his wallet on the hall table.

'Where are you?' came his bark of reply. A thread of unease wound its way through Skye. She slid further down in the tub, water lapping at her collarbones.

'Up here,' she replied, careful to keep her own tone light. Feet sounded on the stairs, and a moment later, the bathroom door was pushed open. Martyn appeared in the gap, cheeks flushed from the cold, eyes flinty. He was dressed smartly in a crisp white shirt and navy trousers, his square jaw clean-shaven, and dark hair brushed forwards.

'What are you doing?' he asked.

'Is that a trick question?'

'It's seven o'clock,' he said. 'Why isn't dinner on?'

Skye pushed herself lower in the water, as if retreating could quiet the discomfort.

'I didn't know that—' she began. 'I thought you were in Dubai overnight.'

'Cancelled. A meeting ran over, so they decided to do a weekend in the city. Left me sitting on the bloody tarmac for three hours. Honestly, these people.' His features curled into a scowl. 'You would've been aware of all this, if you ever bothered to check your phone.'

'Ah.'

Skye's phone was charging in the kitchen, silent mode activated so as not to disturb her peaceful evening.

'Sorry,' she said meekly. 'I'll remember to keep it with me in future.'

Martyn dropped the toilet seat with a deliberate clatter and sat, elbows on knees, watching her with a stillness that made her skin crawl. He hadn't bothered to close the door behind him, and a cold draught drifted into the room. Skye watched the steam filter out onto the landing.

'Do you want to get in with me?' she asked.

'No,' he said flatly.

'I'll get out then—'

'What's this?'

Too late, Skye spotted the magazine on the floor. She lunged for it, but Martyn got there first. The story she'd been reading was one about a woman who'd had her own whirlwind romance, only to later discover the man she loved was a wanted serial killer living under a false identity.

'I found it in the staffroom,' she said, hating that the apology was already lined up in the back of her throat. 'I know it's silly, but it's just a bit of fun.'

'A bit of fun,' he repeated coldly. 'Rotting your brain is amusing to you, is it?'

'That's a bit judgemental,' she said, instantly regretting it. Martyn got to his feet and ripped the magazine in half, then in half again, every movement precise, controlled, deliberate. Torn bits of paper floated down onto the mat. Skye brought her knees up to her chest. The bubbles were beginning to disperse, the water rapidly cooling, though she didn't want to move. He stood over her while she cowered, soaking wet, naked, at a loss as to what to do next.

'I won't be much longer,' she said quietly. 'Why don't you go downstairs and fix yourself a drink? There's a bottle of red open in the—'

He moved so fast that she had no time to react, his hand swinging round in a great arc that sent her glass spinning off the edge of the bath. Wine spread like blood into the water, and Skye gasped as a piece of broken glass sliced into her thigh, another catching her ankle. She tried to collect the pieces only to cut open her hand, and then her wrist, each of the wounds trailing red-ribbon streams. With a cry, she lurched upright and out of the bath, only for her foot to slip on the torn magazine. Martyn caught her as she fell, but she wrenched herself away from him.

'Get off me,' she cried, pawing desperately for a towel.

'You're injured,' he said, all trace of anger gone, colour draining from his face as he took in the state of her. There were tiny slashes everywhere, eyelash-thin nicks on her chest and arms. Skye picked up a roll of toilet tissue and pressed squares of it against the deepest cuts while Martyn hovered, biting his lip.

'I don't know what came over me. I'm so sorry. I'll make it up to you. I love you.'

Skye ignored him and pushed her way from the bathroom and into their bedroom, before slamming the door behind her. The full-length mirror on the wardrobe door caught her, dripping and pale, hair slicked to her scalp, thin trails of blood running down her legs.

Martyn knocked on the door. 'Can I come in?'

'Go away.' Skye turned from the mirror.

'I didn't mean it.'

She sighed. 'It's fine.'

It wasn't fine, but what choice did she have? What was the point in prolonging the argument? All she'd heard growing up was arguments, her mum snapping at her dad, him biting back, the vitriolic exchanges, the clunk of the whisky bottle against a tumbler, the tearful promises followed by days of silent resentment. It wasn't how she wanted her marriage to end up.

Skye unlocked the door and let her husband take her in his arms. She did not move away when he unknotted the towel, nor when he laid her down on the bed and kissed every injury he'd caused. She believed him when he told her it would never happen again.

But it had.

So many times.

Each one worse than the last.

32

Joy used the sleeve of her turquoise beach shirt to dab at her eyes.

They were still in Skye's bedroom, sitting side by side, the sunlight a fallen sail across the stripped wooden boards.

'Bloody hell,' Joy said at last.

'I know.' Skye put her face in her hands. 'The whole situation is such a mess. You probably think I should've stayed, stood up to him and—'

'No.' Joy put a steadying hand on her knee. 'I think you did exactly what you had to, exactly what that bastard forced you to do. I could kill him,' she added harshly. 'I would, given half a chance.'

Skye lowered her hands and let out a helpless laugh.

'I was weak,' she said. 'I am weak.'

'Stop that,' Joy scolded. 'You're here, aren't you? You escaped. That must've taken guts.'

Skye glanced down at her friend's hand, still resting on her knee. She wore rings on every finger, including her thumb, a jumble of silver, amethyst and amber surrounding the plain gold wedding band. Skye's own band was somewhere in the depths of the Aegean.

She had kept hold of her diamond engagement ring, though, fully prepared to sell it if or when her funds began to run out.

'I didn't tell Martyn about this place,' she said. 'The house, the island, the lottery – he doesn't know about any of it, or at least he didn't. But now, with the story being in the newspaper, it's only a matter of time before he tracks me down. He could be on his way here already, and if he does come, and finds me, then he—he'll be so angry. That's why I have to go.'

She got up from the bed. Restlessness had taken hold, and it felt as if the room was shrinking around her.

'You might hate me for saying this,' Joy began, 'but if you leave, he wins.'

'Finding me is the only way he wins,' Skye argued. 'If I stay here, I'll only lose.'

'Lose what?'

'Everything,' Skye said, the word pushed out on a breath. She leaned towards her friend, willing her to understand. 'Everything I've built here, he'll ruin it.'

Joy continued to meet her gaze. 'Ruin it how?'

'You don't understand,' Skye said, her voice catching. 'Martyn's a master manipulator. He won't just turn up here all guns blazing, he'll have a plan, a way to destroy me if I don't do as he says.'

'He can't force you to do anything,' Joy said, her tone gentle but firm. 'We won't let him.'

Skye shook her head and began to pace up and down.

'Things are different now,' Joy went on. 'You're not

in his house any more. This isn't his domain, it's not even his country. If he does come, he'll have no power here. Can you imagine what Andreas would do if some fella turned up making threats against you?'

Skye halted abruptly.

'I don't want Andreas involved,' she said. 'I don't want him to know anything about this.'

Joy's lips parted slightly. She pressed her palms flat against her thighs.

'Can I ask why?'

'Because it isn't his fight,' Skye replied. 'It's not his problem to solve, and it's not yours either. If I go now, the problem goes away with me.'

Joy tilted her head, the corners of her mouth tight. She was not convinced, that much was glaringly clear. Skye felt the guilt begin to swallow her like quicksand.

'The last thing I want is to be a burden to any of you,' she mumbled. 'You came here for a quiet life, remember?'

At this, Joy gave in to a small smile.

'In the time you've known me, have I ever been remotely quiet?' she said. 'Truth is, I love being in the middle of everyone's business. Bobby used to joke that he'd order a giant bug-swatter if I didn't stop buzzing around all our friends, getting involved in their lives. I didn't come to Greece to be lonely,' she went on. 'And I don't think you did either.'

'I came because I won the house,' Skye said.

'Yeah, but it wasn't only the house you came for, was it? I read the paperwork, too, you know. The whole idea of the scheme was to bring new life to this small village, build a community. You can't very well live in a place like Ano Meria and not become close to your neighbours.'

'I know that, but—'

'You're a part of this community now, chook. It's your home, and we – me and the girls, and Vicky and Adam, and Theo and George, and Andreas – we're your family. Nobody can hurt you here because we won't let them.'

'I don't want to drag anyone else into my mess,' Skye said again, the wretchedness making her weary.

'You didn't cause this mess,' Joy insisted. '*He* did, that bloody mongrel husband of yours.'

Skye turned away. Beyond the square window, a bird soared, skimming its wings along the current of the wind, free in a way she no longer remembered how to be.

'There'd be so much I'd miss if I left,' she murmured. 'The view, the mountains, the sea, the sunshine; waking up to the sound of church bells; the smell of wild herbs and the early evening chorus of the crickets – and that's before I get to all of you.'

Joy came to stand beside her.

'If you don't want anyone else to know about Martyn, that's fine by me,' she said. 'I'll keep your secret for you, and if he does show up here, I'll help you get rid of him.'

Skye gave her a sidelong look.

'Get rid of him?'

'Yeah,' Joy replied. 'Not in the Mafia way, obviously. I'll just have a quiet word, woman to brute, tell him to sling it or else.'

Skye tried to imagine that precise scenario and found she couldn't. If she left the island tomorrow, boarded a morning ferry and abandoned her little house, she'd need to have a destination in mind. Going back to her mother's place in England wasn't an option, and anywhere else would require spending money she couldn't spare. To run now would be condemning herself to a lifetime of running, of living with fear at the centre of everything. Joy was right, that path constituted a win for only one person, and it certainly wasn't her.

She thought of Katerina, who must have been scared by the prospect of war. Many Greeks had fled before the occupying forces caught up with them, but not her – not Kat.

She had stayed.

Skye crossed the room and picked up her suitcase, laying it flat on the bed.

'Does this mean you've changed your mind?' Joy asked.

'It means I've run out of options,' Skye said. 'I figure I have to face Martyn somewhere, and it may as well be here.'

'You won't have to do it alone,' Joy assured her. 'I'll be right here, and Andreas, too, if—'

'No Andreas.' Skye was firm. 'I mean it.'

Joy's face fell, though she managed a weak smile.

'He cares about you, you know?' she said. 'He cares

about all of us. That's just who he is. A good man, a man you can trust. They're not all bad.'

'I don't think he's bad,' Skye said. 'I just . . . Promise me you won't tell him?'

Joy breathed in deeply, pressing her lips together before nodding once, almost to herself.

'All right,' she said. 'I promise.'

33

April 1941

The girl was hunched on a low stool in Leni's kitchen, a cup of coffee clutched in both hands. She looked caught between child and adulthood, innocent and haunted at the same time. Draped in a black dress of the kind a grandmother would wear, she met Katerina's eye as she and Stefanos made their way into the room, only to glance hurriedly away.

'Come,' Stefanos said to her. 'Do not be afraid. Kat is a friend, you can trust her.'

When the girl did not respond, Katerina looked across towards her sister. Leni was preoccupied with ladling soup into five bowls and kept her head down, while at the table, Michalis sat silently, feet restlessly tapping against the floor. His spectacles lay discarded, one lens veined with a spiderweb crack.

Stefanos lightly touched her arm as he stepped around her, removing his hat and tossing it down. Michalis jumped violently at the sound, eyes wider than a snared rabbit's, though when Leni rushed to soothe him, he shooed her away, muttering impatient words.

'Sorry,' she said meekly, retreating to fetch a spoon for each of them. Katerina saw the flare of colour on her sister's cheeks, felt the sting of rejection as keenly as if it had been her own. At one time, she would have been quick to leap in and defend Leni, though something told her this would be unwise. Her brother-in-law had changed; been reduced to someone smaller, harder, more unyielding.

Stefanos beckoned for the girl to move closer.

'This is Esther,' he said. 'Her brother, Daniel, was with us in the mountains.'

'Where is he now?' Katerina asked, taking a seat.

'Gone,' Stefanos said. 'Killed during an ambush.'

The girl, Esther, sniffed as she sat. She had neat, symmetrical features, rosebud lips that she pursed to stem her tears, curls of black hair and watchful eyes.

'He had given us a letter to pass on to her if anything were to happen, and when we reached the village, we found that the Germans had been through already. Many people were dead.'

'They killed my mother and father,' Esther said.

It was the first time she had uttered a word in Katerina's presence, and her voice was tight with defiance.

'The soldiers demanded to know who in the village was of Jewish faith, and a traitorous neighbour pointed to our house. I did not know what to do, and so I hid. There was a hut at the back, where we kept the chickens, and I lay on my stomach beneath the straw, heard the gun shots and the screams.'

Leni reached across and placed a hand on the girl's shoulder.

'It was not safe to leave her,' Stefanos went on. 'Daniel, he saved me more than once, and so, it was only right that I save the sole surviving member of his family. The Germans had burned her house to the ground, and they have also sworn to kill anyone who defies them by concealing those they seek. There was no one in that village with the courage to help Esther. It was not a choice.'

Michalis picked up his spoon but made no move to begin eating. It was as though he was not there at all. Katerina had once found the skin of a snake on the hillside, and was reminded of it now, that impression of a living thing, left behind.

'I am very sorry for the loss you have endured,' she said to Esther.

'You will be safe here,' Leni added. 'We will look after you.'

Michalis banged his fist against the table. 'Safe?' he spat, with a mirthless laugh. 'Nowhere is safe any more, you foolish woman.'

'Don't speak to her like that,' Katerina snapped, ignoring Stefanos's sigh of displeasure. 'You are the fool who went to fight in the first place, who wanted to play at being a man.'

'Kat,' Stefanos hissed. 'That is enough.'

Michalis pushed his bowl away, soup spilling over onto the tabletop.

'All we have done,' he said slowly, 'is provide Esther with a stay of execution. When the Italians and Germans arrive here, they will find her, and they will punish those who keep her.'

'Then they cannot be allowed to find her,' Katerina said loudly, as Esther folded further into herself. 'There are plenty of places to hide on this island, and nobody knows them better than I do.' She turned to Stefanos. 'I did as you asked in your letter,' she said. 'I have hidden tools, food, medical supplies, everything I could collect. I will show you, we can go right now.'

'Wait.' He stilled her with his eyes. 'First, we eat.'

'I do not want anyone to die because of me,' Esther said. Her words were steady enough, though the tremor in her voice gave her away. Michalis stood abruptly, his chair toppling backwards and crashing against the stone floor.

'I need to sleep,' he said, and stalked towards the door. Leni hesitated for a moment, then went to follow him, only for her path to be blocked by Stefanos's outstretched arm.

'Leave him,' he said. 'Your husband has not slept properly for many months now. He is home, and for tonight, at least, that may mean he feels safe enough to rest.'

'Yes.' Leni lowered herself shakily into her seat. For a while, the only sounds were the scraping of their spoons against the bowls. Katerina wondered if it was hunger that drove them to eat, or merely the desire not to converse. Though there was much to say, there was also a benefit to allowing some time for new information to settle. To give in to the fear would be to lose the fight before it had even begun. She was afraid of the rapidly approaching war, and what it would mean for her community. Would neighbours turn on one another? It felt impossible, and yet it was happening all over Greece. It had happened to Esther.

When the bowls were empty, she and Leni collected them, wiping the table and pouring Michalis's abandoned soup back into the pot on the stove.

Katerina turned to Esther. 'Come home with me,' she said. 'I have clothes that will fit you, a bed in the attic where you will be safe tonight.'

Stefanos nodded his approval, ushering the girl outside, and Katerina turned to Leni.

'Will you be OK,' she asked, 'with Michalis? I can stay here if—'

'No, no.' Leni unfastened her apron. 'I must look after him myself. Stefanos is right, he will sleep, and tomorrow, he will feel better, more like himself.'

'Of course.' Katerina gripped her sister's hands, the silence between them saying everything. They had always spoken in this way, conveying through touch alone how they were feeling. In that moment, all Katerina felt was uncertainty. She wanted to offer reassurance, but it would have been a lie. Instead, she simply squeezed harder.

Stefanos was waiting by the boundary wall her grandfather had built, rolling a cigarette. He had been inside with Esther, shown the girl how to reach the attic bedroom, and given her a small amount of whisky to sip, in the hope that it would ease her into slumber.

The hour was late, midnight mere breaths away. Katerina led the way up the hillside, retracing the steps she had taken a thousand times or more, comforted by the tread of his boots, the trail of smoke that followed them. When they reached the ridge, she stopped and looked back across the island, squinting into a darkness that would have been total, were it not for the few remaining lights burning in windows. Sleep would be a hardship for many on this night, as it would on every night until the war concluded.

Stefanos lowered himself to the hard earth with the groan of a man who might have been ninety, and lay back, his gaze locked on the stars.

'What are you thinking?' Katerina asked, folding down beside him.

'That it is a miracle,' he said. 'I dreamed so often of being on this hillside again with you.' He turned to her, reached up and stroked her cheek. 'I did not believe that God would answer me – how could he hear me, amongst all the other noise, all those poor souls begging for mercy?' He closed his eyes briefly, refocused them on the sky.

'Perhaps it was me He heard,' Katerina said. 'Because I was asking for the same miracle.'

Stefanos shifted onto his side, drawing her close against him.

'You are my miracle,' he murmured. 'The only brightness in this black world. You belong up there with the stars.'

Katerina tightened her hold on him.

'I belong down here with you.'

She hoped he would kiss her, but instead, he let out a soft, broken sigh.

'How soon will you go?' she asked, for she knew he would. She felt the truth in the way he held her, in the urgent pressure of his fingers against her skin.

'Tomorrow,' he said. 'If we wait any longer, it may become impossible. You know that if they find me here, they will kill me?'

'We?' She blinked, daring to hope, to envisage a future without separation.

'I must take Michalis with me,' he said. 'He has become . . . it would not be safe to leave him. Some of the other men from the village will also accompany us – Constantine, Giorgos.'

'The brothers?' she asked. 'Atlas and Zephyr. Surely they will also go?'

'No.' His gaze remained set on hers. 'That is what they want, of course, but I convinced them to stay here. We need someone to lead the resistance, to protect the people and fight if necessary. However, they cannot remain in the village. Will you take them to the place you have found, show them where to hide?'

'Of course,' she said. 'Anything. But I don't understand why it has to be them – why not you?'

Stefanos rested his forehead against hers. He was near enough that she could feel the soft brush of his eyelashes on her cheeks.

'I am not from this island,' he murmured. 'The men, they will not follow me.'

'The brothers are not from here either,' she said, heat creeping into her voice. 'They are exiles, not even relations of anyone on Folegandros.'

'But they are respected, yes? They are liked?'

Katerina blew out a sharp breath through her nose. 'You are liked,' she insisted, and he smiled.

'Only by you, Katsikaki. And I fear that you and I alone cannot beat an army.'

'I want to come with you,' she said, though even to her, the statement sounded hollow, despondent. Stefanos pressed his lips to hers and kissed her once, very gently.

'I spoke to the priest tonight,' he said. 'In the church, when everybody else had gone.'

'About Esther?' she guessed.

'Not about her. I think it is best to keep that truth as close to the family as we can. War can turn even the oldest of friends into enemies, and you will discover that many will do whatever they must in order to survive, even if that means condemning another.'

'Then what were you talking about?' she persisted. 'Were you asking for absolution?'

A flicker of sorrow crossed his face, there and gone.

'I was asking for something more important than that,' he said, his fingers once again digging deep into her flesh. 'A blessing.'

'For what?'

'For us,' he said, as if it was the most obvious thing in the world, as if he'd told her once before, and she had forgotten it.

'What do you mean?'

'Katerina,' he said. She had never heard him use her full name. It was always 'Kat' or 'Katsikaki'. The brevity of his tone, the way he was staring at her with such intensity, made her chest flutter.

'If your father were here, I would be asking him this question,' Stefanos said. 'When he returns, when Greece has won this war, I will beg for his forgiveness.'

Katerina could barely breathe.

'Forgiveness for what?' she asked.

'For marrying his daughter.'

She sat up, pulling him with her, laughing out loud through her shock.

'Kat.' He seized her hands. 'Will you become my wife?'

She did not have to think. The answer flew out of her in a rush, repeating over and over until the words became a torrent of pleasure, of joy, of love. Stefanos leaned back, smiling as she fell to the ground in a mock faint.

Her, married? It was absurd!

She had believed love to be nothing more than a trap, though this love, *his* love, had set her free. Katerina was sure that if she were to run as fast as she could off the highest cliff on the island, she would soar through the air. All was light, all was glorious colour.

'When?' she asked, as they scrambled upright and she crashed into his arms. 'Now?'

'Patience,' he chided with affection. 'The ceremony will be tomorrow morning, before I go.'

It dawned on her then. He had not returned to bring

Michalis back to Leni, or even to hide the orphaned sister of his fallen comrade – Stefanos was here for her. To abandon the fight when he did was an act of rebellion, though it was one driven by a need to close the circle they had begun to draw together, to attach himself to her in the eyes of God and the law.

'I love you,' she said, and the smile he gave her then was wide enough to swallow the world.

'I love you too, my beautiful little goat.'

There was no longer a need for words, and as the wind broke ash-coloured clouds across the distant mountains, they let their bodies take over.

She was his.

He was hers.

For as long as eternity lasted, they would belong to each other.

34

June passed its baton to July, and the new month strode out under a banner of blue.

For the first few days after the article appeared, Skye remained close to the house, preferring the security of doors she could lock and windows that fastened. The weekend came and went again, bringing with it no sign of Martyn, though he was not the only man to be notably absent from her life. Andreas had not returned, and his replies to her messages were cool and detached.

When she rang to ask if he would collect some tins of paint for her, his response was a sullen '*nai*', and it was Stamatis, not him, who'd turned up at her door with them that morning.

'Where's the boss?' Skye asked.

Stamatis shrugged. 'Gone to the mainland.'

'Do you know when he'll be back?'

'Perhaps a few days, perhaps longer.'

'Is he there for work, or . . . ?'

Stamatis yawned.

'Never mind,' Skye said.

She was still brooding that afternoon when George arrived for his Wednesday lesson, followed soon after by Iris and Ajax, chaperoned over from the mini market by Joy.

'Found these two nippers driving their mum up the wall,' she said, as the three children ran out into the back garden. 'Thought it wouldn't hurt to bring them to class a bit early.'

'If only I had a classroom,' Skye said.

Joy bent to inspect the stack of paint cans, the straps of her brightly patterned dress slipping from her shoulders.

'Conche,' she read aloud. 'Why they can't just call it peach, I'll never know.'

'I thought you'd approve of poncy names for colours,' Skye said. 'Don't all artists go on about burnt umbers and morning room greens?'

'Some,' Joy agreed, 'but not all – and not bloody me. A spade's a spade, a shrimp's a shrimp, and this colour is one hundred per cent peach.'

'I hope I ordered enough,' Skye mused. 'It's going to take me for ever to paint the entire bedroom.'

Joy broke into a grin. 'Not if you bag yourself a few helpers,' she said.

Skye rounded up George, Iris and Ajax, while Joy hurried home to pick up some paint-stained T-shirts for the children to wear over their clothes. Once upstairs, they spread dust sheets across the floor and pushed the furniture into the centre of the room.

'This is your wall,' Skye told George, handing him

a brush. 'It's up to you what you do. You can paint something, or practise your fractions, or write a poem. Whatever you want.'

George shook his mop of unruly curls from over his eyes.

'And I can just paint it, all over the wall?'

In answer, Skye dipped her own brush into the open tin and drew a large, rather crude daisy below the window.

'Sick,' George said. 'I'm going to do a rocket.'

Ajax withdrew his finger from his nose, while Iris fussed with the hem of her oversized T-shirt. The fabric fell well past her knees, her bare feet poking out beneath it.

'Joy is going to paint some animals,' Skye told them, 'and I'm going to teach you the English names for them.'

In a few quick strokes, the head of an elephant appeared on the wall in front of them.

'*Eléfantas!*' Ajax cried.

Skye printed the word below the image and encouraged the two children to do the same. Soon they had a cat, dog, chicken, crocodile and giraffe alongside, and one wall was almost entirely covered in paint. George was close to completing his rocket and was busy adding faces to the small windows.

'That's me, Dad, and Mum,' he said.

Skye and Joy exchanged a look.

'Shall I do some planets?' he went on. 'Did you know it's really windy on Saturn? Dad said it might even be windier than it is here.'

'Surely not!' Joy said, squatting to paint a beetle.
'*Skathári!*' Iris chimed.

'We make a good team, don't we?' Skye said to Joy a few hours later. The children were sitting happily on a blanket in the back garden, slices of fresh watermelon on a plate between them. Ajax squealed as a butterfly landed on his outstretched leg, and George lent in towards Iris, whispering something that made her giggle.

'Their English is coming along quick,' Joy appraised.

'I think that's probably due more to George than me,' Skye said. 'They have far more desire to talk to him, and he's picked up a lot of Greek from Theo, which makes it easier.'

'You'll make a teacher out of him yet,' Joy replied. 'I'd be willing to bet there are loads of Greek kids on this island that would benefit from lessons here with you.'

'I'd love to open my own little school,' Skye admitted. 'But where?'

Joy fell silent, her eyes wandering past the edge of the garden to the house beyond, with its large, empty outbuilding.

'Do you think they'd let me?' Skye said.

Joy's expression was caught between caution and optimism. 'All you can do is ask,' she said.

Skye left her in charge of the three children and ventured the short distance to Adam and Victoria's front door. Nobody came in answer to her knocking, though she could hear music playing inside, along with a woman's voice, low and sultry.

'Press firmly into your forearms, drawing the shoulder blades down your back.'

Skye rapped her knuckles against the wood once more, and this time, the door opened.

'Sorry,' Victoria said, her face flushed. 'I was just attempting a Pincha Mayurasana, but I've lost so much core strength since I—Anyway, what can I help you with?'

'A Pincha Mayu-what?' Skye said.

'Oh, sorry, I forget you're not a yogi. That's a forearm stand, pretty standard stuff. I used to do them all the time, but I guess I've lost the knack.' She tugged at her hairband, sweat glinting on her chest and shoulders. In a sports bra and skin-tight shorts, she looked as though she could outrun the sun. Skye became keenly aware of her paint-splattered shorts and T-shirt, glad she'd put on trainers to hide her unmanicured toenails.

The recorded voice was still talking.

'From Dolphin Pose, shift your weight into your forearms and begin to lift your hips towards the ceiling.'

'I'm interrupting you.' Skye started to retreat, but Victoria made a grab for her.

'Please stay. It'll give me the perfect excuse to take a break. Between you and me, this woman is making me feel pretty rotten about myself. Any more advanced yoga, and I'll be about ready to scream, and I don't think that's quite the vibe I'm supposed to be going for.'

Skye followed her through the airy living space, which had been tastefully furnished with expensive-looking rugs, tile-topped side tables, a vast blue sideboard and several oversized lamps. Instead of sofas, there was a tan leather recliner and a patterned chaise longue, each draped with soft cream blankets. In the top corner, an air-conditioning unit hummed gently.

'It's been so hot, hasn't it?' Victoria said, bending to pause the video playing on her laptop. The woman on the screen was frozen in place, head down and a single leg in the air.

'I've been down to the beach most mornings for a swim. It's the only time of day that I can bear it. Have you got down there much?'

'Not as much as I'd like,' Skye admitted, as they headed into the kitchen.

'Want a smoothie?' Victoria offered.

'Oh, no, thanks.'

'It's my own concoction,' she needled, waving a banana at Skye. 'You wouldn't think it to look in my fridge, but I'm actually not a great fan of fruit. I get around it by adding a ton of honey. Enough of that, and you can crush up whatever you want and put it in there – calcium, collagen, beta carotene, a little melatonin.'

Skye raised an eyebrow. 'I'll take your word for it,' she said.

Victoria dropped several ice cubes into a jug, along with a slosh of almond milk and a heaped tablespoon of smooth peanut butter, which had taken on a rather tar-like consistency.

'There was a time when I was taking so much

medication, I had to make a chart,' Victoria said blithely. 'I used to say to Adam, "Shake me and I'll rattle."'

'Were you ill?' Skye asked.

'Nah.' Victoria opened a cupboard, rifled around for a while, then let out an 'aha, there you are' before re-emerging with a bag of protein powder. Banoffee pie flavour. Skye's stomach churned along with the blender.

'Sure I can't tempt you?' Victoria said. The smoothie was the exact colour and consistency of wallpaper paste.

'I'm sure,' she said hastily. 'Shall we go outside?'

The only shaded area was towards the back of the long garden, between the outbuilding and the mottled wall beyond.

'Any idea what you're going to use the barn for?' Skye asked, careful to keep her tone neutral.

Victoria tapped a finger against her lips, brow furrowing. 'Adam has some kind of idea about a dark room, but I don't know. Feels a bit silly to me, when everything is digitalised these days. I guess it could be an exercise studio, but that would be expensive, and we may not even stay here past the two years.'

Skye crossed to the outbuilding and peered through one of the dust-coated windows. Inside, the wide space was clear of junk, and she could see no holes in the walls nor cracks in the ceiling. All it would require would be a sweep, a spruce, a few bits of furniture.

'I was wondering . . .' She turned back to Victoria, who had taken a large sip of her drink and seemed to be having some trouble convincing herself to swallow it. 'If you'd let me use it from time to time?'

'Sure,' Victoria said through a grimace. 'I mean, I'd have to check in with Adam, but I can't see it being a problem. What do you want it for?'

'That's the thing,' she said. 'It's not strictly for me. I don't know if you've heard that I've been teaching George?'

Victoria shifted in her flip-flops. 'I heard.'

'Well, it would be great to have a classroom. Somewhere where I can set things up.'

'You want this whole area just for George?'

'And Iris and Ajax – you know, from the shop? I've started teaching them English, and I suspect there might be quite a few children on the island that could benefit from some extra schooling. If I had the space then—'

'I don't think so,' Victoria said.

'It wouldn't be every day,' Skye hastened. 'Only a few times a week, and I'd make sure we kept the noise down.'

'One kid is fine,' she said. 'A whole bunch of them? No way.'

'How about three?' Skye said tentatively, but Victoria shook her head.

'Sorry,' she said, 'it's not that I—I just—You'll have to find some other place.'

'Oh. OK.' Skye fell silent, at a loss for how to respond. Victoria's entire demeanour had changed, her easy slouch replaced by a stillness that felt almost brittle. Was it Adam she was worried about? Was he so averse to noise that he wouldn't be able to focus if a few children occasionally passed through? But that made no sense, not from a couple who until recently had been living in one of the busiest – and loudest – cities in the world. Maybe they simply didn't like children, although that seemed ridiculous.

'I should get back to my yoga,' Victoria said briskly. 'Unless there was anything else?'

Skye shook her head, words scattering before she could gather them. Moments later, she found herself out on the hillside again, the sky too bright, too empty.

She had the creeping sense that whatever had passed between them, whatever had sharpened the edges of Victoria's mood, was only the surface of something much deeper.

35

It was two weeks before Andreas returned.

From her spot high on the ridge, Skye caught sight of his truck winding along the road, a flicker of relief sparking before uncertainty took over. It was still early, not yet nine, but she'd been awake for hours, roused from sleep by the insistent clang of church bells.

Sunday again. No ferries. No Martyn.

Dust rose as the truck crunched over the hillside, pulling up not at her house but at the sisters'. Andreas climbed out, his dark hair catching the light. Skye watched him throw a quick glance over his shoulder before heading for the door. She didn't think he'd spotted her up on the mountainside. There had been no wave, no nod of greeting, no signal whatsoever.

The warmth of the morning seemed to slip away as he disappeared inside. Skye lowered her gaze and traced a crack in the earth with the toe of her shoe. Not far from where she sat, rock roses had opened their delicate pink faces to the sun, small bursts of colour against the wide, arid-gold landscape.

A rustle in the near silence made Skye turn in time to

see a lone goat making its way across the loose stones towards her.

'*Geia sou*,' she murmured.

The goat fixed her with its pale, marble-like eyes. One of its long ears was black, and the other brown, though its flanks were predominantly white. As it lowered its head to nibble half-heartedly at a tuft of dry grass, the bell around its neck gave a soft jingle.

'I hope you're not lost,' Skye said, though she doubted it. There were enough trails of goat dung around the village to convince her that the animals went wherever they pleased, and on more than one occasion, they had followed her back from the shop, muzzles pushing into her bags in search of food.

'I don't have anything for you,' she said now, as the goat began to nudge at her side. 'The only thing in my fridge is leftover pasta, and I don't think even you would want that.'

She and Joy had finally attempted to prepare the matsata dish the previous evening, but it had ended in disaster. The pasta had adhered itself to the bottom of the pan, while Joy's decision to add 'a decent glug of voddy' rendered the sauce inedible. In the end, they'd opened a packet of Lay's crisps and dunked them into aubergine dip.

The goat nudged her for a second time, hard enough that she toppled to one side.

'You're right,' Skye said, reaching over to stroke its neck. 'I should get up.'

From somewhere below came the waspy buzz of

a moped engine. No wind today, only heat, the sea a glittering carpet of fallen stars.

She did not plan on a route that would take her past the sisters' house, but her legs carried her there regardless. She wanted to see Andreas even if he did not want to see or speak to her.

The front door was ajar. Skye stepped inside and was about to call out a tentative 'hello' when she heard raised voices.

'You must do as I say.'

A man – probably Andreas.

'Oh, I must, must I?'

A woman – almost certainly Dusty.

Skye moved across the living area, with its mess of mattresses, tangled sheets and piles of discarded clothing, and cut through the minuscule kitchen into the garden beyond. Mia was there, sunbathing in a deckchair, while Louisa stood rigidly in the shade, a panting Bruno by her feet. Dusty and Andreas were a short distance away, postures set, her hands on her hips as he gestured past her towards the extension.

'What's going on?' Skye asked.

Louisa yelped in fright and spun around, a hand pressed to her chest. The green sundress she wore complemented the richness of her fox-red hair, though the worry etched on her face dulled its shine. Mia, by contrast, did little more than open one eye.

'Oh, hi,' she said, readjusting her bikini bottoms.

'You scared the life out of me,' Louisa added, in her musical Bristolian accent.

Skye flashed her a sheepish grin. 'I would've knocked, but the door was open.'

'It does that,' Mia said through a yawn. 'Dusty keeps promising to fix the latch, then forgetting. She's *so* obsessed with the extension, although it appears our resident builder has taken issue with it.'

'I thought as much,' Skye said, casting a glance in Andreas's direction. 'Don't tell me, it's to do with a lack of steel supports?'

'That's only part of it,' Louisa replied wearily. 'Today, it's something about permits or restrictions. I'm not sure, to be honest. It's all gobbledegook to me.'

Andreas had unfolded a document of some kind and was tapping it with an insistent finger as Dusty looked on, radiating insolence.

'Should we do something?' Skye said.

Mia stretched her arms above her head. 'Nah,' she said. 'I'm enjoying being a spectator.'

'I'll go and make some cold drinks,' Louisa said. 'Cool everyone off a bit.'

Mia slid deeper into the deckchair and closed her eyes.

'If there are any of those margarita ice lollies Joy made for us, can I have one of those instead?'

Louisa paused at the door. 'Remind me what your last slave died of?' she muttered.

'Exhaustion,' Mia replied sweetly.

Skye suppressed a smile as she watched the easy way the sisters teased each other. She hadn't been lonely as a child, not exactly, just aware of how much she would've loved an ally, someone to stand with her when the atmosphere at home became tense. However, the absence of a sibling had left her skilled at diplomacy, and she felt confident enough in herself to approach the warring duo further down the garden. Andreas was facing away, but Dusty saw her coming and waved.

'Thank God you're here,' she said to Skye. 'You can help me talk some sense into this oaf.'

Andreas blinked irritably. 'Oaf? What is oaf?'

'It's you,' Dusty said, folding her arms across a threadbare T-shirt. Her distinctive hair was crammed under a baseball cap, and a spray of mosquito bites dotted one cheek.

'Now, now.' Skye adopted her best teacherly tone. 'Let's not resort to name-calling.'

Andreas thrust a sheet of paper under her nose. 'Building regulations,' he said. 'The document contains many references and terms that are specific to Greek law, and she does not understand Greek law.'

'I know how to read a permit,' Dusty said icily.

'This land is *agrotemachio*,' Andreas said, his boots agitating the dry ground. 'That means the extension must join to the house there' – he pointed – 'and be constructed using the same materials. Not this foreign timber and cheap plasterboard.'

'It's not cheap,' Dusty fumed. 'Once it's up, you'll never notice the difference.'

Skye watched Andreas, noting the lines carved across his brow, the way he kept chewing at his lower lip. It wasn't anger she saw, but concern.

'Are you saying these stipulations are the law?' she asked.

Andreas turned to her, though he wouldn't meet her eye.

'*Nai*,' he said. 'There is a danger that if she continues to build in this way, the municipality will find fault, and she will be forced to tear the whole thing down.'

'You're just cross because I'm doing the work myself instead of paying you,' Dusty accused. 'It's a male pride thing,' she added to Skye. 'Men can't bear it when they see a woman doing a job better than they could.'

'I don't think that's true,' Skye began, but Dusty wasn't finished.

'Ever since he found out what I did for a living, he's been sticking his beak in, looking for reasons to undermine me.'

'You are mistaken,' Andreas said firmly. 'I do not want you to get into trouble with the authorities and—' He broke off as Louisa approached, a tray balanced in her hands. A large jug of water, bright with slices of lemon and cucumber, sat beside four glasses and a bowl of pistachio nuts. Dusty reached across and helped herself to a handful, while Skye poured each of them a drink.

'Here,' she said, offering one to Andreas. He hesitated, then took it, careful to avoid touching her fingers. For a few moments, nobody spoke. Ice clinked against glass, the only other sound the faint crack of pistachio shells being prised open.

'You were going to say something else,' Skye prompted, with a glance at Andreas. 'No,' she added quickly, as Dusty started to interrupt, 'let him finish.'

'What was it you wanted to say?' Louisa asked, her voice steady but her gaze almost too direct. She no longer blushed at the mere sight of Andreas, but something in the way she looked at him still gave her away. Skye took a sip of her water, the coolness doing little to ease the complicated knot of feelings she swallowed down with it.

'The law exists not to be difficult,' he said, 'but primarily because of safety. How do you think this structure will survive the conditions on Folegandros? The wind, the winter rain.'

'I've built plenty of the same in England,' Dusty threw back. 'And the weather is far worse there, believe me.'

'Why don't you just do as Andreas suggests?' Louisa said. 'The extension barely exists yet – it's just a floor and two walls. I don't see why you can't make a few changes.'

'I don't see why I should,' Dusty replied.

'This is getting us nowhere,' Skye surmised. 'Surely there's a compromise we can reach?'

'No,' Dusty and Andreas said in unison.

'Bravo!' Mia called from her deckchair. 'You've finally found something you agree on.'

Andreas pressed his lips into a thin line. Thrusting the paperwork at Dusty, he stalked past the three of them towards the house.

'See yourself out,' Dusty said in satisfaction, only to be immediately reprimanded by Louisa.

'I'll go after him,' Skye said, turning away before either of them could argue. She caught up with Andreas as he reached the truck, putting a hand on his arm that he immediately shrugged off.

Skye stepped back, feeling stung. 'Are you OK?' she asked.

Andreas nodded curtly.

'And are we OK?'

He sighed. 'I have something for you.'

'That's not an answer.'

Andreas ignored her, moving around to the passenger side and opening the door. Skye knew what was coming, though the dismay still landed like a stone.

'I thought you were going to translate them,' she said, staring down at the bundle of letters.

Andreas rubbed a hand across his roughly stubbled jaw.

'I think it is better that you ask Theo, or perhaps Cora to help with this. I am very busy. My friend has bought a bus and needs my help converting it into a pizza restaurant.'

'Oh.' Skye was taken aback by the unexpected detail. 'I see.'

'*Ela.*' He placed the small package on her upturned palm. 'It is better this way.'

Was it? Better for whom? Not for her, certainly. Skye's mind drifted back to that evening after they'd first discovered the letters, sitting together in his truck as he read aloud, lost in a past that he'd painted so vividly for her. It had felt like a treasure, a portal into another time, and the thought of unpicking the mystery without him seemed wrong.

'I don't mind waiting,' she said. 'Until you do have time.'

Andreas clambered into the truck, slamming the door behind him. His hands gripped the steering wheel, eyes locked on something far beyond her, or the hillside. The engine spluttered into life. Skye stood back, the sting of unshed tears burning her face as she watched him drive away. It wasn't possible to lose someone you never wanted in the first place, but somehow, that was all she could feel. Andreas had been hers. And now, he wasn't.

36

April 1941

Katerina stole from her bed before the light emerged. She had woken in the stark darkness, pulled from slumber by the strangeness of warm breath against her neck. Not a baby goat in her bed on this night, but a man. One that would soon become her husband.

Stefanos looked peaceful, the deeply etched lines softened, his battle-weary heart at rest.

It was the day of her wedding, but the chores must still be done. Animals knew not of impending conflict, nor celebrations of unity conducted by humans. The ovens at the bakery would not light themselves, the dough that had rested would be impatient for shaping. Would they even have time to eat after the ceremony? Break bread as husband and wife.

Curse this world, and this war, and the criminals who sought to take the lives and lands of others. Katerina aimed a kick at a loose stone, the dust rising as it ricocheted across the hillside. It shattered a silence that was near-complete, save for the hushed whisper of the sea; rhythmic, steady, soothing.

'*Kalimera.*' It was Leni, closing the door to her house, her movements quick and soundless. She wore her hair in a thick plait over one shoulder, the dress below it patched yet clean. There was something clutched in her hands that she offered to Katerina.

'I made these for you,' she said. 'They are only olive branches. I wanted to use roses, but it is too early. They will not bloom for weeks.'

Katerina stared down at the tightly wound crowns. The leaves appeared grey in the murk of pre-dawn, though in truth, they were green. The colour of life, of nature, and of hope. From each crown trailed a long white ribbon.

'I thought that—' She faltered.

Leni smiled with an indulgence that had been absent from her sister's face for months.

'Thought that what? You would get married without the crowning? *Ela re, agapi mou*, it is the most important part. How else do you intend to show God your promises?'

'God has abandoned us,' Katerina said sulkily, only to receive a sharp look.

'You are here,' Leni said, grasping her sister's wrists. 'Alive. The man you love is alive. These are gifts. Nothing is for certain in this world, but faith is important. You must not lose your faith. Whatever path we are on, it is our responsibility to walk along it, not to question, not to feel resentful at being on this earth.'

Katerina sighed in defeat.

'It is OK to be afraid,' Leni went on. 'There is no shame in fear, only in despair.'

'I am not afraid,' Katerina said harshly. 'I am angry.'

Leni let out a low chuckle. 'Only you,' she said, 'would find a reason to be cross on your wedding day. Now, go and see to the goats, and then, we will dress you.'

Several hours later and true to her word, Leni ushered Katerina into their parents bedroom. A pail of warm water had been set to one side, a bar of olive oil soap on a small dish. While Katerina washed herself, Leni arranged a brush, pins and a bottle of scent on the bed. When she laid a dress down next to them, Katerina's heart caught in her chest.

'That is Mama's,' she said.

'*Nai*,' Leni agreed softly. 'She is small like you. I would have given you my wedding dress, but the hem of it would trail through the dirt. It is what she would want,' she added, as Katerina continued to shake her head. 'Before she went to Thira, Mama told me to look out for you, to be a mother if I must. This is me, being a mother.'

The words should have been featherlight, but they landed heavily. Katerina knew that children were what her sister longed for more than anything else, though she had not yet been blessed with them. And now, Michalis was about to leave again, taking that chance away with him.

She put up no further argument, raising her arms as Leni slid the silken folds of the dress over her head. It had a scooped neckline, with long sleeves that tapered to a point. Katerina stood still as her sister shuffled around on her knees, pinning the dress in at the waist, arranging the material just so, her eyes moist as she fussed and fiddled.

'You look so beautiful,' she said. 'Stefanos will not be able to believe his eyes.'

Katerina did not agree.

'What if he laughs at me?' she said, as Leni began to braid her hair. 'He has only ever seen me in my work clothes. That is the girl he fell in love with, not this doll, trussed up like a cake decoration.'

'Woman,' Leni chided gently. 'You are about to be a wife, *agapi mou*. You are no longer a girl.'

They walked through the village with their heads down, smart outfits shrouded beneath dark cloaks. Stefanos had gone ahead to the church with his *koumbaros*, choosing Atlas to be his witness in place of Michalis. Katerina did not question her brother-in-law's choice to stay behind, though it was impossible to miss the wobble in Leni's lower lip.

'He is not himself,' was all she would say.

The day was bright and the skies clear, a tepid wind blowing in across the silvery sweep of sea. Boats dotted the water, fishermen armed with hooks and lines, while ahead, the domed church roof beamed its upside-down smile towards the heavens.

Katerina paused at the door, a pulse thudding in her ears. Leni took her trembling hand and squeezed it.

'Ready?'

She nodded, just once. 'I am ready.'

Stefanos was there, his beard trimmed and hair brushed back. Around him, candles flickered, shadows dancing on the pale walls. She moved as if drawn by a thread, as if their souls were already conjoined. She had felt it the previous night, as their bodies came together; the throb of him inside her, a sensation of love so pure it made her cry out.

She took his hands, the world retreating around them. The priest murmured words, placed the crowns on their heads, beckoned for Leni and Atlas to fasten the ribbons together. A ring was slid onto her finger, cold and solid; she spoke of duty, fidelity and obedience. Around the altar they danced, once, twice, three times, her skirt swinging. She heard the bleat of Leni's sob as the priest made his blessing. Stefanos drew her into his arms. The uniform he wore smelt faintly of smoke, his breath when he kissed her was sweet.

'How long do we have?' she asked him afterwards.

He cupped her face in his hands, dark eyes searching hers. There were flecks of gold in his. She tried to count them.

'Minutes,' he whispered. 'The men are at the port. They are waiting. I cannot—'

'I understand,' Katerina said. Not because she did, but because he needed to hear it. Her gift to him would be to let him go knowing that she would survive, would wait, would love him. When he walked away from her, Stefanos did not look back.

There was suddenly not enough air in her lungs. She gasped, coughing and spluttering. The ground came up to meet her and she dug her hands through the mud, and the dust, her fingers gouging the earth as she wept into Leni's shoulder.

Neighbours and friends stared as they climbed the

hillside, trading looks Katerina refused to meet. All she wanted was to slip back into the silence of their room, into the space that still held his shape, and close her eyes to this new world without him.

Then the screaming began.

37

The sun was already high when Joy appeared, a vast straw bag slung across her shoulder and sunglasses perched in her freshly washed hair.

'It's the perfect day for an outing,' she declared.

Skye hesitated in the open doorway. She was still half-tethered to the heavy mood that had hung over her since the encounter with Andreas two days ago.

'An outing to where?'

'To Chora,' Joy said brightly. 'I need to pop in and see Sander at his gallery, and thought I might chuck a sickie from life after that, play tourist for the day.'

'I'm not sure,' Skye began.

'Oh, come on,' Joy needled. 'It won't be half as fun on my own. I haven't even been up to the church over there yet, have you?'

Skye gave a small shake of her head. 'Not yet.'

'That settles it then. Come on, Theo said he'd give us a lift.'

As usual with Joy at the helm, resistance didn't stand a chance. Skye hurried upstairs to change out of the stained T-shirt she wore for painting and into a cotton dress patterned with palm fronds, brushing her hair as she followed Joy across the hillside to the idling jeep. George sat in the passenger seat, headphones on, iPad playing, his bare legs swinging in the footwell. When Skye's 'hello' went unanswered, Theo turned, his hand on the gearstick.

'Sorry about him,' he said. 'George has discovered the NASA Johnson Space Station on YouTube. He's barely come up for air since breakfast.'

'All that's never interested me much,' Joy remarked. 'Too many little green men down here on Earth, if you ask me.'

Theo stared at the dashboard for a beat before starting up the engine, the corners of his mouth twitching.

'Speaking of men,' Joy continued, turning to Skye. 'Have you seen Andreas lately?'

'Not for a few days.'

'Mia filled me in on the row him and Dusty had. The pair of them are like a couple of bloody kangaroos, fighting all the time. I'm sure his heart's in the right place and all that,' she went on, as Skye started to protest, 'but he really needs to work on his delivery, you know? There's a way of speaking to women, and that's not it. No wonder the bloke's single.'

In the rear-view mirror, Theo's eyes widened.

Not wanting to be disloyal, Skye changed the subject, pointing out a herd of goats at the roadside. Her friend from the ridge was among them, showing off nimble hooves as it hopped over a wall. They drove slowly through the village, pausing to wave at Pantelis in the taverna, and at Louisa, who was outside the mini market chatting to Klodi. Warm air flooded in through the open windows, and Joy extended an arm, her hand surfing on the current of wind. Having dropped them within walking distance of Chora, Theo carried on with George to the port. They were taking a lunchtime ferry across to Santorini, where they would picnic at the beach and explore the island's capital, Fira.

'Won't it be sardines over there?' Joy asked, darting a look towards George.

'Probably,' Theo allowed. 'That's why I'm taking the jeep, so we can make a quick exit if it gets too much. It's a big place – more than twice the size of Folegandros. If we need to find somewhere quiet, I don't think it'll be a problem.'

'Still can't believe his wife left him,' Joy said as she and Skye watched them drive away. 'Man like that, and a boy as sweet as George? Makes no sense to me.'

'Matters of the heart rarely do,' Skye replied. 'A lot of people probably looked at Martyn and me, and thought I'd landed the jackpot. He's handsome, charming, rich . . .'

'Sociopathic,' Joy finished.

The sound Skye made was halfway between a laugh and a groan.

'Like I said,' she mused, 'a total catch.'

Chora was as busy as Skye had ever seen it, the narrow lanes bottle-necked with visitors. She waited outside the gallery while Joy caught Sander up on her progress, showing him photos of the portrait she'd been working on. It had come as no surprise that Victoria looked divine as a Greek goddess, though Joy confessed she'd had more fun painting Bruno.

'People move around all the bloody time,' she said. 'That dog could turn sleeping into an Olympic sport, he's the dream subject.'

The two of them passed a few hours meandering through the streets, picking through knick-knacks and trying on Grecian-style dresses threaded with gold. Joy chose an evil eye ring for her pinkie, while Skye treated herself to handmade leather sandals to replace the rubber-soled pair that had finally given up.

'You hungry?' Joy asked, as they drew level with a French-style patisserie named Le Petit.

Skye eyed the window display, where rows of cakes, chocolates and marzipan fruits were lined up like jewels.

'I am now,' she said.

'Have the cops been back in touch at all?' Joy said, as they re-emerged minutes later, each with a potted dessert in hand. Skye had chosen tiramisu, the cocoa-dusted top giving way to layers of mascarpone and soaked biscuit. Joy's millefeuille cracked beneath her spoon, spilling cream between its flaky, golden sheets.

'Not with me,' Skye said between mouthfuls. 'It was Andreas they called last time, and if he'd heard anything, he probably wouldn't even tell me.'

'But you two are friends,' Joy said.

'I'm not sure we are any more. Ever since that day when the newspaper article came out, he's stayed away. He's angry with me for not telling him the whole story, but it's complicated. Putting my trust in a man – any man – after what happened, just feels like too much of a risk.'

'Give it time, chook,' Joy said, scraping her spoon around the pot. 'He'll come around.'

He may well do, thought Skye. But would she?

They pressed on, the wind tugging at their clothes as the town slipped away behind them. The path grew steeper, winding up the mountain towards the church, and Skye felt her breath shorten with each step. A young Greek couple strode past, as unfazed by the incline as the donkeys watching from the other side of a low wall. Among them, a man in heavy boots and a cap scattered grain from a bucket, while in the undergrowth, crickets sang. At the final bend of the pathway, Skye paused. Chora lay sprawled below them, a scatter of sugar-cube houses stitched into the gold and green hillside. Amid it all, the old fortress clung to its cliff-edge perch, defiant against the drop.

Joy led the way through a small gate and into the grounds of the church. They were not the only visitors; a queue of tourists was clustered in front of an arched doorway, and more were wandering around, cameras and binoculars raised, sunglasses covering eyes that were dazzled by the bleached walls. They waited until there was space before moving quietly into the church's cool interior. Skye found her eyes drawn upwards, to where the domed ceiling was bathed in soft yellow light; large decorative candelabras swung gently above head-height, and the air was fragranced with wood polish.

A short distance away, a group was gathered around a slim, dark-haired woman, listening intently. Skye glanced at Joy, and the two of them sidled closer to eavesdrop.

'You see the icon behind us here,' the woman said, gesturing to a silver image on the wall. 'The legend is that an Ottoman pirate cut away the face of the Virgin Mary and stole her. From that night, and on every night that followed, she visited the man in his dreams and begged him to take her home. The pirate was so tormented that he threw his treasures into the sea, where they were discovered by a captain from Ios. He had heard the story, and knew to return her here, to Folegandros.'

The story was greeted by a series of 'ooh's and 'ahh's from the assembled tourists, many of whom raised their phones to take photographs. The woman told them she would wait outside, flashing a quiet smile at Skye and Joy as she passed them.

'What is it about churches that always makes me feel as if I've done something naughty?' Joy whispered, as a bearded priest in black robes and a kamilavka hat appeared through a side door.

'Because you usually have,' Skye replied, keeping her voice low.

In the end, their giggles became too loud for the muted silence, and they burst back out into the sunny courtyard clutching their sides. It had been weeks, maybe longer, since laughter had taken her by surprise. She felt breathless and weightless, as though something inside her had slipped free from its shackles.

The tour guide who'd told the pirate story was watching them, seemingly bemused. Skye dabbed at her eyes, glancing up as a bird soared into view, its dark silhouette a small rip in the faultless blue.

'Eleonora's falcon,' the woman said, following its flight with a tilt of her head. 'She is hunting.'

'Neat,' Joy said. 'What does she eat?'

The woman's shoulders rose in a small, careless gesture. 'Perhaps mice,' she said, 'but she would prefer to find a rabbit, another, smaller bird, or a bat. You do not see them very often here. Most of the time, they remain close to their nesting ground, and most of these kinds of falcons are on Tilos.'

'You sound as if you know a lot about them,' Skye said.

The woman turned to her. Up close, she was striking in a way that caught Skye off-guard. Her features were finely drawn – a small, upturned nose, full mouth, and serious eyes framed by lashes so dark they looked inked on. She wore a pale-grey trouser suit despite the heat, while a delicate silver cross glinted at her throat.

'Not me,' she said. 'My ex-husband. He is a . . . how do you call it in English?'

'A twitcher?' Skye supplied.

She let out a throaty roll of laughter. 'A twitcher, that is it. He likes to watch the birds, observe their behaviour, learn about their habits. It is a passion of his.'

'You said he's your ex-husband?' Joy asked. 'What happened? Did he run away with another twitcher?'

'No, no.' The woman shook her head slowly. 'It was nothing like that.'

An image came to Skye then, a snapshot of a bookcase, spines facing out that she'd read in turn. One of them, the largest and most colourful, had been about birds.

The tour group had begun to filter out of the church.

'Sorry,' the woman said, stepping aside, but as she moved to pass them, Skye lifted a hand.

'This might sound like a strange question,' she said carefully. 'But what's your ex-husband's name?'

There was the briefest pause, no more than a flicker, before the woman replied.

'It is Andreas,' she said. 'Andreas Vithoulkas.'

38

Andreas had been married.

Married, and he hadn't said a word.

He'd looked at Skye with disappointment, frustration, even anger for not opening up to him, and yet *this* was what he'd kept from her?

'Did you know?' she asked Joy as they made their way back along the winding mountain pathway.

'No, but come to think of it, I don't think I've ever asked him outright. So, he hasn't exactly lied, has he?'

Heat flared in Skye's cheeks as she recalled doing exactly that when Joy had first asked her.

'I guess so,' she allowed. 'But we've had so many conversations over the past six weeks – he could have told me at any time.'

She stumbled in her haste, the bag containing her new sandals bashing against her legs.

'He must've had his reasons,' Joy said. 'Maybe it was a painful break-up? A raw subject for him. He might've been unfaithful, or she could have. Relationships are always bloody complicated. Even me and Bobs had our trials over the years.'

'But Andreas is so direct,' Skye persisted. 'All this . . . secrecy, it doesn't sit right with me. It's not like him.'

'No,' Joy agreed flatly. 'It isn't.'

Skye stopped short. Joy took a few more paces before turning back, her brow furrowed. 'What are you d—'

'Maybe we should go back,' Skye said.

'Back where? Not all the way up there?'

'You don't have to come. Go on ahead and wait for me in town.'

Joy drew in a long breath and folded her arms. 'You want to ask his ex what happened?'

'Maybe.' Skye stared at the stony ground.

'And you reckon she'll be quite happy to spill her guts to you – a complete stranger?'

Skye puffed air into her cheeks.

''Cause I wouldn't,' Joy added. 'Especially not when I was in the middle of leading a tour. And you know what I'd do, the minute you walked off with your tail between your nethers? I'd be straight on the phone to Andreas.'

Skye conceded that she had a point.

'Just ask him yourself,' Joy said, with mild exasperation.

'But he's been acting so cold towards me.'

'And you reckon going behind his back to gossip about him with his ex will help that?'

'Stop being so reasonable,' Skye said, groaning her way into a helpless laugh. 'You're supposed to be the naughty one, remember?'

'Yeah, I know. But now it looks like I'll be handing over that crown to Andreas.'

They did not linger long in Chora. The early-afternoon ferry had docked, bringing scores of daytime tourists along the road from Karavostasis.

'The next bus isn't for an hour,' Joy said. 'Shall I give the girls a call, see if one of them will come and get us? I don't much fancy the walk, do you?'

'It's far too hot,' Skye agreed.

Joy dug her phone out, trying first Dusty and then Louisa.

'No answer,' she said.

'What about Mia?'

'She's working today. I could try Andre—'

'No,' Skye interrupted. 'I'll ring Victoria.'

Twenty minutes later, they were buckled into the four-by-four, skirts arranged carefully to protect their bare skin from the hot leather seats.

'I'm glad you called,' Victoria said. 'I know things have been . . . that I've been a bit quiet. I want you to know, it's not on you. I just have some stuff going on.'

'No need to explain,' Skye assured her. 'I hope we didn't pull you away from anything important?'

'Fat chance of that.' Victoria leaned over the wheel, checking for oncoming traffic. The indicator clicked into the quiet. In the passenger seat, Skye caught the edge in her voice and wondered at the sudden shift in tone.

'You look nice,' she said. Gone were the leggings and trainers, replaced by a dress the colour of sunlit sea. Her dark-blond hair was loose, brushed smooth, and gold shimmered at her ears, throat and wrists.

'We were supposed to be going out for lunch,'

Victoria said, pressing her foot to the gas pedal with enough force to make the tyres screech. 'But then Adam had an emergency at work.'

The way she said 'emergency' made it sound anything but.

'We could all go for lunch?' Joy suggested. 'Why don't we stop at the taverna on the way back?'

Victoria flipped down her sun visor. 'That's kind of you,' she said in a brittle voice. 'But I wouldn't be the best company. I've been a bit up and down since— Well, since what feels like forever, to be honest. I guess I'm just homesick or something.'

'Are you sure it's only that?' Skye asked gently.

Victoria drummed her fingers. 'The thing is,' she said, staring straight ahead, 'we've had a rough time of it, Adam and me. We've been trying to start a family for years now and despite spending a small goddamn fortune on IVF, we're yet to stay pregnant more than a few months. The other day, when you mentioned a school, I don't know, I just flipped out a bit, you know? Like, I didn't want to be reminded of what we didn't have. You probably think I'm an awful person.'

'No, no – God, no,' Skye said. 'I totally understand.'

'Sounds like you've really been through it,' Joy added. 'Poor little chook. Bobby and me, we tried. Never got very far mind you. If you ever want to talk—'

'Thanks.' Victoria shook her head. 'But let's just drop it. I'll only get all maudlin on you both.'

Beyond the windows, the landscape was a blur. A journey that should have taken fifteen minutes took less than ten, and Skye winced as they rounded the corner up to the hillside and almost collided with two people dragging suitcases. Victoria pulled up outside her house at an angle, dust pluming around the truck. Skye hopped out, followed by Joy, the two of them staring after Victoria as she stalked away without a word.

'Crikey,' Joy said. 'I wouldn't want to be in Adam's thongs tonight.'

Skye wheeled around. 'Adam wears thongs?'

'Yeah, on his feet, you 'nana.'

'Thongs as in knickers made mostly of string?'

Joy untangled her sunglasses from her frizzy hair.

'As in flip-flops, or whatever you bloody Brits call them.'

'Oh . . .' Skye said, the word vibrating over a laugh. 'That makes far more sense.'

'Listen,' Joy said, as Skye struggled to control her mirth. 'I need a piddle. Beers back at yours in ten?'

'Mine is full of paint fumes,' Skye replied. 'I'll come to you.'

She watched Joy walk across the hillside, her laughter draining away as thoughts of Andreas intruded. There was no sign of his truck, though she hadn't expected there to be. Disappointment was fast becoming her companion, pushing its way to the front, ahead of the fear and anxiety that had plagued her for so many months. She glanced up at the ferocious sun, but the sky offered no answers.

A movement caught her attention. It was Tigri, emerging from the side of the house and sidling towards her. The cat rubbed his slim body against her leg, mewling with the unique indignance that only cats could muster.

'You daft animal,' she said affectionately, stooping to stroke him. Tigri writhed for a moment, then he froze, yellow eyes fixed on a point in the near distance, fur rising as he arched his back.

'What's the matter?' she asked, toppling backwards as the cat bolted, his claws catching her ankles on his way.

Skye winced, dabbing at the scratches. Blood smeared her fingertips.

She looked up, squinting into the distance.

Not one figure, but two.

A man *and* a woman.

Her breath caught.

No.

It couldn't be.

39

Mum?

Skye wasn't sure if she'd said it aloud, or if the word had simply echoed through her, breaking loose as her world slanted. Her limbs turned leaden, heavy with shock. She wanted to run, but her body wouldn't respond. All she could do was stare, mouth slack, as her mother and Martyn walked towards her.

They didn't belong here. Not in this place. In *her* place.

Nausea surged. Her breath came shallow and quick.

The past and present were pulling tight together, leaving nowhere to hide. Martyn looked wrecked but smug, like a man who'd crawled over a finishing line and still thought he'd won. Her mother, as ever, looked inconvenienced. She batted away a fly with a sharp flick, eyes locking onto Skye with steely focus.

'There you are,' she said, as if the desolate hillside on a remote Greek island was a pre-arranged meeting place, and all she had done was show up a few minutes late.

Skye opened her mouth, but no words came. Her hands began to tremble.

'There she is,' Martyn intoned, his voice dripping in sarcasm. Skye didn't look at him, *couldn't* look at him. An image of his face the last time she'd seen him flashed through her mind, and she shuddered, repulsed by the memory, enraged by it. It was this sudden surge of defiant anger that helped her to raise her chin and meet his gaze.

'Here I am,' she said, surprising herself with how calm she sounded. Inside, it felt as if all her organs were vibrating in unison. The air, already hot, seemed to crackle.

'We had to wait almost an hour for a taxi,' her mother said, removing her wide-brimmed straw hat and fanning herself with it. There was a faint pink line across her forehead, and her usually immaculate hair appeared damp at the roots. 'And then the driver refused to bring us up here, dropped us off miles away. We had no choice but to carry our luggage up here like a couple of donkeys.'

The two people dragging suitcases along the road. Victoria had almost hit them.

'It's a rough track,' Skye said. 'You need something with four-wheel drive.'

She glanced instinctively over to the sisters' house. Dusty's truck was parked outside, its bumpers caked in dirt, the back a mess of tools, planks and bags of dry cement.

'Well, then,' her mother went on, staring around, 'which one of these is yours?'

Skye looked at Martyn. Fear closed fist-like around

her throat as she took in his mocking smile, the twist of his mouth that told her he'd won.

'I . . . I, er.'

'For heaven's sake, Skye,' her mother snapped. 'We've come a long way – a very long way. The least you can do is invite us in for a cold drink.'

How was this happening?

Skye was torn between the urge to fight and be polite, the need to escape and the importance of standing her ground. She felt suddenly exhausted, every limb a water-soaked log.

'It's over here,' she said faintly. 'The house with the blue door.'

Time thickened. Each crunch of dry earth rang out like thunder in Skye's ears. The key was a weight in her hand, her fingers sluggish, skin tingling with dread. She didn't want him here. He had no right to cross this threshold, to pollute the only space she'd kept untouched by him. He knew that, of course he did. That was why he'd brought her mother. Cassandra MacKinnon – cool, composed, impossible to refuse – was his Trojan horse. His way inside. Martyn meant to trap her.

She couldn't let him.

There was a dull thud as her mum's suitcase rolled down the step. Martyn followed with only a gym bag, the same ostentatious leather one he'd had monogrammed in gold, as if it were a trophy. There was a matching one with her initials back in London, presumably languishing in the bottom of the wardrobe where she'd left it. In Skye's mind, she was no longer an 'SL' – Lockhart now a name she wanted nothing to do with. She fought the urge to slam the door in Martyn's face, stopping just inside with her arms folded to hide the shake in her hands.

When he stepped forward, she stepped back.

'I was going to give you a kiss, but if you're going to be like that . . .' he said. His eyes glittered with something Skye didn't want to name. She turned away.

'Where are the teabags?' her mother called. She had wandered through into the kitchen, and leaving Martyn by the door, Skye went to join her.

'I'll make it,' she said, reaching for the jar.

To her dismay, Martyn followed. He leaned against the doorframe with all the nonchalance of a Roger Moore-era James Bond, though with none of the charm. Cassandra had helped herself to a bottle of water from the fridge and sipped it demurely as she peered out over the back garden.

'Looks as if a bomb's gone off out there,' she observed. 'We read about your little discovery. This mess is down to the authorities, I presume?'

'They didn't want to leave a stone unturned,' Skye replied. 'Not once they'd seen the bones.'

Her mother gave a nod. 'And did they find anything else?'

Skye dropped the teaspoon she was holding and it clattered against the draining board. Her bag was on the table, and she heard her phone buzz from inside. It was bound to be Joy, asking where she was, impatient to sit and enjoy a cold beer with her friend. Skye made no move to retrieve it. The phone was safer hidden away, where it couldn't be snatched from her hand or thrown against the wall.

Steam filled the kitchen. Cold sweat dappled her chest.

'Skye?' her mother repeated.

'Oh, sorry. No, nothing else,' she said, pouring hot water into the mugs. Her mum and Martyn liked their tea barely brewed, a detail she'd always found odd. Skye took after her dad, preferring it the colour of mahogany.

Not that it mattered now. Her stomach had shrunk to the size of a walnut.

'So, were they animal bones?' her mother persisted. 'Or did you win a house built on an old burial ground?'

She made it sound as if the whole situation was a joke. But Skye would not play along, not this time. She'd gone along with too much for too long and look where it had left her. The lessons had come hard, and she was not about to forget them.

'We don't know yet,' she lied, sloshing in milk. 'The police haven't let us know.'

'We?' Martyn said. 'Us?'

'The villagers.' Skye passed a mug across without looking at him. 'It concerns all of us.' Andreas's words came to her then, and she almost smiled.

'We're a community,' she went on. 'It's not like London, where you can live next door to someone for years and never even learn each other's names. Here, we talk to one another, help each other.' She stopped short of saying 'look after each other', though from the disgruntled expression taking shape on Martyn's face, it was clear the implication had been received loud and clear.

Her mother turned from the back door and faced her.

'Is that why you ran away?' she asked.

Skye recognised a cross-examination when she heard one beginning and braced herself.

'So, you're saying the reason you threw away a perfectly nice life, a perfectly acceptable existence,' her mother persisted, 'is because you wanted to be part of a community?'

'No,' Skye said. 'I left because my life was perfectly awful, and perfectly *un*acceptable.'

Cassandra scoffed and tears stung behind Skye's eyes. She stared hard at the ceiling, willing them not to fall.

It wasn't her mum's fault. Cassandra was completely unaware of what had been going on. Skye had never told her, had never felt able to shatter the illusion.

'Now do you see what I mean?' Martyn said purposefully. 'Nothing I do is enough, Cassandra. Your daughter is determined to find faults where there are none.'

'Faults?' Skye was incredulous, her voice wavering. 'I found faults – me? You were the one who—The one who—'

But it was no good. She couldn't say it. Not with her mum in the same room.

Skye's mother had always called her father weak – too sensitive, too idealistic, too easily hurt by the world. Everything Skye had loved about him, her mother had dismissed. And selfishly, Skye hadn't wanted the same judgement aimed at her. It had been simpler to pretend, to play a part. Eventually, that had become easier than being herself.

But since arriving in Folegandros, she'd started to find her way back. To abandon that now would be the worst kind of betrayal, and she was done with that. She had been for a long time.

'Mum,' she began, ready, at last, to speak the truth, to be vulnerable, to trust that the only parent she had left might finally see her pain, understand her fear, and help her carry it.

The words were right there, on the tip of her tongue, so close to setting her free.

And then, a loud crack.

The floor shifted beneath her and the world began to shake.

40

May 1941

They came as the shadows lengthened, a swathe of uniformed bodies as unwelcome as a plague. Katerina watched the military ships from a distance, stretched out her arm as if it were a rifle, and took imaginary aim at the disembarking soldiers.

'Brave and righteous' was how Stefanos had described these men in his letters, though to her, they were the antithesis of that. Invaders and thieves, no more worthy than bacteria. They had barely placed a boot on her island before they began to steal, claiming property, livestock and boats, as well as confiscating anything that could be used or repurposed as a weapon. Only the most meagre of farming tools were left in Greek hands, and the Italians were unscrupulous when it came to searching their homes.

Though Katerina did not venture to Chora or the port village of Karavostasis, news of atrocities filtered back from those places on the wind, reports of beatings, lootings and the swift imprisonment of any soul who dared to resist the enemy's demands. Whispers spoke of a black-hearted German general with a quick temper, who boasted of his closeness to the Führer and had a 'no mercy' policy when dealing with adversaries.

'I would have a "no mercy" policy in dealing with him,' Katerina muttered to Leni, who shushed her with furious irritation.

'Be quiet, silly girl, you will get us both killed. Do not forget what the men told us: the enemy has ears in the walls.'

'But this is our home—' Katerina protested, only for Leni to flap her hand in front of her face.

'Nowhere is safe any more,' she hissed. 'You must keep your thoughts in your mind only.'

Stefanos and Michalis had left three days before the occupiers arrived, accompanied by a clutch of men from the village, Constantine and Giorgos among them. The wails of anguish that had splintered the air as Katerina and Leni returned after the wedding ceremony came from their neighbour Phaedra. She had discovered that her son, Kostas, had disobeyed her wishes and gone with his father to join the fight.

'He is only fifteen,' she'd cried, clutching the baby Elpida against her bosom. 'He cannot hold a gun with a broken arm. How will he survive?'

While Leni and Dafni had soothed the wretched woman, Katerina had been struck by an idea. Initially, she had planned to hide Esther up in the mountains with the brothers, Atlas and Zephyr, but would it not make more sense for the Jewish youngster to remain in the village?

After some discussion, Phaedra agreed to take her

in, and the three women set about disguising the girl, first cutting off her long hair, before dressing her in Kostas's clothes and wrapping her arm in a sling. She was to keep her head down and avoid speaking to anyone. As far as the other villagers and any marauding soldiers were concerned, the teenage Kostas had never left. There would be no suspicions raised if they were careful, no reason to believe that their plan would not work. They knew it had to. The alternative would surely mean death for all of them.

Katerina longed to visit the two brothers in their hiding place, but they had told her to wait. The enemy would be on the lookout for such spies and messengers. It made more sense for Katerina to prove to them that she was no threat, gain their trust as far as she was able, thus allowing herself a better chance at slipping away unnoticed when the time came. Atlas and Zephyr had enough supplies to last them a month or so, and they needed her to be their eyes and ears, map the Italian outposts and military bases across the island, compile numbers of troops, and gather the names of those in command.

'Go as the bees do and gather us the pollen we need to grow our defence,' Atlas told her, to a terse eyeroll from his brother. Zephyr had little patience for poetry or metaphors.

'Do what you must, but be smart,' he advised. 'You will be no help to us dead, Kat.'

The word landed like a slap. It had never occurred to Katerina that she might die in this war, not even once.

'How can you be so naïve?' Leni had asked. 'Is there no caution in your heart?'

'None,' Katerina retorted. 'I leave the caution up to you.'

They were so different in that way. Mama had always said as much, had called them her 'oil and water' for as long as Katerina could remember. She thought of her parents often in the days following the invasion. Santorini had been swamped, earmarked as an important base for the enemy, and there was no way of knowing what fate would befall those living there. She wondered if Baba, who was nearing fifty, would join the resistance fighters, or if he would remain at Giagia's house to watch over her and Mama. She knew any stubbornness in her had been inherited from her father, and worried privately where that fire would lead him.

'Mama will not let him do anything foolish,' Leni reassured. 'All will be well, you'll see.'

Katerina had said nothing.

Folegandros was not a big island, though within only a week of the occupying forces' arrival, it became clear that keeping everyone fed was going to prove a challenge. Crops did not grow well on the wind-battered hillsides, and stocks that had been plentiful were dwindling at an alarming rate. Soldiers, especially those who were removed from imminent danger, had few tasks to occupy them save for daily patrols. Many idled away the evenings drinking, eating, and entertaining one another with music or song.

'*Di più, di più!*' they would shout at the local taverna staff. *More, more!*

Katerina had split her herd of goats, giving two to the brothers before moving several more to higher ground, where they would not be so easily spotted. The mature nanny she kept close for milk, butter and cheese, while Chrysí, the younger goat, barely left her side. Each night, she would carry the animal up the wooden ladder to the attic and sleep with her arms wrapped around her, Chrysí's soft golden fur warm against her cheek.

One afternoon, she and Leni were counting the remaining sacks of grain in the outbuilding behind her sister's house when the sound of engines broke the stillness, low, steady, and far too close.

'I want to see.'

Katerina moved away before her sister could grab her, Chrysí at her heels as she traced the rough stone wall onto the hillside. There were three jeeps, the last of which was open-sided with a large gun fixed to the rear. A soldier leaned against it, the very picture of insouciance, his narrowed eyes boring through her with disdain.

Katerina took in his muddied uniform – not quite grey, green, or blue, but a sludgy mess of all three – and fought to keep her face from twisting into a sneer. More soldiers were climbing down from the other vehicles, rifles slung over their arms, wool straps flapping away from their ankles.

These pathetic men, they could not even dress themselves properly.

Chrysí dropped her head and began to nibble at the sparse patches of grass around Katerina's feet, her tail swishing to ward off flies.

Leni came to stand beside her. 'What is happening?' she whispered, darting a wary glance towards the men.

Two of the group broke away, and Leni grasped Katerina's arm as they approached.

'Good afternoon,' said one. His command of Greek was poor, the tone coarse. Even without the ugly uniform, the Italian could never have hoped to pass himself off as one of them.

Katerina did not return his greeting, though Leni murmured a timid *'Parakaló'*.

'Is this your house?' he asked them.

Leni hesitated. 'It belongs to my—yes,' she said.

'It is our family home,' Katerina told him. 'This one, and the one beside it.'

The soldier translated the information to his companion, who was older and thickset, with the mean, watchful eyes of a snake. He raised a brow, then spoke curtly in his own language.

'We think this is a lot of space, for two young ladies,' the first man said. 'Where are your husbands, your children?'

'Our parents are in Santorini,' Katerina said coldly. 'We do not have any children.'

The heavier man ran a critical eye over each of them in turn. 'Husbands?' he barked, the word warped in his untrained tongue. Katerina willed her sister not to reply.

'They are away,' said a voice, and all four of them turned to find Phaedra approaching. The first soldier pointed his gun at her, and she froze, her hands raised.

'Our husbands are away,' she said again. 'They left many months ago, to fight in the north. We have not heard from them. We do not know if they are alive. There are only women here on this hillside, women and my two children. We do not want to cause you any trouble.'

The soldier grunted, lowering his weapon with a terse nod. Turning their backs, the two men conferred for a few minutes, before striding away without another word.

Katerina reached for Chrysí, knotting her fingers through the goat's shaggy mane.

The soldiers were moving now, trooping as one mass towards the house belonging to Giorgos and Dafni. Leni jolted violently at the bang of a fist against wood, and this time, Katerina made no complaint when her sister grabbed her hand. She had no desire to follow those men, they repulsed her.

The sound of voices floated across the hillside, tempered at first, then louder. Katerina strained to listen, but all she could hear was a pleading cry.

She turned to Leni. 'Let me go,' she said. 'I need to see. I need to—'

A loud crack rang out across the hillside. Chrysí lurched forward out of Katerina's grasp and trotted towards where the jeeps were parked, her small hooves kicking up dust. With a cry, Katerina wrenched herself free and ran after her, rounding the final vehicle in time to see Dafni fall to the ground as she was struck.

'No!' she cried, rushing over without a thought.

The man standing above her fallen neighbour turned. The pistol he had presumably fired into the air was still in his hand. He was more smartly attired than the Italian soldiers surrounding him, and recognising the red panels stitched along his grey trousers, Katerina stalled, her heart leaping up into her throat.

'Please,' she said. 'Don't hurt her.'

The German officer looked at her in bemusement. He had the complexion of wet dough, his neck a livid red. Katerina met his eyes and saw only cruelty within them.

The soldier who had acted as translator stepped forward. 'This woman,' he said, following the German's acidic drawl, 'dared to defy orders.'

From the ground, Dafni left out a whimper. One side of her face was already beginning to purple, though she made no attempt to deny the accusation.

'What orders?' Katerina stammered, looking between the men.

'She has been instructed to give up her house,' the Italian soldier said. 'General Wolff requires it for his wife.'

Dafni muttered something unintelligible and spat into the dirt.

'If you need a house, there is an empty one over there,' Katerina said, pointing across to the dwelling that had until recently belonged to the brothers.

The German pursed his lips. 'That one is no good,'

he informed her. 'Tell your friend, here, to collect her belongings. Anything she leaves inside, she will forfeit.'

Dafni heaved a great breath and got slowly to her feet. *'Nein,'* she said firmly, though her lips quivered.

With a sigh, the German cocked his pistol and pushed it against Dafni's head.

'Stop!' Katerina screamed. 'She doesn't mean it, she doesn't understand. Dafni,' she begged, 'do as they say. You can come to live with me. Please!'

The German officer growled a warning, which the soldier translated.

'He is going to count to three,' he said, and there was a pleading edge to his tone that hadn't been there before. Katerina tried to reach Dafni, but it was as if the older woman was set in stone.

'Eins, zwei . . .'

'No!' Katerina grabbed General Wolff's arm in desperation. He wheeled around and almost fell, righting himself on one of the men who hurried forward. Katerina found herself pinned against the wall of Dafni's house, the German's gloved hand around her throat. Spittle landed on her cheeks as he roared at her. She could not understand the words, though knew what he meant to do.

Her mind went helplessly to Stefanos. If this were to be her final moment, she wanted to spend it thinking of him. She closed her eyes, allowed her body to go limp. Her arms dropped to her sides, the flame inside her doused by terror.

Dafni began to scream.

Katerina made herself look. The older woman was being restrained by the soldiers, shouting that she would do as they asked, that she was sorry, that if they must shoot someone, let it be her, not this innocent girl.

The pressure around her throat was increasing. Katerina's vision clouded with dark shapes and she gasped, trying in vain to breathe past the man's clawing fingers.

The end must surely be soon.

Then, suddenly, there was air. Clean and sweet and rushing into her lungs.

The General fell to his knees. Behind him stood Chrysí, her head down and her front hooves firmly planted. Coughing and spluttering through her tears, Katerina crawled away from her captor. The German was back on his feet within seconds, the faces of the other soldiers a mix of veiled shock and amusement. Katerina stumbled, rolling onto her back only to launch herself up with a raw, splintering cry.

Too late.

Another crack rang out across the hillside. Birds took flight in a flurry of wings.

The body of the little goat landed with barely a sound, her life draining out into the dirt.

41

It began with a low growl beneath the floor.

Within seconds, the roar was deafening.

A sudden, sharp lurch rippled through the house. Skye's legs buckled, slamming her against the oven. She hit the tiles hard. Across the room, her mother's eyes locked with hers, wide with terror.

The walls groaned. The picture Joy had given her fell with a crash, splinters of glass shooting in all directions. Tea splashed, crockery burst, shards skittered like bullets.

Skye grabbed her mother's arm and dragged her beneath the table, their knees knocking as they crouched together in the small space.

Her heart pounded against her ribs.

There was no sign of Martyn.

The ground shifted again, and the windows rattled violently in their frames.

A loud crack split the air like a gunshot. Skye whimpered and pressed her palms to the floor. She tried to count, to focus, but the numbers slid away. A chair toppled, a vase shattered, and metal clattered as the knives and forks jumped in their pot.

Then came a low, guttural moan, unmistakeably male, followed by a crash from upstairs so thunderous that it shook the walls.

The house was going to fall in on them.

Skye bit back a sob as her mum shuffled closer.

'It'll be OK,' Cassandra said. 'It's only an earthquake. It won't go on much longer.'

Even as she spoke, the rocking slowed, softened, stopped. Silence came, eerie and still. Not peace, but the breath before a scream.

'Are you all right?' Skye whispered.

'I'm fine,' her mother replied, though her skin was pale and had taken on a waxy sheen.

'I need to find Martyn,' Skye said. She crawled out from under the table, her knee finding the broken glass.

Swearing, she staggered upright and saw a pair of feet through the open kitchen doorway. Martyn. He had fallen and was not moving.

Skye reached him just as the front door flew open. Andreas staggered in, chest heaving and eyes wild, scanning the room as if scared of what he'd find.

Skye said his name, and he found her, relief turning quickly to confusion as his gaze shifted to the still figure on the floor.

'*Ela*, who is—'

Martyn groaned. He brought a hand up to his head, wincing as his fingers made contact.

'Don't move,' Skye said, kneeling beside him. 'You might've hurt your neck.'

'My ankle,' he said weakly. He attempted to raise his chin only to cry out in pain.

Andreas came closer and stood for a moment before crouching by Martyn's feet.

'I am not a doctor,' he said, 'but the ankle appears to be broken.'

Martyn set his jaw. Despite all the bullying, and the threats, and the coercive control, Skye experienced a pang of sympathy. Nobody deserved to be in pain, not even him.

'What's happened?' Her mother stepped unsteadily into the room. 'Dear God. Martyn, are you all right?'

The shift in Andreas's expression was slight. To anyone else, it might have gone unnoticed. Skye looked at his strong hands. No rings. No sign at all that promises had been made, vows exchanged.

He was not going to ask her.

She would have to tell him.

'Andreas, this is my mum, Cassandra.'

He nodded once, unsmiling.

'And this is Mar—.'

'Her husband,' Martyn interrupted. 'And you're the bloke from the newspaper.'

Skye stilled him as he attempted to sit.

'Are you OK?' she asked Andreas. 'Not injured or—'

'*Ochi*,' he said shortly. 'There's nothing wrong with me. I was talking outside with Joy when we received the alert. Did you not get it?'

The message on the phone, the one she'd ignored. Before she could say as much, Martyn let out another moan.

'We need to call an ambulance,' her mother urged.

She fetched one of Skye's beautiful cushions from the seating area and eased it beneath Martyn's head.

'If we can move him to my truck, it will be better,' Andreas said. 'There is a medical centre in Chora. I will drive him there.'

'I'm sorry,' her mother interrupted. 'What was it you said you did?'

'I am a builder,' Andreas said. He certainly looked the part, in his splattered overalls.

'He did all the work on this house,' Skye told her. 'I'd have been lost without him.'

Andreas glanced at her, his expression unreadable. Was it hope? Forgiveness? Or just confusion? Skye couldn't tell. But then again, did she really know him at all?

Martyn shuffled up on his elbows only to howl in pain. There was blood on the cushion, more congealing in a sticky patch on the back of her husband's head.

'He might be concussed,' she said. 'We shouldn't wait any longer. Mum, can you go and grab a towel from upstairs? You'll know where – there's only one bathroom.'

'You are shaking,' Andreas said.

Skye tensed, her breath catching as he gathered her hands and squeezed them.

'I'm just in shock,' she said. 'The earthquake. I've never—It was scary. Thank God for your steel supports.'

A smile tugged at the corners of Andreas's mouth. 'All the houses here are OK,' he said. 'All but one.'

'Some help here,' Martyn barked.

Skye jumped, pulling her hands away.

'Sorry,' she said automatically. Obedience borne from habit, sustained by self-preservation. Somewhat reluctantly, Andreas got to his feet. They each took one of Martyn's arms, slowly hoisting him upright. His skin had taken on a grey tinge and felt clammy to the touch.

'Do not put any weight on the foot,' Andreas warned, as Cassandra appeared on the stairs.

'It's a bit of a mess up there,' she said, handing over a towel. 'A section of your wall has fallen through along the landing. It looks to me as if there was already a gap there. The bricks appear to be missing behind the plaster.'

Skye looked at Andreas and saw the same question waiting in his eyes.

'Can we get on with it?' Martyn hissed. 'I'm rather in need of some pain relief.'

They headed outside, Martyn hobbling between them.

'*Perimene*,' Andreas said, when they reached the boundary wall. He fished his keys from his overalls pocket and ran to fetch his truck.

'You two seem cosy,' Martyn grunted. 'Did he even know you're married, or have you been lying to your new *community* about that as well?'

Skye ignored him, though she couldn't disregard the sickness that washed over her. She had lied, outrightly and by omission, and even though she'd had a valid reason for doing so, it still didn't feel right, had never sat right with her. When her friends learned the truth, would they ever trust her again? Would Andreas?

'I asked you a question,' Martyn persisted.

The mask was beginning to slip.

He was angry and getting angrier.

Skye started to reply, but her mother cut across her.

'You're in no fit state to be having this kind of conversation, Martyn,' she said briskly. 'Let's get you patched up first, shall we, then we can all sit down and talk properly later?'

The truck pulled up. Andreas got out and helped Skye ease Martyn into the backseat. Victoria and Adam had come out into their front yard. Both looked shell-shocked but were otherwise unscathed.

'This is my mum,' Skye told them. 'Can she stay with you while I go to the medical centre?'

'Of course,' Victoria said. 'The electrics are still functioning, thank God. I'll make us a pot of green tea.'

'Before you go,' her mother said, hurrying towards the passenger side of the truck, 'I found this upstairs, near where the wall collapsed. I know it's not yours – or I presume it isn't. Anyway,' she said, pressing something cool and hard into Skye's palm, 'best you take it. Maybe hide it somewhere?'

'Hide it?' Skye asked. 'Why would I need to do that?'

Andreas put the truck in gear and they began to move away.

Skye glanced down at her hand. The object was a medal. Silver, with rounded edges. One side bore the motif of an eagle, talons curled around a wreath of leaves, while the other showed a three-columned building.

Above it, carved deeply into the metal, was a symbol that turned her blood to ice.

A swastika.

42

It was a clean break.

Martyn sat in mutinous silence as the doctor patiently took him and Skye through a series of X-rays, explaining that the ankle would need to be cast, and that crutches would be provided. His head injury was superficial, although concussion had not been ruled out.

'If you take him home, you must watch him closely,' the doctor told Skye. 'Any dizziness or nausea, the room going into a spin, anything like this, then you must quickly return.'

'*Entáxei*,' she murmured, the Greek coming through naturally. 'I mean sure, yes, of course.'

Andreas made a small noise of appreciation from the corner of the room. He had insisted on accompanying them, and ignored Martyn's terse mutter of 'for God's sake' that followed.

The medical centre was crowded with the walking wounded. Rather than allowing them to wait in the examination room, Skye and the two men were ushered back to the small waiting area, Martyn thoroughly disgruntled to be pushed there in a wheelchair.

'They are saying that the earthquake measured over five points on the Richter Scale,' Andreas said. He was staring down at his phone, brow furrowed. 'There have been some landfalls in the north of the island, a few buildings damaged around the port.'

'Not your house?' Skye checked. He smiled briefly.

'*Ela*, no. That one, I reinforced myself.'

Martyn said nothing, merely continued to scowl into the middle distance. Skye studied his profile. So much about him was familiar, and yet she didn't know the man beside her, had never really known him at all. The version he'd charmed her with was not the same one she'd married, nor the monster that man had swiftly become. Martyn's crow's feet had deepened, and there was more salt than pepper in his dark hair. She had teasingly asked him once if he dyed it and been met with a stony silence.

'I wouldn't care if you did,' she'd said, hurrying to repair the damage. 'I quite like grey hair on men. In fact—'

'I'd quit while you're ahead, if I were you,' he'd snapped, the meanness in his tone coming as a shock. 'Didn't anyone ever teach you that if you don't have anything nice to say, then it's better to say nothing at all?'

She hadn't meant to offend him, and meekly told him so, but Martyn had taken her remark and stewed on it, bringing it up time and time again. It came to a point where Skye herself began to second-guess her recollection of the conversation. Had she deliberately set out to goad him? Was she really as bad a person as he claimed?

'How long does it take to get a goddamn cast done?' Martyn said, addressing no one in particular.

Skye went to reply, only to think better of it, though Andreas had no such restraint.

'There has been an earthquake,' he said. 'There are many people injured, and this is not a hospital. We are on a small island and the resources we have here are limited. Everybody must wait their turn.'

Martyn's neck flushed puce, his lips twitching with what Skye recognised as fury.

'This is going to put me out of action for weeks,' he complained. 'Perhaps even months. I have a full roster of flights booked. I can't very well honour those now, can I?'

Andreas exhaled long enough to count to ten.

'Can I perhaps make an observation?' he said, crossing his legs at the ankles. He was in his thick-soled boots, the laces knotted tight around the bottom of his overalls. 'It appears, to me, that you are not a man who has been told "no" very much in your life. This is not a good thing. We cannot always have what we want exactly when we want it. A good man, a patient man,' he went on, 'understands this, and does not blame other people.'

'I think in this case,' Martyn replied cuttingly, 'the blame can be fairly laid at Skye's feet.'

'You think so?' Andreas scratched behind his ear.

'The only reason I'm on this provincial lump of an island is to collect what is rightfully mine.' Martyn's attention switched to Skye, who shifted on the hard plastic seat. An elderly man with a nasty gash on his cheek limped in and made his way to the reception desk, a teenage girl hurrying after him.

'*Ela re, koúkla*,' she heard him say to the girl, as she fussed around him. '*Eímai entáxei.*'

Skye's father had fallen a few times in the months leading up to his death, the worst incident resulting in a trip to the emergency department. Ten stitches and a strict warning from the doctor not to drink so excessively. It was a plea echoed by Skye, which had been roundly ignored. She should have intervened, done more, moved back in with her parents if necessary – though she hadn't. Work had been time-consuming, her life a merry-go-round of chores, admin, and snatches of respite time. It had all felt vital then, but nothing should've mattered more than her father. When the phone had rung on that awful day and she'd seen her mother's name on the screen, Skye had known. She'd just *known*.

Andreas leaned forward. His expression had hardened. Martyn was the taller of the two, though her Greek friend was heavier, broader, stronger.

'A person cannot belong to another,' he said.

Martyn scoffed. 'Who said I'm here for her?'

Skye sat up a fraction higher. 'For God's sake,' she interrupted.

Martyn turned to her. He looked almost bored, as if he hadn't spent the past few weeks sending threatening emails, stalking her best friend at her place of work, and wheedling his way into her mother's sympathies. *Of course* he was here for her.

'What?' Martyn asked. 'It's the truth. I don't want you. As a matter of fact, I'm beginning to wish we'd never met.'

Skye let out a short, broken laugh. 'I can assure you that the feeling is one hundred per cent mutual,' she said.

'However,' Martyn said acidly, deflating the small bubble of triumph that had bloomed within Skye, 'the truth is, you have something of mine, and I would like it back.'

She looked away, stared hard at the opposite wall, with its posters showing various skin rashes and instructional diagrams for washing your hands. The Greek letters swam as she fought the tremble in her bottom lip. From beside her, she heard Martyn emit a small huff.

'When you chose to steal from me, you really left me with no choice,' he said.

Andreas's phone began to ring and he stood, the mobile in his hand, seemingly torn.

'It's OK,' Skye told him. 'You should answer it.'

Andreas tapped the screen, and bringing the phone to his ear, he said, '*Nai. Perimene.*'

'Go,' she said. 'It's fine, honestly.'

His eyes flicked back to hers. 'I will be outside,' he said, then, turning to Martyn, 'I will stay close – and do not worry,' he added, with a look at Skye, 'I know that he is lying. *Ela*, you are not a thief.'

He'd gone before she could muster a reply, though what could she say? On this occasion, Martyn was telling the truth. She had stolen from him, there was no point in denying it any more.

'Mr Lockhart?' A nurse had appeared in the doorway that led through to the examination rooms. When she saw that Martyn was in a wheelchair, she came towards them.

Skye didn't wait, she fled, out through the door and into the street beyond, her heart a frantic drum, the heat slamming into her like a wall.

Andreas was a few feet away. She could tell at once that something was seriously wrong. His eyes were fixed, features pinched, lips pulled into a tight line.

'What's happened?' she asked, putting a hand on his shoulder. 'What is it?'

Andreas blinked, as if he barely recognised her, and then his face crumpled. 'Karolos,' he said, so wretchedly that Skye stepped back.

'Your neighbour?' she said. 'The old man with the dog?'

He nodded once, teeth biting down hard on his lip. 'His house,' he began, swearing as a tear slid across his cheek. Skye felt his torment as keenly as if it had been her own, though there was little she could do other than be there, stand with him while he struggled to make sense of this new, unfathomable tragedy.

'I knew it was no longer safe,' he said, his voice low

and urgent, the words infused with grief. 'I should have insisted that he let me do the work.'

'Did he—' Skye began. 'Did the earthquake . . . ?'

Andreas swallowed. A second tear chased after the first. '*Nai*,' he said simply, sadly. 'Karolos was inside when it happened.' His eyes met Skye's. 'He is dead.'

43

'I'm so sorry.'

Skye reached for Andreas's hand, her fingers wrapping around the phone that was still clasped in it. There was a crack in the bottom corner of the screen, his wallpaper image one of two young boys on a beach, smiles wide and hair wet. It could only be him and the brother he'd lost.

Martyn didn't have any photographs of his late sister, Beatrice. His mother had thrown them out, he told her, when they drove over to his parents' Richmond house together for the first time; it would be better for all involved if she didn't mention the subject. A strange way of coping with death, but then, who was she to judge? Grief was perhaps the most unique and singular emotion, more so even than love.

'It is my fault,' Andreas mumbled.

'No,' Skye said, 'you mustn't think like that.'

There was a set of wide stone steps leading up to the second floor of the medical centre, and she led him towards them.

'Sit down for a moment, you're shaking.'

Andreas sat, knees bent and face in hands. Skye crouched in front of him.

'Nobody can ever be blamed for an earthquake,' she began. Andreas wasn't listening. He talked across her, muttering Greek she couldn't follow.

'I must go.' He got to his feet. 'But will you be able to get back to Ano Meria?'

'Don't worry,' she said. 'I'll call Dusty, or Victoria. I'm sure one of them will drive over here and collect us. If not, I'll find a taxi. You go.'

He strode away before stopping and turning back to her. 'There are things I must say,' he said. 'To you. I—'

'It's OK.' Skye tried for a smile. 'There will be time. Later.'

After he'd gone, she sat down on the steps, watching as dazed-looking tourists filed quietly along the narrow lane. The earthquake had shaken loose a cascade of red petals from a nearby tree, scattering them across the pale-grey stones and whitewashed walls like drops of blood. That death had visited this beautiful place felt abhorrent, though of course, the island was no stranger to tragedy. Skye's thoughts, as they so often did these days, strayed to the past. To Katerina. She felt a connection to the woman that went beyond the house itself, as if a part of her still lingered. Perhaps it did. There were the letters, the bones, and now – Skye slipped a hand into her bag and withdrew the silver medal – there was something else. A new clue. Who had the Nazi decoration belonged to? And how had it ended up hidden in a hollow space in her wall?

There hadn't been time to discuss it with Andreas – or even show him. They'd both been too preoccupied with Martyn. Her husband was a different kind of enemy to those Katerina must have encountered, but he was an opponent, nonetheless. She'd built him up to giant-like proportions, but in the end, the threat of his arrival had turned out to be far more terrifying than the man himself. He hadn't changed, but she had.

She drew in a steadying breath, warm and peppered with dust, then stood and walked back into the medical centre. There was no sign of Martyn, and no available seats. Instead, Skye leaned back against the wall, the hairs on her arms rising in the chill of the air-conditioning. When her husband finally emerged, he was on crutches, injured left foot swaddled in a cast.

'I need to find a pharmacy,' he grumbled, hobbling towards her. 'They've prescribed something for the pain.'

'How bad is it?' she asked.

'Well, I've suffered a non-displaced ankle fracture,' he replied sardonically. 'So probably unlikely to be doing any cartwheels. It bloody hurts, if you must know, although I suppose that pleases you.'

'Not at all.'

'Where's El Greco gone?' he said, huffing in irritation as he attempted to manoeuvre his bandaged foot through the open door.

'If you mean Andreas,' Skye said, 'he had somewhere else to be.'

'Managed to unhook himself from the elastic of your knickers, did he?'

Skye glared at him.

Martyn was panting at the effort of having made it out into the lane. The cut on the back of his head had been glued, a patch of dark hair neatly shaved away. It didn't please her at all to see him in this state, though nor did Skye experience much in the way of pity. Her days of caring about him had long since passed.

'I'll need to call one of my friends to pick us up, but we'll have to walk back to the outskirts of town again. Do you think you can make it that far or—'

'Of course I can,' he bit back, only to wince as he stubbed his injured foot against one of the crutches. He refused her offer of help, sweat leaking into his eyes as they made their slow way through Chora. Many of the shopkeepers were busy redressing window displays that had presumably been damaged by the earthquake. Had the mini market in Ano Meria survived unscathed? Were the children OK? Iris and Ajax would likely have experienced tremors before, though for George, the experience must have been a frightening novelty.

She should be there with them, in the village. Not here, with him.

The distinctive green cross of a pharmacy came into view ahead. Skye left Martyn on a bench while she went inside with his prescription, collecting the drugs and buying two bottles of Coke at the same time.

'I thought we could both use some sugar,' she said, unscrewing the cap.

Martyn took a long sip, suppressed a belch, then looked at her.

'The Rolex,' he said. 'I need it back.'

Wind whipped along the alleyway in a whistling screech.

'I don't have it,' she said.

Martyn sat back, brows heavy above narrowed eyes. 'It didn't very well up and leave the house on its own, did it? Try again.'

The mocking tone, that phrase he'd thrown at her so many times before: *'This wine you bought is no good, try again'*; *'Your outfit makes you look like a slut, try again'*; *'That apology sounded false, try again'*. Somewhere along the tumultuous path of their relationship, she had gone from being everything he'd ever wanted, to lacking in every conceivable way. By the time she fled, nothing Skye did was deemed acceptable, no matter how hard she tried. Martyn would not have stopped until he'd reduced her to nothing.

The incident that had convinced her to leave began with good intentions. It was a Friday evening, and Skye was in their open-plan kitchen, preparing a meal. She'd planned each element with great care, defrosting two Wagyu steaks that had been languishing in the freezer for weeks and serving them with garlic chips, chargrilled peppers and fresh greens from Epsom's fanciest deli. She dressed the table, setting out flowers, candles and the best crystal glasses before opening a bottle of vintage Barolo.

Martyn arrived home on the dot of seven.

'In here,' she called.

'What's all this?' Martyn pulled at the neck of his navy sweater as he came into the room and unfastened the top shirt button below. He had flown a music mogul and the man's various entourage over to Ireland that day – an 'easy enough hop', he'd told her, which was why Skye had felt confident in going all-out. Her husband was less liable to be in a bad mood when he'd only been required to travel short haul.

'This is dinner,' she said brightly, passing him a glass of the wine. 'Steak done the Japanese way, and there's even dessert. It's only chocolate mousse, but I made it myself. I know how you hate the shop-bought ones.'

'Where did the steaks come from?' he enquired, strolling towards where the pan was still sizzling.

An icicle slid down the length of Skye's spine. 'The freezer,' she said, as casually as she could. 'That's all right, isn't it?'

Martyn stared at her. 'I was saving those,' he said. 'For my father, remember? I promised him lunch after golf on Sunday.'

'I don't remember you mentioning it,' Skye said. 'I'm sure we can—'

She let out a yelp as Martyn threw his wine, the glass crashing against the cabinets and breaking into hundreds of pieces. Skye tried to run but he was on her in a second, dragging her up and pushing her back against the worktop. Clawing frantically behind her, Skye's fingers closed around something small and hard. She swung her arm around in desperation, only to miss. Martyn bellowed, knocking the object away. The small, patterned bowl skidded across the tiles, smashing apart as it hit the wall.

It was the last thing her dad had ever made for her.

A sudden fury surged through Skye. She screamed as loud as she could, writhing and shouting as Martyn forced her from the kitchen and up the stairs. There was a box room at the far end of the landing that he used as a gym, and having flung her inside, he slammed the door shut and bolted it from the outside.

Skye lay among the dumbbells, breathing hard, her sobs coming fast as his footfalls receded. There were scratches on her neck, her wrists sore to the touch. A whirring noise filtered up through the floorboards, followed shortly by the sound of Martyn returning. Skye pinned herself against the wall furthest from the door, turning her face away when he entered.

'Don't be like that,' he said. 'I have something for you.'

She flinched as he knelt before her, clutching a jug from the blender.

'Open wide,' he said, extending a spoon.

Skye stared in horror at the brown mush. 'What is it?'

'Well, it's dinner, obviously. I thought you were hungry.'

Skye shook her head violently. 'I don't want it.'

'Come on, now, this is expensive steak. The very best. We can't have it go to waste.'

'You're insane,' she hissed, and he smiled.

'Behave like a baby, and I'll treat you like a baby.'

'I'm not going to eat that, Martyn.'

'Oh, you will,' he said, pushing the spoon hard against her chin. 'Unless you want to spend the entire weekend locked in here.'

'I don't understand,' she pleaded. 'What did I do wrong? Why are you being like this?'

Martyn didn't reply. He held the spoon aloft, waiting for her sobs to cease.

'Do you want me to pretend it's an aeroplane?'

Two days later, Skye saw the story about the one-euro lottery.

Today, she faced the man who had become her tormentor.

'That's the thing, Martyn,' she said. 'I did try. But I'm done playing this game with you. You don't scare me, not any more.'

'What's that supposed to mean?' he said sourly.

Skye got up from the bench.

'There are plenty of hotels in Chora,' she said. 'I suggest you book into one of them.'

'Hang on a minute,' he said, grunting in pain as he struggled to stand. 'Where do you think you're going?'

'Me?' she said, her smile spreading with the sweet surety of what came next.

'I'm going home.'

44

Skye arrived back in Ano Meria as the day dipped towards evening. The light had grown mellow, the heat loosening its grip.

Her neighbours were assembled in a small huddle on the hillside. Joy hurried over to greet her, a flood of questions pouring from her lips.

'I met your mum'; 'I can't believe Martyn's here'; 'Where is he?'; 'Bloody hell'; 'Are you OK?'; 'Has he hurt you?'; 'Where's Andreas?'

Skye held up a hand to silence her.

'Sorry,' Joy babbled. 'I was on my way to look for you earlier when Andreas rolled up. He'd just got the alert, and we didn't have time to reach your place before the earthquake started.'

'There was an accident at the port,' Skye told her. 'One of Andreas's friends was killed.'

Joy's features clouded with sympathy.

'And Martyn is still in Chora. I told him to book into a hotel.'

'You did?' Joy brightened. 'Good on you, chook. I'm proud of you.'

'He was pretty pissed off,' Skye admitted. 'But

Martyn doesn't give up. He's not going to back off until he gets what he came for.'

'And what's that?' Joy asked, but Skye didn't get a chance to answer. The others were walking towards them. Victoria, still in her blue dress, and Adam, with his shirt unbuttoned to reveal a livid sunburn. Louisa stood pale and stiff, her arms wrapped around her middle. Beside her, Dusty bristled in her cement-spattered combats, fists clenched and eyes blazing. Theo rubbed at his temple, shoulders tense. George, by contrast, lit up the moment he saw Skye, bouncing from foot to foot and grinning like the proverbial cat.

'Where's Mia?' Skye asked.

Dusty and Louisa exchanged a strained look.

'She's with Bruno at the clinic,' Dusty said. 'Daft old thing was taking a snooze in the front yard when the quake hit and didn't so much as stir, not until part of the wall came down on him. He should be fine,' she added. 'Mia reckons it's a dislocation rather than a break, but she's not sure and—' She broke off as Louisa let out a sob.

'Sorry.' Louisa flapped her hand in front of her face. 'Ignore me. It's just that Bruno was our mum's dog and if anything were to happen to him . . .'

'He's in the best hands,' Joy said soothingly, patting Louisa on the back.

'Has anyone seen Tigri?' Skye asked. 'He was around earlier but ran away when—Before the earthquake.'

'Cats are resilient,' Joy said, cursing as she attempted to untangle her sunglasses from her windswept hair.

'He probably knew what was coming earlier than we did,' Victoria said. 'He'll show up soon enough.'

Skye smiled distractedly. Another figure was approaching, her pace smooth, unhurried.

She was still wearing the cream slacks and wide-brimmed straw hat she'd arrived in.

Victoria followed Skye's gaze. 'Oh, hey Cassandra.'

Her mother's expression remained carefully neutral. 'Hello, everyone,' she said, looking at each of the group in turn.

Skye made rapid, muttered introductions.

'What have you done with Martyn?' Cassandra asked.

'He decided to move to a hotel.'

'Who the hell is Martyn?' Dusty asked, glancing at Theo, who shrugged.

'Mum, you must be starving,' Skye said, her cheeks flaring. 'Let's go inside, shall we?'

They made it fewer than ten yards before George shot past them at speed, pursued by Theo.

'I just saw him, Dad. He's over here!'

'The cat,' Theo called as he passed them. 'We've been looking for him.'

They were heading straight towards the only house on the hillside yet to be claimed.

'If those two are going in there for a snoop, then so am I,' Joy exclaimed.

Dusty, Adam and Louisa murmured their agreement, but Victoria stood apart from them, her arms folded.

'Wait a sec, guys,' she said. 'We don't know that it's safe. We should wait for Andreas.'

'I vote we risk it,' Joy said. 'Dusty here can take charge, let us know if anything is on the verge of collapse over there.'

Skye hesitated. There was something undeniably enticing about the empty house. Not even Andreas had been granted access to it yet. She had already crept around its perimeter on several occasions, trying in vain to peer through the boarded windows. Both the front and back doors were padlocked, so it was unlikely that Tigri had managed to get inside.

'You don't have to come,' she said to her mother.

'What, and miss all the fun?' Her brows lifted slightly. 'What was it your father used to say? Nae chance, lassie.'

The sweetness of the remark disarmed Skye, and she managed only a nod. The two of them fell into step behind the others.

'I might run back for my camera,' Adam said.

'Why don't you just get the damn thing surgically attached?' Victoria said snippily.

'Oh dear,' Cassandra said in an undertone to Skye. 'I see it isn't only the earthquake causing cracks to appear today . . .'

'Mum,' Skye hissed, increasing her pace. 'They'll hear you.'

'I'm only saying what I see.'

It was one of her go-to lines. Skye had grown up hearing it on repeat.

'Your mam's only a nitpicker because she cares,' her dad would say. Skye disagreed. The 'cruel to be kind' persona her mother had cultivated had always baffled her. Why, if you truly cared about someone, would you go out of your way to tear them down? It made no sense.

They reached the empty house and paused outside. It was single-storey, with dirt-streaked once-white walls. Two front windows were set between the entrance and a built-in nook, where a pile of rotten logs was stacked. Unlike the other dwellings on the hillside, there was also a terrace area with open sides, and a wood-panelled roof that had long since been eroded by the elements.

Joy tried the front door. 'Locked,' she said, over the rattle of the padlock.

'We're back here,' Theo called, sticking his head around the side of the house. 'You're not going to believe what we've found.'

Dusty went first. Skye picked her way over cracked pots and shrubbery, offering her mum a hand as they scaled the low wall that encircled the rear garden. There was Tigri, nonchalantly washing himself in the shade of a fallen lime tree. A large hole had opened up below the exposed roots and George was peering into it, eyes wide behind his glasses.

'The earthquake must have felled it,' Theo said. 'It was still standing the last time I came this way.'

'What's down there?' Louisa asked. Skye had a feeling she already knew. Another grave, it had to be. She took a moment to prepare herself, though her mother had no such qualms. Crouching beside George, Cassandra let out a low whistle.

'Definitely human,' she said with authority. 'And looks to be intact.'

'No way.' Adam tripped in his haste to take a photo, and Skye hurried out of shot.

Not that it mattered much any more.

'We'd better call the police,' Louisa said, though she made no move to do so.

'I'll do it then, shall I?' Victoria said, stalking off in the direction of the house.

'Dad,' George piped up, 'when the police have finished looking at the skeleton, do you think they'll let us keep the skull?'

Theo took his glasses off and rubbed at his eyes. 'Probably not,' he said evenly. 'I don't think you should get your hopes up on that one.'

Skye moved closer to the grave. What was it Andreas had told her? That a body should be buried with its feet facing east. Taking out her phone, she switched on the compass function, moving until the dial was pointing in the right direction. That was strange. This person, whoever it was, had been positioned facing not east but northwest. She didn't pause. Her thumb hovered for only a second before it tapped Andreas's name.

He should know about this; be kept in the loop.

But Andreas didn't answer. She hung up before the voicemail could finish, stowing her phone as Victoria rejoined the group.

'The cops can't get here until tomorrow,' she said.

'They told me to make sure the grave is covered up, and that nobody should touch the bones.'

'Fine by me,' Dusty said. She already had her hands in her pockets.

'We can use the old tarp at mine,' Skye said. 'I'll go and fetch it.'

Nobody had been into the house while she was in Chora. The kitchen was still a disaster area, the bloodstained cushion abandoned on the floor where Martyn had fallen.

Instead of going straight into the garden, Skye went upstairs and was immediately confronted by a pile of rubble. The hollow where part of the landing wall had fallen in was a little above head height. Skye stood on her tiptoes and felt around inside.

There was something there. More letters, perhaps?

She stretched further, her fingers closing around a small, lightweight bundle. It came free easily. The pouch was made from coarse sacking cloth, its top tightly cinched with twine. Hands clumsy with anticipation, Skye worked at the knot then slowly eased it open, tipping the contents into her other hand. There were two items: a gold cross pendant on a fine chain, and a slim, rectangular metal tag, around the size of a matchbox.

Skye squinted at the inscription. There were a series of numbers, below which was punched a name: MUTI, GIULIO. Not German, like the swastika-stamped medal, but Italian. A dog tag. Could both have belonged to an occupying soldier? And if so, why had they been hidden here, sealed inside her wall?

Her phone began to vibrate. Skye slipped the items back into their pouch, her heart lifting as she saw Andreas's name.

'You called me,' he said.

'I did,' she agreed. 'I probably shouldn't have. I know you're busy.'

'I am with the police.'

'Oh. Is everything—Are you all right?'

'It is not the best time to talk now,' he said. 'But you are well?'

'I'm fine,' she said, the words sounding empty. 'How about you – are you OK?'

'*Ela*, I have to go.'

'Of course. Sorry, I—'

But Andreas had already hung up.

45

September 1941

Katerina was beginning to show.

In war, she had learned, possessions were no longer something that belonged to you. They could be taken at any time and frequently were, the occupiers on her island grasping always for more. Precious jewellery was traded for bags of grain, animals taken and slaughtered to fill the bellies of an idle army, families ripped from their homes with only the clothes on their backs.

It was for these reasons that Katerina did not wish to share the news of her pregnancy. The baby was hers, and it was Stefanos's. She cherished the comfort of knowing their child was there, growing inside her. A secret she must keep for as long as possible, even from those closest. Though in a community where food was scarce and becoming more so, the protrusion of her stomach would not go unnoticed for much longer. Katerina was, for once, eager to bid farewell to the summer. She looked forward to cooler days that would warrant thicker layers of clothing.

Life had settled into a routine of sorts, one which saw her rise each day before the dawn. She and Leni had so far been permitted to keep their one remaining goat, though the soldiers were first in line when it came to any milk the nanny produced. The bakery was still open, though Leni prepared only the most basic breads, substituting ingredients and adjusting the size of loaves so that everyone could get their fair share. Katerina ate more for the life inside her than to satiate her own hunger. She foraged for wild herbs as she wandered the hillsides, scouring the edges of walls for fallen fruit.

Leni barely seemed to take a morsel.

'There are others who need it more than me,' she would say, nibbling half-heartedly at a tomato. 'Many who do not have my health or youth.'

The school in Chora had been closed, its building taken over as a military barracks. Leni, having sought permission from the officer in charge of their village, had converted the grain store at the rear of her house into a classroom. The island's children were welcome to come and go as they pleased, encouraged to read, or draw, or merely escape the watchful eyes of their captors for a few hours each day. Katerina was no scholar, though she was able to teach the basics of farming, while Dafni took care of the rest. When she was not tending to her oven, Leni also helped.

'The children give me a purpose,' she told Katerina. 'When I am around them, watching them play, it does not feel as though we are at war.'

Their small school did not draw only the young

inhabitants of the village. Ingrid, the wife of the General who had so callously murdered Chrysí, would often come to stand in the doorway, her slim arms clasped and head bowed. She did not attempt to speak to them, which was just as well. Katerina could not abide the idea of having to exchange pleasantries with such a woman. She was living in Dafni's house, had wriggled inside it as a maggot would into a wound – yet somehow, their neighbour had made peace with her presence.

'Look at her,' she said to both sisters one afternoon, when Ingrid had materialised in her usual place. 'She is a broken soul. There is no hate in her heart. It is her husband who is to blame, not this waif who moves around as if she has already passed over.'

'You pity her?' Katerina muttered, eyes narrow and indignant.

Dafni sighed. 'I pity any woman who has been abandoned by a man that promised to look after her,' she said. 'I pity her as I pity us.'

'There is a difference,' Katerina said cuttingly, 'between men who choose to leave and those who are given no choice. Her husband, that *téras*' – she snarled the word – 'is an invader. He dragged his wife here with him for no other reason than his own stupid pride and selfishness. Why bring her at all if he was planning to rejoin the fight on the mainland?'

'I have heard that she was a nurse,' Dafni said. 'Travelling with the German army to tend to the injured soldiers. Something bad must have happened to bring her here. It is not usual for the wives of fighting men to accompany their husbands.'

'I do not know what to think about her,' Leni said. 'But I am glad he is gone. My sister is right, that man is a monster.'

'A monster that Ingrid chooses to love,' Katerina pointed out. 'That is why she will never receive any pity from me.'

When she was not required at the school or bakery, and the few chores she had were complete, Katerina concentrated on what she and the exiled brothers had come to refer to as pollinating. Some days, this simply meant collecting morsels of food in secret, ready to transport to the mountains, while on others, she passed messages between men on other parts of the island, some of whom were hiding, others that were protected by their profession.

In the months since Stefanos had left, she had helped Atlas and Zephyr build a radio by carrying each separate component to them, disguised within the carcass of a maza loaf, or strapped against her body below the folds of her skirt. The patrolling Italian soldiers took pleasure in stopping anyone they happened across on the roads and pathways – especially if it happened to be a lone female. Katerina had been subjected to their filthy pawing hands on more occasions than she could bear to recount, though she was careful not to complain. Battles had to be chosen wisely, and each time she walked away having got another item of contraband past them, it was with her head held high.

A lot of the men were barely men at all, their faces pocked with adolescent acne, downy fluff where a moustache should be. They did not frighten her.

Others did, older lieutenants with mean eyes, ready fists and belligerent smiles. Of the five assigned to Ano Meria, three were of the first kind and two like the second – including the man who had leaned so nonchalantly against his gun while the general nearly strangled her. The men called him 'Lio' – a name Katerina associated with a lion – and he was every bit as predatory.

'Do not antagonise him,' Leni would hiss, whenever they emerged from the bakery to find him loitering in the lane outside. Lio had a pipe, not dissimilar to those Baba and his friends used. He kept it in his mouth, even when he wasn't smoking. Katerina had come to loathe hearing the soft clack of it against his teeth almost as much as she hated the cold, shark-like stare he fixed on her.

'*Signorina*,' he would say to each of them, in the kind of mocking tone that made Katerina want to spit into the dirt. On every occasion, Leni smiled, replying with a timid '*kalispera*'. Katerina refused to engage. Why should she greet the enemy as if he were a friend? To do so would not only dishonour her husband, but her country. Lio did not take kindly to her indifference. The more she ignored him, the more it seemed to fuel his desire to pursue her, to prod her, to taunt her with crude remarks.

'When Stefanos returns to me, that man will be sorry for what he has said,' Katerina brooded.

It was always 'when', never 'if'. Neither she nor Leni had heard from their respective husbands, though it did not mean they hadn't tried. The Greek postal service had been all but cancelled on the mainland and was non-existent out among the islands. Everyone was aware that the flow of information was being strictly controlled by the occupying forces.

'How will we know if something has happened to them?' Leni fretted.

'I would know if Stefanos had been killed,' Katerina said. 'My heart would tell me.'

On the final Sunday of the calendar month, Katerina was making her way down from the mountains several hours later than planned. She had gone that morning with a food package, arriving worn out and dehydrated to discover a group of newcomers at the cave.

'Do not worry,' Zephyr said, as he hurried to greet her. 'These people are with us. They are part of the resistance.'

Three men she did not recognise, all young, and a woman of around her own age.

A woman, alone with five men?

Katerina was shocked into momentary silence at the sight of her. She said nothing until Atlas approached, embracing her warmly while his brother unwrapped the parcels.

'There is not enough here,' Zephyr said, turning to her. 'We need more.'

'There is not enough anywhere,' Katerina told him, aggravated by his tone, by the hovering flies, by the tenderness in her breasts. 'The blockade has not moved, and no food has reached the island for many months. I told you this.'

Zephyr went to argue but his brother silenced him with a look.

'We understand,' Atlas assured her. 'And we are grateful to you. I know you risk a lot, coming up here.'

The woman stepped forwards. 'Selena,' she said. 'I am a bee, the same as you.'

'In Chora?' Katerina asked.

'All across the island, but yes, mostly in Chora. I can speak Italian,' Selena explained. 'I hear what they say about us, how they wish to defile us. To them, we are common peasants, though they underestimate us at their peril. The soldiers' lips grow looser each day, and the wind blows secrets from these men as easily as it spreads seeds for harvest. Their bravado and arrogance will destroy them,' she added with malicious relish.

An hour later, when Katerina was preparing to leave, Atlas drew her to one side.

'If you see Selena in the town, or by the port, you must not acknowledge her,' he said. 'Do you understand, Kat? Not even if you think she's in danger.'

'I will always help my friends,' she said, only to fall silent as an image of Chrysí appeared in her mind. She had buried the brave little goat in her garden, her neat hooves pointing east, where she would be greeted each morning by the sun. She looked back at Atlas and nodded. 'I understand.'

The way he had elicited that promise from her roused a suspicion in Katerina. She mulled it over as she crept down the hillside in the near darkness. Could it be that Atlas had developed feelings for Selena? She was certainly brave, and beautiful too, with all that wavy hair the colour of tamarisk bark and those piercingly blue eyes. The idea of anyone finding love amid the horror of war made her limbs feel lighter somehow, and as Katerina rounded the corner that would lead her home, she broke into a skip.

'*Buonasera, signorina.*'

A dark shape emerged from the shadows and Katerina staggered sideways, a scream escaping her lips. Lio removed his pipe from between his teeth and considered her. It was past curfew – long past it. Katerina did her best to dredge up a smile.

'*Buonasera, signore,*' she said, hoping her use of Italian would appease him.

Lio came slowly towards her. She saw the glint of something gold at his throat as he extended a languid finger into her basket.

'It is sage,' she told him, 'for eating.'

When he didn't immediately respond, Katerina lifted a bunch and made as if to eat them. The soldier cocked his head to the side, watching her, and then, with a ferocity that caused her to cry out, he knocked the basket from her hands and began to stamp on it, mashing the precious herbs into the ground beneath his boot. Katerina turned and fled, though she only got a few yards before he caught her, his arm snaking around her waist and pulling her roughly back against him. She became sharply aware of two things: the hard, unyielding shape of his pistol, and – far worse – the vile pressure of his arousal.

'Please,' she begged, first in Greek and then again in his native tongue. '*Per favore.*'

Lio ignored her. He dragged her off the pathway and over to a low wall, one hand creeping up to her throat, the other burrowing lower. She threw her head back, trying to smash it against his nose, but he dodged away. With a grunt, he removed his hand from between her legs and slapped her hard across the face.

Katerina reeled, momentarily stunned by his violence, and then she erupted. She clawed, and bit, and screamed. She tried everything she could to wrench herself free. Lio grabbed her left breast, squeezing it so hard that Katerina thought she would throw up. He had torn open her shirt and was attempting to raise her skirt, all the while hissing 'Shhh' into her ear. A light appeared in the window of a nearby house, a woman's voice shouted, 'Who is there? What is happening?'

Lio loosened his grip only a fraction, though it was enough for Katerina to break away from him. She fell onto her back, her ripped shirt gaping open, skirt pulled up around her thighs.

'*Bastardo!*' she yelled, aiming a kick at his ankle.

Lio stared down at her for a moment, then readied himself to retaliate. There was no time to run, to speak, even to think. It was pure instinct that wrapped her arms around her stomach. Nothing mattered more in that moment than the precious cargo growing inside her.

Lio's boot struck her in the ribs. The next strike landed higher, smashing into her shoulder. The harder he kicked, the tighter she curled herself. On and on it went, blow after blow, until at last, panting with effort, he slid down against the wall.

Katerina watched through a haze of pain as he removed a pouch of tobacco from his pocket, the scent of it bringing with it an image of Stefanos.

The corners of her mouth lifted. She tasted blood.

Smoke clouded the air. The Italian sucked his pipe, regarding her with what – disgust, amusement? Katerina did not care. He had beaten yet not beat her. She said nothing as he continued to stare, nor did she move or look away. Eventually, with a bored-sounding sigh, Lio got to his feet and spat in the dirt where she lay.

'*Puttana*,' he said, almost regretfully, as if by being pregnant, blessed in the purest and most natural of ways a woman could be, she had become a disappointment.

Katerina knew, then, what she must do. The truth struck her with such clarity that she whispered the words, sending them off into the wind as a promise.

'*I will kill you.*'

46

Skye stared down at the tarpaulin.

The wind had picked up, tugging at its corners, the plastic snapping softly against the rocks that held it in place.

The mood amongst those gathered around her was one of excitement, as Theo and Dusty traded ideas about who was in the grave, and how they'd ended up there.

'It could be an Ottoman pirate,' he suggested.

'Or his wench!' she chimed in.

'I think it's a time traveller,' George said. 'Someone from the year 2050. Maybe they came here and got stuck? Or someone in the olden days saw their futuristic clothes and got so scared that they killed them.'

'Brilliant idea,' Adam enthused. 'What do you think, Vic? Time traveller, pirate or wench?'

Victoria looked up from where she had been scrolling on her phone. 'I think this game is dumb,' she said.

Skye caught Louisa's eye. They exchanged a quick, awkward smile, then Louisa turned away, tucking a loose strand of red hair behind her ear.

'It's getting late,' Skye said to no one in particular.

She hadn't shown the pouch to the others yet, nor what was hidden inside it. A quick online search had returned numerous matches for the name Giulio Muti, though nothing relating either to wartime, or any person missing since. Could the bones beneath the tarpaulin belong to him? Or was the Italian linked in some way to the remains that had been uncovered in her own garden? She must read more of Katerina's correspondence, scour the letters for clues.

George began to yawn widely.

'Come on,' Theo said, putting his arm around his son's shoulders.

Mia pulled up in Dusty's truck as they were walking back to their respective houses, a comatose Bruno beside her on the front seat.

'How is the poor little mite?' Joy asked.

'His back paw is fractured,' Mia said, her voice strained.

Theo offered to help her carry the dog inside, and Joy looked on, wringing her hands.

'What a bloody day it's been,' she said. 'I'm ready for a beer. Anyone else?'

'I'm afraid we can't,' Cassandra cut in before Skye had a chance to reply. 'My daughter and I have things we need to discuss.'

Darkness was closing in. The moon shone bright in a cloudless sky, while far beyond, the sea churned, silvery-black beyond the hillside.

'I sent Martyn a message.'

Skye froze in the process of unlocking her front door. 'Saying what?'

'Telling him to come back here.'

'What?' Skye drew back, as if the words had struck her. 'Why would you do that?'

'He has a suspected concussion,' Cassandra replied. 'It's not safe for him to spend the night alone. You'd never forgive yourself if something happened.'

'Well, I hope you're willing to sit up all night with him then,' Skye said, slamming the door behind them and going through into the main living area. 'Because I won't be.'

'You still haven't told me what all this is about,' her mother persisted. She removed her straw hat and held it in front of herself like a shield. 'According to Martyn, you gave him no prior warning. He says you simply upped and left in the middle of the night.'

Skye went into the kitchen. There was a dustpan and brush hanging from a hook by the back door, and she set about sweeping up the shards of broken glass and crockery. More smashed items, another scene of devastation. She had dealt with so many. Too many.

Her mother appeared in the archway, lips pursed.

'It wasn't the middle of the night,' Skye told her.

'You still left. Still treated him as if he was some kind of sordid one-night stand, rather than your husband.'

'I wish I had stopped at one night,' Skye retorted, tipping the contents of the dustpan into the bin. 'If I'd known what he was really like, I'd never have gone on a second date, let alone married him. It was the worst mistake of my life.'

Cassandra said nothing, her jaw tight, gaze pointed.

'I mean it, Mum. Martyn isn't the man you think he is.'

'Do you want to know what I thought when you introduced me to Martyn?'

Skye steeled herself.

'I thought, thank goodness. She's found a man who has his life in order, a man who will provide for her, who has the means and the maturity by which to do so. An adult, essentially.'

'But he—' Skye began.

'No, let me finish. Fact is, I fell for your dad because he was a dreamer. And that, well, that turned out to be *my* biggest mistake. You have no idea what it was like being married to a man like Cosmo. I know he could do no wrong in your eyes. But let me tell you, he did.'

Skye strode right past her mother without a word. Her body trembled, adrenaline radiating as she braced for the next blow.

'You need to hear this,' her mother called after her. 'The truth is hard to hear sometimes, but you can't keep on living in this pattern of denial and avoidance.'

The air caught in Skye's throat, her mouth falling open. She turned around.

'Nothing Dad did was ever good enough for you, was it? I was there, Mum. I saw it every day, saw the way you found fault with everything, correcting his grammar when he spoke, talking down to him as if he was a child. For God's sake. He was miserable – you made him miserable.'

Cassandra's eyes went wide, her nostrils flaring.

'I don't know why we're discussing Dad anyway,' Skye said, snatching the cushion off the floor. The blood from Martyn's head wound had stained right through the cover, and with a muttered curse, she threw it in the direction of the kitchen. 'He has nothing to do with me and Martyn. Dad never even knew him, more's the pity. If he had, I bet he'd have seen straight through him.'

'Straight through what?' her mother asked. She folded her arms, crushing the straw hat in the process. 'For Christ's sake – what has been going on with you two?'

Skye's shoulders sank. 'I don't know where to start,' she said wearily.

'Start with why you ran away; why you entered a lottery to win a house on a remote Greek island.'

'I needed to get away.'

'From what – Martyn? Because of his job? Were you lonely, is that it? I assumed he must have been unfaithful, but he's assured me that isn't the case.'

'And you take his word as gospel, do you?' Skye said.

Her mother bristled. 'His word was the only word I had. You had done a flit.'

Skye rubbed her temples. Only Cassandra MacKinnon could reduce what had been a desperate escape into something as whimsical as 'a flit'.

'OK,' she said, drawing in a breath. 'I entered the lottery because I wanted a place to run away to, somewhere Martyn wouldn't know to look. I had to leave because . . . because . . .'

Why was it so hard to say the words?

'I was lonely,' she said finally. 'But not in the way you think.'

Skye walked across to the built-in seating area and lowered herself down against the one remaining cushion. After a few moments, her mother followed.

When had they last done this? Sat together side by side? Never as adults. Skye had always gone to her dad. It was he who lent a sympathetic ear, ruffled her hair, pulled her close for a bear hug. Her mum had been there sometimes, but only ever on the periphery.

'I'm listening,' she said now, with such unexpected tenderness that Skye felt a lump rise in her throat.

'It's hard,' she began. 'Talking about it, about him.'

Her mother nodded slowly.

'Martyn was—He preferred keeping me all to himself. After I was made redundant, it got worse. I'd noticed a few things, and there was an incident one night, when he came home early and found me reading a magazine in the bath.'

Her mother leaned closer. 'A magazine?' she repeated. 'What's wrong with that?'

'Nothing,' Skye said, with a bitter-sounding laugh. 'But he took offence to it. We had an argument, a glass got broken, and, well, it was scary. *He* scared me. I put it down to stress, or him having a bad day, but honestly? That was me making excuses, hoping it was a one-off.'

'And wasn't it?' her mum asked.

Skye sighed deeply. 'No,' she said. 'It wasn't. He never actually hit me, but he was violent. There were plenty of occasions when he shouted and made threats. A few nights before I found out about this house being available, he dragged me upstairs, locked me in the box room. I'd made us this special meal and he blended it up into mush, as if it was baby food, force-fed me with a spoon. It was so awful, so humiliating. I knew then that if I didn't get away from him, I might not be so lucky the next time. He enjoyed it. The bastard took pleasure from tormenting me.'

Her mother had gone very still. 'How long was it going on for?' she asked.

'Over a year, almost to the day.'

'Why didn't you tell me?' she asked. The words were thin, breathless. 'You should've told me.'

'I'm telling you now.'

'But you should have told me sooner.'

Skye fell silent, caught in her mother's unyielding gaze. The skin around Cassandra's pale eyes held only the faintest lines, her barely-there brows darkened with pencil, a sharp cupid's bow and the faintest trace of freckles across her cheekbones. Delicate, beautiful.

'I didn't tell anyone,' Skye admitted. 'Not until I got confirmation on this house. Then, I told Sal. I wanted at least one person to know where I was, in case you needed to reach me.'

'I have been trying to reach you,' her mother said. 'When I realised you'd blocked me, I didn't know what to do. I know you're angry with me for showing up here with Martyn, but I had no idea he was the reason you'd left. There was no one else willing to do anything. I only had his word. If I'd known . . .'

Her expression hardened. 'If I'd had even the slightest inkling of what he'd been subjecting you to ... I wish you'd told me. I would've helped you, protected you—'

'Really?' Skye said. 'You'd have believed me? Without question?'

'Of course I would.'

'That last dinner party we came to, Martyn and me, did you not notice that I barely spoke? That I barely ate?'

'I did actually.' Her mother looked suddenly thoughtful. 'I wondered if something might have happened, if perhaps you were pregnant even. When I was expecting you, those first few months were torture. I was so sick.'

Skye had heard this tale of woe before. She didn't want to listen to it again.

'You didn't say anything to me,' she pointed out.

'No, but I assumed if there was something to tell, then you'd tell me. I didn't want to speak out of turn, mention the "P" word in case I was wrong. That sort of thing is private and—'

'But you're my mum,' Skye said quietly, firmly.

'Yes.' Cassandra turned to face her. 'I am, and when you become a mother, you'll see that nothing matters more than your child.'

Skye's throat thickened. 'How did we get here?' she murmured. 'How did we stray so far apart from each other?'

The smile her mother offered was watery, a tremor running through her lips as she tried to hold it steady.

She began to speak, but before the words could leave her mouth, Skye's attention was snatched elsewhere.

A dark shape moved past the window, its limp unmistakeable.

Her husband, the enemy, had returned.

47

Martyn stood in the doorway. His shirt clung to his back in damp patches, creased as if he'd slept in it, while his skin had taken on a mustardish tinge. Deep lines bracketed his mouth, and there were more around his eyes. It was a far cry from the neat and put-together version of her husband Skye was used to seeing. The contrast elicited something in her that she wasn't expecting, though the flash of pity was there for less time than it took her to draw breath.

'I need to sit down,' he said. 'Keep the ankle elevated.'

Sky stepped aside without a word, her expression flat. Martyn shuffled into the room awkwardly on his crutches, grimacing with every step.

'I'm never going to get used to these things,' he grumbled, as he lowered himself down.

Skye's mother got to her feet. 'I'll make us all a hot drink, shall I?'

'I'd rather have something more medicinal,' Martyn replied.

'Don't be absurd,' she said coldly. 'You have a suspected concussion, not to mention a stomach full of painkillers.'

'I don't have any alcohol in the house anyway,' Skye said. 'Not unless you want ouzo?'

Martyn pulled a face. He waited until Cassandra had gone, then turned to Skye.

'You left me,' he said. 'Again.'

'You patronised me,' she countered. Tiredness slammed into her. Skye was sure that if she closed her eyes, she would sleep where she stood. From inside the kitchen came the burble of a kettle beginning to boil.

'What do you want?' Martyn said. 'An apology?'

'How about a divorce?' she replied.

He rolled his eyes over a drawn-out sigh. 'On what grounds?' he demanded, wincing as he shifted position.

Skye stared at the floor, counted to five, tried in vain to calm the chaotic rhythm of her heart. Every part of her felt coiled tight, tension running across her shoulders and back, stiffening her legs and locking her knees. Where had this strength been before, when she'd needed it?

'I think,' she said, a slight tremble to her deliberately mocking tone, 'that it's referred to as "unreasonable behaviour", though that's a euphemism if I've ever heard one.'

'*I'm* the unreasonable one?' Martyn rocked back in his seat. 'How about abandonment? You're the one who walked out, remember.'

'Let's ask my mum, shall we?' Skye replied, as Cassandra came back into the room, a tray balanced in her hands. 'She's the lawyer.'

Martyn glowered.

'I suppose you've spun your mother quite the yarn,' he said. 'Told her some sob story about how awful it was for you, being with someone like me, who supported you, believed in you—'

'Abused me,' Skye interrupted. 'That's right,' she went on, as Martyn shook his head in a show of disgust. 'What you did to me, the bullying and belittling, that was abuse.'

Martyn turned to Cassandra. 'See what I mean? She's a fantasist.'

Skye took a mug from the tray, deliberately selecting one Andreas had given her. Chipped, faded, yet oddly comforting, much like the man himself. Her mother handed another tea to Martyn, then took her own and sat a few feet away from him.

'My daughter tells me you locked her in a room,' she said, in the even-tempered yet mildly condescending tone Skye always imagined she employed in a court setting. 'Do you deny it?'

An ugly shade of beetroot crept across Martyn's neck. 'That was a joke,' he muttered. 'We were fooling around.'

Sky's mouth fell open. 'You dragged me up the stairs and threw me in there,' she cried. 'How could that ever be classed as "fooling around"?'

'Listen,' he said, eyes darting from Skye to her mother. 'Couples bicker all the time. Didn't you and Cosmo have the odd run-in, Cassandra?'

'That's your summation, is it?' she said pleasantly. 'That dragging someone through a house and locking them up against their will is merely what all married couples do?'

'I never hit her.' Martyn pouted. 'Tell her,' he ordered Skye. 'Not once did I raise my hand to you.'

'What do you want?' she snapped. 'A medal?'

'So I get angry sometimes,' he said defensively. 'So what? Haven't either of you ever lost your temper after a bad day? My job is extremely high pressure.'

'Well, yes,' Skye said, 'the pressure tends to be high when you work at thirty thousand feet.'

'Now you're being facetious.'

Cassandra cleared her throat. 'You hurt her, Martyn,' she said stonily. Her face remained impassive, devoid of emotion, though the anger was there in the rigid set of her jaw. 'You hurt her and you scared her – that's not acceptable.'

The dark-red flush spread to his cheeks. Martyn took a furious sip of his tea only to splutter as the hot liquid went down the wrong way. He had never apologised to Skye, not since that first incident with the wine glass in the bath. Was he truly not remorseful, or was it that to say sorry would mean admitting he was at fault? Skye flexed and unflexed her fingers, moved her half-empty cup from one hand to the other.

'Did you ever consider trying therapy?' she asked him.

Martyn widened his eyes in theatrical disbelief. 'Why in God's name would I do that?'

'For your grief,' she said. 'It must have been difficult for you after Beatrice died.'

He let out a huff and tilted his head away.

'Who's Beatrice?' her mother asked. Skye hadn't

divulged the story about Martyn's sister. He'd made it clear that nobody must ever mention her name to his parents. Not that Skye had seen Mr and Mrs Lockhart much since the wedding. She recalled their stiff smiles, the way his mother always set the table with quiet precision, as if a single fork laid incorrectly would be intolerable. Conversation at their few lunches drifted like background music, quiet and polite, entirely forgettable. Skye had no reason to respect their wishes in this scenario, yet as she started to speak, Martyn cut across her.

'We don't talk about Beatrice,' he said.

'No,' Skye corrected, '*you* don't talk about her – not nearly enough. Don't you think you should? Don't you wonder if all those repressed emotions, the anger and grief and frustration, could be the reason you have so many – what was it you called them – bad days?'

'Grief has nothing to do with it,' he shot back. 'It's stress, plain and simple. After a long day of dealing with halfwits, I don't want to come home and find another one waiting for me.'

Skye blurted out a laugh. 'I'm a halfwit now? Wow. I mean, wow, Martyn. That's a nice thing to say about your wife.'

'Listen,' he said again.

Yet another command.

'It doesn't do any good to keep dredging up the past. It may suit you to talk about your dad every goddamn opportunity you get, but not everyone is like that. Some of us would rather draw a line under the unpleasantness.'

What a strange word to use. More and more, it occurred to Skye that this man she'd married, whom she'd believed herself to love, was an actor. An enigma. She had no idea who Martyn was, though a phrase her father once said to her came to mind – *'When people show you who they are, hen, believe them.'*

'Do you have a photo of her?' she asked. 'In your wallet, or on your phone – anywhere?' Turning to her mother, she added, 'Beatrice was Martyn's sister. She died in an accident when he was—'

Martyn leaned forwards. 'I said,' he growled, 'that I don't want to talk about it.'

'I want to see her,' Skye persisted. 'There must be photos.'

'My mother burned the lot, you know that.'

'Do I? All I know is what you told me, and I'm afraid that doesn't hold much value, not any more. In fact,' Skye said, putting down her empty mug and taking out her phone, 'I might just call your parents now and ask them.'

'Don't you dare,' he said, grabbing for her.

Skye was too fast, and far nimbler than him. She swept her phone easily out of reach, fingers already swiping through the list of contacts. Martyn swore under his breath.

'Fine,' he said. 'I'll agree to the fucking divorce, OK? Now put the phone down.'

Skye lowered her arm, catching sight of her mother's intent expression. Martyn adjusted his shirt cuff, the movements brisk, almost challenging. His eyes were trained down, looking anywhere but at her. And she knew then. She just knew.

'Beatrice,' she murmured. 'She isn't real, is she?'

A muscle flickered in his jaw.

'I'm right, aren't I? She doesn't exist. She never did. You made her up.'

Even her mother had paled.

'You made her up to get closer to me, to make me feel as if we had something in common.'

Martyn said nothing, though his scowl deepened.

'I knew it.' Skye rubbed her hands across her face. 'I knew something wasn't quite right.'

'I won't fight you on the divorce,' he reiterated, spitting the words out through clenched teeth. 'And you can keep this place.' He glanced around her lounge with a faint sniff, his lip curling. 'I won't try to take half of it from you, even though I'd be well within my rights.'

'Debatable,' Cassandra interrupted.

'And you'll agree to leave me alone?' Skye said. 'We can do this thing amicably?'

'That depends.' Martyn took a sip of his tea and pulled a face.

It must have gone cold, just as his heart had, somewhere along the line.

'On what?' she asked.

'The Rolex,' he said, matching her glare with his own. 'Either you give it back, or I'll fight you all the way to court. I'll force you to give up this house. You won't be able to stay here, with your new *community* and your halfwit Greek boyfriend. You'll have to move back in with your mother here, and we both know that's the last thing you want, given how much you hate her.'

Skye began to fiddle with the frayed hem of her dress. She cast a quick look in Cassandra's direction. Her mother's hands had frozen mid-motion, one resting on the rim of her cup, the other curled tight in her lap. A moment later, she got swiftly to her feet and began to gather up the mugs.

'Mum,' Skye began, the word clanging like a bell into the silence. But her mother had gone, cream slacks rustling as she hurried into the kitchen.

Skye turned slowly to Martyn. 'If you push this, you won't win,' she told him, steady on the surface, though she could feel the tremor beneath.

'Won't I?' he drawled. 'You don't have any proof of my supposed abuse,' he said. 'It'll be my word against yours, and my pockets are deeper. Or you can simply give me the watch back now, and I'll be on my way. You'll never have to see me again.'

'I told you,' she said with emphasis. 'I don't have it. I sold it.'

Martyn recoiled. 'You sold it? Theft *and* fraud – what a naughty girl.'

'You barely ever looked at it. And I only got back what I put into your house, so as far as I'm concerned, we're even.'

'We are not even,' he snarled, reaching for his crutches. 'Not even close.'

Skye shied away as he hauled himself upright, getting to her feet at the precise moment her mother reappeared.

'Where are you going?' she called, as Martyn reached the door.

'To call for a taxi that will take me back to my hotel,' he said. 'There's a ferry tomorrow at five o'clock, so you have until then to contact whoever it was you sold my watch to and organise for it to be returned.'

'And if I don't?' Skye said faintly.

'Then I'll have no choice but to report you,' he said. 'Like I said, wifey, you can run, but you can't hide.'

48

November 1941

Katerina could not stop her hands from shaking.

The temperature had cooled, though that was not the cause. She could not place the blame solely on the shoulders of Gaia. Mother Earth was not the one who had blocked the seas, she had not seen fit to starve the people of Greece alongside their captors.

A splatter of ink dropped onto the letter. Katerina cursed quietly. There was a pencil in the pocket of her skirt and she drew it out, tossing the pen into the dirt. A puddle of blue spread like a squashed berry. Two words. That was all she had written.

Dearest Stefanos,

Nobody other than she ever wandered this far across the mountains of Folegandros. She was alone, yet the urge to look carefully around was insistent. The Italians had made it clear: anyone found to be writing letters, diaries, or other accounts of the occupation would be marked for death.

'There is no reason to take such a risk,' Leni had warned. 'We cannot send these letters, even if we write them.'

It was true. Stefanos could not be reached, but writing to him was something. A line cast out with an empty hook.

The scratch of the pencil was soft, rhythmic.

*When at first the invaders came, strong lines were
drawn between us and them, though the hardship of
these months has blurred them. We are united now,
foe and friend, by hunger.*

Katerina stared at the words she had written.

It was not only the line between Greek and Italian that was fading. Her own neighbours had become thieves. The bakery windows had been smashed, the wood panels nailed across them ripped apart by those seeking sustenance.

She bent her head to the paper once more.

*The brothers tell me it is worse on the mainland.
The German army has mounted blockades that
prevent the farmers from moving produce into
the cities. In Russia, the horses are being eaten.
Cats and rats hunted. Glue made into a meal.*

Even as she noted them down, Katerina could not quite believe these reports. Whispers that had begun their journey so far away must have become distorted. A tale grew each time it was shared, the storyteller adding a flourish, a salacious detail, something new for their audience.

People would not eat glue. It was an absurdity.

Where are you, I wonder, my travelling warrior, my stubborn patriot, the beat in my heart?

She froze. The pencil immobile.

Had she imagined it?

Katerina held her breath, every muscle pulled tight. Then it came again, gentle, certain, a nudge from somewhere deep within. She pressed a hand to her abdomen.

'*Geia sou, thavmataki mou.*'

Her baby. Their little miracle.

She must tell Leni.

Her skirt flew out behind her as she ran, arms wide like the wings of a bird. The path was dry, stones tumbled away to be caught by thickets of coarse grass. Katerina clambered over a wall. The Aegean winked a greeting. Shimmers of light no less beautiful below a sky that had borne witness to war. She no longer asked the sea to return her lost love. She whispered that plea to the wind.

Ano Meria came into view, homes the colour of feta, the land around them burnt toast. Even in this moment, with hope blooming rose-pink in her heart, Katerina saw food where there were only rocks and earth. Hunger had become the nightmare none could wake from.

She slowed as she neared the base of the hillside, pulse drum-loud in her ears. A crowd had gathered not far from the road, hunched shoulders and bowed heads.

'What's happened?' she asked, hurrying towards them.

A man turned. Grey beard, thin spectacles, cracked lips.

'Go,' he said, pushing at her.

Katerina took a step closer, her chin high. 'Do not touch me,' she said.

A boy swung around, no older than ten. Hollows beneath his eyes, meanness painted by desperation.

'She does not need these things,' he said, gesturing to a figure on the ground.

Katerina crouched, her blood turning to ice in her veins. The woman who laid there was a friend of her mama, the same wretched mother who'd had to bury her son when he fell from the mountain. A basket was beside her, its contents strewn. Coins, papers, a comb with only four teeth remaining, a single dark hair snagged between the fragile wooden fibres.

The boy shoved her roughly aside and Katerina half-fell, catching herself on the dead woman's body. She was not yet cold, her eyes stared up, clouded and unblinking, trapped in a moment that would never move forward. Below her skin, the bones pressed sharply, as if her body had already begun to vanish. She did not stir when the man knelt to untie her boots, did not flinch as the boy's eager fingers tore a silver brooch from her shawl. Katerina recognised it. The meander symbol had been chosen to represent the eternal love the woman felt for her lost child.

She stood, her legs trembling. The burn of rising bile scoured her throat.

'*Aionia mnimi,*' she murmured. *Memory eternal.*

Then came the warmth of someone's touch, hands steadying her, words in a language she did not understand. Katerina turned, jerked away as if burned.

The wife of the German general lowered her hands and stepped back a few paces, her head down. Katerina had only ever seen her at a distance, skulking around the school outbuilding. Prejudice had tainted her opinion of the woman, though even that could not dull the truth of her beauty. Her skin was pale as porcelain, her eyes an open, clear blue, like the sky before sunrise. A single lock of her hair had slipped free from its severe bun, the loose golden curl a trail of sunlight across her cheek.

'Sorry,' she said in Greek.

Katerina curled her lip into a scowl. '*Echthroi,*' she muttered. *Enemy.*

The woman gave her a searching look, then tapped her fingers to her chest. 'Ingrid,' she said.

The foolish woman believed that Katerina's name was Echthroi. The audacity of these people, who came to rule when they could not understand the language, did not respect the people whose lands they sought. It was not her responsibility to help, nor point out the error. She owed this Ingrid nothing but contempt.

Women from the village had begun to swarm, shooing the men away from the body, scolding the boy, whispering prayers.

'She will be with her son now,' one said to another.

Katerina moved away, pressed a hand to the swell of her stomach, yearning for a flicker, a flutter, anything. Stillness. Quiet that morphed into dread. Was the baby seeing this, too, through her eyes? Were they trapped in this moment, bearing witness before they'd drawn so much as a breath?

She stumbled in her haste to get away, feet slipping on the path, air caught in lungs that seemed incapable of expanding. She was yards from Leni's house when Phaedra appeared, Esther close at her heel. The young Jewish runaway wore a cloth cap pulled down, threadbare trousers and waistcoat over a boy's buttoned-up shirt. She kept her gaze fixed on the ground.

'Are you ill?' Phaedra asked. '*Ela*, you look pale.'

Katerina shook her head, dismissing the woman's concern.

A head taller than many and slim as a match, Phaedra had piercing pale-grey eyes and the roughly hewn complexion of someone who spent the majority of their time outdoors. She'd always seemed unbreakable to Katerina, as if the core of her neighbour had been whittled from iron.

'You do not need to worry about me,' she said. 'Where is Elpida?'

'Ah.' The tight line of Phaedra's lips softened. 'She is sleeping. My daughter will be two before December, but she does not have the strength her brother had at that age. How could she,' she added mutinously, 'when there is barely a thing to feed her?'

'The allies will move the blockade soon,' Katerina said dully.

They all said it. None of them believed it.

'Why don't you come to the house?' Phaedra said. 'I have made a pot of nettle tea. It is no match for coffee, but it is better than nothing at all.'

'I need to speak to my sister.' Katerina nodded towards the door.

'Leni? She is at the bakery.'

The was something about the way she said it, almost too quickly, her voice high, different.

'It is a Monday,' Katerina told her. 'The bakery does not open today.'

Phaedra put a hand on her arm.

'Come,' she urged. 'Won't you have tea with me? I was going to give you some baby clothes that I found.' As she spoke, she took a series of small steps to the side, only stopping when she had blocked the door. Esther glanced up for the first time. Her dark eyes crinkled as they caught Katerina's. It was as if she was trying to communicate something.

Then movement, shadows behind the shutters. A male voice, low and urgent. Another sound, this time a cry.

Phaedra flinched, and Katerina saw it – the fear, raw and sudden – before she shouldered past her without a word.

'Leni!' she cried, advancing into the room at speed.

No. It made no sense.

That could not be her sister splayed out across the table, her arms thrown wide, her eyes devoid of light. Not her sister with her skirts pulled high, a man between her thighs, his hand roving across her chest. Lio did not cease his grotesque pawing. He thrust harder, grunting like a ram, trousers pooled at his ankles, a vile smirk slashed like a wound across his face.

Katerina opened her mouth. No sound came. The scream stayed locked inside, a shrill vibration in her skull. When Lio had beaten her, when his boots had found bone and she had tasted blood, it had not hurt like this.

A sob escaped.

She turned.

And ran.

Behind her, the door slammed, sharp and final. Across the hillside, it cracked like a gunshot.

49

Skye awoke suddenly, heart hitting her throat as if flung from a slingshot.

The floor was hard beneath her. Disorientation muddied her thoughts. She rubbed her eyes and looked around. She was downstairs, on the deflated airbed, a sheet tangled by her feet.

Martyn. His threat. The argument.

Each memory landed heavily, a booted foot on her chest.

Her phone was within reach, its long white cable snaking up into a socket. Skye pulled it towards her. It was Wednesday the sixteenth of July, and the time was seven fifty-nine a.m. As she stared at the screen, the clock slipped forward to eight, and her alarm began to tinkle.

Nine hours until Martyn's ferry left the island.

Nine hours to either return the Rolex to him or watch him leave, knowing the fight that would follow, the trouble she could be in if he reported her, the determination with which he would dismantle and destroy her life.

She could not let him. *Would not* let him.

Upstairs, she knocked on her bedroom door. 'Mum? Are you up?'

No answer.

Skye went inside to find the bed neatly made, her mother's suitcase tucked away in a corner. She was about to try calling when she heard the growl of approaching vehicles. Through the window that overlooked the hillside, a police car appeared followed closely by a van. They had arrived to remove the bones from the garden of the empty house, remains that would be collected, tested, investigated.

Twenty minutes later, Skye had dressed and was tugging on her trainers when someone knocked on the front door. Immediately, she thought of Andreas. But it wasn't him. Instead, Theo stood there, sunlight catching his dark curls and turning them conker-bright.

'Of course!' She clutched her head. 'It's Wednesday. George's lesson. Is it OK if—'

'You need to cancel?' Theo said. 'I guessed as much, given that your mum is here.'

'It's not that,' Skye began. 'I just have something I need to take care of.'

'Say no more,' Theo assured her. 'I don't think even astronauts from the International Space Station would be able to drag my son away from peering over the wall at what the police are up to. He hasn't stopped going on about those bones we found.'

'Have you already been over there?' she asked.

Theo slipped a rucksack off his shoulder.

'Everyone's over there except you and the girls,' he said. 'Dusty's had some sort of construction disaster,

Mia's watching over the injured Bruno, and Louisa' – he paused, frowned – 'actually, I'm not sure where she is. Anyway,' he went on, 'I had a quick word with the lead officer over there, and he said something I thought you'd want to know.'

'Oh?'

Skye was part way through tying her hair back with a toggle, and only half heard him.

'The remains in your garden,' he went on. 'What have the authorities told you about them?'

'Nothing,' she said. 'Andreas spoke to them, and all they said was that the grave contained a mixture of both animal and human bones. Why?' she added, as Theo cast a look towards the empty house. 'What do you know?'

'Well, when I spoke to the police a few minutes ago, they told me it was likely that the remains over there would turn out to date from the war. When I asked the man why he'd come to that conclusion, he said it was because of the other bones, the ones at your house.'

Skye felt a tingling in her fingertips.

'Do you think the two could be linked?' she asked.

'I can't be sure,' Theo admitted. He unzipped his rucksack and produced a manilla folder. 'The letters,' he explained. 'The originals are all here, along with translations. I did the last few this morning.'

'Oh, wow. That's amazing,' Skye enthused. 'Is there anything mentioned in them that might shed a light on any of these discoveries?'

'Yes,' Theo said, drawing out the word.

'Sounds like there's a but...'

'The girl,' Theo said, 'Katerina. She wrote most of these letters, but none of them were ever sent. They're all addressed to the same person but most read more like passages from a diary.'

'That makes sense,' Skye said. 'There was no postal service in the Cyclades islands during the occupation. I looked it up.'

'Sad really,' Theo replied. 'It's hard to imagine a world where you can't simply pick up a phone or send a quick text, isn't it? Not that some people even bother to do that,' he added bitterly.

Skye accepted the folder.

'There's a lot of information in there,' he said. 'I think it's only right that you have a chance to see everything first, before we show the letters to the police.'

'The police?' Skye's eyes widened.

'You'll see what I mean once you've read them.' Theo shouldered his backpack. 'I'd better get back to George. I left him with Adam. They were taking photos of a colony of beetles last I saw. Will you be coming over?'

Skye shook her head. 'Not right now. There's something else I need to do first.'

The urge to read every single word Katerina had written was so strong that it dragged a groan from her. Reluctant to leave the precious bundle behind, she retrieved a tote bag and slid the folder inside, locking the front door behind her.

Skye knew her mother, and Cassandra MacKinnon was a woman who insisted upon quality. The freeze-dried coffee granules in her daughter's kitchen would not have passed muster. Far from having no idea where her mum could have gone, Skye knew exactly where to look.

She set off down the hillside and joined the main road. It was hot enough that she could feel the sun-warmed tarmac through the soles of her trainers. The air tasted thick and metallic. Nature was everywhere, raw and unrestrained, surviving despite the wind, the heat, the dryness. She, too, must find a way to endure, as this island endured.

With renewed purpose, Skye increased her pace, reaching the taverna entrance only to bump into Louisa coming the other way. She was laden down with blue carrier bags from the mini market, and there were larger bags below her eyes.

'I know, I look awful,' she said, by way of a greeting.

'Impossible,' Skye told her. 'I've never seen you not looking like a modern-day Rapunzel.'

'Mia keeps on at me to cut this off,' she said, with a disdainful swish of her long red hair.

'Don't you dare,' Skye said, with mock severity.

'Do you have any siblings?' Louisa asked. 'No? Lucky you. I mean, I love my sisters, but sometimes I think I'd have a quieter life living with a hive of bees. I had my own place in Bristol, but after Mum died . . .' She trailed off. 'Anyway, I shouldn't hold you up. I only came out to get some snacks for Dusty. She's in the most furious temper. The earthquake cracked all the concrete she'd laid in the extension. It's not salvageable, apparently, so she's having to start all over again.'

Skye winced. 'What did Andreas say?' she asked. 'I presume he knows?'

'I've been trying to call him,' Louisa said. 'I don't suppose you've heard anything from him?'

'Not much,' Skye said mildly. 'I'm sure he'll reappear soon enough.'

'Maybe he's upset,' Louisa ventured.

Skye looked up sharply. 'Upset?'

'Well, you know, what with your husband turning up . . .'

'That's not the reason,' Skye said firmly.

A spot of colour glowed on each of Louisa's cheeks.

'I thought that you and he were—'

'We're not.'

'Oh.' She readjusted her grip on the bags. 'Sorry.'

'It's a complicated situation,' Skye said. 'Between me and my husband, I mean, not Andreas.'

'Say no more.' Louisa smiled fleetingly. 'It's none of my business anyway. I haven't been gossiping about you, I swear. I just . . . I watch people. I always have, it's the way I am. I notice things, the small stuff. Whenever I've seen you and Andreas together, the pair of you seem so close. I shouldn't have assumed, I suppose, but it didn't feel as if I was, if that makes any kind of sense?'

Skye's mouth opened, then closed again. She settled on a nod.

'I've gone and put my foot in it, haven't I?' Louisa sighed. 'Dusty's right. I should keep my stupid opinions to myself.'

'They're not stupid,' Skye said quickly. 'And I'm not at all offended, I promise. But I really do have to go.'

'Right you are.' Louisa moved aside. 'If I do get hold of Andreas, is there anything you want me to tell him? Any message I can pass on for you?'

Tell him I'm sorry. Tell him I didn't mean to lie. Ask him why he never told me the truth – why I can't stop thinking about him.

Skye's finger curled around the strap of her bag. She took a breath, held it.

'No,' she said. 'Nothing.'

50

Skye spotted her mother immediately.

She was sitting at one of the indoor tables, a laptop open in front of her and a look of studied concentration on her face.

'Oh, good,' she said, barely glancing up as Skye slid into the seat opposite. 'I was hoping you'd roll up at some point this morning.'

'I got held up,' Skye said. She explained briefly about the police. 'I thought you might've been having a lie-in.'

Her mother blinked at her. 'When have you ever known me to have one of those?'

'Well, not often, but—'

'There's far too much to do to waste time sleeping. I've been here since six. Luckily, Pantelis was here. He very kindly let me in and made me coffee. In fact, I've had rather a lot. They make it strong here, don't they?'

At the mention of his name, the taverna owner materialised beside the table. Solidly built with large, wide-apart eyes, full lips and thick, straight hair, Pantelis had the easy charm of a Labrador. Skye was sure that if he'd had a tail, it would be perpetually wagging.

'*Kalimera*,' he said, propping a menu in front of her. 'Frappé?'

'Please. I mean, *parakaló*.' She smiled up at him. 'Milk and sugar.'

'*Entáxei.*'

He turned towards her mother, pencil tapping against his small notepad.

'I'm fine for now,' she trilled. 'We've been chatting at length,' she told Skye, as Pantelis strode briskly away. 'Did you know, for instance, that Folegandros began as an asylum for those banished from Crete? It started life as a place for runaways and miscreants.'

'I guess that's appropriate.'

'I rather thought so,' her mum said cheerfully. 'Now,' she went on, 'we had better discuss this situation with Martyn.'

She had slipped seamlessly into professional mode, and looked the part, too, with her blond bob neatly straightened, the blouse and slacks immaculately pressed. In her crumpled shorts and tatty trainers, Skye felt teenaged by comparison.

'What he said,' she said hesitantly, 'last night, about me hating you, it's not true.'

A flicker of pain passed across her mother's face, gone almost before it surfaced.

'I mean it,' Skye went on. 'I know we've had ups and downs, that things have been strained between us, but I don't hate you, categorically not.'

Her mother nodded, though her eyes darted away, fixed on something beyond the boundaries of the taverna. Silence hovered for a moment, only to be shattered by a returning Pantelis. He put down Skye's frappé, along with bowls of fresh fruit topped with yoghurt and honey.

'On the house,' he said. 'To welcome your mother to the island.'

Cassandra began to flap her hands in protest.

'There's no point arguing,' Skye said. 'The first thing I learned when I moved here was that real Greeks like to eat. The wisest thing you can do is enjoy it.'

'Bravo!' Pantelis agreed.

Skye picked up her spoon as he weaved away through the tables.

'I think it's best if I come clean,' she said, 'about the Rolex.'

Her mother closed the lid of her laptop and pushed it to one side. 'Yes,' she agreed. 'I think you'd better.'

Once Skye began talking, the words spilled out more easily than she expected. She began with the watch, how she'd taken it, sold it, used the money to escape. Then, more slowly, the rest followed. The way Martyn's small complaints had started to build. How, over time, his niggles had become demands; how she'd let them grow until they crowded out everything else.

'I feel as if I sleepwalked into it,' she admitted. 'After Dad, I just felt so numb. The grief took over, it dulled my instincts. I knew, deep down, that there was something not quite right with Martyn, but I ignored it. I feel embarrassed, to be honest. You and Dad raised me to be independent, to have self-respect, to not put up with anyone who'd set out to do me harm.'

'Well,' her mother said quietly, 'you didn't, did you? Look where you are now.'

Skye pushed segments of orange around in her bowl.

'I suppose so,' she said. 'But it shouldn't have taken me as long as it did.'

'For what it's worth, I think what you've done is very brave,' Cassandra said, 'though I still wish you'd told me.'

The taverna was growing busier. Holidaymakers who'd strayed from Chora, locals with newspapers tucked under their arms. At the deep bellow of a familiar Greek voice, Skye swung around, but it was only Klodi, handing over a delivery of fresh fish.

'I didn't think I could tell you,' she said. 'The few times me and Martyn argued in front of you, you always took his side. That was how it felt. I thought that if I told you about my plans to leave him, you'd convince me to stay – or worse, drop me in it. I'm sorry, but I couldn't risk that happening.'

'No,' her mother said. 'It's me who's sorry. Sorry that you felt you couldn't trust me, but also that you went through all this. Honestly, I could wring his bloody neck.'

Shocked laughter burst from Skye.

'Please don't do that,' she said. 'I'm not sure I'm rich enough to fly over every month to visit you in prison.'

'Yes, well,' her mum said darkly, 'violence is never the answer. Fortunately, I have something far more satisfactory in mind. I've been doing some research into your estranged husband this morning. As it transpires, there's been quite a few bad reviews posted online about the charter company he works for.'

Skye pushed her empty bowl aside.

'Tell me more.'

'There are a handful that mention awful food, late departures and all the usual stuff you'd expect to see. However, this one caught my eye,' she said, pushing the laptop round. 'Have a read. Tell me what you think.'

AVOID SKY HIGH AT ALL COSTS (0 out of 5 stars)

I booked a private round trip with Sky High for myself and my family, flying from Dublin over to Cheltenham in March, and while the trip itself was smooth and the plane comfortable, we came away extremely upset.

An item of luggage belonging to my elderly mother-in-law was deemed 'too large' to fit into the cabin, and the steward removed it not long before take-off to stow in the hold. We were assured the case would be safe, though when we returned home having collected it, a number of pieces of jewellery were missing, including a rare antique diamond ring my mother-in-law inherited from her late grandmother, and an emerald pendant bought as a birthday gift by my wife.

Upon complaining to the company, we were assured by the pilot himself that an extensive search would be made, though neither item was recovered. Luckily, we have a robust insurance policy, though damages alone cannot replace treasured heirlooms or gifts. I am not usually one to cast aspersions, though it appears clear to me that someone either working for Sky High or adjacent to the company is operating as a thief.

Skye looked at her mum. 'So, someone at Sky High is stealing.'

'Indeed,' Cassandra said. 'That someone being Martyn?'

'Are there any more reviews?' Skye asked. 'Any that mention a watch going missing?'

'No,' her mother said thoughtfully. 'Though you know what they say about smoke. And it's odd, the way he's being so utterly insistent about that watch in particular. You said it was an unwanted gift?'

'That's what he told me,' Skye confirmed. 'I agree that it's odd. But even if we're right, and he did steal the Rolex, there's no possible way we can prove it.'

'Maybe not,' her mother said, 'but we can try.'

Skye checked the time. It was nearing eleven.

'We haven't got much time,' she said. 'I could try to make him admit it, perhaps record him confessing and use it as leverage? He's unlikely to fall for that, though.'

'Perhaps all you need do is mention your suspicions?' her mother suggested. 'Might be enough to get him to back off.'

'But if he is a thief, we can't let him get away with it,' Skye protested. 'What about the future customers of Sky High, and the next woman he charms into trusting him? He needs to be stopped.'

'You're right.' Her mother closed the laptop. 'But how?'

'I think,' Skye said cautiously, 'I have a plan that might just work. But we won't be able to do it alone.'

'OK, so do you know anyone who might help us?' she asked.

Skye gave in to a slow smile.

'Oh, yes,' she said, 'I know a few people.'

51

December 1941

Leni was at the stove when she fell.

She had been wilting horta to serve with the snails that Dafni collected that morning. The older woman had returned with a small pail and dirt beneath her nails. Katerina, who was no longer able to stand up without first bracing herself on an item of furniture, reached her sister too late to catch her.

'The food,' Leni croaked. 'Do not let it burn.'

Katerina tutted. 'You are more important,' she said. With some difficulty, she crouched down, slipping her arms beneath Leni's. They were as thin as twigs, and coated with soft, downy hair. Katerina settled her into a chair before lifting the pan from the heat.

'This,' Leni said, her skeletal hand coming to rest on Katerina's bump. 'This is the most important thing.'

They were the same words her sister had used on that awful day. Katerina had returned home under duress, forced back by curfew, driven to her bed by fatigue, and found Leni waiting.

'How could you let him do that to you?' Katerina

had hissed. 'He beats me half to death and you let him touch you, let him defile you? It is sick. You are sick.'

'He brings me food,' Leni said simply. 'If I did not let him do these things to me, we would starve.' Her eyes had strayed down. 'There are things more important than my body. It is not my soul. He will not have that.'

Katerina could only weep.

'Do not worry, *agapi mou*.' Leni pulled her close, stroked her hair. 'In those moments of violence, I close my eyes. I go elsewhere to when the war is over, and our husbands have returned. I picture your child. I see their smile. I believe in that future.'

'But why does it have to be you?' Katerina cried.

'It has to be somebody,' Leni said, her voice becoming harder, firmer. 'Would you want that I let him rape Phaedra? She has children, and I . . . There is less risk for me.'

Katerina had not raised the issue again. She wrote about it, though, putting into words what she could not say aloud, talking to Stefanos on the page as if he were there beside her.

Leni leaned back in her chair, eyelids fluttering.

It had been raining at almost every moment for the past four days. Katerina slipped as she hurried outside in search of Dafni. The older woman was standing at the boundary wall, staring into the middle distance. Her once grey-blond hair was almost white, and tendrils blew around her face as she turned.

'Come quickly,' Katerina said. 'I need your help.'

It took some convincing, but eventually, Leni agreed to let them carry her through into the bedroom. She barely seemed there at all, ribs and collarbone rising like peaks beneath the weight of her shawl.

'When was the last time she ate?' Dafni asked, as they returned to the kitchen. Katerina filled a cup with water and cast around for a lemon, finding nothing but a few dry rinds.

'I do not know,' she replied. 'Perhaps a few raisins last night, the heel of the acorn loaf she baked for the children.'

Dafni's hands twisted together.

'It is not enough,' she said, 'not when your sister works so hard.'

Katerina winced as a painful spasm rippled across her lower back. The baby had continued to grow, safely cocooned inside her, though they had yet to turn. It was a quiet worry, one she kept to herself.

'None of us has enough,' she said, scraping the snails and greens from the pan onto a dish. 'I will try to make her eat this.'

Leni could not hold her cup. Katerina held the rim to her lips, heard the tap of her teeth chattering against it.

'You are cold,' she said, removing her own shawl and laying it over her sister. Leni accepted the spoonful of horta, though could not seem to chew it.

'You must try,' Dafni urged, but Leni's eyes were closing, sleep stealing her away.

'She needs milk,' Katerina said.

The Italians had long ago stolen their nanny goat, though there were a few surviving animals up in the mountains. It had been weeks since Katerina attempted the climb. If she could make it to the caves, the brothers would help her. They would give what they had to save her sister.

'Stay with her,' she told Dafni, pulling on an old overcoat of Baba's. 'Do not leave her alone, not for one minute.'

'Where are you going to go?' the older woman called, but Katerina was already closing the door behind her. It was nearing dusk – a foolish time to be seen on the roads or hillsides, where she would become a target for restless soldiers looking for sport. A cross-country route would be much more difficult, though this was the direction she took. Drizzle fell as she scaled the first slope, damp seeping through her coat, its weight pulling at her shoulders. Katerina's breath misted the air, each step tugging pain through her joints. The months of famine had sapped her strength and shrivelled her muscles. She had lost so much, yet what remained felt forged, not broken.

The allies must move the blockade soon. If they did not, all they would find when eventually they reconquered these islands would be bones. Two days ago, Katerina had sat and watched as a man no older than her father walked out into the sea. There were many who wandered the shallows, searching the rocks for molluscs and urchins. She assumed he was another.

'*Kalimera*,' she'd said, as he walked past her on the beach.

The man glanced at her, smiled, said nothing.

By the time his intention had become clear to her, he had ventured too far out for her to reach.

Katerina checked her bearings. She was halfway,

equal distance from her home and the caves. It was safe enough to talk to her child.

She did this often, speaking of the land, of the birds that soared above, the summer winds and the tremors that shook her awake.

'You will never know hunger, *agapi mou*,' she whispered. 'That is my promise to you.'

The night crept up on her as if it were a thief, stealing the last of the light, throwing her on the mercy of her recollections. She had made the journey often enough to find her way in the dark, though it felt as if the mountain had tripled in size. When she finally saw the familiar outline of the caves ahead, it was all she could do not to fall to her knees in the wet earth.

'Atlas,' she called, careful to keep her voice low. 'Zephyr. Are you there? It's me, Kat.'

No reply came. The hum of silence was deafening. She could detect no fire, nor the ashy scent of one that may hastily have been extinguished. She called the brothers' names again but received not so much as a murmur.

Katerina struck one of her last precious matches as she stepped into the cave, its flicker casting uncertain shadows into the emptiness beyond.

No brothers. No food. No goats. They had all gone.

The tears that fell were few, though her body rocked as if buffeted by waves. She had come so far, and it had been for nothing. She would have to return home with nothing for her sister.

Katerina cursed the heavens, scorned the god she no longer believed in. Her boots struck the stone as she stormed down the mountain, muttering vengeance under her breath, on the invaders who had taken everything, on the island itself for betraying her.

Rage surged through her, so hot and blinding that she didn't see the ember glow in the dark.

Did not see the figure, motionless.

Not until he stepped from the shadows, silent as smoke.

Katerina screamed.

52

The Aquarius bar was tucked down a narrow side street in Chora. Skye arrived early, a little before one thirty, and chose a table facing the lane. She wanted to see him coming.

The past few hours had rushed by in a blur. There had been a lot to do. A lot to say.

Skye uncrossed her legs, pressed her hands on her knees to stop them jiggling, took a napkin from the dispenser and tore it into strips. She had changed into a white dress and sandals, applied make-up and brushed her unruly hair.

Looking the part was important.

Martyn arrived fifteen minutes late, shuffling awkwardly on his crutches. As he neared, Skye stood, greeting him with a chaste kiss on the cheek.

'Thanks for coming,' she said. 'I thought we should talk, just the two of us.'

'So you said in your message.' Martyn stifled a yawn. He was in a black polo shirt and trousers, the bottom of one leg rolled up over the cast. A waitress appeared, and he ordered a beer, eyebrows lifting when Skye opted for a cocktail.

'Bit early, isn't it?'

She shrugged.

'How did you sleep?'

Martyn pulled a face. 'Not well, though the painkillers did the trick. I don't even know if they'll permit me to fly with this goddamn thing on my foot.'

'You should check in with the doctor before you go,' she said. 'That's unless you decide to stay a while.'

His gaze swept over her, flat and unimpressed.

'Why would I do that? You've made it pretty clear that you aren't interested.'

'I know,' she said, putting her elbows on the table, 'but I've been thinking. Maybe I've been too hasty.'

Martyn narrowed his eyes. 'Is that so?'

Their drinks arrived. Skye's cocktail glowing a lurid blue, Martyn's local pilsner sporting a goat's face on the label, the word 'Katsika' stamped beside it.

'It was wrong of me to just disappear on you,' she said, removing the pineapple garnish from her glass and taking a bite. 'You must've been worried.'

'Of course I was,' he said, picking at a scab on his knuckle. 'I went all the way to Australia in search of you.'

'I heard.'

'You made me look like a fool,' he said, turning to her. 'A cuckold.'

Skye did not trust herself to reply. A couple strolled past in matching Hawaiian shirts, the tropical print clashing with the soft white of the buildings.

'Why this sudden change of heart?' Martyn demanded. 'Yesterday, you couldn't wait to be rid of me, and now you're, what, sorry?'

She would choke before she uttered that word in his presence.

'We're married,' she said instead. 'We made vows. I guess this is me trying to honour them.'

She thought about those promises, 'to love and to obey'. Skye no more wanted to obey Martyn than climb into a basket with a cobra.

'What are you saying?' he barked. 'That you want us to try again?'

'First, we need to reach a truce,' she said carefully. 'We can't try again if things are going to be like they were before. You'd need to agree to anger management counselling, or some sessions with a psychotherapist. Preferably both.'

'I see.' Martyn took a long draw of his beer.

'We'd also have to start being honest with each other.' Skye's foot began to tap underneath the table. 'About everything.'

Martyn leaned closer, his head tilting to one side.

'The thing is,' she said. 'I started lying to you because I was scared of how you'd react.'

A yawn broke through and he let it. Skye ground her teeth.

'I had a reason to lie,' she continued. 'A valid reason. But why did you?'

Martyn ran a hand over his stubble.

'Why did I what?' he asked, in a bored-sounding voice.

'Lie,' Skye pressed, her own tone neutral. 'The whole thing with Beatrice, your imaginary sister.'

When he didn't immediately reply, a twinge of unease passed through her. Had she pushed him too far? But then Martyn's shoulders drooped, and he hung his head.

'I don't know why I made her up,' he said, not looking at her. 'I didn't plan to, I just . . . I could sense that you weren't all that interested in me and I suppose I thought it would give us something in common. A foundation we could build on.'

The galling thing, of course, was that it had.

'Well, I had made grief my entire personality,' Skye said, and it felt strangely good to admit it. She hadn't judged herself for it then and didn't now. But naming it helped. She'd wallowed, let the sadness rise around her like water, and done nothing but float until it finally began to recede.

A faint smirk tugged at Martyn's mouth. Whatever softness she'd glimpsed in him moments earlier was gone, replaced by something harder, more acerbic.

'You tricked me with that story about Beatrice,' she went on. 'I thought your anger and aggression came from loss, but if that's not the case, then where does it come from?'

'Maybe you bring it out in me,' he suggested.

The beer bottle was empty. Martyn picked at the label, dropping slivers of the goat's face onto the tabletop.

'I think,' she said, sliding her still-full glass closer to him, 'it might be a simple case of guilt.'

Martyn scoffed, though he did not get time to reply.

A woman was striding purposefully towards their table, a man a few paces behind her.

'Martyn Lockhart,' Victoria exclaimed, with a swish of her ponytail. She had put on an expensive-looking kaftan and designer sunglasses, while Adam had swapped his shorts and flip-flops for chinos and boat shoes. Neither paid Skye the slightest bit of attention.

'Do I know you?' Martyn asked, in the oiled tone of a man well accustomed to turning on the charm.

'You were our pilot,' Victoria gushed. 'Took us from the city out to the Hamptons. Must have been the summer of 2019, before the world went damn crazy. I knew I recognised you.'

'Of course,' he lied seamlessly, grinning from one to the other. 'I remember your faces, of course.'

'And I remember yours,' Victoria simpered. 'I said to my husband at the time, what is it about pilots that makes them so darn attractive?'

'She did say that,' Adam agreed heartily. 'If I wasn't so rich, Marty old boy, I'd have been extremely envious.'

He had adopted a clipped aristocratic diction for the role and was clearly enjoying himself.

Martyn's fixed smile failed to hide his wince.

Victoria put her bag on the table and made a show of fanning her face with her hands.

'That was the same summer we lost your late mum's pearls – do you remember?' she said to Adam, who nodded gravely. 'It was the oddest thing. We put them in with our luggage, and then, when we got back to Park Ave, they were gone, vanished from the box. I always assumed someone at the depot had stolen them.'

Skye had found the story by scrolling through the replies below the original review. Every detail was the same, except for one: that couple had not been Victoria and Adam.

Martyn stared up at them both, bug-eyed and pale. He looked as if he might be sick.

'What a shame you misplaced them,' he said. 'Anyway, great to bump into you both. I should—' He gestured towards Skye and Victoria slapped a hand to her forehead.

'Of course,' she said. 'So sorry to have interrupted your day.'

She picked up her bag, and the strap – surreptitiously looped by Skye over her cocktail glass – snagged, sending it flying into Martyn's lap.

'Fucking hell!' he exploded, leaping to his feet as quickly as the cast on his foot would allow. The front of his shirt was soaked, and dribbles of blue ran down his trousers.

'Your phone!' Skye gasped, snatching the handset up from the table. 'I'll go and put it in rice,' she said, heading for the door of the bar before Martyn could react. She heard Victoria's saccharine cry of 'Oh no, I hope it doesn't stain,' and suppressed a laugh.

In the cramped, tiled space of the ladies' bathroom, Skye shut and locked the cubicle door. The phone was dry, unscathed, as she had planned. Her heart pounded as she tapped in Martyn's pin code – the same one he'd used when they first met – a rush of relief flooding through her as the home screen flashed up. Her fingers moved fast, almost of their own accord, clicking into his emails with a surge of anticipation.

There, in a folder marked 'WORK', she found exactly what she'd been looking for.

53

Four emails.

Each one short, precise, no-nonsense. The true owner of the Rolex was apparently far too prominent a business mogul to send correspondence himself and had instead tasked a personal assistant by the name of Caspar Newbolt with the job of contacting Martyn. The message was clear: return the watch by the date stated or the consequences would be dire. The mogul in question was keen not to involve the authorities or the press, but it was made clear that he would do so if pushed.

Skye skim-read each email, eyes wide, chest constricted, then she forwarded them to her mum. With her own phone, she sent a follow-up text: *Check your inbox.*

Cassandra MacKinnon was not one to dally. Within three minutes, Skye had received a reply.

*Part one of the plan complete. Funds transferred.
Be there in 5.*

Her breath slowed, steadied. She unlocked the cubicle door and crossed to the basin, washed her hands methodically, smiled back at her reflection in the mirror. A real smile. One of triumph.

Back at the table, Martyn was seated, a wad of blue-stained napkins pressed against his crotch. Victoria had pulled up a third chair, but Adam remained standing. He caught Skye's eye and she nodded, just once.

'Must visit the little boy's room,' he said, sidling away as Skye returned to her chair.

'Give me that,' Martyn snarled, grabbing his phone from her hand.

Victoria's mouth fell open, but she quickly shut it again.

'I dried it for you,' Skye told Martyn. 'Seems to be working fine.'

He ignored her, his head down over the screen. Someone came out to clear the table, and Victoria insisted on ordering another round of drinks.

'It's the least I can do after drenching you in cocktail,' she said.

Martyn grunted. 'Fine. I'll have a whisky – double.'

'Is that a good idea with the painkillers?' Skye began, only to be silenced with a thunderous glare. Victoria began to fidget, her fingers tapping against the tabletop, colour rising in her cheeks.

When the waitress returned, so did Adam, his phone pressed to his ear, a studied expression on his face.

'That's right, Mr Newbolt. A courier has been arranged. The package will be with you by end of play.'

Martyn paused in the motion of raising his whisky glass to his lips. It really was fascinating, Skye mused, how often a person's complexion can change colour. In the past half-hour, Martyn had gone from pink, to puce, to near grey, and was now close to being devoid of any discernible shade.

'What's going on?' he hissed at Skye, as Adam ended the call.

Victoria raised her coffee cup to hide her smile.

'Why don't you let me answer that one?' a voice said. Cassandra advanced towards the table, her large straw hat shading features that were laced with disgust. Behind her came Joy, a fiery vision in a jumpsuit patterned with red, yellow and marigold-orange swirls.

'Good to see you, chook,' she said, crouching beside Skye's chair and staring pointedly at Martyn. 'This your great big twerp of an ex, is it?'

'We're actually still married,' Martyn muttered.

'Sure,' Joy replied. 'For now.'

Cassandra dragged a chair over from a neighbouring table, the metal scraping across the stone slabs with a screech that set Skye's teeth on edge. Surrounded on all sides, Martyn could only gawp at each of the people circled around him.

'I think we should start with a thank you,' Cassandra said coolly.

'To whom?' Martyn replied.

'Well, how about to Skye, for starters. It's thanks to her that the watch you stole was sold on to someone reputable who was prepared to return it to its rightful owner. If she'd put the thing up on Vinted, we probably wouldn't have been quite so fortunate. Although by "we", what I actually mean is you. You're the only one standing to lose in this scenario.'

'But she stole the watch from me,' he argued. 'She was the one who—'

'No,' Cassandra corrected patiently. 'My daughter was desperate. She needed to find the means by which to escape you and your abuse of her. She has an excuse – what's yours, I wonder?'

Martyn pressed his lips into a thin line.

'Mr Newbolt was surprisingly agreeable about the whole thing,' Adam put in. 'So you probably owe him a thank you – and me, for smoothing things over with him. While we're at it,' he went on, as Martyn began to fluff up like an angry parrot, 'you can thank my wife, too.'

Victoria raised a hand. 'That's me,' she said. 'I always knew that drama class I took in college would come in handy one day, and tipping that drink over you, that was just a nice bonus.'

Martyn rounded on Skye. 'You set me up,' he said.

'*We* set you up,' Cassandra interrupted. 'These are Skye's neighbours. Her community.' She lingered deliberately on the word, daring him to mock her. Martyn said nothing. He picked up his glass and drained it, made as if to stand.

'Oh no you don't.' Adam put his hand on Martyn's shoulder. 'We're not done yet.'

'Get the fuck off me.' He shrugged hard, twisting out of the other man's reach.

'Read the room, Martyn,' Cassandra drawled. 'You're

not in charge here, and if I were you, I'd listen to what your wife has to say.'

Skye took a breath, made herself face him.

'You have to sell the house in Epsom,' she said. 'My mum and Jonathan have paid for the Rolex to be returned, and I need the money I put into that property to pay them back.'

'And if I refuse?'

'Then she'll call the cops on you,' Joy put in gleefully. 'Sounds to me as if you've been a bit of a naughty boy, haven't you, Marty?'

'I won't only report you,' Skye said. 'I'll speak to your parents, tell them what you've done to me, and the story you made up.'

Martyn deflated a fraction, his chin dropping towards his chest. 'Fine,' he snapped. 'You can have your paltry contribution back, but—'

'I want a divorce, too. No contest. Pay me what I put in and you can have everything else.'

'You think I'd want to stay married to you?' he spat. 'After this?'

'Skye isn't the bad guy here,' Victoria said. 'You should be ashamed of yourself. For God's sake, go to therapy, sort your shit out. Women aren't punchbags – you don't get to push us around, not any of us.'

'Here, here,' Cassandra chimed.

Skye bit back the tears. They were all here for her. She had asked for help, and they had come without question. These people. *Her* people.

'I'll sort out the paperwork,' her mother went on

briskly. 'All you have to do, Martyn, is sign. If it was up to me, of course, the police would already have been informed, but fortunately for you, my daughter inherited her father's heart, not mine.'

'That might be true,' Joy said, 'but I think we can all see where she got her strength from.'

Skye reached down and took her friend's hand, squeezing it. Martyn rolled his eyes.

'Is that it?' he said tersely. 'Can I go now, or are you going to torture me further? Tar and feathers. One hundred lashes in the village square.'

'Facetious idiot,' Adam snapped.

Martyn used his crutches to hoist himself up, letting the chair fall to the ground with a clatter. He shuffled out from behind the table and moved into the lane, turning to scowl at them all one final time.

Skye stared at him. Her fear was gone. He was pathetic. A sad, lonely, spiteful man.

'This is your last chance to say it,' she called out.

Martyn turned.

'Say what?'

'Sorry.'

His shoulders rose as he drew in a long breath. Then he spoke, low and venomous.

'I am sorry,' he said. 'Sorry that I ever met you.'

54

December 1941

The Italian soldier stood facing her. He was scrawny from hunger, black-eyed with loathing.

Katerina did not dare move. Her arms went protectively over the swell of her stomach. They were not far from the ridge where she had first set eyes on Stefanos. Those days felt otherworldly to her now, trails of a dissolving dream.

'*Buona sera,*' he said.

She would not speak to him, not after what he had done to her, to her sister. Katerina turned away, but Lio reached out a hand and clamped it on her wrist, pulling her round to face him. He was still strong – far stronger than she. She could smell alcohol on his breath and wondered where he had found such contraband, whom he had hurt in order to get hold of it.

'Leave me alone,' she said, with as much authority as she could muster.

Lio sneered at the Greek words and spat on the ground. She watched as he slowly slid his pipe into the pocket of his army-issue coat and drew out another object. A blade. Katerina's breath caught in her throat as she looked at it, gleaming in the thin light of the half-moon.

Lio gestured behind her, his meaning clear. Lie down, submit, allow me to do what I want.

Katerina did not move. She pictured her sister, frail and sick, waiting for her to return; she saw Stefanos, somewhere on the mainland, fighting for freedom; she imagined their baby, who would surely die with her if she did not succumb to her enemy's demands. Yet she could not bring herself to cower, her limbs would not obey her.

Lio raised the sabre, drawing it slowly through the air, showing her how she would meet her end. She could give in to him, lay back and let him crawl across her as an insect would, although Katerina suspected that he would murder her whether she did so or not. Better to die undefiled than give him the satisfaction of having bettered her.

'No,' she said, the word loud, unequivocal.

A breeze tore across the hillside, whispering its awe.

'No?' Lio's brow tugged upwards, a slug caught on a hook. The sigh he relinquished was one of disappointment. He had a particular game in mind, and she was in no mood to play.

The baby kicked and Katerina glanced down, her hand tightening on her abdomen.

'No,' she said again, and with a sudden burst of energy, she pushed him hard on the chest. Caught off guard, Lio stumbled backwards.

It was enough.

Katerina put her head down and ran, ignoring the scream of pain in her joints, the burn in her lungs, the fear that snapped at her heels. The house was in sight, a glow of amber light at a downstairs window, salvation within grasping distance. She cried out as Lio thundered towards her, felt his boot connect with the back of her legs, saw the glint of his blade as she fell, tumbling over and over. He loomed above her, straggly hair obscuring the stars, malevolent grin opening wide. Katerina groped desperately at the ground, gathering nothing but wet turf until, at last, she found something.

She had one chance, only one. Katerina took it, hurling the small rock at Lio's head as hard as she could. A crunch sounded, then a grunt as he staggered backwards, falling to one knee.

She crawled onto all fours; transformed, a snarling wildcat hunting for prey. Lio touched his head. A damp patch of blood was spreading, and his bewilderment turned instantly to fury. With a great roar, he swung the sabre, missing her face by a mosquito's breath. Katerina ducked away, flattening herself into the mud as he advanced. She raised an arm, the hot fire of the blade slicing through her flesh. It cut from wrist to elbow and she cried out in pain.

He would slice her into pieces where she lay; they would find her corpse in the dawn light, battered and bloody, the baby dead inside her.

Stefanos's words came to her: *'You must use your head, not your body.'*

But he was not here. Nobody was. She was the one who must protect their child.

Before Lio could raise the sabre again, Katerina surged up from the ground. A raw cry tore from her throat as she hurled herself at him, driving him backwards. He hit the ground with a sickening thud, air ripped from his lungs.

Her breath rasped in her ears.

Lio twitched, his legs kicking out like a severed puppet, and then nothing. Stillness.

Katerina approached slowly, kicking away the blade he had dropped into the dirt. The rain began to gather pace, droplets streaming across his frozen cheeks, his open mouth, his staring eyes. She dropped to her knees, saw the rock she had thrown beneath his head, understood that it was over.

'No,' she said quietly, to him, to the world, to whatever god that may have been watching, 'means no.'

Another sound came, the scuffling of feet, hushed voices.

Katerina scrambled upright. It was too late to run, or to hide. The Italians would not believe it had been an accident. They would take her to the square in Chora and shoot her. With a sob, she bent and raised the sabre, the blade trembling in her hands. Two figures emerged on the shadowy pathway, and she charged forwards, letting out a wail of relief when she saw who had come.

Phaedra, her cloak swaddled around her, the young Esther by her side.

'We heard screams,' Phaedra said. 'What has ha—' She fell silent as Katerina stepped aside.

'He was going to rape me,' she said. 'Kill me. I pushed him. I did not—It was not—'

'He is dead?' Esther asked, her tone measured; curious not afraid.

'Yes,' Katerina whispered.

Esther nodded. The moonlight had painted her eyes into something feline. 'Good,' she said. 'I am glad.'

Katerina glanced at Phaedra.

'We cannot leave him here,' her friend said. 'If the soldiers find him . . .'

'I know,' Katerina agreed. 'How shall I do it?'

Phaedra put a hand on her arm.

'*Ela*,' she said. '*We* will do it. There is a cart. I will fetch it, and some cloth to put around the body.'

She turned and went back down the hillside, leaving Katerina and Esther alone. The young Jewish girl was crouched beside the body, examining the wound. With careful fingers, she eased the rock from beneath Lio's smashed skull and held it out.

'Take this,' she said, with quiet authority. 'Hide it or throw it away.'

The girl was only fourteen. How could she be so calm?

Katerina's hands would not stop shaking. Blood ran out from the cut on her arm, dripping into the earth. She took the stone, weighed it against the flimsy blade she still held. The enemy had come from a foreign land with a foreign weapon, and Folegandros, her island, had provided the only tool required to defeat him.

She heard the crunch of wheels. Phaedra was back, pushing a small cart.

'Take his feet,' Esther said. 'If you drag him from his head, he will soil himself.'

'How do you know this?' Katerina asked, as they moved into position. It was difficult for her to manoeuvre around her bump, but she managed to grab Lio's boots.

'My father was an undertaker,' Esther explained. 'I would help him sometimes, with the bodies.'

'Is it best that we bury him?' Phaedra asked.

The girl shook her head. 'If there is no body, there is no crime,' she said firmly. 'A buried body can be discovered. No, we must put him into the water. Let the sea take him.'

It took them some time to lift Lio into the cart, and longer still to make the slow journey out to the highest cliff point. Esther ran ahead, checking for patrolling soldiers, but the island was theirs, clear but for the scraggly outline of trees, the humpbacked line of low walls.

Katerina threw the rock in first. She did not hear it land. It was impossible to hear anything but the roar of the water, the whistling wind, the irregular beat of her frightened heart.

'We tell nobody,' she said, turning first to Phaedra, then Esther. Each gave her a solemn nod. 'Not even our families.'

'What family?' Esther said. She kneeled beside the cart and began to unbutton the dead man's coat.

'What are you doing?' Phaedra asked in alarm. 'Leave him.'

Esther tugged hard at something, rocking back onto her heels. 'Take these,' she said to Katerina.

A dog tag, and a gold cross on a fine chain.

'Hide them, bury them, burn them – do whatever you must. They cannot remain on the body. If the tide brings him back to shore . . .'

'I understand.' Katerina slid both into the pocket of her skirt. She had planned to throw the sabre off the cliff, though that seemed foolish now. It had been his, just as the other items had been his. She would keep it. Bury it in the garden of the house that the brothers had abandoned. Nobody would find it there.

'Should we say a prayer?' Phaedra murmured.

Katerina looked at Esther.

'No,' she said.

Another hour passed before Katerina made it home.

She had left the house as one woman and returned as another. Would her sister know, she wondered, as she hung up her father's coat? Would she take one look and see her for what she was now – a killer?

But Leni did not look.

She did not speak.

In the time Katerina had been gone, her sister had died.

55

The mood on the hillside was one of giddy frivolity.

Skye accepted a rare beer from Joy, laughing as her friend clambered up onto a patio chair.

'Careful!' she cried, as it wobbled precariously.

'Time?' Joy asked, looking around at her assembled guests. They were all there – Theo and George, Adam and Victoria, Dusty, Louisa, Mia – and Cassandra. The sun blazed in a sky scrubbed free of cloud. Smoke curled from the barbecue, tugged apart by a teasing breeze that carried the scent of charred meat and roasting pepper through the garden.

'Two minutes to five,' Dusty replied, her phone in her hand.

'Let us know when it's thirty seconds,' Joy told her. 'I want us all to join in on a countdown.'

Skye frowned for a moment, then she realised. The ferry would leave at five p.m., taking Martyn with it. She smiled, waited, raised her beer, chanted along to the chorus of 'ten . . . nine . . . eight . . .' Joy gave a great whoop as the hour passed and held her bottle aloft.

'To freedom!' she said.

'And victory,' Adam put in.

They all looked expectantly at Skye. She hesitated, then took a slow, deliberate sip.

'To justice,' she said.

'Do you think we should've gone down to the port, made sure he really did leave?' Mia asked. She had arrived with Bruno in her arms, Louisa following with a large, rather tattered dog bed. When Skye had brought the sisters up to speed on the day's events, their three mouths had fallen open in unison.

'Shame I don't have that sabre any more,' Dusty brooded now. 'I could've brandished it at him.'

Louisa caught Skye's eye. 'I'm not sure that would have been a good idea,' she said mildly.

'You gave it to the police, then?' Theo asked, coming towards them with one of Joy's hastily constructed halloumi kebabs.

'Yeah,' she said, rather forlornly. 'They said I can have it back once it's been tested. I might mount it on the wall, you know, like a Samurai sword.'

Mia scrunched up her features. 'What are you now, Mr Miyagi?'

'He was into karate.'

'Potato potarto.'

Theo laughed, then turned to Skye. 'Did you read the letters yet?'

'No,' she said. 'I haven't had a moment. But I want to. I will. Soon.'

'Andreas should be here,' Joy said, swiping Cassandra's wide-brimmed hat and plonking it on George. 'I'm going to call him.'

She raised a theatrical hand for silence, selecting

speakerphone so they could all listen in. Andreas, when he eventually answered, did so with a dour sounding '*Nai*'.

'What are you doing?' Joy said. 'Nah, scratch that. It doesn't matter what you're doing. Your plans are cancelled. You're coming here to my house for a barbie.'

Silence on the other end of the line.

'Andreas? You there?'

'You are having a party?' he asked, though it was delivered more as a statement of fact. Skye felt a twinge of unease, her whole body tingling unpleasantly.

'Not a party exactly,' Joy said. 'More a gathering of friends. We're celebrating, you see, and—'

'I am not in the right mood to celebrate,' Andreas said. 'Goodbye.'

The dial tone sounded. Joy grimaced.

'Ah, well,' she said, reaching for her beer. 'His loss, I reckon. Shall we put some music on?'

Nobody mentioned Andreas again, but he remained in Skye's subconscious as the evening wore on, his mood a dark slash through an otherwise colourful tapestry. When her mum stood up at nine thirty, yawning widely and brushing off Joy's cry of 'Stay, stay', Skye was only too glad to accompany her back to the house.

She still had her tote bag, the bundle of letters pressed enticingly against her side.

'Hot drink?' she offered.

Cassandra smiled through a shake of the head. 'No, thank you. I might just go on up, if that's OK with you?'

Not once, at any time that Skye could recall, had her

mother asked permission before doing anything. The thought brought a smile to her own lips.

'Of course, Mum,' she said. 'And thank you, again, for today. I couldn't have done it without you.'

Cassandra paused, a foot on the bottom stair.

'I wouldn't have wanted you to,' she said.

In the kitchen, Skye boiled the kettle, adding a handful of fresh mint and a slice of lemon to her chipped *I don't need therapy, I just need a trip to Folegandros* mug. She'd picked up a foldable canvas deckchair from the mini market and set it up now just beyond the back door, angled towards the view. The air held the last warmth of the day, soft against her skin. Insects hovered low but made no sound, as if the hush of approaching night had silenced them. The sun hadn't quite set, and the sky behind the mountains was tinged in gold. A fading spill of light, slipping away.

She needed to message Sal. Tell her what had happened. But that could wait.

Skye opened the bag, took the first translated letter from the pile, and began to read. It did not take long. Within moments, her dusky garden faded and the past rose up around her, Katerina's words unspooling like the notes of a song inside her head. Theo had been right, the letters read more like diary entries. Only not the kind you write to yourself. These had been meant for someone else. For 'S'.

Stefanos.

Skye caught her breath at the sight of his full name. She whispered it into the quiet, as if the sound might summon him, draw him home, coax his secrets into the present.

> *Stefanos, my love,* Katerina had written. *I am alive. I begin with those words, because they are how I begin each day. It is always a surprise to open my eyes and discover that I am still here, that the night did not take me, cloaked by darkness, to whatever it is that awaits us in the life after this one.*

Skye squinted down at the words, dark and deliberate, the paper tinged yellow by the light spilling out through the open back door. She read on, tears stinging as she learned of a woman collapsing in the road, a boy taking her purse, her shoes, a brooch she wore in honour of her lost child. She read about famine. How the wife of a German officer lurked like a ghost around the school Katerina's sister, Leni, had opened. The outbuilding mentioned could only have been the one still standing in Victoria and Adam's garden – the very same space Skye herself had imagined as a classroom.

Goosebumps dappled her arms.

The water in her cup had gone cold, yet Skye barely noticed. She was enthralled. Outraged yet tantalised. Katerina's accounts a horror film from which she could not tear her eyes.

> *There was a time when I believed that death marked the beginning of a journey, one that would carry the soul from this world to another. Today, I fear that I*

was wrong. How can death lead to beauty when it is this brutal? How is pain considered a pathway to any form of salvation?

And on it went. Reams of fear, and yearning, and anger – much of the latter reserved for the occupying invaders, though Katerina seemed to be angry at the entire world. She was plain in her account of having lost faith in God, foolhardy in the derisory way she disregarded curfew, risking her life to ensure her friends, the two brothers, did not starve.

There was a lot to take in, so much devastation. An elderly man walking into the sea, livestock taken and slaughtered, bags of grain traded for precious gems. Skye brought the pages closer, reading and re-reading until the images burned into her mind. More than once, tears blurred the words. As night settled thick and still around her, a quiet melancholy took hold.

She had read many accounts of war over the years, though none so raw, so unashamed in their fury and indignation. Katerina was undoubtedly brave, though as her letters continued, it was clear to Skye that her edges had begun to fray.

I try to work, try to eat, try to hope, she had written. Leni gives everything away – her food, her time, her affection to the orphans whose parents have been killed or starved to death. She says that they are her purpose, the innocent souls that spur her on. It matters not what we do, she tells me, but why we do it.

When Skye turned over a page and found a short passage, not more than three sentences in length, her hands began to shake.

Katerina had been beaten. Leni had been raped. The same man had committed both crimes. An Italian soldier. In the letters, he was referred to as either 'Him' or 'the pig'.

Could his name have been Giulio Muti? Was it his body buried in the garden of the abandoned house? Had something happened to mean that Katerina ended up with his dog tag? The temptation to read ahead nagged at Skye, but she forced herself to continue chronologically, a smile finding its way onto her face as she read the words of love that Katerina had scribbled to her and Stefanos's unborn child.

After our baby comes, I will begin spying for the brothers again. He or she will be the perfect decoy. It is an amusing thought, a child of yours being a soldier before they can even think for themselves. I can picture your smile, my love. Hear your laughter in the dark.

Skye stretched, checked the time. It was two a.m. She was wide awake, perhaps more so than she had ever been. Had freedom done this to her, or was it discovery?

Only three more letters remained.

She sat for a moment, head tipped back, gazing at the stars. The last time she'd done so, Andreas had been beside her. Later that same night, he'd read the first letter aloud. It was in those moments that something had taken root between them, a bond shaped not just by feeling but by a story. Their story, folded into that of two others long since gone.

Whatever had become of Katerina and Stefanos, she and Andreas belonged to it now – they all did, every one of them on the hillside – theirs a new chapter in a tale buried for decades, hidden inside a house that had saved Skye in more ways than one.

The same instinct that had led her to Folegandros stirred again.

It urged her to keep reading. To go deeper. To reach the end.

But as Skye was about to learn, Katerina's final letters weren't the end at all.

They were only the beginning.

56

The house looked much the same as it had on her last visit. Pots of herbs on the steps up to the door, terracotta tiles, a mosaic patio table with matching chairs.

Skye bent and lifted the edge of the doormat. Andreas hadn't been joking about leaving the key under there, though its presence likely meant he was not at home. She knocked regardless, several times, pressing an ear to the wood and listening for any sign of movement. There was nothing, the house quiet, white walls turned tangerine by the rising sun.

She had borrowed Victoria and Adam's shiny truck, parked it by the port and walked the rest of the way. The earthquake that had shaken the isle had wrought devastation in Karavostasis.

Areas where rocks had fallen were roped off, while a section of the narrow beach had been piled with splintered planks, broken pots and items of damaged furniture. A few houses bore livid cracks, though all had remained standing. Save for one.

Skye had paused when she reached it, peered through into the mangled mess of masonry, shattered glass and twists of wire. Steel rods poked up at odd angles, and scalloped roof tiles sat dormant, still as a shoal of piranhas. Her foot slipped on something half-buried beneath the remains of an interior wall. A dog food bowl, flakes of dried-on meat stuck to its sides.

It looked as if a bomb had hit it.

She didn't cry. There were no more tears. Skye had wept through the final letters until her skin felt tight, her eyes raw. Now, only numbness remained, a hollow space inside her, as if something had been emptied out.

Andreas's patio chair groaned as she sat.

Where was he?

Getting up again, Skye went down the steps and checked the beach for any sign of him. There was no one around, though strains of music drifted out from a nearby window. She took out her phone and recorded a brief voice note for Sal, bringing her friend up to date, recalling with relish the expression on Martyn's face when he realised the game was up. Another six or seven weeks, and Sal would be here. She could not wait to show her friend the island; take her out in a boat and sail past the caves; climb the winding pathway to the Church of Panagia, watch the birds swoop, and regale her with tales of Ottoman pirates, mythical treasures and spiritual miracles.

Five more minutes, then she would try to call him.

Skye returned to her chair on the patio. From her bag, she retrieved the last letter. It was dated 22 December 1941, and the final few lines crushed her each time she read them.

*History is erased by time, though the memory of what
I did, what I had to do, will remain with me always.
You told me I was strong, Stefanos. Why did you lie
to me? I hate you. I need you. I love you.
   Kat.*

When Skye looked up again, the first thing she saw was Andreas. There was a fishing rod in his hand, a tackle box dangling by its handle. At his ankle, a small, grey, scraggly dog.

'You are here,' he said.

'I am here,' she agreed.

Andreas looked worn thin. His shoulders sagging, his clothes rumpled, fatigue pressed into every line of his face. Even his movements were slower, heavier. Though as he climbed the steps, he managed a faint, faltering smile.

'Is that Filia?' Skye asked, crouching to stroke the dog.

'I collected her from the vet clinic late last night,' he confirmed. 'No injuries, though she was traumatised after—' He fell quiet, gaze skittering away.

'I'm so sorry,' Skye said. 'You both look as if you could use some sleep.'

'I could not sleep,' he said, holding up the rod. 'So we fish, Filia and me. Although I do not think she likes the boat very much.'

'I can go if you want,' she went on. 'I only came to see if you were all right and' – Skye peered at him more closely – 'are you all right?'

Andreas shrugged. 'I will be. After coffee. Will you stay?'

'Yes. *Nai*.'

He retrieved the key and pushed open the door. Filia trotted inside and began to make an inspection of the room, sniffing every item of furniture and testing the rug to make sure it could double as a scratch pad. Andreas vanished into the kitchen, returning a few minutes later with small cups, one of which he held out to her.

'Let us sit outside.'

'I have so much to tell you,' Skye began, taking the seat beside him. Her hands were possessed. She fiddled with the hem of her dress, the strap of her bag, the ends of her hair.

Andreas sat down and began to unlace his boots.

'To tell me,' he echoed. 'I know about the bones at the empty house. The police . . . it is a small station. I overheard them talking about it.'

'Why were you at the police station?' she asked.

Andreas tugged off a sock.

'To identify the body.'

'Oh,' she said, a coldness stealing through her. 'That must've been awful.'

'I did not think it would be a problem, but' – he sighed – 'when my brother drowned, my parents were too distraught to do what had to be done. I offered to do it, and when I was called to do the same thing again for Karolos, it was as if the years were swept away in a great whoosh. I lost the ability to breathe, to stand up. I was no help.'

Without thinking, Skye reached over and took his hand.

'I'm so sorry you had to go through that. I wish I could've been there with you.'

He stared at her, eyes unblinking. 'You were busy,' he said slowly, 'with your husband.'

Skye removed her hand. 'He's gone,' she said.

Andreas cleared his throat. 'Gone?'

'Away. Back to England. Out of my life for good. We're getting divorced.'

He took a sip of his coffee but said nothing.

'I should've told you about him,' she went on, addressing the floor. 'I came here to escape from him. Our marriage was . . . Martyn had become abusive. I just thought if I could hide here, stay out of his way, then I could forget about all of it. But that was never going to happen. It was as if I had a huge gaping wound in my side and was trying to go about my daily life as normal. I had to face him, confront him, but I wasn't strong enough to do that in London. Coming here, meeting you, and all the others, that was what gave me the strength I needed.'

'He abused you?' Andreas's voice was ice cold. He muttered something in Greek. 'I will not translate that,' he added. 'It is very rude.'

'Whatever it is, I've probably thought it myself,' Skye told him.

'This, I think not. The Greeks are very creative when it comes to insults.'

'Well, I'm sure Martyn deserves it. He isn't only a bully and a liar, he's also a thief. He left here believing that he'd get away with it, but my mother had other ideas. She got in touch with Sky High – that's the charter company Martyn works for – and told them everything we knew. His boss was furious, said he would suspend him with immediate effect and report the matter to the police in the UK. I can't imagine anyone will employ him to work as a pilot again – that's if he manages to avoid a custodial sentence.'

Andreas made a low whistle. 'That does not explain how you convinced him to leave you alone,' he said.

Skye rubbed her hands over her face.

'For you to understand that,' she said, 'I'll need to tell you a little story about a watch . . .'

57

Skye went back to the start.

She told Andreas everything, ignoring the temptation to gloss over the less palatable parts she had played. Lying, pretending, faking – they were all past tense. Honesty had stepped up and eradicated the lot.

He said little, though listened intently, head bent towards her, his lips slightly parted.

Filia wandered out to join them. The dog pressed her cool snout into Skye's hand before crossing to Andreas's discarded socks to give them a sniff.

'Do you think I'm a bad person?' she asked.

'No,' he said. 'What I think, is that you are a brave person.'

'I might've agreed with you yesterday,' Skye said. 'But then I read the rest of the letters.'

She glanced down at the tote bag on her lap.

'I brought them here to show you,' she said. 'Also, when the earthquake happened, part of the wall upstairs at my house fell in. There's a hollow on the landing, between the two bedrooms. I felt around inside and found a pouch containing a dog tag, a gold cross and a Nazi medal. I don't know who the last one belonged to, but I think I do know how the other things got there.'

'They were all together inside your house?' Andreas frowned.

'It's all linked,' she said. 'The remains in my garden, the sabre Dusty found, the dog tag. The only puzzle still to solve is that of the person buried under the lime tree in the empty house.'

'It is not the same man who wore the tag, and the cross?'

'No,' she said. 'Something else happened to him.'

Andreas cocked an eyebrow. 'Will you tell me?'

Skye inched the bag towards him.

'I think it's better if Katerina does that herself.'

Andreas stretched his arms above his head, yawning widely.

'Must be catching,' Skye said, nodding towards Filia. The little dog was turning around in ever-decreasing circles, trying to find a comfortable spot on Andreas's socks. 'Do you want me to go so you can sleep?'

'*Ela*, no.' Andreas reached down and patted her hand. 'I want you to walk with me.'

They went together down the steps and crossed onto the beach, his arm brushing against hers, a light morning breeze blowing loose strands of hair across Skye's cheeks. It was still quiet, though more of the surrounding shutters had been opened, the new day welcomed inside. Filia followed them, her nose to the ground, stubby tail wagging.

'Will you keep her?' Skye asked.

Andreas made a soft tutting sound. 'I am too busy. But she is a nice dog. I am sure she will find a new home soon.'

'Maybe she could come and live in the village – although, I'm not sure how Tigri would feel about that. He already has Bruno to contend with.'

'Bruno is more of a log than a dog,' Andreas said.

His hand was close to hers. It would be so easy to reach out, slide her fingers through his.

'I love it here,' she murmured. 'I feel safe, I guess. As if I'm finally in the right place.'

'That is exactly how I felt, the first time I came to the island,' Andreas said, though his words were weighed down. There was something below the surface, a barrier that had not been there before. Skye held back as they drew closer to what remained of Karolos's house, but Andreas pressed on. He crouched and began to root through the rubble with his fingers, tossing aside chunks of masonry and broken picture frames. A flash of gold caught Skye's eye.

'Is that another idol?' she asked.

'Saint Nektarios, the miracle worker.' Andreas lifted the small treasure, used his thumb to wipe away the dust. 'This was my fault,' he said. 'I knew it was unsafe. I should have forced the old man to let me do the work.'

'No, no.' Skye was beside him in an instant. 'How could you ever have known what would happen?'

Andreas shook his head.

'It was an act of nature,' she insisted.

Filia picked her way past them, nosing through the debris. A moment later, she froze, her tail upright, rigid. Skye moved to comfort her, but the dog shied away, sticking her muzzle in the air and letting out a mournful-sounding howl.

Andreas got shakily to his feet. They stood, facing each other.

'It's not your fault,' she said. Slowly, she moved towards him. Placed her hand against his chest. Pressed until she felt his heart. It was beating out of time.

'I was distracted,' he said, his own hand coming up, a thumb finding her cheek.

Skye's mouth went dry. 'Distracted by what?' she whispered.

The way he touched her cast her adrift from herself.

Andreas moved his thumb softly over her lips.

'You,' he said. 'Always you.'

He leaned closer, but Skye jerked away.

'What is the matter?' Andreas asked, his arms falling limply to his sides.

'You were angry at me,' Skye said, unable to keep her tone neutral. 'Why?'

He kicked at a stone, swore.

'*Ela*, because you did not trust me. I told you about my brother, Sotiris, and still, you sent me away.'

'That was because I was scared. In that moment, I wanted to confide in someone that I knew would understand, not fly off the handle.'

'What is fly off the handle?'

'It's when someone loses their temper, gets angry. It's what Martyn did all the time, it's what men do *all the time.*'

Andreas opened his mouth, then closed it again.

'It wasn't that I didn't trust you,' Skye said. 'It wasn't really about you at all. It was about me. What I needed in that moment. It doesn't mean I don't care about you. I do. I—I've missed you.'

Andreas took a breath, fixed her with his steady gaze.

'And I've told you now,' she went on. 'About Martyn, about all of it. Doesn't that count for something?'

He folded his arms.

'This isn't fair, Andreas. You haven't been honest with me either.'

'What do you mean?'

'I mean you were married. That's right,' she added, as his eyes went wide, 'I know about your ex-wife. I saw her at the church in Chora. There was a bird and—Never mind, the point is, I know. When were you going to tell me about that, huh? After you kissed me? After we'd had sex? When? Because, I'll be honest with you, I've been with one colossal liar in my time, and I'm not about to fall for another.'

Andreas stared at her, jaw hanging open, skin a blotchy red.

'You ask me about Eurora now?' he said icily. 'I am standing in the ruins of my dead friend's house and you want me to talk about the ruins of my marriage?'

Skye faltered, her breath catching. 'I just want to know you,' she said softly.

But he was already turning. Already walking away. Already gone.

Skye was left alone, in the silence he didn't stay to fill.

58

January 1942

Katerina knew only darkness.

The pale light that streamed in through the windows of the house each morning mocked her with its optimism. A dawn that had once felt so promising now a cruel reminder of all she had lost. She pulled the blankets over her head, closing her eyes to it.

Dafni came, as she had taken to doing, her tread soft across the cracked boards. Each day, she would bring a morsel to tempt Katerina – dried fish she had traded in the village, root mash with a little oil, a thin broth with lentil sediment. Today, it was a single boiled egg.

'You must eat,' she said. 'For the baby.'

Katerina took the dish from her. There was no salt or bread, but the egg was fresh, its yolk the melting yellow of the sinking sun.

'You will want to know how I got it,' Dafni said proudly. 'I heard about a woman in Chora, who has been permitted to keep chickens. Most of the eggs go to the soldiers, but she manages to hide a few each week and will let them go for a price.'

She waited for Katerina to ask what price, frowning slightly when she did not.

'It is different for each person. There is a rumour that one of the rich landowners gave her two donkeys for two eggs – can you believe it?'

Katerina could believe it. She was taking only the smallest bites, wanting to savour it, hating how ardently her body demanded the food. Why should she eat, when Leni had not?

'For me, she asked only my name, and who the eggs were for,' Dafni continued. 'I tried to pay her, said that I could clean for her, perhaps brush her donkeys' – she chuckled to herself – 'but she would not hear of it.'

Katerina chewed slowly.

'The rain is having a day of rest,' Dafni said, looking back towards the door. 'I thought that I might go down to the beach, try to find an urchin for supper. It is too cold for the Italians – they do not walk down to the water, and I prefer to be away from their scrutiny.'

The shell of the egg was empty, every piece of the white scraped away. Katerina passed her empty dish and spoon back to the older woman and lay down.

'You should try to get outside, *agapi mou*,' Dafni said softly, putting a hand on her arm. 'There is still life for you to live, a life growing inside that is going to need you very soon.'

A hot spike of anger speared through Katerina. Life without her sister was no life at all.

She must have slept, for when she next opened her eyes, the room was frigid, the fire in the grate long ago burned out. Wood had become scarce on the island, and they had taken to burning clods of earth, the thick smoke coating the walls with dirt.

Katerina swung her feet to the floor and stood. Every movement was difficult, her belly protruding from her body like a ripe grape. The baby had been quiet, sleeping when she slept, docile since the death of his or her aunt. That Leni would never get to meet the child was an unfairness that had ripped away the final vestiges of Katerina's faith. What kind of a god punished a soul as sweet as her sister's?

In the days following the meagre funeral, she had sat and read each of the letters Leni had written to Michalis, full of false cheer and anodyne tales, and then, she had burned them. If he ever came back, she planned to tell him the truth of what had befallen them, the horror he and Stefanos had walked away from when they chose to rejoin the fight.

Dafni was not in the house, nor the yard. The clock on the wall of her bedroom told her it was nearing four thirty p.m. – the sun would set within the hour. Katerina was struck by a sudden urge to see it, to sit as she once had on the hillside in the days before the occupation. Before love. Before tragedy.

Wrapped in two shawls with her boots laced tight, she raised the latch and stepped out into the cold afternoon air, pausing for a moment at the grave she had made for Chrysí. Her beloved goat. The first casualty of a war that was determined to take away everything she loved. Katerina used the wall to steady herself, stared up through the bare branches of the overhanging tree towards a sky the grey of a young gull's feathers. Walking hurt, but she had come this far and pressed on, ignoring the low pulls of pain across her back, the cramps that squeezed bile into her throat.

The ridge was ahead, though she could no longer go to that spot. Lio's face was a frequent visitor, coming to her in the blurred world between wakefulness and slumber, eyes wide and mouth agape. His death had shocked both of them, and though the rain of that night had washed away any trace of blood, Katerina feared his ghost would be standing guard where his body had fallen. Waiting for her, as he had in life.

She stopped as a ripple of discomfort travelled through her. A new pain, as if someone was pulling her insides together. Sweat beaded on her upper lip, her skin damp despite the chill.

It had been a mistake to climb up here, she should never have strayed so far from the house.

Katerina gave in to a sob, stumbling on legs that felt weak as matchsticks. Her hair fell in tangles over her eyes. Pebbles tumbled away. The path was slick, the light fast-fading. Below her, the village came into view, her relief tainted by agony as a violent cramp took hold. She clutched her stomach, cried out as a gush of liquid flooded the inside of her legs.

The baby was coming.

She fell to her knees and crawled towards the closest house. Not her own, Dafni's. In her delirious state, she had forgotten that her friend no longer lived there, had not lived there for many months. If she could only reach the door, find the strength to bang against it – but then the burning came again. Katerina could no longer move, nor breathe, nor think coherently.

Warm light fell across her. A voice, gentle but firm. Hands moving, examining. Words she did not recognise spoken with hushed urgency. Katerina was afraid, more afraid than she had ever been, and though the woman looking down at her did so with kindness, she shut her eyes. And did not open them again. Not during the pain, nor the agony; not when she was tearing, ripping, screaming. Not afterwards, when all was quiet, and the darkness she craved came again to steal her away.

She dreamed of Stefanos. His hand in hers. Laughter on his lips. Light in his eyes. They were on an island. Not Folegandros, but another, smaller, cut off from the rest of the world. The sun warm against their skin as they lay together, side by side, on a beach of sugary sand.

It was all she wanted, but there was something wrong. Something missing.

Katerina sat and stared out across the water. It was not blue but black. A great swirling beast rising nearer and nearer until—

She awoke thrashing, kicking, a rasping cry scouring her throat.

Dafni appeared in an instant. She sat on the edge of the bed and pulled Katerina against her, holding her tight, rocking her back and forth.

'Where is she?' Katerina stuttered. 'Where is my daughter?'

Dafni did not reply. She loosened her grip, shook her head.

'What have you done with her?'

'I am sorry, *agapi mou*.' Dafni began to cry. Her face crumpled like paper in the rain. 'Ingrid, she did everything she could. The baby came the wrong way, the cord was around her neck. I am sorry,' she said again.

What use was sorry? What good could sorry do?

The door into the room creaked open. Ingrid emerged, a bottle in her hand. Her face was flushed, blotched with tears. The dress she wore stained in blood.

'Koniák,' she said, unscrewing the lid.

'Drink it,' Dafni urged. 'It will help with the pain, the shock.'

Katerina was too numb to refuse. The brandy tasted sweet. She took another sip, then another. She drank until the room turned to water, until the horror of her reality had been erased. She craved only oblivion.

The days passed.

Sun rose, darkness fell.

Somehow her heart continued to beat.

Ingrid and Dafni stayed close. She was never alone. Even when she stepped outside to relieve herself, their boots waited just beyond the wooden door, standing guard, watching, caring. In the quiet hours, the German nurse read thick novels, slowly working through Greek words. Dafni, endlessly patient, offered gentle corrections with a smile.

Katerina was in the room, but not truly present. The world felt distant, muffled, as if she was watching through the wrong end of a telescope. She was a ghost in her own skin, untethered from life.

It was several weeks before she ventured back to the place where her daughter was buried. Not in the church grounds, or the cemetery in Chora, but with Chrysí. Katerina had been adamant.

'We will have a proper funeral when her father returns,' she said, in answer to Dafni's timid argument. 'I am the only home she ever knew. She belongs close to me.'

Phaedra and Esther had stood alongside them at the small grave on that bleak morning, heads bowed, faces set. Katerina had weighed them down with one secret. Now, she had burdened them with another.

When February arrived, it did so with news. The British had listened to the plea of the Greeks and would allow humanitarian aid to pass the blockade. At last, food would come. Too late to save the hundreds that had perished on Folegandros, the rumoured tens of thousands who'd starved on the mainland. Too late to save her sister. Katerina yearned for her baby, yet Leni's absence was the boot on her throat.

She no longer feared the enemy, not their guns or bombs. It was sorrow that terrified her. Grief a parasite that was consuming her from the inside out.

'I must leave this place,' she said.

Dafni and Ingrid turned abruptly to face her. They were sitting as they often did, in the garden of Katerina's home, a pot of herbal tea curling steam into the still air. It was March, yet spring was nowhere to be found. Winter had become an enemy, holding hostage the season of hope.

'What are you talking about?' Dafni replied. 'Leave and go where?'

'To the mainland.'

Ingrid lowered her cup.

'*Ela*, you cannot,' Dafni chided. 'It is forbidden.'

'Let them shoot me,' Katerina said. 'I do not care.'

'That is exactly what they would do,' Dafni said. 'But they would rape you first. Beat you. Make an example of you.'

Katerina raised her eyes to the muted sky. 'There is nothing here for me,' she said quietly. 'My parents are gone, my sister is dead, my child is dead, my heart—' Her voice snagged on the word. 'My heart has turned to ash. If I stay here, I will die.'

'No.' Dafni reached across and took her hand. 'You will not die, Kat. You will live.'

'I need to see him,' she said firmly. 'I must find Stefanos. I must tell him about—He is the only one who can save me. The only person I have left.'

'You have us,' Dafni said urgently. 'You have Ingrid, Phaedra, Es—Kostas. Your parents will return when the war is over and—'

'They are gone,' Katerina said. 'I can feel it.'

'Even if you could escape this island, you do not know where to find Stefanos. He could have been captured, or be hiding, or even killed.'

'He is alive.' Katerina met her gaze. 'If he had died, I would have died with him. No. He is alive, and I will find him. No matter what it takes.'

Ingrid stood to refill their cups.

'Your husband,' she said. 'He is a soldier?'

'He fights for freedom,' Katerina said, puffing out her chest. 'For Greece.'

Ingrid nodded. 'It is probable that he will be on the mainland,' she said, stumbling slightly over the words.

'The mainland!' Dafni cried. 'There is no way to reach it. You must forget this nonsense.'

But Katerina was looking only at Ingrid. She saw how the woman's focus had drifted, her ice-blue eyes locking on to an unseeable future.

'I can help you,' she said.

Heat flooded through Katerina. 'What do you mean?'

Ingrid sat down, folding her hands in her lap. 'My husband has sent for me,' she said.

Katerina could not be sure, but it looked as if the woman shuddered as she spoke.

'He is in Athens and will remain there for some time. I have been instructed to prepare for a boat that will leave in two days' time. If I tell the soldiers that you have become my nursemaid, they will not question it. The General's rule is absolute, and I am his wife.'

'You would do that?' Katerina said breathlessly. 'For me?'

Ingrid faced her. 'You love this man, Stefanos?'

Katerina smiled. It was the first time she had since Leni's death.

'As the clouds love the sky,' she said softly. 'As the trees love the sun, the waves love the shore, the night loves the stars.'

'Then you must find him,' Ingrid said.

Katerina fell to her knees, seized the woman's hands, and pressed her lips to her fingers.

'You mean it? I can come with you?'

Ingrid rose slowly, drawing Katerina up until their eyes met. Two women, face to face.

Equals.

Friends.

Survivors.

'Yes,' she said. 'I mean it.'

59

The call from the police came early on Saturday morning.

Skye was on her way across the hillside when her phone rang, and she paused to answer it.

The officer at the other end of the line had a mercifully good grasp of English, and did not indulge her in any small talk before coming straight to the point.

'We believe that the animal remains belong to a goat,' he said. 'Not a very big one, but yes, a goat.'

Chrysí. Katerina had written an account of what happened to her much-loved animal in the letters. Skye steeled herself, braced for a wave she couldn't dodge.

'The other bones are human. A very young infant. A baby girl.'

Sadness settled over her, a sudden weight, stones sewn into her clothes.

'Do you know who she was?' she murmured.

'There is no DNA match on our systems here in Greece. However, we made contact with the owner of the house where the other bones were discovered, to make a request for a sample. If there is a match there, we will also test the infant remains using the same DNA. They may be related.'

Unlikely, but not impossible.

'Did the other bones belong to an adult?' she asked.

'*Nai*. The pathologist report has determined that he was a man, probably the age of forty to forty-five, something like this. There are injuries on the bones that suggest he did not die in a natural way.'

'You mean he was murdered?' Skye said, glancing up to find Theo striding towards her. The dog tag she'd given him not ten minutes previously was dangling from one hand. Having heard her question, he cocked an enquiring brow.

'There is evidence that the body was in the ground for more than eighty years,' the officer went on.

'So, whoever he was, he died at some point during the war?'

'We will try to find a list of all the people that lived in the area. However, during wartime, there were many people whose homes were taken over by the occupying forces. It was a time of much chaos, a lot of death. But we will do our best to find out more.'

'What will happen to the baby's remains?' she asked.

'If we do not manage to trace the family, we will make a public announcement. If that does not lead us to any conclusion, the bones will eventually be reburied.'

'Will you tell me?' Skye said, gripping the phone more tightly. 'If there's a funeral or anything, I'd like to be there.'

'*Entáxei*. Of course.' She heard the smile in the officer's voice. 'If you discover any further remains during your renovations, please inform us immediately.'

'I will,' she told him. 'Thank you—I mean, *efcharistó*.'

'*Parakaló*,' he replied briskly, and the line went dead.

Skye turned to Theo. 'I feel awful,' she said. 'If I'd read the letters sooner, I'd have known straight away who was buried in that grave.'

'The police confirmed it?' Theo winced as she nodded. 'Ah. Poor Katerina. But you mustn't blame yourself. The rain did the damage. The bones would've come to light sooner or later.'

'That's not all,' Skye said. 'The other body, at the empty house, it has signs of an unnatural death.'

'Another murder?' Theo blew air into his cheeks.

'I'm not sure the Italian who tried to kill Katerina was murdered,' Skye said. 'In the letter, she says he fell, hit his head. It was an accident.'

'OK.' Theo rubbed his temple. 'And they didn't bury him, did they?'

Skye shook her head slowly. '"We gave him to the sea", was how it's worded in the letters.'

Theo passed her the dog tag. 'I found him,' he said, sliding a folded piece of paper from his pocket.

Skye raised a hand to shield her eyes from the sun. It wasn't yet nine, but the heat felt absolute, pressing down from above, rising up from the ground beneath her feet. She'd forgotten to put on sunscreen, and her skin prickled, tight and raw, as if the air itself was sandpaper.

Theo cleared his throat. 'Giulio Muti, born 1916 in Cornacchio, Emilia Romagna, Italy.'

Frowning, Skye did the maths. 'That would make him, what, twenty-four or twenty-five when the war reached Greece?'

'Sounds right to me,' Theo agreed.

'Well, that one hundred per cent rules him out as being the body buried in the garden. The police just told me that man was likely in his mid-forties.'

Theo nodded sagely. 'That makes sense,' he said, refocusing on the lines of text. 'Giulio joined the army and became part of the 50th Infantry Division, Regina, detachments from which were stationed across the Cyclades islands during the occupation, between 1941 and 1943. He died in December 1941, and the cause of death is stated as drowning. Katerina might've given him to the sea . . .'

'But the sea gave him back.' Skye ran her forefinger over the tag. 'Perhaps that has something to do with why all these houses were abandoned? The Italians must have asked questions. It might have been enough to scare the residents into fleeing.'

'Another mystery,' Theo said, not unhappily.

'We should tell the police,' Skye said. 'They want to test the DNA of the baby against whoever it is that owns the empty house, but we know whose baby it is. It feels important that she be reburied.'

Theo nodded sagely. 'Reburied here?'

'No.' Skye thought for a moment. 'There's a cemetery, isn't there, close to Chora?'

'I believe so, yes.'

'How likely do you think it is that Leni was buried there?'

The corners of Theo's eyes crinkled as he smiled. 'You think the baby should be laid to rest with her?'

'I do,' Skye said. 'I think Katerina would have liked that.'

'I wonder if she ever found Stefanos,' Theo said.

Skye glanced up. Two birds had swooped in low across the hillside, the tips of their wings stretched out as if yearning to touch one another. They rode on the current of the wind, dipping and diving, heading out together across the wide expanse of sea. She could not tear her eyes away, watching until they were little more than dark smudges against the glittering blue.

'My head tells me no,' she said. 'But my heart . . .'

Dust rose from the road. A truck came into view.

Skye jolted, her skin tingling as a thousand volts of anticipation hurtled through her.

She had asked her dad once. They were at Neist Point on the Isle of Skye, sitting together below the looming lighthouse. Rods in hand, a Thermos of cocoa between them.

'How did you know that you were in love with Mum?'

Cosmo MacKinnon had given her a sideways look.

'That's a big question for a wee lass.'

'Fifteen isn't wee,' she replied. 'You're never too young for love, remember?'

'Aye,' he agreed. 'The more you can get of the stuff, the happier you'll be.'

'But how do you know when it's real?' she pressed.

He tilted his head, eyes fixed on the horizon.

'It'll feel like a door swinging open. One that's always been there, only locked. When you step through, there's no going back. But that's all right. Because it's warm in there. It's safe. It's home.'

And that was it.

When Skye was with Andreas, that's exactly how she felt.

Like she'd stepped through.

Like she'd finally come home.

60

The overalls were gone, as were the heavy workmen's boots. Andreas's hair looked damp beneath his red baseball cap. He was wearing a faded T-shirt and the same shorts he'd had on the day she bumped into him at the beach.

When he saw her walking towards him, he smiled.

'*Geia sou*, Skye. *Ti canis?*'

How was she?

She was so many things, none of which she knew how to put into words.

'I'm ...' Instead of finishing her sentence, Skye shrugged.

Andreas nodded. 'I am the same,' he said.

A furious yapping startled the two of them.

'*Ela re*,' Andreas grumbled, opening the door of the truck. 'I brought Filia with me.' The wiry little dog hopped down, strutted importantly to Skye for some attention, then scampered off into Victoria and Adam's front yard. They were both outside. Victoria looked wan and puffy-eyed. She was wearing pink Crocs, Bermuda shorts and a vest with *Venice Beach California* printed across it. Adam, meanwhile, was stripped to the waist, a shovel in his hands that he'd already used to dig several large holes.

'Still hunting for buried treasure?' Skye asked. Adam pulled a face.

'Not so much as an earthworm yet,' he said with a sigh.

Victoria bent to stroke Filia. 'Oh my word,' she said. 'She's a darling. Is she yours?'

Andreas and Skye exchanged a look.

'She is not mine,' he said, 'but she can be yours. If you are willing to take her . . .'

'Sure we are,' Victoria said, over Adam's tentative 'Maybe'.

'She belonged to my friend Karolos,' Andreas explained. 'He unfortunately died during the earthquake' – he glanced at Skye – 'it was an accident.'

'So she's an orphan?' Victoria cried. 'The poor little thing.'

Filia rolled over onto her back, paws in the air, tongue lolling out from the side of her mouth.

'I think she likes you,' Andreas said. 'She never behaves this way for me.'

'Come on, gorgeous.' Victoria clicked her fingers and the dog promptly leapt to attention. 'Let's go and see if there's any leftover chicken in the fridge.'

Adam watched them go, his smile lingering. 'Thank you,' he said. 'That's the first time I've seen her looking properly happy in a while.'

'Perhaps she and Filia can mend each other's broken hearts,' Andreas said, his eyes drifting to Skye once again.

'Hope so.' Adam raised his shovel. 'Better get on.'

'Where is your mother?' Andreas asked, as Skye followed him back towards the truck.

'I woke to find a note saying she'd gone for a swim with Joy.'

'So, you are alone?'

Skye turned in a slow circle, her arms outstretched.

'Do I look alone to you? I moved from one of the most overpopulated cities in the world to this tiny Greek village, and I've never felt less alone in my life.'

'Ah,' he said, pulling down the tailgate. 'It happened. The island worked its magic on you.'

'Yes,' she said with a laugh. 'It really did.'

'I have something for you. A gift.'

He slid a paint tin off the truck and held it out to her.

'*Ela*,' he said. 'Let us go to the house.'

When they reached her front door, Skye put down the tin and Andreas knelt. He extracted a penknife from his pocket and used it to pry open the lid.

'I thought it would be nice for the shutters,' he said. 'This door as well, perhaps.'

The paint was not the bright, deep blue of the Santorini domes, nor did it have the rich intensity of the Aegean. This blue was velvety soft, and it stirred something within her.

'It is the colour of the sky,' Andreas said. 'In Greece, it represents a fresh start.'

'It's perfect,' she said, her voice catching. 'But you've given me so much already. I've barely given you a thing.'

'*Ochi*,' he said. 'What you have given me is more than anyone ever has.'

The air thickened. The wind, for once, had fallen away.

'Shall we walk?' she said.

They went side by side up the winding path, their steps quiet on the uneven ground. Skye had always felt the pull of the ridge, a place that held her secrets, where she could lean against the sun-warmed stone and let the world fall away. Below, the sea stretched vast and sparkling. A boat cut across it in the distance, trailing a ribbon of white foam.

She sat, and so did Andreas, his knee grazing hers.

'You are pink,' he said. Before she could reply, he had taken off his cap and placed it on her head.

'Thank you,' she said, as he raked a hand through his curls, mussing them up.

'I like to do this,' he said, tapping the tip of her nose with a finger. 'I like to look after you, even if you don't need me to.'

Skye searched his eyes. They were flecked with gold, shooting stars on a night sky.

'I am sorry,' he said. 'Eurora was my wife for only one year. She was not faithful. I discovered very soon after the wedding that she was no longer in love with me. Perhaps she never was. We were young.' The words sailed out on a sigh. 'My ego was very bruised. The problem is that I am proud, and I am stubborn. I did not want you to think of me in that way, as a man who had been rejected and humiliated.'

Skye's jaw tightened. 'She's the one who should feel humiliated,' she said. 'She had you, and she cheated? What an idiot.'

A smile found its way to his lips.

'What about after Eurora?' Skye asked. 'Have there been others?'

Andreas tugged at a tuft of grass.

'Some. But it was never serious. I learned that it is better to be alone than with the wrong person.'

'How will you know when you find the right person?'

A beat passed. Shorter than a breath, but long enough for Skye to see his answer before he gave it. It was there in the tenderness of his gaze, the fullness of his lips, the heat of her own longing.

'For me,' he said, 'it was there at the very beginning. I saw you, outside the house, a key in your hand, and the moment you turned around, I was lost. From that second to this, I have been yours.'

Skye drew in a long, shuddering breath. 'And you're only getting around to telling me this now because?'

Andreas flicked up the peak of her cap and leaned in closer. 'In Greece, we have a saying: Everything in its own time, and the mackerel in August.'

She snuffled with laughter.

'It reminds us,' he said, 'that things happen best when they are supposed to, and that certain fish taste better if you eat them in the right season.'

'Clearly, I still have a lot to learn about being Greek,' she mused.

Andreas smiled broadly. 'You teach the children, and I will teach you.'

'Wait, children?'

'*Nai*. The children on the island. Unless you want me to give you some of your own?'

'Oh my God!' she said. 'We haven't even kissed and you're taking about babies.'

'Come here then,' he said, hooking a finger.

'Just like that?'

'Do you want me to beg?'

He started to shift onto one knee and Skye grabbed his shoulders, pulling him forwards until they toppled back into the dust. Andreas propped himself up on an elbow. Slowly, he removed her hat. Her hair fell across her cheeks, and he brushed it away. His fingers traced her eyebrows, her lips, the soft pulse on her neck. When he kissed her, he did so gently. Barely a touch, a taste.

Skye dissolved into him.

She was liquid.

She was fire.

When they finally opened their eyes, it was to brilliant light. The sun had searched and found their hiding place. It had split the clouds in two purely for them.

Andreas wrapped his arm around her shoulders.

'Will you come with me to the mainland?' he asked. 'I want you to meet my family, my parents, and especially Elpida, my *giagia*. After I read the letters you brought back to me, I took photos, sent them to her. She has never spoken about the war – not to me or anyone in my family – but now, she says she is ready at last. She wants to tell us more about what happened here, in Folegandros.'

Elpida. The baby girl belonging to Katerina's neighbour, Phaedra. She was only mentioned once in the letters by name, but Skye had remembered it, had been sure she'd heard it before. Could that child have grown up to become Andreas's grandmother? In all that had happened, it did not feel beyond the realm of possibility.

'Of course I'll come.' She leaned her head against his. 'Do you think they'll like me?'

'No,' he said simply, laughing at her expression of mock outrage. '*Ela*, they will love you.'

Skye moved closer. 'How do you say "I love you" in Greek?' she murmured.

'*S'agapó*,' he said. 'Easy to learn, difficult to say.'

She laced her fingers through his. 'I'd best start practising in that case.'

'All this love,' he said, with a theatrical roll of his eyes. 'I am crazy with it.'

'You'd better kiss me again then.'

'*Perimene*,' he said as she leaned in. 'No more kissing until we discuss baby names.'

The sun had nothing on the heat blooming in her chest. Skye felt as if she might burst with it – love, laughter, the dizzying thrill of all that lay ahead.

'Go on, then,' she said. 'You can choose first.'

Andreas smiled. There was lightness to it, but something deeper too. It settled inside her like a promise.

'If we have a boy,' he said, 'can we name him Sotiris, for my brother?'

Skye nodded, her smile catching as she squeezed his hand.

'Yes,' she said. 'And if it's a girl, we'll call her Katerina.'

Acknowledgements

The House of Hidden Letters is my thirteenth novel, though the first to be published under the name Izzy – as opposed to Isabelle – Broom. Now, I don't know whether it was this tweak, or my brand-new publishing team, or the fact that I dipped a toe into the past, or perhaps the magic of Folegandros itself, but everything about this novel felt special from the start. I hope that if you've made it this far and are still reading, it means a smidgeon of that passion has found its way into you, too, my dearest reader.

My Editor in the UK, Susannah Hamilton, has infused this project with insight, energy and unbridled cheerleading at every stage of the game. Nobody reads faster, instils confidence better, or makes me want to strive harder than she. I feel extremely lucky to be working together with her on this and future books.

The wider team at Century are all incredible. I must thank Camila Ilardia Jimenez in Editorial, Jade Stratton in Production, and my Managing Editor, Conor Hodges. I hope The Clumsies' negronis lived up to my hype.

This novel would never have found its way into the hands of readers without the sterling efforts of marketing genius Isabella Levin, not to mention the persuasive prowess of publicity guru Aoifke

McGuire-France. My sales team of dreams, Alice Gomer, Kirsten Greenwood, Phoenix Curland, Emily Harvey, you all deserve medals – and a Greek holiday. Ditto Emma Grey Gelder for her artistic brilliance and rights warrior Amelia Evans, without whom this novel would have far fewer translations.

Jill Cole, thank you for being the best copyeditor in the biz. I'd like to keep you for all my books, if you please.

My US Executive Editor, Esi Sogah of Penguin Berkley, helped me put a big tick on my bucket list when she came on board with this novel. Thank you, Esi, for believing in me – especially after that first awkward Zoom when, unsure of how best to end our meeting, I simply zoomed out of shot. You must have known I was a weirdo then, yet you persevered. There will never be a time when I am not grateful. Thanks also to Kiera Bertrand, Genni Eccles, Naira Mirza, and everyone at Berkley who has worked so tirelessly on this book. I appreciate you all more than you could ever know.

Heartfelt gratitude, as ever, to my agent Alice Lutyens, who is unfailingly kind and wise, with a wit that stings like a whip. I don't know what I'd do without you, but I know it would be a lot less fun. That goes for everyone at Curtis Brown, especially Rakhi Kohli, Emma Jamison and Samuel Loader.

Efcharistó to Kostas Kapsaskis, who not only took me out for the best souvlaki in Athens but also talked to me at length about Greece during World War Two. Your insights and quirks gave this book and those that will follow so much more depth and authenticity. The people of Greece are a big part of why I love it so much, and when I was on the island, its residents could not have been more welcoming and generous with their time. I'd like to give a special mention to Elpida at H Kouzina Ths Giagias (Grandma's Kitchen) café in Ano Meria, Anna at the Folklore Museum of Folegandros, and Melissa at Flomos, Chora.

To those authors who agreed to read an early draft of the novel – Chris Whitaker, Cesca Major, Cathy Bramley and Veronica Henry – thank you, so much. Your generosity is unparalleled. Chris, when I got that message from you that simply read: 'I love Katerina so much', my heart swelled to twice its normal size. I will always put up with you.

To Katy and Katie, my voice note queens, where would I be without you both? Writing can be a lonely profession at times and you both make it less so. That goes for you, too, Cathy. Nobody makes me cackle more and watching your love story with Mr F unfold these past few years has been a source of such inspiration and joy.

Thanks to Louise (LJ) Ross for allowing Kate Gray, Sophie Cousens and me to stay in your stunning Coach House back in January 2025. That writing retreat proved to be the perfect springboard for this novel, and your warmth and hospitality meant the world.

Book people are the best people – it's a common saying because it's true. There simply isn't space for me to list every one of you who has supported me and my books, so please take these words as a kind of love confetti cannon and consider yourselves covered in the stuff.

To all the booksellers – special mention to Grace and Grace at Waterstones Sudbury – panel chairs, event organisers, bloggers, BookTokkers, press reviewers, Instagrammers, library frequenters and anyone with a passion for books and reading, thank you for what you do.

Sadie, the Appleby to my Peake, the Lady Shady, my favourite person on planet earth, let's never stop finding the stupidest things funny. I love you more than a scribbled 'Jimmy'.

Lastly, but never leastly, I must thank my family, every eccentric, challenging, hilarious and brilliantly unique one of you.

Mum, remember when you said I was born to write this novel? Well, here we are. I did it all for you, as I do every time. With love.

Izzy Broom

The House of Broken Promises

Don't miss the thrilling sequel to *THE HOUSE OF HIDDEN LETTERS*, coming 2027

Pre-order now at penguinrandomhouse.co.uk

On a station platform, with nothing to read,
and a four-hour train journey stretching ahead of him...

That's where the story began for Penguin founder Allen Lane.
With only 'shabby reprints of shoddy novels' on offer,
he resolved to make better books for readers everywhere.

By the time his train pulled into London, the idea was formed.
He would bring the best writing, in stylish and affordable
formats, to everyone. His books would be sold in bookstores,
stationers and tobacconists, for no more than the price
of a ten-pack of cigarettes.

And on every book would be a Penguin, a bird with a certain
'dignified flippancy', and a friendly invitation to anyone who
wished to spend their time reading.

In 1935, the first ten Penguin paperbacks were published.
Just a year later, three million Penguins had made their
way onto our shelves.

Reading was changed forever.

—

A lot has changed since 1935, including Penguin, but in the
most important ways we're still the same. We still believe that
books and reading are for everyone. And we still believe that
whether you're seeking an afternoon's escape, a vigorous debate
or a soothing bedtime story, all possibilities open with a book.

Whoever you are, whatever you're looking for,
you can find it with Penguin.